Pop's office was at the top of a steep flight of stairs separated from the rest of the store by a rope. His big mahogany desk was there, surrounded by piles and piles of cardboard boxes teeming with old books. One day, I was playing in there alone, and I summoned my imaginary friend, Posey Darling. I asked her whether she wanted to play hide-and-seek and was stunned to hear a little voice respond, "OK." I looked around a little fearfully and was relieved to see a tiny doll-like girl peek her head around the door.

"Hi, I'm Jess."

"I'm Verity, Verity Wolf."

Her eyes widened. "Wolf? Is . . . is this your shop?"

"It's my grandad's," I had said, a little airily. Feeling bold, I added, "By the way, you're not allowed up here."

She put her hands on her hips and glared at me. "Then why did you ask me to play hide-and-seek with you, stupid?"

From that day on, we were inseparable. I have barely any childhood memories without Jess in them. One time we built a fort by stacking piles of books like bricks. It took days, but all the effort was worth it. We called it the Book Cave. Nan helped me furnish it with sleeping bags, blankets, and pillows so we could stay the night. We took turns reading *Deenie* out loud by flashlight. When I got to the part where Deenie mentions her "special place," Jess once interrupted me, "You know she's masturbating, don't you?"

"Duh!" At the time, I had no idea what masturbating meant and got a funny reaction when I asked Pop about it the next day.

Jess's mother, Mei Lyn, was a barrister who worked around the clock. She was hardly ever home, and when she was, her mind was preoccupied with work. Their apartment was small and filled with expensive antique vases, so we had to be careful not to knock anything over. That's probably why Jess spent so much time at our place, where we could run wild and not have to worry about all that stuff.

We stuck together all through our school years, passing notes to each other in class and spending our lunch breaks plugged into Jess's phone, chilling to her latest playlist on Spotify. Jess had a knack for curating popular music lists from every genre imaginable and somehow making it all work. Whenever a school dance came around, she was always the one asked to DJ.

On weekends, we'd cycle out to junk shops, markets, and garage sales, searching for rare books. If we stumbled on something valuable, Pop would be over the moon—like the time we found a copy of *Kiss Kiss* with Roald Dahl's autograph on the inside jacket. We didn't get lucky all that often, but when we did, the look on Pop's face was priceless. He kept a glass cabinet behind the counter especially for his collection of autographed books. He swears he will never sell a single one, even though we could really use the money.

PART ONE

"something secret is going on,
so marvelous and dangerous

that if you crawled through and saw,
you would die, or be happy forever."

—**Lisel Mueller,** *"Sometimes, When the Light"*

One
(Sydney)

On a blue-sky day in Centennial Park, I sat on an old tartan rug with my best friend, Jess, who had her head buried in the latest poetry book by Mena Rhodes. It had just hit the shelves, so the first thing we did that morning was race to our local bookstore, Berkelouw. We were thrilled to see a stack of Mena's books on a table up front, carefully arranged like a Jenga tower. We made a beeline and picked up a copy. Now it was barely noon, and between the two of us, we had practically torn through the entire book. "Her best one yet," Jess hugged it to her chest.

"I loved the one about—" I started.

"The rings of Saturn?"

We looked at each other and sighed in unison.

Jess put the book down, and we stretched out on the rug, faces soaking up the sun. It had gotten cold early this year, as if someone had flicked a switch. We didn't mind, though. It meant we could break out our sweaters. We were obsessed with them. The cable-knit ones we wore today were identical, apart from hers being mustard yellow and mine a retro red. Sweaters were the only item of clothing we could agree on. Otherwise, our choices were in complete contrast. Take now, for example. I had on pale denim jeans and ballet flats. She was in tiny shorts, fishnet stockings, and combat boots. My chestnut-brown hair was thick and unruly. Jess's jet-black locks hung straight and glossy all the way to her hips. She was tall and rakishly thin; I was petite and curvy.

I wanted to be a poet like Mena Rhodes. Jess dreamed of being a famous artist, someone wild and provocative like Tracey Emin.

She'd turned nineteen six weeks ago, which is the same age I would be next week. But from the beginning of our friendship, it always felt like she was so much older. It probably had to do with how Jess was always looking out for me. I knew I could count on her no matter what.

I met Jess when I was seven, shortly after my parents were killed in a car accident and I had to move into Nan and Pop's small apartment above Pop's secondhand bookstore, Wolf Books. It was an old, rambling establishment with a network of nooks and crannies. Customers likened it to a maze.

One summer, Pop built a window seat in my room, which overlooked the courtyard. Jess and I often saw Nan pottering around her bonsai garden. She put her heart and soul into that tiny patch of sunshine.

Years went by, and the tiny trees grew fractionally taller, their branches thickening and twisting into knots like Nan's hands as she faithfully tended them. Now she moved slower and was often out of breath. But that didn't stop her from hiding packs of popping candy in our pillowcases or jumping out at night with a sheet over her head to scare the bejesus out of us.

During all those years, Jess and I were always there for each other. I was with her the first time she fell off her bike and took the skin off her knees. And when she was dumped by her first boyfriend, I was there with ice cream and tissues. I held her hand that day at the doctor's clinic when she asked for the morning-after pill in a shaky voice. And she was there to talk me through my first period (she got hers the year before). When I got blind drunk at a party, she sat with me on the bathroom floor, holding my hair back as I retched into the toilet bowl. And just last year, when Nan died suddenly of a stroke while tending to her beloved Japanese maple, Jess was there. More than my best friend, she's family. We know every last thing about each other, and she's the only person in the world I have ever allowed to read my poetry.

I started writing poetry after Mum and Dad died. It became a way for me to feel closer to them. Whenever

I had a pen in my hand, it was like they were still with me, even though so much time had gone by. When we lost Nan, I started writing for her as well. I suppose it was a way for me to deal with the sad things in my life. I never thought much about it beyond that. It wasn't until recently, when poetry came back into vogue, that I dared to believe I might write a book someday. I owed this dream to Mena Rhodes, who was the first poet I knew to post her poetry online and unwittingly start a movement.

"Do you think Mena has a muse?" Jess's voice cut through my thoughts, bringing me back into the present. "She writes about love so convincingly. Do you think something happened in her life—or there was someone who inspired it?"

"Who knows? She's so tight-lipped about her private life. But she did mention once in an interview that she's inspired by 'the collective human experience.'"

"But her work is so powerful—especially the dark stuff. I don't know how you could write about something realistically unless you've lived through it."

"What about authors like C. S. Lewis? I bet he's never been to Narnia."

"I get how stuff like scenery and dress-ups can come from pure imagination—how it can be manufactured. I mean, our lecturers go on about it all the time." Jess had just started her first semester at the College of Fine Arts, while I was taking a gap year to help Pop with the store. "But I think visualizing something is completely different from writing about a feeling that you've never felt before. Remember that time I broke my leg?"

"Totally! You were in a foul mood for the whole summer."

She laughed. "I was such a brat."

"Understatement of the century! I told you to cheer up, and you threw a potted plant at me."

"Wasn't it just a plastic plant?"

I glared at her. "It was a cactus, Jess. It grazed my arm, and your mum had to pull out the spikes with tweezers. Remember?"

She gave me a sheepish look. "Oh! Now I do. You gave me the silent treatment for days afterward. You had no idea what it was like. It felt as though my leg was a hunk of lead and fire ants were crawling under my cast. I was hardly getting sleep, and the worst thing was I was stuck at home. It was hell! Anyway, that's my point. Even though you were there with me, you weren't me. You've never broken a bone, so you could feel sympathy for what I was going through, but you couldn't feel empathy for me. I think that would be possible only if you'd experienced it yourself. Then again, you write some of the most heart-wrenching love poems I have ever read, and I know for a fact your only muse is a certain boy in a K-pop band—"

"Oh my God, you're never going to let me forget that, are you?"

She giggled. "Never! Busting you making out with your phone was priceless."

I cringed. Jess knew way too much about me.

"Seriously, though. How do you do it, Vare? With art, it's vague. Everything is open to interpretation. But writing is definite. Nowhere to hide. Nothing else— not film, music, or art—gets down to the bare bones like poetry."

I chewed on my bottom lip. "It's hard to explain. I get this emotion way down in the pit of my stomach; I feel it welling up. Then my chest gets heavy. It happens when I think about Nan."

Jess looked sad. She loved Nan as much as I did. For ages after Nan died, we had moments when we'd talk about her as if she were still there. Then the pain would hit us—she was gone, and we'd never see her again.

I continued, "It's like your entire body is pure emotion—fluid, like music. That's the only way I can describe it. Then words appear, like lyrics that complement the music. The words don't always reflect the feeling, even if they seem to hold true to the sentiment. That means the thought originally was about missing Nan, but the poem is about much more. I think it's because loss is universal."

"Exactly! When you lose someone you love, it makes no difference whether they're a family member or your soul mate. It hurts the same."

"The feeling is like the ocean. Sometimes calm and still; other times, it's a hurricane. So maybe it's like that for Mena, too."

"You know, I think your poems are just as good as hers."

"You're only saying that because you're my friend."

"Well, if you'd stop being so damn stubborn and share your work on Instagram, I bet you'd get a second opinion."

"No, I don't think I'm ready—not yet."

"I know you, Vare; you're never going to be ready." She sat up, her eyes scanning the park. "There!" She said pointing to a random girl, cycling by on her vintage bike.

I propped myself up on my elbows. "Why are you pointing at her?"

"I bet you five bucks she would love your poetry. I bet you anyone in this park would love it."

I groaned. "You're high."

A young mother walked by pushing a stroller. "There!" Jess pointed again, and I swatted her hand down before we caught the lady's attention. "She'd love your poetry, too."

I sat up straight. "Jesus Christ, can you stop pointing at random people?"

Jess turned and grabbed my shoulders, giving me a little shake. "Seriously, Vare! Even my mother loves your poetry, and that woman hires a professional to get in touch with her emotions."

I smirked. The first time we saw the movie *The Terminator*, we couldn't help but draw similarities between its killer robot and Jess's mother. Mei Lyn was a fast-talking, always-on-the-go powerhouse of a woman. God knows how she ended up with a daughter like my bohemian, free-spirited best friend.

Then a group of sulky-looking schoolgirls walked by. Jess's eyes lit up. I glared at her. "Don't even think—"

Her hand shot out. "There!"

One girl looked directly at us, and I wanted to die.

"Great," I muttered under my breath. "She's coming over."

"Stop freaking out. It's a schoolgirl, not Pennywise."

Easy for her to say, I thought, my heart in my throat.

The girl stopped at the edge of our rug, staring down at Jess. "Do I know you?"

"Definitely not."

"Then why were you pointing at me?"

I glanced nervously at her friends, who had stopped and were looking over at us with a hint of animosity.

"Do you like poetry?" Jess asked. The girl's eyes narrowed. "What the hell are you talking about?"

Jess picked up Mena's book and flashed it at her. The girl's face lit up. "Oh my God! Is that her new one?"

Jess nodded. "Fresh off the shelf."

"I love Mena; like, I'm literally obsessed with her! I follow her on Instagram and Twitter."

"Well, if you like Mena's work, you might want to check out Verity Wolf."

The girl wrinkled her brow. "I've never heard of her."

"You're in luck! Because she's right here, sitting in front of you." Jess jabbed my shoulder with the tip of her finger, and I groaned out loud.

The girl rolled her eyes. "Is that right?"

"She's going to be famous one day—just you wait and see!"

"Don't listen to my friend—she's crazy." I gave the girl an apologetic smile.

"Could you read a few of her poems? I want to know what you think, and you can be brutally honest," Jess asked.

The girl smirked. "Sure, I'll read some of her poems."

"Seriously, can you just ignore this raving lunatic—" I started.

The girl crossed her arms and glared at me. "Hey, I walked all the way over here, so you'd better show me something."

I blinked at her and considered my options. I couldn't think of a way out, so, reluctantly, I reached into my back pocket and pulled out an old receipt book and passed it to her. Pop kept a stack of them in his office and didn't mind when I used the odd one to jot down my poems. I always kept one handy, in case a poem came to me out of the blue.

I watched the girl's face as she flicked through the little book, but her expression gave nothing away.

I snuck a glance at Jess, who was now grinning like a Cheshire cat. Finally, the girl looked up, and my heart practically stopped.

"Hey, you're, like, actually good! Do you have an Instagram?"

"Um, yeah, I do! If you want to add me, my name's Verity Wolf."

She had her phone out before I even finished my sentence.

"Followed you," she said. "But you haven't posted anything yet."

"I'll post some poems today," I promised.

"Cool," she said, before sauntering back to her friends.

My heart was pounding so loud in my chest I felt as if it were going to burst. "I swear, one of these days, I'm going to kill you, Jess."

She gave me a smug look. "I think you owe me five bucks."

Two

THE OLD, RUSTY bell clanged noisily as I pushed through the glass door of Wolf Books. The bell had been a fixture in there ever since the store opened—even before I was born. Jess told Pop he should replace it with a modern door chime, but Pop thinks the bell gives the store character. He's probably right. The bell sometimes even got a mention when someone blogged about the old-world charm of our bookshop. But the real star is Pop. Five foot eleven and broad shouldered, he could come across as slightly menacing when we had unwelcome visitors like salesmen or religious zealots. He had a shock of white hair that made him look slightly mad and gray-green eyes that were full of either contempt or love depending on who or what was in front of them. Right now, he had just finished stringing up a banner.

His eyes twinkled when he saw me.

"There's the birthday girl! What do you think?"

We stood back to admire his handiwork.

A VERITY HAPPY BIRTHDAY TO YOU

I snorted.

"I had it specially made up."

"Must have cost a fortune!" I felt guilty. Wolf Books had been going through some tough times, and even though Pop kept a brave face, I knew how much strain he must be under.

"I have a fund for purchases like this."

"You know my birthday's not until next week."

He looked at me warmly, shaking his head. "Can't believe my girl's nineteen. Time sure does fly."

He was right. My mind drifted back to a birthday years ago when I stood in this exact spot. I remembered it like yesterday. Jess was holding a cardboard box out to me, with Pop and Nan grinning behind her. Inside, I found a tiny Snowshoe kitten mewing up at me, a dark patch stretched across his eyes like a mask. "You should name him Zorro," Jess had suggested, and the name stuck. For as long as I could remember, I had begged for a kitten, and it was one of the happiest moments of my life. Just as I was reminiscing about Zorro, I felt a soft pressure at the base of my ankle, and I looked down to see him rubbing his head against me. I bent down and picked him up.

"Nan would have loved the banner, Pop."

A sad look fell across his face. It was my first birthday without her, and I knew it must be on his mind, too. Pop and Nan met and fell in love when they were teenagers. Up until her passing, they had barely spent a day apart. For him, the loss was huge, and it took a toll on his health. Pop was such a strong, capable person— it frightened me to see him age almost overnight. It took a lot of convincing, but finally he agreed to a checkup, and tests showed that his heart wasn't exactly up to scratch. The doctor warned him to slow down, but if you knew what Pop was like, that was easier said than done. Today, he looked almost frail, and I was worried about him climbing up stepladders. "Jess would have helped you put up the sign, Pop."

He waved me off. "I'm not an invalid. Besides," he shot me a mysterious smile, "Jess is busy working on something else."

"So now, why don't you go upstairs and finish that book you're reading? I'll bring up a cup of tea for you."

He narrowed his eyes. "I know what you're doing."

"Doctor's orders," I grinned.

"Well, a new box of books came in today, and I was just about to—"

"Deny your one and only granddaughter the joy of sorting through old books?"

He smiled and shook his head. "OK, you win. It came via FedEx this morning, and it's over by the counter. It was a blind bid, but there could be something valuable there—you never know. So this is a white-glove operation."

"Noted," I said with a firm nod. "Leave it to me, Pop."

☆

AFTER I LEFT Pop settled into his favorite armchair with a mug of Earl Grey, I raced downstairs. The box was sitting on the floor, and I dived straight in. This was my favorite thing about working in a bookstore. Every time we got a new shipment, it was like Christmas. My eyes lit up when finally I got it open. It filled with old leather-bound books, with intricate gold lettering on the covers, authored by obscure poets. What a treasure trove! I sat cross-legged on the floor and eagerly flicked through them while Zorro jumped into the box and curled up into a ball. "Don't get too comfortable, buddy," I warned.

I'd had a long-standing love affair with poetry. When Pop had wanted to replace the poetry nook with travel books, I made an impassioned plea to keep it. After days of my cajoling and foot stamping and a short-lived hunger strike, he finally agreed to keep the poetry section, but only so long as I promised to look after it. Since then, it's been my own little corner of the world. I liked to imagine the poets themselves when I arranged their books on the shelf. I pictured Óndra Lysohorsky in long, rambling conversations with Rumi about sundials and flowers. Dorothy Parker would talk to Emily Dickinson about rhyming meters and cats. We became the last bookshop in Sydney with a poetry section. It seemed inevitable that this most beautiful form of our language was dying, but then Mena Rhodes wrote her book and turned it all around. Soon, other aspiring poets followed her lead, and poetry grew into a trend no one saw coming. At first, the establishment ignored it, chalking it up to a fad. But as book sales broke into seven figures, they dubbed the group the pop poets, legitimizing the movement. After Mena Rhodes, there came Rita Singh, Samira Ahmadi, K.C. Gray, and Sara Woo. Each had amassed a global social media following, and their signing events were like rock concerts, with crowds that would put some pop idols to shame. Soon, the poets were mixing with musicians, models, and movie stars. Their Instagram feeds became a constant parade of flashy hotels, rooftop parties, paparazzi, and exotic island holidays.

I took out the newly arrived books one by one, trying my best not to disturb Zorro, who was now glaring at me, tail twitching in the air. I gave his head a scratch, and he flipped onto his back, stretching his paws out. Then a book caught my eye, and I reached for it.

The book looked ancient, like it had been made by hand. The cover edges were worn, the pages yellow and brittle. It was thick and heavy, bound in black cloth, with a single word embossed onto the cover. I ran my fingers over it, and a shiver went down my spine.

"*Poemsia*," I whispered.

I turned its pages carefully, reading verse after verse, each one lovelier than the next. I stopped on a page and sucked in a breath. Before me was a poem so arresting I couldn't help but read it over and over.

The poem was a love letter to a literary character. And it made me think of my first fictional crush and how sad I'd felt at the close of the final chapter when the time came to say goodbye. Nostalgic and bittersweet—it was possibly the most beautiful poem I had ever read. I snapped a picture and sent it to Jess.

She called me right away. "That's gorgeous, Vare! Your best one yet."

"I didn't write it, silly."

"Oh, it looks like something you would write."

"I wish! I found it in a really old poetry book."

"What's the name of the book?"

"*Poemsia*," I said.

"Weird. I got goose bumps when you said that."

"*Poemsia?*"

"The word sounds so familiar. Like I heard it in a dream."

I felt a tiny fluttering in my chest like anticipation—although for what I wasn't sure.

The bell clanged loudly, and I snapped to my feet. "Jess, I've got to go. A guy just walked in."

"Is he cute?"

I gave him a glance. Probably in his early twenties, jeans, gray sweater, tall, and clean-shaven. Not bad.

"Maybe. I'll call you back." I hung up.

He sauntered to the counter and said, "Hey." Up close, he not only was pleasant to look at but smelled great, too. Like soap and sandalwood. His dark, rumpled hair fell against his forehead in waves. And I couldn't help but notice his eyes. Green—and not a light green, or a gray-green, or a green bordering on blue. Definitively green, like the color of envy.

"Can I help you?" I asked.

"I'm looking for an ultra-rare book. Chances are you won't have it."

"Try me."

"*Door into the Dark*, by Seamus Heaney."

"Poetry!" I could hardly contain my delight.

His eyes widened. "So you do have the book?"

I sighed. "Yes and no."

He raised his eyebrows.

"Hold on a second." I turned and walked over to the cabinet where Pop kept his treasured books. Among them was a first edition of *Door into the Dark* signed by the author. I went back to the counter and handed it to him. He looked radiant, like he couldn't believe his luck. He turned the page and whistled.

"It's autographed and—holy shit, there's even an inscription."

"My granddad found it at a flea market in Brussels. Can you believe it?"

He shook his head. Then his expression changed from one of utter delight to disappointment.

"It's a first edition," he said flatly. "No way can I afford this."

"Well, that's the thing—it's not for sale."

"Fantastic," he sighed. "I've gone to every store in town, and I can't find a copy."

"I'm sure you can get one online."

"Yeah, but shipping takes forever, and I'm in a hurry. My friends and I have this tradition where we try to make a big deal out of each other's birthdays. I don't know how it started, and to be honest, it is getting out of control. For my last birthday, they organized a party at my parents' house. They took me out into the yard, and there was a donkey standing there."

"What the hell?"

"Exactly. Then they blindfolded me, spun me around, and shoved a paper tail into my hand. There were bits of Velcro attached to it, and I literally had to pin the tail on the donkey."

"How did that go?"

"Terrible! It's a lot harder than you'd imagine. I almost ended up in the pool. But I have to admit it was fun. The only thing is . . . how do you top that? How do you top a donkey in your backyard?"

"No idea," I said, wondering what all this had to do with Seamus Heaney's book.

"Anyway, our friend Penelope's birthday is coming up, and we had the idea to redecorate her studio apartment as a surprise. She's turning twenty-two, and she's a huge fan of black. So we're going to find twenty-two items that are black. So far, we have a lamp, a bedspread, a rug, umm . . . a notepad, a photo frame . . ." He counted each item off on his fingers.

"OK, dude, I get the picture. But what does this have to do with *Door into the Dark?*"

"It just happens to be Pen's favorite book, and I wanted to scan in some pages and make a collage to hang on her wall."

"That's a nice idea, and personally, I'd rather have my place redecorated than get a donkey in my backyard."

He sighed. "The donkey was great, but between you and me, I would have preferred something modest, like an iTunes gift card and my friends singing around a cake. At this point, we're just in competition to outdo each other."

I laughed. It was the opposite with me and Jess. We downplayed our birthdays. Usually, we did the same old thing, and I'd treat myself to something special like two shots of espresso in my mocha instead of one.

"You know, it just so happens my birthday is next week." I pointed at the banner Pop had strung up earlier.

"Cute! I'm guessing you're Verity?"

"Uh-huh."

"Any plans for the big day?"

"Not really, and anyhow, I don't think anything could top the year I got my cat, Zorro." On cue, he jumped up onto the counter and regarded the guy with a suspicious glare.

"Is this him?" The guy held his hand out in a loose fist, and Zorro rubbed his head against it. That was weird because my cat usually has trust issues.

I nodded.

"Hey, little guy," he said to my cat. "My name's Sebastian, but you can call me Sash."

Zorro let out a half meow and rolled onto his side, purring.

And just like that, this guy Sash had won me over.

"Look, I can see you're under a lot of stress, so I'll tell you what. I'll lend you the book, but you have to bring it back before Pop—my granddad—notices it's missing. So I'll need your phone number and some ID so I can hunt you down if you don't show up." I narrowed my eyes at him. "And I will hunt you down."

"Deal!" he said, enthusiastically. "I'll guard it with my life."

He reached into his back pocket and pulled out his wallet. He put his driver's license on the counter, and I took a snap of it.

"OK, now pass me your phone, and I'll pop my number in," he said when I was done.

I handed my phone to him, and he punched in his number. I smiled when I saw he had put it under "Sash book guy."

I told him, "This is a one-off, OK? We're not running a library here."

"Gotcha! Thanks, Verity, and happy birthday for next week."

"Good luck with your decorating."

As soon as he left, I remembered the promise I had made to the girl at the park. It had been ages since I'd logged on to Instagram, and the only two people I followed were Mena Rhodes and Jess.

On my feed appeared a picture of Mena posing with her French bulldog named French Fry, captioned with #loveofmylife #furbabyforever and a string of heart emojis. I smiled at French Fry's goofy expression. With an Instagram page boasting thousands of adoring fans, the cute puppy was a celebrity himself.

I checked my notifications and found a new follower named Mallory. I recognized her as the schoolgirl from the park and followed her back. Then I posted half a dozen of my best poems. It looked kind of bare, so I put up a snap of Zorro and that poem I found in *Poemsia*, tagging it with #poemsia, #inspo, and #notmine.

I remembered to call Jess. "I've put some stuff on Instagram," I said when she answered.

"Oh, cool, let me check it out." There was a pause. "Wow, you've been busy!"

"And guess what? The schoolgirl from the park just liked a bunch of my poems!"

"I'm super proud of you, Vare! I've been trying to get you to post your work for ages."

"I know, and you were right. But it's so scary having my poetry out there. What if everyone hates it?"

"There's already someone who doesn't." Jess was referring to Mallory.

"I guess. I just feel so . . . exposed. What if someone comes along and steals my work?"

"And what if they do? You'll just keep writing better stuff."

"Hey, you're totally right Jess!"

"Of course, I am," she chirped. "By the way—what were we talking about earlier?"

"*Poemsia*—the book I found. And then the cute guy walked in."

"So he was cute, huh?"

"Well, he wasn't bad looking." I thought about his emerald-green eyes. They were ridiculously pretty. Admittedly, so was the rest of him.

"Did you get his number?"

"Yes."

"Way to go, girlfriend!" She sounded impressed.

"It's not what you're thinking, Jess." I gave her a brief summary, starting from the elaborate birthday surprises organized with his friends to him leaving with Pop's prized copy of *Door into the Dark*.

"So you have a snap of his photo ID. Hmm."

"Forget it, Jess; I'm not sending it to you."

"Hey, do you think this could be the start of something?"

"Please. We only spoke for, like, two minutes."

"There's such a thing as love at first sight, you know. Literally millions of cases recorded. And it's been ages since you've even looked twice at a guy."

Jess was such a romantic. Once she organized a blind date for me and her cousin Ed, and he spent the entire time bombarding me with questions about whom she liked, where she went, and what she ate. It felt more like an interrogation than a date. "I think your cousin's in love with you," I told her afterward. To her horror, I had added, "And I'm pretty sure he's reading your diary."

"It's not like your love life is action-packed, either," I pointed out.

"Exactly, and if a couple of cuties like us are still single, that proves there's a shortage of men."

"You've got a point," I admitted. "But how do I know he's single?"

She countered with, "How do you know he's not?"

Three

I WOKE UP on the morning of my birthday to see Pop at my bedside cradling a muffin with a candle stuck in it. "Happy birthday to you," he sang in his low, gravelly voice.

"Thanks, Pop," I smiled, sitting up to blow out the candle.

That was when I noticed the package wrapped in red paper on my bedside table.

"For me?"

"Go ahead and open it."

I tore through the wrapping and gasped. It was a hardcover of *Cult of Two*, the book that had rocketed Mena Rhodes to fame. Her autograph was on the title page, scrawled in black ink. I ran my fingers over her signature and felt a thrill knowing Mena had actually held this book in her hands. "Where did you get this?"

"I had to pull a few strings."

"What kind?"

"The eBay kind," he winked.

I laughed. "This definitely is going into the cabinet."

"No. This one's for you to enjoy." He tapped the top of my bedside table. "You keep it right here."

LATER I MET Jess at Last Chance, our regular café and the pride and joy of Jonesy, a twenty-something hipster with red retro-styled hair. He was a glass-full kind of guy—eternally optimistic—even though things didn't go his way much. That included dates from hell, frequent and unexplainable dents in his car, and his shady landlord who kept upping the rent whenever he pleased, which meant Jonesy was always on the brink of going out of business. If that were to happen, we would be just as devastated as Jonesy. And we wouldn't be alone. Jonesy was a most important part of our community. In the few short years Last Chance had been operating, it truly had become our second home. There were the rainbow macarons, the chaotic furniture with not a single matching table or chair, and the large magnetic wall dubbed the Altar. It was where Jonesy proudly displayed his amazing collection of fridge magnets. Over the years, his loyal customers kept adding magnets they found on their travels. It was no surprise Jonesy inspired such thoughtfulness since he was such a thoughtful guy himself—always making a point to remember someone's allergies or how they liked their coffee and eggs. He was particularly fond of Jess and me, often keeping our favorite table over by the window free for us.

Jess went to grab the latest issue of *Who* from a pile of magazines Jonesy kept by the counter. We loved our ritual of flipping through and discussing the lives of the rich and famous.

"Karla Swann's on the cover again—I just adore her!" Jess gushed, pushing the magazine across the table toward me.

Karla Swann was the undisputed voice of our generation. Years back, she shot to fame when her hilarious body-positive videos went viral. Since then, she's ruled Twitter with her fresh, witty commentary on everything from current affairs to feminism and climate change. She was dating K-pop sensation Henrietta Blue, and not a week went by that the two weren't photographed at glamorous events like the Met Gala or doing regular everyday things like picking up their morning coffees. I flipped through the magazine to pictures of the couple shopping at the exclusive LA boutique Money for Jam.

"Oh my God! How cute are they?" I said, holding up the magazine to Jess.

She sighed. "Tell me about it. Look at the expression on the shop assistant's face."

"You can tell she's a fangirl," I said, scanning the article. "According to her, they were just pulling clothes off the rack and taking them straight to the counter."

"They didn't even try them on?" Jess said, incredulous.

"Jess, they didn't even look at the price tags!"

"Wow, I heard a single T-shirt in Money for Jam can cost, like, hundreds. Imagine being that rich."

"I wish," I sighed. I thought about my wardrobe, which consisted mainly of hand-me-downs from Jess and things I picked up from eBay or op shops. With the mounting cost of Pop's heart medication and other bills, there was hardly money to spare for luxuries like designer clothing.

"Karla really does have it all, doesn't she?" said Jess.

"Imagine being flown around the world to speak on issues you're passionate about."

"Or walking into a store with the knowledge you can buy literally anything you want. That's like having a superpower."

"And on top of all that, being in a cute relationship that the entire Internet obsesses over."

"Speaking of cute relationships, have you heard from that guy Sash?" Jess asked.

"He texted to let me know he dropped by, but he saw Pop manning the store and was too afraid to go in."

"Ha ha, who could blame him?"

"But says he'll come back tomorrow."

"Any other developments?"

"Jess, I'd practically forgotten he existed until you brought him up."

"Please, Vare—yesterday, you spent over ten minutes describing his eyes."

"He does have nice eyes, though. Sparkly."

"How sparkly?"

"Sparkly like a wine glass in a dishwashing liquid commercial, like teeth in a toothpaste advertisement, like a pair of cubic zirconia earrings in an infomercial, sparkly like—" I stopped and narrowed my eyes at her. "Just because I think his eyes are sparkly doesn't mean I'm hot for him."

"What do you think of Jonesy's eyes?"

"Puppyish."

"What color are they?"

For the life of me, I couldn't remember. Luckily, Jonesy chose that moment to appear with our coffees. I sneaked a quick look at him, then smirked at Jess. "Brown."

She gave my ankle a swift kick under the table.

"Girls," he said, setting down our coffees, "still playing footsie at your age?"

"Is it turning you on, Jonesy?" Jess said in a low, sultry voice, and he blushed a deep red.

"This is for you, birthday girl," he said, ignoring Jess. He put down a plate of his famous macarons.

"Aw, that's sweet of you," I cooed, fluttering my lashes at him.

"No—no worries," he stumbled and disappeared before we could give him any more grief.

We bit into our macarons, sighing with pleasure. Jess did a little shimmy and pointed at me. "Birthday gal, birthday gal," she sang tunelessly, and I joined in. "Birthday gal . . . birthday gal . . ."

The yuppie guy sitting at the next table cast a disapproving glance at us, and we clamped our hands over our mouths, laughter bubbling up behind them.

I made a grab for the last macaron, but Jess whipped it away, popping it straight into her mouth.

"But it's my birthday!" I protested.

"Vare, I love you to death, and I would give you my kidney if I had to. But please keep your hands away from my food."

I rolled my eyes. Jess was the most generous person I knew, except when it came to food. There were times she'd almost knocked me over in her hurry to snatch the last slice of pizza.

"Your present!" she announced, ruffling around in her bag and pulling out a book-shaped package. "Open it!"

I tore off the wrapping. When the book was in my hands, I did a double take. "What the hell . . . ?" I said slowly. I looked up at Jess. "That's my name on the cover."

"It's a book of your poetry!"

I frowned. "But how did you do this?"

"Well, I designed the cover, and my professor helped me put it together using InDesign."

I traced my fingers over the bold sans serif font. It looked so slick and professional, and I was simply in awe of my best friend's talent. "This is amazing, Jess! Like, seriously, you could enter this into a design competition."

"My professor said as much," Jess smiled proudly. "Oh, by the way, I've uploaded it onto Amazon CreateSpace, too!"

"Oh my God," I breathed. "That's how—"

"Mena got started—I know."

When Mena wrote her first book, there wasn't a publisher who would even look at an emerging poet. Growing more and more frustrated, she decided to go the self-publishing route, and it was only when her book started making best-seller lists that she was picked up.

I flipped through the pages in wonder, seeing my words reflected back at me. "It looks just like a real book!"

"That's because it is a real book. I got you an ISBN, too, which means it's official. And it's even listed on Amazon. You can buy it and everything. I have a box of them in my car."

"Seriously? You can buy the actual book?"

Jess grinned. "Go to Amazon and search for your name."

I did it, and my jaw dropped. My book was there, on Amazon, with a brief and somewhat inflated description of me. I shook my head. "I can't believe this."

"Why not, Vare? I've always believed in you."

Tears filled my eyes. "Jess—"

"C'mon, I want to show you something." Jess put a ten on the table and stood up.

She grabbed my arm. "Follow me."

She led me across the street to Berkelouw Books and took me straight to the new arrivals.

"Give me your book," she demanded, and I handed it to her. She walked right up to a shelf and placed it next to Mena's book. Then she stood back and grinned at me. "Imagine, Vare, your book on the shelf next to Mena's."

"Oh my God," I whispered, my voice heavy with emotion. "I had never realized how badly I want this."

"And you know what? You're going to make it happen."

I shook my head. I was so touched by what she had done for me—seeing my most cherished dream in front of my very eyes. "I don't know what to say . . . you're the best friend a girl could have."

"Oh, don't get all sentimental. Just promise me you'll do it, OK?" She gestured at the shelf.

"I promise," I said. Seeing my book next to Mena's gave me a burst of determination unlike anything I'd ever felt. That powerful vision before me was a reminder of what was possible if only I believed in myself.

"You swear you'll get your book on that shelf someday—that you will do whatever it takes?" Jess pressed.

I reached out and curled my little finger around hers. "Pinky swear."

☆

THE NEXT DAY, I was reorganizing the poetry section when the bell clanged. I poked my head around to see Sash walk through the door.

"How did it go?" I asked, as he handed back the book I'd loaned him.

"Awesome. Pen was over the moon. She loved the collage best, which was possible only because of you. I owe you one."

I went behind the counter and put Seamus Heaney back in his rightful place.

"Do you think you managed to top the donkey?"

"No doubt in my mind. Want to see pictures?" He took his phone out and handed it to me.

"Whoa," I said, as I scrolled through the photos. It looked like a scene from a home makeover show. A studio apartment was transformed into a gothic wonderland. I focused on a close-up of the collage, and my eyes widened. Poems by Seamus Heaney marched like ants across a monochromatic landscape. Layers of paper were cut like waves between the lines of words to form an intricate collage.

"Are you or your friends interior designers?" I asked.

"Not exactly. I studied architecture, but I'm not doing much with my degree."

"The collage is awesome. I was expecting a few pages from the book comped together, but what you've done is a work of art."

"I'm glad you like it."

"Are you taking orders? I want one!"

"No, but I can make you one, if you'd like."

"Are you serious?"

He shrugged. "Sure. Like I said, I owe you one."

"Well, in that case, I'll take you up on your offer."

"Do you have a favorite book or color?"

I thought for a minute. "I like green. As for the book, why don't you surprise me?"

"OK, sounds like a plan. After this we're even steven —deal?"

I stuck my hand out. "Let's shake on it."

☆

LATER THAT WEEK, Jess helped me set up a little display for my books using an old pamphlet holder. We put it on the front counter by the cash register. Every time the bell sounded, I looked up hopefully, thinking it could be my first sale. But by the end of the week, I still hadn't sold a single copy. On the flip side, my newly opened Instagram account had close to twenty followers, mainly because Mallory had shared my work with her friends.

I just had the idea to put up a link to my Amazon page when I was interrupted by the bell. I looked up to see Jess walking in with a board tucked under her arm. "Guess what I made in print class today?" I gave her a questioning look.

"Ta-da!" she declared, holding it up for me. Printed on the board in a bold cursive font were the words "Poetry in the Park." "Remember that day we were in the park and I bet you five bucks that anyone there would love your poetry?"

I knew exactly where she was going with this, and I wanted to put a stop to it then and there. "No. Absolutely not."

"I thought we could set up a table and put your books out, and you could maybe read some of your poetry—"

"Are you crazy? I'd rather die."

"Mum even agreed to lend us her gold microphone."

I stopped. "Are you serious?" I asked in a hushed voice.

Mei Lyn was, to put it mildly, a karaoke enthusiast. When Jess and I were kids, we'd watch her croon away into the night while we jumped up and down, angling for our turn. Mei Lyn would clutch the microphone tighter in one hand, batting us away with the other, never once missing a beat.

"Yes. I had to swap her a whole week's dish duty to get her to agree."

"That's sweet of you, Jess, and I am so, so grateful for your sacrifice. Too bad it was all for nothing because the answer is still no."

She let out an exasperated sigh. "But you've got to start somewhere!"

"I got another follower on Instagram today— we've moved into double digits now. When will you ever be happy?"

"Vare, remember that day in Berkelouw when you promised you were going to get your book on the shelf next to Mena's? That you would do whatever it takes?"

"Yes, but I don't understand how reciting my poetry to a bunch of strangers is going to help."

"It's part of putting yourself out there—right? You just never know who could be in the audience. Besides, what's the worst that can happen?"

"That's my point. For me, there's nothing worse than public speaking."

Jess was a natural performer, and loved the stage. I was the exact opposite. On the rare occasion I had to give a speech, I'd break out into a sweat, and my mouth would go dry. The idea of reading my work to a bunch of strangers was enough to send me into a panic.

Jess put the sign down on the counter and looked me squarely in the eye. "OK. I didn't want to do this, but you've forced my hand. Do you remember the spider?"

I groaned. "Seriously?"

"I still have it—the contract. With your signature on it."

A few years back, Jess was staying over for the night. We were about to switch the lights out when I turned and saw a large blob out of the corner of my eye. My head snapped toward it. At first, I thought Zorro had brought a bird into the house, and it had escaped his clutches. That had happened occasionally—Pop and I had to chase it with a butterfly net while Zorro watched the ensuing chaos with intense interest. But this wasn't a bird. My mouth opened in horror. It was a gigantic spider the size of my hand. Meanwhile, Jess had followed my horrified stare, and when her eyes fell on the spider, she gasped and grabbed my arm. "What the hell!" she hissed under her breath.

It scurried up a beam, and we had to cover our mouths to keep from screaming. We didn't know what to do. Waking Nan and Pop was out of the question. It was well past lights out, and we'd get into trouble for staying up so late.

"What the heck are we going to do, Jess?" I whispered desperately.

She looked at the spider, mesmerized. "We can't sleep with that thing in the room—it will kill us."

"This is a possible life-and-death situation," I agreed. The thought of the spider crawling across my face while I was fast asleep gave me a jolt of revulsion.

We kept our eyes glued to the spider while we worked out a plan.

"What if we did sentry duty—two hours each. You watch my back while I sleep, then I'll watch yours," Jess suggested.

"OK, sounds good."

"You go first," she said as she snuggled down.

"Hang on a second! It's two in the morning, and we stayed up only because you wanted to watch *Finding Nemo* for the hundredth time. Plus, I pulled an all–nighter yesterday to finish my English assignment. So I think I get the first two hours, OK?"

"Verity, this is your house, which means you solely are responsible for that monstrosity. If it was my house, I would be more gracious."

"That's not fair!"

"Fine." She sat up. "Only one way to settle this." She balled her fist at me.

"Fine." I balled my fist, and we said in unison, "Rock. Paper. Scissors."

Her rock beat my scissors.

"Best out of three!" I cried.

She balled her fist again, and I bit my lip in concentration, trying to anticipate her next move. But in the end, Jess still won.

"Well," she said, a little smugly, "I guess I'll be seeing you in two hours. Nighty night!"

"Jess . . . " I said, feeling desperate. By now, I was past exhaustion. Every cell in my body was screaming for sleep. "Please, I'll do anything."

"Anything?" Her eyes glittered.

"Yes, anything."

She grabbed her copy of *Hating Alison Ashley* and a pen. She scratched something into the back of the book and handed it to me.

This is a binding contract between Jessica
Lui and Verity Wolf. Jessica agrees to
do sentry duty for the first two hours
to guard Verity against the ginormous
spider in Verity's bedroom. In exchange,
Verity will grant Jessica one wish-

I looked up at her. "A wish? What am I—a genie?"

She took the book from me, crossed out "wish," and replaced it with "favor."

"There. Happy?"

I continued reading.

Verity will grant Jessica one ~~wish~~ favor,
for as long as she (Verity) shall live.

"What kind of favor?" I asked, suspiciously.

She shrugged. "Who knows what the future has in store for us or when I might find you useful?"

"That's too vague," I protested.

"Vare, I would never ask you to do anything life-threatening."

"That's really comforting."

"Well, it's up to you." She stretched and yawned.

I glared at her. "Fine, give me the pen."

As she handed it to me, a wicked smile broke across her face. I signed, feeling like I had just sold my soul.

"Ha, I own you now," she crowed. "Enjoy your nap,

Verity." I'm sure if Nan and Pop weren't fast asleep, she would have started cackling.

"You are your mother's daughter."

Soon, I sank into a deep sleep and only realized what I had done when Jess woke me a few hours later. By then, it was too late.

Now, years later, Jess had brought out the promise I made, and she was going to play her hand. She watched me, a grin on her face. Her eyes flickered to the Poetry in the Park sign. "So let's plan it for . . . Saturday?"

"You are pure evil," I said and felt dread in the pit of my stomach.

She smiled at me sweetly. "You'll thank me one day."

Four

I woke up Saturday morning with butterflies in my stomach. By the time Jess picked me up in her little white Honda, the butterflies were more like a swarm of angry bees.

We packed an old trestle table into the trunk along with a black tablecloth, a table easel, and a box of my books. Jess had made a couple of posters and coerced Jonesy to stick one up at his café. She'd also pinned one to her college noticeboard.

We got to Centennial Park just after noon and chose a spot under a tree. I had hoped for bad weather so I'd have an excuse to cancel, but no luck. It was a beautiful day, warm and sunny with a whisper of a breeze.

We set up the trestle table and draped the tablecloth over it. Jess put her Poetry in the Park sign on the easel and placed it on the tabletop alongside copies of my book. "There," she said, a look of solid satisfaction on her face.

A small group of people gathered around watching us. I turned to Jess, and she had Mei Lyn's prized microphone in her hand. It made a small hissing sound when she switched it on.

"What do we do?" I whispered.

Jess straightened and spoke. "Hello, everyone. Welcome to Poetry in the Park. Today, we are featuring a rising star in the poetry world, Verity Wolf. Please watch this face of hers, ladies and gentlemen, because she is going all the way to the top! Verity now has her book for sale." Jess held up a copy for everyone to see. "They are ten dollars each, and our lovely poet will be happy to autograph your copy. You can also find her on Instagram, at Verity Wolf—all one word, lowercase. And please don't forget to tag all your friends as well! Now, everyone, put your hands together for Verity Wolf!" There was some light clapping and a couple of hoots, and the commotion got the attention of other passersby. The group was growing into a small crowd, and suddenly, all eyes were on me. I gulped and took the microphone from Jess.

"Um, hi. I'm Verity—Verity Wolf. Thank you for coming out to see me. Ah . . . today, I will be reading a selection of poems from my, um . . . book. I hope you like them!" I took a deep breath. I was shaking, and I wanted to run and flee, but Jess handed me a copy of my book and mouthed, "Good luck." All I could do was turn to a random page and clear my throat.

As I read, a strange thing happened. The people all somehow faded away, and I wasn't nervous anymore. I read poem after poem, growing bolder and more expressive with each one. My audience listened, rapt, and I felt pure adrenaline rush through my veins. Hey, I'm actually good at this, I thought. Out of the corner of my eye, I could see Jess. She looked like she was over the moon. I saw that the book pile was smaller and realized with a jolt that she must have sold some.

Finally, I stopped, took a few big breaths, and thanked the audience for listening and Jess for organizing the event. There was more applause and hooting before the crowd began to disperse.

A girl came up to me, clutching a copy in her hand. "Mallory!" I said, delighted.

"Can you sign this for me?" she asked, handing me a glitter pen.

"Sure."

I worried that I'd pass out with all this excitement. I couldn't believe what was actually happening. I autographed Mallory's copy, and I looked over at Jess, who was watching us with a huge grin on her face. I felt a big, warm wave of affection sweep through me. She was the one who'd made this possible. I was so damn lucky to have her in my life.

"I love all the poems you've posted " said Mallory.

I beamed at her. "Thank you!"

"My friends really like your stuff as well. Keep posting!"

As she wandered off, I felt my heart filling up like a balloon. I didn't know why I had been so resistant to this idea and vowed that from now on I would be more open to Jess's crazy schemes.

"Morning!" A gruff voice interrupted my thoughts. I looked up to see an unfriendly looking police officer glaring down at me.

"Morning," I gulped, taking a step back.

He took off his aviator shades, popping them into his front pocket. "Are you running some kind of business here?"

"Um, no. We're—it's just an art project," I said nervously. He raised his eyebrows at me and gestured toward Jess, who was just exchanging a book for a ten-dollar bill.

"Looks like a business to me. Do you have a permit?"

Jess looked over at us, and her eyebrows shot up in alarm. She came over in a flash.

"Hi, officer, is there a problem?" she asked cheerfully.

"You bet there is. You're not allowed to operate a business in this park without a permit. You know, you could be liable for a hefty fine." He puffed out his chest and glared at us. There wasn't a lot of action in the park, and it was just our luck to have a run-in with a cop on a power trip.

"Hold on a minute," said Jess. She whipped out her phone and dialed a number. Then, without a word, she handed the phone to the officer. "Here, it's for you."

He raised his eyebrows and brought the phone to his ear, wincing as he was attacked by Mei Lyn's wordy assault. "Lady . . . lady, your daughter is operating an illegal business in the park—"

We sensed Mei Lyn rattling away while the cop tried in vain to get a word in.

"Yes, but—liable for massive fines . . . uh, no I did not know that. No, of course not . . . there's no need to escalate this matter . . ." He shot us a wary look. Then, as Mei Lyn continued to fire away, I noted a slump in his shoulders, almost like he was visibly shrinking right before our eyes. "Yes, OK, I understand, ma'am."

With a sigh, he handed the phone back to a now-triumphant Jess. When he spoke again, the cockiness had left his voice. "OK, girls, pack it up and don't let me catch you out here again."

☆

WHEN WE GOT back to the store, Jess and I were on a high, laughing and hanging onto each other. Pop was at the counter, talking with great impatience to some unlucky guy. When the guy turned around, I saw it was Sash, and my heart did a little skip.

Pop's head swiveled toward me. "Verity, this young man here says he's your friend. Is that true?"

"Uh, yeah, kind of," I stammered.

"Then why is he trying to sell me something from his college?"

Sash shot me a helpless look, and I saw he had a rectangular-shaped package in his hand. "I've just, um, finished your collage and thought I'd drop it by."

"Oh!" In all the excitement leading up to my reading in the park, I'd completely forgotten about our deal. "Pop, I think he meant 'collage,' and he's not trying to sell us anything. Sash makes really cool collages, and he offered to make me one as a thank-you—" I stopped.

"A thank-you for what?" Pop asked.

I gave him a sheepish grin. "I kind of loaned him one of your signed books."

"You did what now?"

"He needed to scan in a few pages to make a collage—it's a long story."

Pop looked from me to Sash, who was fumbling with the brown paper wrapping. Once it was free, he handed it to Pop.

Pop's expression softened. "Gee, well, this isn't bad—not bad at all." He looked up at Sash. "You made this?"

Sash nodded.

Pop motioned me over. "Come here, Verity—see whether you recognize this book."

"*The Green Wind*," I breathed. "I love that book!"

"Hey, that's really something," said Jess, who had come up behind me.

I had seen only a photograph of the collage Sash had made for his friend. Now, holding one in my hand, I saw it was something else entirely. Carefully, I ran my fingers over the ridges and grooves made from layers and layers of paper. It had green text on white paper and white text on green. Slivers of the cover peeked through in a fractured composition that looked random yet somehow deliberate. It was as though the book was made of glass and someone had dropped it from a great height then captured the moment it had shattered.

I looked up at him. "This is incredible! How did you know I so love this book?"

"Lucky guess," he shrugged, with a grin.

I was so absorbed in the collage I forgot that Jess and Sash hadn't been introduced. I put it down and turned to him. "Oh, by the way, I see you've met Pop, and this is my best friend, Jess."

Jess smiled at him. "You must be Sash. Verity has told me so much about you."

I looked at her with daggers in my eyes, and all my warm feelings from this morning evaporated.

Sash raised his eyebrows. "She has?"

"I told her about the donkey," I said quickly. "I thought it was a funny story."

"How did you girls do at the park?" Pop asked.

"Awesome!" Jess crowed. "Couldn't have gone any better. Vare kicked ass. You should have seen the audience when she read her poetry. Everyone was dead silent. You could've heard a pin drop. Also, we sold, like, half a dozen books!"

Pop reached over and pinched my cheek. "Well done!"

I grinned at him.

Sash shot me a quizzical look. "You write poetry?"

"Lucky last copy! Here, it's all yours," Jess said, handing him my book. He turned it over in his hands, looking impressed.

"Thanks."

"Also, a cop came by and practically tried to arrest us for operating an illegal business, but Jess called her mother, and she sorted him, quick."

"She basically murdered him—it was beautiful to watch," Jess laughed.

"Jess's Mum is a barrister," I explained to Sash. "She's a killer in the courtroom and has a reputation for reducing grown men to tears."

"A talent I wish I had inherited," Jess sighed.

"Sure wouldn't want to be in Mei Lyn's way when she's on the warpath," Pop agreed. "Remember when they tried to force me into selling this old place and she put a stop to it?" His eyes lit up at the memory.

Jess smiled proudly. "That's my mother, all right."

"All in all, a fantastic day," I said. "We sold some books, I got some new Instagram followers, and we got to witness Mei Lyn in action, which is poetry in itself. Poetic justice."

"Aw!" Jess clapped her hands. "Verity just made a little joke."

I giggled.

"Anyway, we should go out tonight to celebrate." Jess turned to Sash. "Want to join us?"

"Ah, I'd love to, but I'm meeting some friends at Fidelio."

"Isn't that the bar where they hold those life-drawing classes?"

"Uh-huh. Nude models every Tuesday."

"I've been meaning to check it out," Jess said.

"Why don't you two come along? My friend Penelope writes poetry, too."

For situations like this, Jess and I had a signal. One cough meant yes. Two meant no.

I coughed twice.

"Yes!" she said. "We'd love to come."

My mouth fell open. "But Jess, don't we have to do the thing?"

She shot me a wicked grin. "The thing can wait, Vare."

Sash looked from me to Jess and back again. "So I'll pick you guys up here at seven?"

"Seven is perfect," said Jess.

I KNEW FIDELIO was a bar on the outskirts of the city in an old converted warehouse with high ceilings and exposed beams. Round paper lanterns and tabletop candles gave it a soft ambience. A bar ran down the whole length of the establishment, and tables, barstools, and armchairs were arranged haphazardly across the polished wood floors. The far wall was decorated with sketches and poems on coasters donated by the artists, writers, and musicians who were regulars at the bar. Tonight, we found it buzzing with conversation and laughter.

Jess and I followed Sash to a table where two guys and a girl were in a heated debate about karma.

"—associated with Buddhism, along with reincarnation, so wouldn't karma apply to all your lives, not just the one—"

"Maybe it's cyclical; it applies to each individual life as well as holistically, over the entire map of your existence."

"But it's based on action, right? And behind each action, there's a choice that affects the outcome of your circumstances for better or worse. Unless you're telling me our lives are predetermined and we're just following some kind of template."

Sash cleared his throat, and the trio looked up at him. He lifted his hand in an awkward wave. "Hey, guys."

"You're late!" said the girl. She looked at us. "Didn't know you were babysitting tonight, Sash."

"Don't be rude, Pen. This is Verity and Jess—Verity is the girl from Wolf Books who loaned me *Door into the Dark*." He turned to us with an apologetic smile. "These are my friends, Penelope, Teddy, and Tom."

He pointed around the table. "Teddy and Tom are engaged," he added.

Penelope smirked while Teddy and Tom smiled at us.

"Don't mind Pen; she's an acquired taste," said Teddy. He had long caramel locks and a shadow of a beard. His eyes had a mischievous look, as if he was about to play a trick on you. He touched his hair often, and you could tell he was vain about it. His fiancé, Tom, had striking catlike eyes and the longest lashes I had ever seen. His hair was impossibly black and lustrous.

As for Penelope, she was a natural beauty. Not a stitch of makeup on her face, yet her skin was clear and dewy. Her champagne-blond hair was swept up in a tight ponytail. She wore black trousers and a jacket over a white T-shirt. She looked like a violinist ready to step onto the stage.

Suddenly, I felt self-conscious in my jeans and sweater emblazoned with the phrase "I am the crazy cat lady of your dreams."

We exchanged a few words of greeting before settling into seats. I glanced over at Jess and winked. She tapped my foot under the table and winked back.

Teddy leaned toward me. "So you're the girl from Wolf Books."

"Sure am."

"Gosh, that place has been around since I was a kid. It's such a relic." Teddy shook his head and smiled.

"How did you manage to score a copy of *Door into the Dark*?" asked Tom.

"My grandad found it at a flea market in Brussels."

"Talk about find of the century!" Teddy leaned in and gave me a conspiratorial wink. "What else have you got?" I rattled off a list that Pop had collected over decades, and he let out a whistle. "A first edition of *Notes from the Underground*? Whoa. Is there anything you don't have?"

"Well, there is one thing. Pop's favorite poet is Sal Dollinger, and it's one of his life goals to get an autographed book." Dollinger was one of the most celebrated American poets of all time. In addition to serving two terms as the poet laureate, he'd won practically every literary prize there was. He was openly gay and a prominent activist for LGBT rights.

"Oh, I love Sal Dollinger!" Teddy squealed. "His book *Grape* was literally my bible. I read it at sixteen, and it was the perfect backdrop for my sexual awakening."

"Mine was *Love Is a Dog from Hell*," said Jess.

Penelope made a face. "Bukowski? Ugh."

Jess looked at her. "What's your problem with Bukowksi?"

"I can't stand all that pulp fiction bullshit."

"What poets do you like, Penelope?"

She shrugged. "Calmine Verdue."

"Who is that?" Jess asked.

Penelope shot her an incredulous look. "You don't know Calmine Verdue? He was a sixteenth-century poet, son of an English aristocrat—a genius! Wrote in complex stanzas that corresponded with prime numbers. His subject matter centered mainly on fractals, mirrors, and death. His greatest masterpiece was his seminal poem written from the point of view of a worm making its way through the carcass of a wild boar."

"Sounds like fun." Jess's voice dripped sarcasm.

"I find Verdue a bit dry. I don't mind Bukowski, though," Tom piped in. "Granted, he doesn't have the best batting average, but when he gets it right, ball's out of the park."

"Tom, we've discussed this! As far as I'm concerned, there is not an ounce of merit in his entire body of work. What's more, he paved the way for the shit they're calling poetry these days."

"You mean pop poetry?"

She looked at him as though he had said a dirty word. "Pop poetry is not poetry; it's—" She threw up her hands. "It's something a monkey with a typewriter can do."

"Can a monkey with a typewriter sell millions of books?" Jess quizzed. If there was one thing she couldn't stand, it was a poetry snob.

"Pop poetry is just a stupid fad—like coloring books for adults."

"Isn't that what they said about Ginsberg and the whole Beat poetry movement?" Sash countered.

"Are you seriously drawing that comparison?"

"I don't see why not. The Beat movement attracted the same criticism they're heaping on pop poetry now. Maybe we just need to give it time before we call it."

Penelope rolled her eyes.

"Verity writes poetry!" Jess blurted. "In fact, she's just written her first book."

Penelope turned to me. "Really? Who's your publisher?"

I blushed. "Um, it's sort of self-published."

She snickered.

"Isn't that the way most writers start out?" Teddy said kindly.

"Someone's going to pick her up—it's just a matter of time," said Jess.

I flashed her a grateful smile.

"Is your book on Reader, Verity?" Tom asked.

"No—should it be?" I asked.

Reader was an online platform where you could review and recommend books. I'd never gotten around to signing up and wondered whether it was time I did. It could be a great place to promote my poetry.

But Tom quickly dispelled my idea. "Ah, I would stay away if I were you. It started out as a place for booklovers to share books they love, but now it's swung the other way. Many on the site read books purely to hate on them. It's become a spectator sport. They seem to have a special vendetta against pop poetry."

"Oh," I said, surprised. "Thanks for the heads-up. I'll be sure to avoid it like the plague."

"That's probably best. It's like certain reviewers are in competition to outdo each other when it comes to trashing books. For some people it's a serious hobby. Others are making a career of it. Isn't that right, Penelope?"

She rolled her eyes. "Don't put me in with that rabble just because I'm the top reviewer on Reader. So what if I'm tough on books? I'm just being honest. That's why they gave me the lit section on Billy." She smirked. "I mean, it's only the largest online news and media site in the world."

"It has nothing to do with the fact that Daddy golfs with the editor?" Teddy winked.

"Shut up, Teddy."

"Bashing authors has become such a trend now," Tom sighed. "There's even a phrase for it. It's called 'hate reading.'"

"Oh God, Tom, don't even start with all that shit. Authors shouldn't be so thin-skinned. If you put your work out there, you have to be open to criticism."

Tom drummed his fingers on the table. "That's all great, honey, if it was an even playing field. But you know that you and your friends sometimes play dirty."

"Who me?" She fluttered her eyelashes at him.

"Remember what you did to Anna Suzuki's latest book? You got your mitts on an advance copy and ripped it to shreds. Then everyone else followed in your footsteps, and her book ended up in the bargain bin. Which is a real shame—I liked it a lot."

"Oh, please, that book deserved everything I threw at it."

I gaped at her. "But I loved that book! It was definitely her best. I mean that twist at the end—"

"Oh my God, I did not see that coming!" said Jess.

Penelope let out an exasperated sigh. "That was the worst part of the book. It made no sense and was obviously written purely for shock value."

"On the contrary, I think it was genius, and it tied up the story nicely," I insisted.

Jess nodded in agreement.

Penelope fell silent, eyes locked onto mine. "What did you say your name was again?"

"Verity Wolf."

Teddy looked up sharply. "Pen, don't even think about it."

I looked from him to her. "Think about what?"

"If I know Penny like I do, she's just thought of writing a review for your book. But you're going to leave this one alone, aren't you, darling?" Teddy gave her a pointed look.

"Pen, please keep your opinion to yourself this time." Sash sounded wary. "Remember Verity's been really kind, lending me the book for your collage."

Penelope smiled sweetly at him. "Anything for you, my love."

A short silence fell over the group, and I had to wonder about Sash and Penelope's relationship. He referred to her as his friend, but I sensed an underlying tension between them, suggesting they were more than that. Not that it was any of my business.

A waitress came over to take our order. "We're drinking Deep Sea Diver," said Penelope, winking at Teddy.

"Ooh! I've heard about that beer, and I've been meaning to try it," said Jess.

The waitress grinned at her. "You do know these two adorable guys created Deep Sea Diver?" She waggled her forefinger between Teddy and Tom.

Jess's mouth fell open. "No way!"

"It's our baby." Teddy took Tom's hand, and they smiled at each other.

"I know, right? My friends are wildly accomplished, and I'm making collages," Sash said ruefully.

"Teddy and Tom started up a microbrewery straight out of business school," explained Penelope. "They worked like hell in the beginning, and now it's taking off. That's also great for me, considering I put up the capital to get the ball rolling."

"We'll be forever grateful, darling." Teddy blew her a kiss.

"So Deep Sea Diver all 'round?" prompted the waitress.

"Everyone except for me. I'm the designated driver," said Sash.

Penelope rolled her eyes at him and stood up. "Excuse me, I have to go to the ladies'."

Once again, I was struck by how gorgeous she was. Practically every head turned to watch her as she made her way across the bar.

"She's in a shitty mood tonight," said Teddy.

Sash sighed. "Pen submitted a manuscript of her poems awhile back, and she got the rejection letter today. She thought she had a chance this time because they took ages to get back."

"What's her poetry like?" I asked.

"Kind of like James Joyce, with a dash of Ayn Rand."

Teddy grimaced. "Not exactly the content that's flying off shelves nowadays, but hey, it's a sign of the times."

"I love that you're all book nerds. I'm guessing that's how you met?" Jess asked.

"Nope," said Sash. "We met at Jitterbugs Dance Academy. We were part of the same crew that won the state championships for three consecutive years."

"We ruled the nineties with our unique blend of ballet and hip-hop," Teddy laughed.

"Our teacher, Mrs. Parker, was an absolute tyrant. The world of competitive dancing is a dark, sadistic place. We clung to each other like bewildered circus children. There are stories we can tell."

"Like the time Parker caught Pen munching on a Hershey bar and the witch smacked it out of her hand. Pen was only nine!"

"Or when I was the only one in our group who couldn't do a perfect handstand and she brought out the gong," said Teddy.

"Oh, the gong!" Sash moaned, his head in his hands.

"The gong?" I asked.

"She'd wheel this huge gong out onto the stage, and each time we displeased her, she'd bash it. The noise was excruciating. It went right through your entire body."

"That gong still makes it into my nightmares," Tom shivered.

"I can't remember having a free weekend from the ages of seven to twelve. We literally had our childhoods stolen from us but there's—" Teddy started.

"No time for fun if you want to be number one!" The boys joined Teddy in chorus. They broke into laughter.

"It was Parker's mantra. Crazy bitch." Teddy shook his head. "But anyway, that's how we all got together. We're forever bound by the deep psychological trauma that was dance school."

"So what did I miss?" Penelope came back and took her seat.

"We were just reminiscing about Parker and our dance school days."

"Jesus Christ, let's not take that trip down memory lane. I still get panic attacks every time I catch my niece doing a pirouette."

AT LAST CHANCE, the next day, my eyes were glued to my phone, and Jess was trying to get my attention.

"Vare! Hello?"

"Just a second—almost done replying to a comment." My thumbs went into overdrive.

"But we haven't had a chance to talk about last night."

"You mean Fidelio with Sash and his friends?"

"Of course!" Jess clicked her fingers in front of my face. "Eyes here, Vare."

I grinned at her. "Sorry! But you're the one who started me on this Instagram thing."

"I've created a monster," she laughed.

"OK, I'm taking a break from Instagram. I'm all yours, Jess." I put my phone face down on the table.

She gave me a wistful look. "I've missed you, Vare."

"Ha, ha, very funny."

"OK, so last night . . ."

I bit my lip. "What do you think of Penelope?"

"Well," said Jess, brushing her hair back, "honestly? She's kind of a bitch."

"Agree."

"I googled her this morning. She's pretty influential in the book world, being the top reviewer on Reader. According to Forbes, she has the power to make or break a book."

"Great," I sighed. "Hopefully, she'll stay the hell away from mine."

"You know what I think? She's jealous of you."

"Me? But why?"

"She kept looking from you to Sash. And while we're on that subject, I think he likes you."

"Don't be stupid."

"Oh, come on. The guy could barely keep his eyes off you the whole night. And he kept defending you."

"OK, so let's say you're right. Why would Penelope have an issue with that? They're just friends. Plus, she's drop-dead gorgeous. She could have any man."

Jess shrugged. "No, no, don't sell yourself short. You've got this sex kitten look about you."

"Especially when I'm coughing up hairballs."

"Moron," she said, flicking a straw at me.

I laughed. "Well, don't stop there. Say more good things about me."

She squinted at me. "I would say your hair is your crowning glory. It's thick and wild and makes you think of snow-covered forests and wolves howling at the moon. You always look like you just got back from a summer holiday—I need a whole bottle of bronzer to get anywhere near the perfection that is your skin. Not to mention you're smart and funny. And you're kind. You see the good in people, which is rare. You say the first thing that pops into your head; you have no filter."

"Except when I'm on Instagram."

She roared with laughter. "See what I mean? You're so corny—I love it! And don't even get me started on your luscious boobs."

"Swap you my boobs for your metabolism."

"Deal."

We giggled.

"So do you like him?" Jess asked.

"I don't know for sure," I said honestly. "I don't not like him."

"When do you see him next?"

"He's coming by the store tomorrow. Pop found a book he was asking about."

"Pop likes him, and that is saying something."

A notification buzzed on my phone. Jess slapped her hand over it and looked me dead in the eye. "Stay with me, Vare."

"Teddy and Tom are cute, aren't they?"

"Total couple goals."

"Hope they'll invite us to the wedding."

Jonesy came by with our coffees and a basket of fries.

"Um, Verity? Sorry I couldn't make it to the park yesterday, so, like, I was thinking that if you want, I could put some of your books on the counter."

Jess's face lit up. "Jonesy! You're such a sweetheart!"

He gave her a nervous smile. "Su—sure."

"We love you, Jonesy." I blew him a kiss.

He smiled down at his feet before hurrying off.

"See the power you have over men?" said Jess.

I reached for my coffee just as my phone pinged. I grabbed it.

"You addict!" Jess laughed.

I glanced at the screen and let out a small yelp. "Jess! I've just been regrammed."

"What? By whom?"

"Poetry Seen."

She clapped her hand over her mouth. "You mean the one with over a million followers?"

I nodded, and she plucked my phone from my hands.

"Jesus Christ!" she breathed. "Vare, your notifications are going off. You've put on, like, hundreds of new followers!"

"I know, but the poem they put up—"

"It's the one from *Poemsia*," Jess finished.

I nodded. "And they've credited it to me."

Jess rolled her eyes. "You literally said it wasn't yours—it's right there in the caption!"

"I know, but they're so busy I guess they missed it. I should let them know."

Jess passed my phone to me. "Why don't you leave a comment? Hopefully they'll see it."

I tapped out a quick comment, feeling light-headed. It was a wild stroke of luck to be noticed by Poetry Seen—the largest poetry account on Instagram—I just wished with all my heart they had shared one of my poems instead.

"Don't worry about it," Jess said, peering at me from across the table. "You look pretty damn sorry for yourself for someone who's just been discovered!"

I bit my lip. "I know, I know, but—"

"No buts! The fact is you made it crystal clear it wasn't your poem, and you've left a message for Poetry Seen. There's not much else you can do."

"I guess . . "

Jess plainly heard the uncertainty in my voice because she reached over and squeezed my hand. "Besides, look at what's happening! People are liking and commenting on your poems! Your poems, Vare. Look at what this one girl said. 'Just found your page through Poetry Seen. Your poems are beyond beautiful! New forever fan!'"

I looked at Jess beaming at me, and I knew she was right. As usual, I was overthinking this. And Jess, God bless her, had worked so hard to make this happen—she had more faith in me, than I had in myself. I couldn't ruin this moment for her.

"Can you believe it, Jess?" I broke into a grin. "I have fans."

She squealed, and the couple at the next table shot us a fresh round of dirty looks. Jess threw her shoulders back and glared at them. "That's my friend, Verity Wolf! Remember that name, folks; soon it will be on everyone's lips!"

Five

BY THE NEXT day, my following count had grown to a thousand, but it still hadn't sunk in. I found myself compulsively checking my account to make sure it wasn't all a dream. I'd been too wired to sleep, so I stayed up and wrote some new pieces, then posted them. The feedback was addictive. I got such a rush when someone liked a poem or made a comment. Messages were flooding in faster than I could answer them. It was exhilarating.

Just before lunch, Sash came around and caught Pop staring despondently at a light fixture that had come loose—again. Right now, it was dangling from the ceiling. "Want me to fix that for you?" Sash asked.

Pop looked taken aback. "You can do that?" He had always been handy around the store, but in the past few years, he hadn't been able to keep it up—especially if it involved climbing ladders. He was under strict instructions from the doctor to avoid anything strenuous.

The store was hardly earning enough for us to get by, so we couldn't afford to hire anyone. The place had always looked a little worn—that was part of its charm. But now it was starting to look shabbier than ever since Zorro treated the place like his own personal scratch post.

"Sure, I can fix it. You have a ladder and some tools?"

Pop looked delighted. "Follow me, young man."

I left to pick up sandwiches for lunch. When I returned, Pop and Sash were flicking the switch of the newly fixed light. "Ah, that makes it less gloomy," said Pop with satisfaction.

"Awesome! We can actually see what we're doing now."

"You know, if you put up a skylight, it would brighten up this entire room," Sash said thoughtfully.

Pop and I exchanged a look.

"He's quite a handyman, your friend," said Pop, admiration in his voice. "You wouldn't happen to be a builder, would you, son?"

"My dad's in construction and got me work on some sites during my summer break. I studied architecture at Sydney U, but I work part time as a drafting monkey now."

"Well, that makes a lot of sense. Thank you for helping us with the light."

"Anytime." He was still looking intently around the store, no doubt making a mental checklist of all its safety hazards.

Pop let out a dramatic yawn. "It's time for my nap, so I'll leave you kids to it."

"Don't you want your sandwich?" I asked, surprised. Pop had never been this hospitable when it came to boys.

He smiled. "I'll take it upstairs with me."

☆

I TOOK SASH through a tiny window that led up onto the old tin roof of our store. I'd spent so much time out here, it was like my second bedroom. An awning stretched out underneath, and that meant you could watch the busy street across the road and be shielded from view. Further along the horizon, you could catch a glimpse of Centennial Park.

"Tuna or egg?" I asked, unpacking our lunch.

"Tuna."

We ate in silence, looking down at the tree-lined street across the road. It felt nice, sitting there with him, the cool wind against our faces. The sun kept ducking behind the ominous clouds, and it looked like a storm was brewing. Zorro hopped through the window and plonked himself squarely between us. Sash reached out and stroked him at the same time I did. My hand brushed his, and I quickly withdrew it.

"I don't have cooties, you know," he teased.

"How do you know I don't?"

He grinned. "I'll take the risk, Wolf."

There was an awkward pause as I tried to think of something to say. "Thanks for helping Pop today. It meant a lot to him."

"It was the least I could do. He went through a whole lot of boxes before he found the book I wanted."

"What was it?"

"*The Black Tulip.*"

"I adore that book!"

"I know. It had a bunch of passionate annotations written by a twelve-year-old kid named Verity."

I blushed, suddenly remembering how I had felt the need to express my thoughts and feelings at the end of every chapter.

"It was cute," he said, seeing the look on my face. "I love coming across old notes in books. It's like a message in a bottle."

"That's a nice way to look at it." I smiled and took another bite of my sandwich.

"Can you believe how crazy the Dutch went over tulips?"

"It's mind-boggling," I agreed. "But I liked how Rosa saved the day because she had learned to read. I think it was the first time I realized the power of words."

"Is that why you wanted to be a writer?"

"I've never thought of it like that, but you could be on to something, Freud."

He grinned. "Did you know that at the height of tulip fever, one single bulb was swapped for loads of wheat and rye, a couple of pigs, an ox, stacks of butter, a silver cup, gallons of booze, and a barrel of cheese?"

"An entire barrel of cheese? Wow."

"How long do you think it would take you to eat a barrel of cheese?" he asked.

"Probably six months to a year. How about you?"

"I really like cheese, so I could beat you to it—at least by a month or two."

"What's your favorite cheese?"

"Old Socks makes a great Stilton."

I wrinkled my nose. "Yuck!"

"But it's so delicious," he protested.

"Do you know what's delicious? Kraft Singles."

He laughed. "Sure, if you like plastic."

"I'd take plastic over mold any day."

The sound of a car horn blasted from the street below, and Zorro scrambled onto Sash's lap.

"Don't worry, little guy," he said, scratching under Zorro's chin. "We're safe up here."

I felt something warm bloom in my chest as I watched the two of them.

"I liked your book, by the way," Sash said suddenly.

"You read it?"

He nodded. "I think you write really well. I envy people like you."

"What do you mean?"

"It's almost as though you were born with a talent, and this talent is something that leads you, quite naturally, down a certain path. It's the same with my sister, Marcia. She's always wanted to help people. Her heart is so big, and now she's started her first year as a nurse. It's like she's doing what she was always meant to."

"It's the same with Jess. She's always had a knack for art. She can make something amazing from scraps. Once she sewed an evening gown out of Ferrero Rocher wrappers."

"See what I mean? Like Jess, you've never questioned what you wanted to do with your life, have you?"

"Well, I've always felt this inexpressible need to write, but it wasn't until Mena Rhodes came along that I thought I could do something with it. I think maybe it's because I needed a benchmark, someone to prove it could be done. Otherwise, it's like a treasure map without the X. Now I know definitively—I want to be a poet just like Mena."

"Your work is different from hers, but in a good way. It feels aged, like someone wrote it a long time ago."

"Maybe that's because I've spent my life in a secondhand bookstore."

"I'm sure all those authors you love are rooting for you."

"Do you know what? I've always thought of them as my mentors."

"I like that idea."

"So what do you want to do, Sash? Design grand buildings?"

He groaned. "To be honest, I don't know. I don't have a straight line to anywhere. I'm still a treasure map without the X, but I had a funny thought today when I was working on the light fixture. It would be nice to own a bookstore someday. That's a perfectly good dream to have, isn't it?"

"It most certainly is."

A gust of wind rustled the leaves on the rooftop, and Zorro darted from Sash's lap to pounce on one like a ninja. Sash leaned back on his elbows, a serene expression on his face.

"It's peaceful up here. I like it."

"It may look that way, but there's more than meets the eye."

"How so?"

"Well, you see that hat shop across the street, the one with blue lettering in the window? It's run by a lady named Margo—in her late thirties and never married. She's desperately in love with Paul, who owns the bakery two doors down. He's up at four every morning, baking. She goes in for the hot rolls, and they sit and have a coffee out front. You'll see her walk by several times during the day. She stops and agonizes about whether to go in. Sometimes she walks right up the street and then back down again."

"Sounds like love is in the air."

I sighed. "If only it were that simple. See, Paul is in love with Sandra, the florist next door. But Sandra's got a mystery guy—tall, dark, and handsome. Picks her up in a red Maserati. They're on-again, off-again. Maybe he's married; who knows? Sometimes she stands at the curb for ages after he drives off, with a sad look on her face. Once they had a massive argument right there on the sidewalk, and she smacked him with a bouquet. Rose petals flying all over the place."

"It's a love triangle, then."

"Exactly. One that's been developing over years."

"Your very own saga unfolding right here in Paddington."

"I've been keeping a record of it. I changed the names and businesses for privacy reasons. The hat shop is a mirror store and the bakery an arthouse cinema. Also, instead of Paul, the guy's name is Raul."

"I like how you say that."

"Raul?" I rolled the word on my tongue.

"Uh-huh, it's like you're growling."

I laughed. "You give it a try."

"Raul," he said, in a deep, rolling voice.

"You sound like a villain. We'll have to get you an eye patch."

"And a tattoo."

"Yes, Raul has a tattoo of a spider."

"He does?"

"On his face."

Sash laughed, and I noticed that his eyes crinkled in the corners. Pop always said that was the way you could tell someone was laughing for real.

"Well, I have to give my leading man a certain edge. He's got to be dangerous." My voice dropped to a whisper. "I'll let you in on a secret. Raul's a spy. The bakery is just a front. He bakes secret messages into the bread so it's literally impossible to catch him because the messages are edible."

"That is genius."

I nodded. "It's quite a sophisticated operation. That's why I have been meticulously recording all of this. I've also been adding my own embellishments."

"Of course you have."

I grinned. "Between you and me, I'm rooting for Margo. She's sweet. I like Sandra, too, but she's tempestuous—Slavic, you see. Her accent is alluring, and I can understand why Raul—I mean Paul—is attracted to her. But he doesn't realize Margo is the one for him. Sure, she dresses like a little old lady while Sandra prances around in slinky dresses and heels. She's a bombshell, for sure. If Margo would only pop in some contacts and let her hair down, I just know Paul finally would realize it was her all along. Jess disagrees. She thinks Paul needs a woman who stirs his imagination as well as his loins."

Sash raised his eyebrows at me.

"Her words, not mine."

"So she's team Sandra, and you're team Margo."

"That's where it stands now. How about you, Sash? Since I've let you in on our melodrama, it's only fair that you weigh in. Who would you choose if you were Paul? Plain-Jane Margo or sexy temptress Sandra?"

He gave me a devilish grin. "Sandra."

☆

AFTER THAT DAY, Sash came over often to fix things. I was worried we might be taking advantage of his generosity, but Pop wasn't the least bit concerned. "If the boy wants to work, let him work. He's not doing it for free, is he?" Pop was referring to the arrangement he now had with Sash—they traded books for maintenance services.

"Most people want to be paid money, not books," I said, eyebrows raised.

"Out-of-print books," Pop corrected me. "I'd gladly have done the same at his age. Anyway," he lowered his voice, "he's doing a good job. Don't go and ruin it for us."

I heard the now-familiar banging noise in the next room and rolled my eyes.

Sash worked Tuesdays and Thursdays at Das Haus, an architecture firm downtown. I found myself dreading those days, since I'd gotten so used to having him around. The place somehow felt livelier when he was here. I loved hearing the banter between him and Pop when they watched old war movies or played a game of chess. Sometimes they would spend hours discussing historical events from the fall of the Roman Empire to the invention of Gutenberg's printing press.

Aside from keeping Pop company, Sash was teaching me a lot about building. For example, now he was on a stepladder, hanging on my bedroom wall the collage he'd made. Most people just bang a nail in, but not Sash. He had all sorts of contraptions for drilling and measuring, and I'd ask, "What's this for? What about that?" so he'd patiently explain. I particularly liked his story about the bubble leveler that was invented by a Frenchman who was also responsible for popularizing the breast stroke. I loved the randomness of it all. Now Sash was frowning with concentration as he held the collage up to the wall.

"How's work?" I asked.

"It's going OK, I guess. They offered me a full-time job at Das Haus."

"Wow, congrats! Are you going to take it?" I was happy for him, even if it meant he'd have less time to hang out here.

"I don't know, Wolf. It's like what we talked about. I'm not sure my heart is in architecture. It's gone so digital, and I've always loved working with my hands. I mean"—he motioned to the task he was doing—"if there's such a thing as job satisfaction, this would kind of be it."

"Well, we'd hire you in a heartbeat, kiddo, but you know we can't afford you."

He looked down and grinned. "I know, Wolf." He went back to the wall. "I think everyone is toughing it out nowadays. I was walking down Oxford Street this morning and noticed so many stores with 'For Lease' signs tacked to their windows."

"It's sad, isn't it? Just a few years ago it was buzzing, but now it's so quiet. A whole lot of businesses have gone under—it's a miracle Wolf Books has held on so long. We had a few close calls, but Jess and I always managed to keep our doors open somehow. We've done bake sales, gotten council grants. One time when things looked particularly grim, we even set up a GoFundMe page, and a generous donor came along and saved the day. Despite all that, we're still hanging on by the skin of our teeth."

Sash sighed. "I think lots of people are in the same boat. That's why I should take the job. My parents have been dropping hints about me going into full-time employment. I'll bet they're keen to have me out of the house. But what if I accept the offer and a year goes by, then two? All of a sudden, I'm this architect, and that's my life? On the other hand, what if I turn it down and the opportunity never comes up again? It's such a great firm, and I know there are graduates lining up for my position."

"I know how you feel. If Wolf Books goes under, I'm in real trouble. This is my safety raft, but it's leaky. The water's rushing in, and I don't know how to stop it. I'd get a side job but all my time goes to helping Pop with the store. It's touch and go—you get a box of books that don't sell, and you're dipping into your emergency fund to get through the next month. It worries me a lot, because other than this old place—I don't have a backup plan. I don't know what I would do."

"You have your poetry," Sash pointed out.

"Ever since Mena's massive success, everyone is jumping on the bandwagon and flocking to Instagram to share their poems. I'm just one of many hopeful poets."

"I think you're being modest, Wolf. There is something really special about your work, so it's no surprise you're building a following. I showed your poems to my sister, Marcia, and she loves them! So do Teddy and Tom. In fact, everyone seems to love—"

His sentence cut off, and I knew exactly why.

"Everyone except for Penelope—right?" I teased.

He sighed. "Penelope's kind of specific about what she likes."

"Are you and Penelope . . ." I trailed off.

He looked a bit embarrassed. "Um, we were actually together for a while—on and off. But we're just friends now."

"Oh, I see." I wasn't sure how I felt about that. It wasn't a huge surprise, but I found myself wishing their relationship had been purely platonic. At that very moment, I realized I was falling for him. Damn it, why did Jess have to be right about everything?

"Can you hand me the drill?" Sash asked, interrupting my thoughts.

"Sure!" I found it in our toolbox and passed it up.

He squinted at the pencil mark, then switched on the drill. At that moment, Zorro raced in, bounded off my bed, and crashed into the stepladder. Sash's grip on the drill slipped, and it grazed his finger. He let out a bloodcurdling wail as the drill fell to the floor with a thud.

My hand covered my mouth. "Oh my God! Sash, are you OK?"

He was staring at the trickle of blood running down his finger.

"Oh," he said weakly, "I think I'm going to pass out."

Somehow, I got him off the ladder. He was unsteady on his feet, so I had him lie down on the floor. I took off my jacket, rolled it up, and stuck it under his head. Then I took a closer look at his injured finger. It didn't look too bad—worse than a paper cut, but not too much more.

"OK, take a deep breath, soldier."

He did as I said, and I went to fetch our first aid kit from the bathroom.

"You OK?" I asked, as I dabbed his wound with a soaked cotton ball.

He grinned. "Still alive, Wolf."

I wrapped a Garfield Band-Aid around his finger. "Thought we lost you there for a minute."

Then I lay down next to him, and we stared at the ceiling.

"Well, that was embarrassing," he said eventually. "I'm not great with blood."

"Who is?"

"All this work to prove my masculinity—ruined in a single moment."

"It's OK. That high-pitched wail was in no way a threat to your manliness. While we're on the subject, do you need me to loosen your corset?"

"Ha ha, very funny."

"Seriously, masculinity is overrated. Even Superman has a weakness."

"And what's yours?" Sash asked.

"Cockroaches. I go hysterical when I see one."

"I think most people react to them that way."

"Not Jess. She'll wack one with a shoe while I'm standing there, screaming and hopping from one foot to the other."

"I don't like the idea of killing anything, so I would probably just learn to accept it. Once a praying mantis lived in the corner of my shower for weeks. I named him Henry."

I laughed.

After a short pause, Sash said, "Thanks for helping me."

"Couldn't let you bleed to death," I teased.

He held up his bandaged finger and grinned. "You did a nice job. My sister would be proud. Nurses appreciate stuff like this."

"It is a masterpiece," I agreed. "Look how neat and stuck down it is. Not a single air bubble."

"It's firm but not so tight that it's cutting off my circulation."

I took his hand so I could again admire my handiwork. As I did, he squeezed mine gently, and our eyes met. My heart started pounding in my chest, but Zorro decided this was the moment to walk up and plant himself squarely on Sash's chest.

I withdrew my hand and glared at my cat. "Look at all the trouble you've caused," I reprimanded. "You could have killed us."

His eyes grew wide, and he looked from me to Sash. Then he threw his head back and let out a loud, mournful meow.

Sash grinned, scratching behind his ears. "Apology accepted, little guy."

Six

"Apparently, Sash and Penelope used to go out," I told Jess.

"Ugh," she replied. "Now it makes sense why she was so rude to you. Anyway, you have to watch her. She's up to no good for sure."

We were now at the mall to pick up a new charger for my phone. My old one, held together with bits of electric tape, had finally given up last night. My phone battery had been dead all day, and I felt restless thinking of all the Instagram messages I'd left unanswered.

"Do you think Sash still likes her?" I asked.

"How long were they dating?"

I shrugged. "No idea. He said it was on and off."

"Uh-oh, you know what that means. When an on-off relationship isn't on, it's never really quite off either."

I groaned. "Great. Why can't I just like someone who doesn't come with baggage? Especially when the baggage is as gorgeous as Penelope."

Jess went silent, and when I turned to face her, she was staring at me openmouthed. "Young lady, did you just admit to me that you like Sash?"

"Yeah."

She beamed at me. "Well, this is an exciting development!"

"I kind of had a weird dream about him last night. We had to paint a room bright yellow, but the paint rollers were corncobs."

"Not surprising. You guys have been doing all this DIY stuff. It's practically foreplay."

"I don't know. I'm not really getting any vibes from him."

"Vare, it is painfully obvious to anyone with eyes that you're hot for each other but neither one of you wants to make the first move."

I thought back to when Sash squeezed my hand. Was it my imagination, or had we shared a moment? I wish I had the same confidence as Jess, but I couldn't be sure how he felt.

We got to JB Hi-Fi and were making our way to the wall of chargers when Jess grabbed my shoulder so hard I yelped.

"What the hell, Jess!"

"Did I just see what I think—" She turned to me. "Vare, look!"

She pointed at a row of flat-screens showing an episode of *E! News* with a jubilant Karla Swann sitting next to Henrietta Blue. The crawl at the bottom of the screen read "Karla Swann engaged."

Karla was answering a question posed to her by the host. "The moment I read the poem," she said, "I just felt this crazy love for my girl."

Henrietta reached over and took her hand. "Then she showed me the poem and said, 'This is so us.'"

Karla beamed at her. "So I said, 'Hey, what are we waiting for? We know we want to spend the rest of our lives together.'"

The host smiled dreamily. "Oh, that's so romantic. Who proposed?"

"Actually, I'm not really sure," Karla laughed.

"We pretty much proposed to each other at the same time," Henrietta confirmed.

"And to seal the deal, Karla, you posted the poem on Instagram. Is that right?" The camera panned over Karla's Instagram page, and there it was. The poem from *Poemsia* captioned with, "OMG just found my wedding vows!!! Thanks @veritywolf."

I gasped and grabbed Jess's arm.

"Yeah, and everything went kind of nuts after that."

"You can say that again. The post only went up last night and already has half a million likes!"

"Oh, it's probably because the poem is so beautiful," Karla said modestly.

"Who is the author?"

"Verity Wolf—she's amazing! I found her through Poetry Seen and love everything she writes." Karla sighed and clutched at her chest. Suddenly, the television screen was filled with an image of my Instagram page.

"That can't be mine," I said, numbly. "I don't have ten thousand followers."

"Check your phone!" Jess cried.

"It's dead—remember? That's why we're here!"

"For Chrissake!" Jess fumbled in her pocket and took hers out.

"OK," she said deadpan. "OK, we need to stay calm. We're in a public place. Let's not freak out."

I glanced at her screen and nearly passed out. Sure enough, my following count was now in the tens of thousands.

"What do we do?" I said, panicked.

"Why are you asking me?" Jess's voice was shrill.

"Jess!"

"Vare!"

"Oh my God."

"Oh shit!"

"Look!" I cried, pulling up my sweater sleeve. There were goose bumps along my arm.

She did the same.

"Holy crap," I breathed.

"Mother of God."

We looked at each other, eyes wide and bewildered. I didn't know whether to laugh or cry.

"Jess, could this be a joke? Am I dreaming?"

She reached over and pinched the top of my arm.

"Ouch!" I glared at her.

She grinned. "Nope—not a dream!"

☆

At Last Chance, Jess and I stood at the counter relaying the exciting news to Jonesy. It was just beginning to sink in.

"Then we saw Verity's Instagram on all the television screens, and she was like, 'I don't have ten thousand followers.'"

"We were calm, though; we didn't lose our shit."

"But I have to admit it's mainly because we were in shock."

"We're not now."

Jess and I looked at each other and squealed at the top of our lungs.

Jonesy grinned. "OK, I guess you had to get that out of your system."

"It's, like, trending on Twitter and everything."

"How did she find your poem?" Jonesy asked.

I cleared my throat. "Ah, well, it's not my poem, which kind of sucks. I found it in this old book, *Poemsia*."

"But you did make that pretty damn clear, right from the start," Jess pointed out.

I nodded. "Karla said she loves all the other poems on my Instagram, and they are most definitely mine."

"Vare's Instagram is insane at the moment!"

"Congratulations, girls. Verity, don't forget me when you're famous."

I reached over and pinched his freckled cheek. "You? Never."

He grinned.

"Anyway, dear Jonesy," said Jess, "we'd love to stay and chat, but we'll need our coffees to go. Vare and I have some serious work to do!"

Seven

"VERITY WOLF—THAT'S GOTTA be a pen name, right?" I was on a FaceTime call with Sierra, a twenty-something journalist from BuzzFeed. She had ash-gray hair in a messy bun; wide, expressive eyes; and upturned lips that looked ready to spill over into laughter. I'd been nervous before our call, but her funny and bubbly personality had put me right at ease.

"Yes, Verity Wolf is my actual name. Like, it's the one I was born with," I explained.

"Wow, that is so cool—I love it! My name is just, ugh, lame." She rolled her eyes.

"But Sierra is such a pretty name!"

"Oh, please, I sound like a Crayola. But we're not here to talk about me, right? Let's talk about you."

I smiled. "OK."

"Excellent! It's been about twenty-four hours since Karla Swann shared your post on her Instagram. How did you hear the good news?"

"Funny thing is I hadn't checked my Instagram for ages because my charger died, and I didn't have a spare one. So I was in JB Hi-Fi—an electronics store—with my best friend, Jess, and we saw it on *E! News.*"

"Oh my God! That must have been so surreal."

"It felt like something out of a sci-fi movie!"

"How did Karla find your Instagram?"

"Poetry Seen regrammed me awhile back."

She nodded. "Right! That makes total sense. Karla is a huge poetry fan, so of course she'd be following them. What self-respecting poetry fanatic doesn't, right? They have a star-studded fan base, and it's no secret celebs are playing their part in making poetry mainstream. Tell me, how are you handling your newfound fame?"

"I don't think it's really sunk in. I keep expecting to wake up."

"Oh, I can imagine! And the poem Karla posted—what inspired you to write something so beautiful?"

I stopped. "Oh, um, I didn't write that poem."

Her eyebrows shot up. "I'm sorry, Verity—did you just say you didn't write the poem?"

"Um, no. I didn't." I then gave her a quick explanation about *Poemsia.* "I mean, I literally said it wasn't mine in the caption, but I guess no one really notices things like that now."

"I see! That's totally understandable. Yes, things are always getting misattributed. It's an easy mistake to make, right?"

"You know, I did leave a comment on their post but—"

She roared with laughter. "You and about a thousand other people, right?"

"I know, I know—a long shot. I'm pretty sure they haven't seen it."

"I had a quick look through your Instagram this morning, and coming from a self-professed poetry nerd, every single poem is as good as the next. That's my honest opinion. Other than the poem you found in *Poemsia*, are all the others written by you?"

"Every last one."

"Wow," she breathed. "Besides Mena Rhodes, I can't think of another modern poet who gets me like you do. I am so happy you've been discovered, even if it's in a roundabout way. Your talent deserves to be shared with the world."

"Oh my gosh, thank you!"

"Thank you for your time, Verity. You can now count me among your thousands of adoring fans. I'll be waiting eagerly for your next post!"

I got off the phone and looked up at Jess, who was sitting cross-legged on the window seat across from me. She had her laptop balanced on a cushion, and her fingers were flying across the keyboard.

"Do you think I did OK?" I asked anxiously.

"You're a natural!" she sang, not even pausing to look up. "By the way, I've set up a new email for you, veritywolfwrites at gmail, like we discussed. I've hooked it up to your Instagram, and you're already getting a whole bunch of emails."

"Wow! Anything good?"

"A couple of media things—the rest is fan mail."

"Should we set up a Twitter?"

"Good idea! I'll get on that now."

"You are a machine!" I said fondly.

When we got back from Last Chance, we made a to-do list and got to work. I was trying to keep from feeling overwhelmed. It was as though more had happened in the past few hours than in my entire life, and in the midst of all that, my mind kept flitting over to another development. If Karla hadn't shared my post, it probably would have been the only thing on my mind. Right on cue, that development walked in.

"Hey, girls." Sash raised his hand in that cute, awkward wave. He had a tool belt around his waist, and God, he looked good. I literally wanted to tear his clothes off with my teeth. He had come in to help Pop fix the vent in his office, the one that kept making a rattling noise.

"Busy day, huh?" he said. "Your grandad has been filling me in on all the exciting news."

"Can you believe it?" Jess looked up at him. "Our little Verity Wolf, an overnight sensation."

"That's pretty damn cool," said Sash, with a big grin.

"It's kind of freaky," I admitted.

"Looks like you're handling it OK."

"I'm lucky to have Jess—she's dynamite." I planted a quick kiss on her cheek.

"Have you uploaded a new poem today?" Jess asked, glancing at our to-do list.

I shook my head. "I know, I know. I need some new material. But it's hard to write on demand; I need inspiration."

"Then get inspired." Jess looked pointedly at Sash, and despite how much she was helping me, I wanted to murder her. Thank God he was distracted by a window on the far wall where the screen had come loose.

"Oh shit!" Jess said suddenly, her voice hushed and urgent.

"What is it?"

"An email just came through from Carry Way Press."

"Aren't they the ones who—" I started.

"Publish Mena Rhodes? Yes."

In a flash, I was on my feet, and Jess turned her screen to face me.

Sash came up behind me and let out a low whistle. "Holy. Christ."

"Is it true, Jess? Are they—" I stopped and put my hand over my mouth. Tears filled my eyes.

Jess looked fixedly at me, nodding slowly. "You've just been offered your first publishing deal."

Eight

JESS AND I sat opposite Mei Lyn at her large oak table while her team of women marched briskly in and out of her office, high heels clacking on wood floors, piling stacks of paperwork on her desk. Before she got her law degree, Mei Lyn had worked as a talent agent, and now I couldn't think of a better person to represent me.

We listened as she took us through the contract from Carry Way Press. She spoke in long, rambling sentences like an auctioneer. The only way you could get a word in was to interrupt her.

"All in all, seems like everything is in order, and the couple of things I need to straighten out should be sorted by this afternoon. I'll make sure they get into section two—"

"Mum! Seriously, this is Carry Way. We're happy to sign anything they want. Why give them a hard time?"

Mei Lyn frowned. "Jess, you're dealing with a corporation. Remember that it's my job to make sure Verity is protected. You'd be surprised how tricky these things get, and that's why there are people like me whose sole purpose is to look out for the interests of my client. Mmm, I know it's all very exciting, and you girls get carried away too easily—"

"Honestly, Mei Lyn, I'm happy to sign the contract. I'm sure—"

"Ah! Ah! Ah!" She stuck her palm up. "I'm handling it, girls. What I'm asking for is more than fair. I'm just making sure our Verity is safe and sound. Yes, now where was I?" She snapped her fingers twice, and a young girl with a pale, eager face came rushing in. "Donna, latte and muffin now, please. My blood sugar is getting low again."

"Right away."

Mei Lyn looked at us. "You girls want anything?"

We shook our heads.

"So, yes, young lady, yes, you are hot, hot, hot at the moment. I've been following the news, and you have cachet, and now's the time to make the most of all this hype. You're OK to get your manuscript to them by the date specified?"

"Yes, it's ready to go."

Jess let out a squeal. "I can't believe my own best friend is going to be a published poet!"

Mei Lyn looked at her daughter as if seeing her for the first time. "Please, this is a place of business, not a frat house. Now if you'll excuse me, girls, I have other work to do."

"Thanks, Mei Lyn. I really appreciate your help."

"She's charging you," Jess blurted.

Mei Lyn winked. "And I'm worth every penny."

☆

THAT NIGHT, JESS'S artwork was part of a group exhibition at her college, showcasing reimagined movie posters. With everything going on, I had no idea how she found time for her design work. I suspected my dear friend was a lot more like Mei Lyn than she would admit.

The show was held at Creep, a gallery down the road from the college. The small, cramped space was packed with arty types and students who came for the free beer. Jess looked radiant in a black strapless dress and nude heels as we pushed through the crowd looking for her poster. Suddenly, she stopped and clutched my arm. "There's mine!"

I scanned her work and had to grin. Even though the poster was all imagery and had no text at all, I knew at once which movie it was. *Finding Nemo!*" I exclaimed.

Jess looked delighted. "You got it!" She did a swimming motion with her arms. "Just keep on swimming, swimming, swimming."

"It's awesome!" I stood back to take it all in. The entire poster was made up of sketches of every sea creature imaginable, and it took me awhile to spot Nemo in the upper left-hand corner. "I just found Nemo! And there's Dory and Nemo's dad. Oh, and Bruce the Shark! How long did it take you to draw this?"

"I scanned in some doodles from my old notebooks and filled in the rest."

I reached over and hugged her. "I love it! I'm so proud of you."

I felt a tap on my shoulder. "Hey, stranger!"

"Teddy! What brings you here?"

"We're sponsoring the event."

I caught the label on the beer bottle in his hand.

"Of course, Deep Sea Diver!"

"They're guzzling all our stock." Tom appeared at his side.

"Bastards!" Jess joked.

"We adore your poster," Teddy declared.

"How did you know it was mine?" asked Jess, flushing with pleasure.

Tom waved the exhibition program. "It's printed right here, along with a glamour shot of you."

"It was our favorite artwork, so we looked it up, and I said to Tom, 'Hey, that girl looks familiar.'"

"Awww, guys." Jess beamed from ear to ear.

Teddy pulled out his phone. "I'm going to get a picture for our Instagram."

"Are Sash and Penelope here too?" Jess asked.

Teddy and Tom exchanged a look.

"They've gone to see *Marrow Morrow*."

"You're kidding me!" Jess's mouth fell open.

When *Marrow Morrow* premiered at the Cannes Film Festival, most of the audience walked out within the first five minutes. Since then, it's been a challenge for movie buffs, bloggers, and the rest of the Internet to see how much of the movie they could withstand. *Marrow Morrow* was said to be so esoteric that no one could make sense of what the movie was about. Half the critics lauded it as a masterpiece, but the other half agreed it was the worst movie ever made.

"They are brave," I said.

Teddy winked. "Thankfully, we managed to dodge the bullet. Poor Sash, I really feel for him. Pen will be in heaven, though. This is her kind of thing."

Tom's phone buzzed loudly. "Oh, speak of the devil!"

"And what does the devil want?" asked Teddy.

Tom passed his phone to him, and his eyes lit up. "Looks like they've left the movie theater."

Jess laughed. "They walked out?"

"They couldn't handle it," Teddy grinned, his fingers tapping at lightning speed on the screen. "I told them where we are, so they're heading over now."

"I still can't believe they put themselves through it." Tom laughed. "But you know Sash has always had a soft spot for Pen."

My stomach dropped. "He has?"

"They're kind of like Ross and Rachel from *Friends*. Always breaking up and getting back together."

I swallowed. "Oh, do you think they still have a chance?"

Teddy shrugged. "Who knows? With those two, you get the feeling they're unfinished business."

"Jess! Congrats!" boomed a voice from behind us. I looked back to see a man in his late twenties with dark, spiky hair and glasses beaming down at Jess.

"Oh, hi, Haden," she said coyly. She turned to us. "This is Haden, my graphic design professor, and these are my friends, Verity, Teddy, and Tom." She pointed us out as she went, carefully avoiding eye contact with me.

"Ah, Verity Wolf, the poet. I helped Jess put your book together. She's told me so much about you."

"Really?"

He flashed me a smile, then leaned in to whisper something in Jess's ear. He touched her shoulder lightly before disappearing back into the crowd.

Teddy shot Jess a gleeful look. "You've been a bad girl, haven't you?"

Jess blushed. "It's not like that."

"Darling, your hand was just in the cookie jar. We all saw it." He looked around for confirmation, and we all nodded.

"And what a fine cookie it is," Tom drawled.

I put my hands on my hips. "Jessica Lui. Why have you failed to tell me your professor is a young sexy god of a man? We will be discussing this in great detail later."

She smirked. "There is nothing to discuss, so you can all get your minds out of the gutter."

"Hey, Wolf!" Sash suddenly appeared, Penelope at his side.

"Hey!" I felt a burst of happiness at seeing him, but then I thought back to what Teddy said, and it was like a punch in the stomach.

Teddy raised an eyebrow at Penelope. "So how far did you make it?"

"Fifteen minutes," she replied.

"Not bad."

She grimaced. "We were hanging on by the skin of our teeth. Arjun Ahuja said it was a masterpiece, so I was excited as hell to see it, but it was excruciating. You know me—I was a slut for *Eraserhead*. *The Cars That Ate Paris* is about as close to commercial cinema as I get. This was on a whole other tier of weird. The movie opened with a man sawing off his own head. Then his severed head started eating the rest of his body. Then it cuts to an old maid in a rocking chair, and she was laughing hysterically. Next the camera took us inside her mouth, where all these people were in the middle of an orgy—dressed in BDSM gear, by the way. We're talking full-body vinyl, gimp masks, whips, the works, screwing each other senseless. Meanwhile, a high-pitched whistle was wailing at us the whole time. That's when we decided to bail out."

"Fifteen minutes is decent—we're proud of you, darling." Teddy smiled at Penelope.

She glanced around the room. "What is this event we're sponsoring?"

"Reimagined movie posters by art students."

"What are you girls doing here?" she addressed us for the first time.

"That's mine," said Jess, pointing to her poster.

Penelope stood back to examine Jess's work. "I don't get it."

"*Finding Nemo*," Sash smiled.

"Oh, I've never seen it."

"You've never seen *Finding Nemo*?" Jess looked stunned.

Penelope shook her head and pressed her mouth into a thin line. Her attention snapped back to the boys. "You guys hungry? Let's go to Mechanical Mango."

Mechanical Mango was an Indian restaurant with a modern twist. It was one of the most popular eateries in Paddington, so we had to wait twenty minutes by the curb before we were shown to our seats.

Inside, we were greeted with an explosion of color. Crimson wood chairs leaned against walls of mustard-seed yellow; draped fabrics hung in splashes of gold and cardamom.

"I'm starving!" Penelope declared, as she skimmed the menu. "Should I just order for everyone?"

"Yes, Mom," said Teddy, in a mock American accent.

"Sash, you want the deconstructed vindaloo, right?" She looked directly at me when she said it.

"Sure," he said, poring over the wine list.

She hailed a nearby waiter. "We're ready to order." She rattled off a list of items on the menu, then snapped it shut.

Jess shot me a worried look. We weren't sure whether Penelope had ordered for us.

"Also, can we have two herb naans and a mango lassi each?" I piped in, crossing my fingers the bill would be fairly split. Neither Jess nor I could afford to pay for Penelope's extravagant order.

"And a bottle of the Riesling—my treat," Sash added.

Penelope raised her eyebrows. "What are we celebrating?"

"Jess's art show."

"And Verity's publishing deal," added Jess.

"Oh," said Penelope, eyes darting to me. She tried to cover up a wince with a smile. "Congratulations. Which publisher?"

"Carry Way Press," said Jess, proudly.

Penelope snorted. "I see."

The expression on Jess's face darkened suddenly, like a freak storm. "What the hell is your problem?"

Penelope looked taken aback. "Well, Carry Way is hardly publishing Pulitzer Prize material, are they?"

"So what? Are you saying we should toss out every book that hasn't won an award? Because that's most of the books in this world."

"No, I don't think we should toss them out. I think we should burn them."

"Who the heck made you the authority on what people should be reading?"

I tugged discreetly at Jess's sleeve, but it was like she was possessed.

"Well, for someone who watches cartoons, I wouldn't hold out much hope for your choice of reading material."

"Oh, you think you're an intellectual, and that means you'll only support books that are pushed by the establishment, which, by the way, gets it wrong half the time. History proves that. To be honest, I don't think you actually know what you like, Penelope—you have to be told. Don't you think it's ironic that you favor one limited genre to the exclusion of everything else? You keep swimming in your own little pool, even though there's an entire ocean out there."

"Are we back to *Finding Nemo* again? Is that the only reference you ever draw from?" Penelope snapped.

"How would you know? You said you've never seen it."

"Whoa!" said Teddy, both palms up. "Girls, come on, this is Mechanical Mango—a place of peace."

"That's right," said Sash. "Why don't we all just agree to disagree?"

But there was no stopping Jess. "I can't stand this elitist crap. It's ignorant, but more than that, it's dangerous.

People like her would have us back in the Dark Ages, when literacy was barely accessible. Words are necessary, and I hate the idea that any faction of the human race feels it is more entitled to language than others when words are a birthright. Yet, there are those who pretend that literature isn't wholly subjective, and they prop up writers who perpetuate that myth. It's like the emperor's new clothes—they all pat each other on the back even if they don't understand their own shit half the time."

Penelope stood up and threw down her napkin. She placed her hands firmly on the table and glowered at Jess. "You think you have me all worked out, don't you? Well, you don't know a damn thing. You and your friend"—she spat out the word—"you might fool the boys, but I see you both for what you are—stupid, shallow girls. One of you got lucky because some vacuous celebrity shared your post on Instagram. You live in a world of bubblegum music, pop art, selfies, makeup tutorials, reality TV, celebrity, instant gratification, instant fucking poetry. You read books about menial topics like boy-meets-girl—the same thing over and over that adds nothing to the collective progress of the human race. It contributes nothing to the greater discussion, and you dare to tell me I am holding the world back? Well, screw you. I don't want to waste another second of my time listening to your bullshit. Enjoy your little party and have a nice life." She pushed her chair back loudly and stormed out of the restaurant.

"That was intense!" Teddy grabbed a napkin and fanned himself.

"Show's over, guys," Tom called to the people throwing glances at our table.

Sash gave us an apologetic look. "Sorry, girls."

Jess shrugged. "You don't need to apologize for her."

"Aren't you going to go after her, Sash?" Teddy asked.

Sash looked from him to me and back again, as if he was conflicted. Then he straightened up and shook his head. "No, not this time. I think I'll just leave her to cool off."

Teddy and Tom exchanged a glance. I could tell they were surprised by Sash's reaction, and I wondered whether this happened a lot: if Penelope ran off, Sash would run right after her. I had to admit, I was glad he didn't this time.

"I wonder why she's so strung up. You didn't tell her about Verity's Instagram, did you, dude?" Teddy asked.

"Nope, we all agreed to avoid the topic, remember? It's a sensitive issue since she's still upset about her manuscript getting rejected."

"How did she find out?"

Sash shrugged. "Maybe she caught the news on Twitter?"

"Or maybe the crazy bitch has been stalking Verity," Jess suggested.

"Hey, no need for that. She might be a crazy bitch, but she's our bitch," said Tom.

Our food came in a cloud of scent and color. The mood lightened as we filled up our plates.

"So, Jess," Teddy glanced at Tom, "we have a proposition for you."

She looked surprised. "For me?"

"You know, things are going really well with our Deep Sea Diver beer. We're going to extend our product to include ciders, too. The problem is that we're not happy with the current designer working on our labels. We'd like to hire you instead—if you're keen."

Jess looked taken aback. "You want to hire me?"

They both nodded enthusiastically. "We loved your *Finding Nemo* poster, and there was a link to your portfolio in the program. We checked it out and really liked what we saw. What do you say?"

"Yes, I'd love to do it!"

"Oh my God, Jess—your first paying job!" I exclaimed.

"I get paid?"

"Of course. We'll send you a brief, and you can quote it up for us. Penelope is footing the bill, so you can pretty much charge us whatever you want as long as you don't go too crazy." Tom winked.

Jess's face fell. "Oh. I forgot about Penelope. Do you think it's a good idea for us to work in the same office after what just happened?"

"No need to worry. When you get to know Pen, you'll realize her bark is worse than her bite. Besides, you only have to come in every now and then. I'm sure we'll be able to stage-manage you both," said Tom, with a chuckle.

"Where are you based?" Jess asked.

"You will be pleased to know Deep Sea Diver HQ is just a few blocks from Wolf Books. It's the pink brick building with the white shutters."

"Oh, I know the one," I said. "It's just by the park."

Jess clapped her hands. "This is so exciting!"

Teddy tipped his glass in Jess's direction. "Welcome to the family!"

IN WHAT SEEMED like an orchestrated move, Jess said she'd hitch a ride home with Teddy and Tom, which left me with Sash. I lived just down the road, so he offered to walk me. He was quiet most of the way, like there was something on his mind. I bumped my shoulder into his. He looked at me and smiled. Then he returned the bump.

"What's this, Sash? Dodgem cars?"

"You tell me, Wolf—you're the one who started it."

We stopped under the lamplight at the entrance of the store.

"Do you want to come in?" I asked.

"Sure."

We went up to the roof and sat on the corrugated tin, looking down at Oxford Street. Laughter, conversation, and live music intermingled with drunken shouts came from a pub down the road. It was a cool, still night, and a handful of stars were scattered sparsely over the city sky. My heart was drumming softly in my chest, and I wasn't sure whether it was the glass of Riesling I'd had at dinner or my mounting feelings for Sash.

"Have there been any new developments?" he asked, nodding at the bakery across the street.

"I think Paul is warming up to Margo. The other day he took a basket of pastries into her store."

"That sounds promising!"

"They were probably just leftovers from that day, but, you know, it's a start."

"He could have just thrown them out or fed them to the pigeons."

"Exactly! But I do have one other theory."

"I'm intrigued. Please share."

"What if he did it purely to make Sandra jealous?"

"Isn't Sandra pining after her mystery man? Why would she be jealous?"

"Because even though she doesn't want Paul, she doesn't want anyone else to have him either. Kind of like Pen—" I stopped when I realized what I had said.

"What?" Sash looked bemused.

I held my head in my hands and groaned. "Forget I just said that."

He nudged me with his elbow. "Aw, Wolf. You've got me curious now. What's this about Pen?"

I slowly raised my eyes to meet his. "Well, I know you've said the two of you are just friends, but I'm not sure she got the memo and"—I felt myself redden— "I think that's why she's been so cold toward me. You've been spending so much time here that she might have the wrong idea." I stopped, realizing how close I'd come to revealing how I felt.

Sash sighed. "Look, me and Pen . . . we were stuck in this loop, you know? We'd get together, then break up, then start all over again. I don't think it was healthy for either of us. We've known each other since we were kids, and you can't ignore that kind of history. She'll always be a huge part of my life, but for now it's definitely over."

"How can you really know for sure? I mean, it seems like she'd be anyone's dream girl."

"There are a lot of great things about Pen, and on paper we make sense. But as a couple, it just doesn't work. To be honest, there's someone else I like now."

I swallowed hard. "Someone even more beautiful than Penelope?" My head was ready to explode trying to picture such an unearthly creature.

He smiled. "She's literally the most beautiful girl I've ever known—inside and out. She's talented, sweet, and kind. She's got a weird sense of humor; she's so random I never know what she's going to say next. I really like that about her."

A lump grew in my throat as he described this mystery girl. I couldn't believe how let down I felt, even though I hadn't liked him for very long. All this time, I thought Penelope was the one I should be worried about when it was someone else. I cleared my throat and tried to keep the disappointment out of my voice. "Who's the lucky girl?"

"Um . . ." He gave me an odd look. "You seriously don't know?"

"Am I supposed to?"

"Well, I thought it was pretty obvious."

"Do I know her?"

"I'd say you know her really well."

Then the realization hit me.

"Jess," I said, with a deep breath. "Of course you like her! She's single, by the way, but I think there's something going on with her hot professor. That doesn't make her any less awesome or available." I put on a brave face, but my mind was actively rearranging itself, putting Sash into the platonic friend basket. I could definitely be happy for them if Jess liked him, too.

Now he was looking at me with an expression of mild incredulity. "Wolf, it's not Jess."

"No? Then who is it?"

"OK, I didn't think this would be necessary but—" All of sudden he looked shy. "It's you, Wolf—I like you."

"Me?" My brain reshuffled again, back to where it began, and my heart leapt with unexpected joy. "Really?"

"Oh, come on, Wolf, it can't come as that big a shock to you."

"It's a shock. Believe me—it is a huge shock."

"But I've been over practically every day—you know, fixing things."

"For free books!" I blurted.

"That was a thinly veiled excuse to see you. Not that I don't like fixing things for Pop. He's awesome and knows a lot about stuff."

"He does, doesn't he? He's like a fountain of knowledge. I keep telling him he should go on a quiz show." I was talking fast now, because Sash was looking at me like he wasn't even listening, like we had gone to a place where words were fast becoming pointless. "I think it's because he's so well read. He reads nonfiction in addition to fiction. Anyway, he thinks he's too old for game shows, but I think age is just a number, don't you? The other day, we were watching *The Chase*, and he got all the answers right." I rambled on as a grin spread across his face.

"Wolf, can you stop talking for a second?"

"But"—

"I can't kiss you otherwise."

My mouth dropped open.

Then his lips were on mine, and it was like all my screws were coming lose. I felt a plunging sensation in my chest as we moved into each other. A soft, involuntary moan escaped from my lips, and he kissed me harder. His breath was heavy when we broke apart, his lips wet, eyes half closed.

"That was kind of . . . hot."

"It was definite—" I started, but he was kissing me again. I swear I felt that kiss in places I didn't even know existed.

"Wow," he said when we broke apart. We grinned at each other like idiots.

"What the hell is happening?" I blurted.

"I don't know, but I'm really into it."

It was my turn to kiss him, and it was pure bliss and absolute torture at the same time. I was in a daze, as if my brain had suddenly packed up and gone on vacation. I could barely string words together in a sentence.

"OK . . . wait. Let me just . . . let's take five," I gasped between kisses.

"Good idea. Let's get our bearings because, honestly, I don't even know what planet we're on right now."

"OK, OK—let's discuss this like responsible young adults."

"So we left Mechanical Mango, then you invited me up. I was hoping you would."

"Then we came out onto the roof, and you dropped a bombshell."

"And you started rambling about Pop."

"After which, your tongue somehow ended up in my mouth."

He laughed. "Then we fell through the fabric of space and time and ended up here."

"Where is here?" I asked, my eyes searching his.

He answered like I had asked him a trick question. "The rest . . . of our lives?"

A tide of emotion swelled up in my chest. "Sash—"

"Wolf," he murmured, and his mouth found mine again. For some reason, I thought of the scene in *The BFG* where Sophie had her first sip of Frobscottle. It was like a sugar rush straight to my bloodstream that ran down instead of up.

He traced my lips with the tip of his thumb. "I think this could really be something. Don't you?"

"I think it could be everything."

☆

THE FOLLOWING DAY, I met Jess outside Mei Lyn's office.

"Sash kissed me!" I announced.

Jess grabbed my shoulders. "And?" she practically yelled.

That morning, I had woken up to two texts. One with a single red rose emoji from Sash and one from Jess all in caps instructing me to get down to Mei Lyn's office ASAP because there was NEWS. Even though I was dying of curiosity, my mind and, not to mention, my body kept drifting to the night before. It was like Sash had flicked a switch somewhere, and I was in a perpetual state of arousal. I literally had to change my underwear twice that morning.

"Told you he was hot for you," Jess beamed when I gave her a quick recap of the night before.

"Speaking of hot, what's with your professor?"

She glanced at her phone. "Whoops, we've got to go in; don't want to keep Mum waiting." We walked through the glass door and into the reception area. Donna smiled at us from behind the desk. "Go straight through, girls."

In her office, Mei Lyn was pacing up and down, talking furiously on her phone. The moment she saw us, she ended the call and threw her arms out for emphasis. "Verity! Do I have news for you—big, big news! Carry Way has been in touch, and they want you—get this—in New York when your book launches next month."

"New York?" I cut in. "New York?"

"New York?" Jess repeated. Our heads kept snapping back and forth, like a pair of squawking parrots, looking from each other to Mei Lyn.

She nodded impatiently. "Yes. New York. Carry Way is teaming up with Barnes & Noble, and they want to put on a show for you at the Sojourn Theatre. They want to capitalize on all this momentum with Karla Swann sharing your post on Instagram. Oh, and one of their poets will be chairing your event—interviewing you on stage etcetera." She glanced down at her writing pad, where a mess of her ineligible writing was scrawled. As she scrutinized it, her forehead creased, lips moving silently as though she was trying to work out what she had written. "It seems here that her name is . . . Meenie Row?"

My mouth fell open. "Do you mean Mena Rhodes?"

"Yes, that sounds about right. She's a huge fan of your work."

I grabbed Jess by the shoulders, and we jumped up and down, shrieking at the top of our lungs. Mei Lyn shot us a look of disapproval, and we settled down.

"You don't understand, Mum. She's, like, our hero. She's totally famous and amazing! Like, she does all this charity work, and she's beautiful and recycles—"

"She's got a Frenchie named French Fry. She knits him these tiny sweaters—"

"I'm following French Fry on Instagram—Mena took him to a café yesterday and got him a puppacino."

I clapped my hands around my face. "I can't believe she'll be chairing my event. Like, seriously, is this really my life? Guess I don't have to worry about no one showing up!"

"Remember when she chaired Sara Woo's event? Sara was literally unknown, and suddenly she was huge, all thanks to Mena Rhodes. They call it the Mena effect. Everything she touches turns to gold."

"Oh my God, Jess. I'm going to get the Mena effect!"

This set us off again.

"Girls!" Mei Lyn clapped her hands, her voice as sharp as a drill sergeant's. We straightened up, heads snapping to attention. "So here is the deal. I managed to wrangle business class tickets for you, Verity."

"Oooh, fancy," said Jess.

"Whoa! I've never flown business before! Can Jess come with me?"

"Um, not sure if you're aware of this, but plane tickets cost money."

A sudden thought popped into my mind. "What if we traded the business ticket for two economy fares?"

"That could be arranged, and I can give Jess a bit of pocket money to spend while she's over there. She can visit Aunty Hoy and finally meet cousin Pei Pei."

Jess shot out of her seat. "Really, Mum?"

Mei Lyn smiled benevolently at her daughter. "Yes, really."

Then Jess turned her head slowly, her eyes meeting mine. The realization dawned like sunlight on her face. "Vare," she breathed.

"MOMA!" I cried.

"Barnes & Noble!" she shrieked.

"Central Park!"

"Times Square!"

We squealed so loud that Mei Lyn had to thump her tabletop several times more than usual.

SASH WAS AT the store when I got back. He looked dangerously sexy in full building gear, hands clamped around a mallet, ready to strike at an old water-damaged wall.

"Hey!" he said, putting it down.

"Where's Pop?"

He took off his goggles and came up to kiss me.

"He's gone to pick up sandwiches."

"Do you know when he'll be back? I have really exciting news!" I couldn't wait to tell him, so I began spilling all the details of my meeting with Mei Lyn.

His face lit up. "Go, you!"

I beamed at him. "And Jess is coming with me, too!"

"Ha! I can just see the two of you, strutting down Fifth Avenue like you own it. Can I take you out to celebrate? It's just occurred to me that we've never been on a proper date."

I clapped my hands. "Yes! I'd love to go on a date with you!"

"Tomorrow night?"

"Why not?"

"OK, I'm going to plan something unforgettable."

"What do you have in mind?" I asked.

"Well, what's the most exciting date you've been on? I want to know what I'm up against."

"In the ninth grade, Vic took me to the gaming arcade armed with a bag of shiny coins and told me I could play any machine I wanted."

"Wow, how can I possibly compete with that?"

"I wouldn't wanna be you."

He laughed. "Thanks for the vote of confidence."

I wrapped my arms around his neck and kissed him hard. "You know what—I'll bet you could take me on the most boring date ever and it would still be the best date."

"Hey, why don't we test that theory?"

I raised my eyebrows. "You want to take me on a boring date?"

"Not just any old boring date—the most boring, blandest, dullest date ever."

I laughed. "OK, you're on. Let's see what you've got, mister!"

☆

OUR DATE KICKED off at the State Library, where we attended an hour-long lecture by Professor Imran Frey, who spoke at length about the subject of topography and its relevance in the urban landscape. Frey spoke in a monotone voice and had all the charisma of the subject matter he was relaying to the audience of mostly middle-aged men. Once in a while, someone would cough, look around self-consciously, and mutter, "Pardon me."

When it was over, we stood on the steps outside, and Sash turned to me with a self-satisfied grin. "How was that?"

"That was fantastically boring!"

"How about Frey, huh?"

"He might as well have been a GPS."

"So have I done OK so far?"

"Oh, you've done more than OK, buddy." I winked at him.

"Well, you ain't seen nothin' yet."

I rubbed my hands with glee. "Ooh! What's next?"

"Are you hungry?"

"Yes! Starving. Where are you taking me?"

"You'll see!"

He took my hand and led me to his car parked at the curb. I was bouncing with excitement as my mind went through every uninspiring restaurant I knew. I wondered whether we were going to that salad place where the staff gave you judgmental looks if you asked for extra dressing.

"Where to, Captain?" I asked.

"We're here."

My mouth fell open. "What?"

He popped the glove compartment. Inside were two pieces of plain white bread wrapped in cling film and a bottle of water.

I laughed. "Well, just when I thought you couldn't possibly outdo yourself."

"Your dinner, madam," he said, with a flourish of his hand. He gave me a piece of bread and a plastic cup. But when he poured the water, he missed the cup and it sloshed onto my thighs.

"Woops," he said and patted me down with a paper towel. His fingers brushed my skin, sending a hot flush of desire through my body.

"Look at how much trouble you've gone to."

"Anything for my girl," he grinned.

We ate our meal, sneaking kisses in between.

"Gosh, this really does suck," he said, chewing on the bread.

"You wouldn't be saying that if you were a pigeon—they totally love this stuff."

"Seagulls, too—they lose their shit over this kind of thing."

"If you could fill your sandwich with anything, what would it be?"

"Three kinds of cheeses."

"What kinds?"

He wrinkled his forehead. "Gee, that's a tough question."

"Is it really?" I teased, and he swatted at me.

"I'd probably have a good aged cheddar, maybe a few slices of Camembert, and, ummmm, just a sprinkle of pecorino. How about you?"

"Tomato and mayo, like Harriet the Spy."

"Good God, I'm dating a nerd!"

"You kind of remind me of a character in that book."

"The Boy with the Purple Socks?"

"Yes!" I said, surprised he'd guessed correctly.

"You're not the first person to tell me that. In grade school, someone pointed at me and said, 'Look! The Boy with the Purple Socks.'"

"Why would they say that?"

"Probably because I was wearing purple socks."

I doubled over laughing. "You're such an idiot."

"To the world's most boring date."

We tapped our plastic cups.

"OK, now for dessert!"

As we approached the ice cream shop, I gave him a sidelong glance. "Uh-oh, looks like we could be playing with fire here."

"Trust me," he grinned.

I scanned the counter packed with an array of tantalizing flavors and toppings like hot fudge, M&M's, and rainbow sprinkles.

"Two vanilla cones, please," Sash told the girl behind the counter.

She stared blankly at him. "And?"

"That's it."

"You don't want any toppings? Gummy bears? Popping candy?" She gestured to the colorful display. "It's, like, the same price."

Sash shook his head firmly. "Nope, just plain vanilla, thanks."

"Vanilla, like our date," I giggled as she handed over my ice cream. I bit into it with glee.

We ate our ice cream on the sidewalk, holding hands. When we finished, Sash said, "And now for the grand finale!"

"Oooooh!" I grinned.

"Close your eyes and follow me."

I did as he asked, keeping my eyes shut tight, even though we had to apologize profusely every time we bumped into someone.

He came to a sudden stop. "OK, you can open them now."

My eyes flew open, and I was standing in front of a park bench.

I burst into fits of laughter. Placed on the center of the bench was a cardboard sign that read "wet paint."

I looked up at him. "What happens now?"

"We end this uneventful date with the most boring activity known to man."

And there, under the soft glow of the lamplight, we stood shoulder to shoulder, literally watching paint dry. Somehow, I was having the time of my life.

Nine

A FEW DAYS later, Sash came over for lunch and Pop had made his favorite—sausages and sauerkraut. We were enjoying our meal out in the courtyard with bottles of Deep Sea Diver. Pop was feeling spritely, buoyed by all the excitement we'd had lately. The small but significant improvements Sash was making to the store also seemed to energize him.

"Bracket looks like it might be loosening up." Sash nudged his head up toward the awning above the door.

Pop followed his gaze. "I think the wood has split right at the joint with the rafter. It's been years since it was treated."

"I'll look at the damage after lunch and see what I can do."

They nodded solemnly at each other.

I slid off my sandal and moved my foot under the hem of Sash's jeans. He jolted, banging his knee loudly against the table.

Pop turned. "You OK, son?"

"Um, yeah. Just felt like there was a spider on me."

"You've got to watch those redbacks." Pop pointed his fork at Sash, looking him dead in the eye. "They can kill you." Sash looked shrunken. "Ah, I think it's gone now."

"Good." Pop nodded and went back to his meal.

Sash kicked me under the table.

I smirked at him.

He glared.

Pop was still under the impression that we were friends, and I was waiting for the right moment to tell him it was more than that. I knew he liked Sash a lot, but Pop didn't always react so well when it came to the subject of boys. It probably had to do with his overprotective nature. That meant Sash and I had to be discreet, sneaking kisses whenever we could. I have to admit it was driving me crazy, and I couldn't help finding every opportunity for us to be alone.

"Verity, could you please pass me the salt?" Pop asked.

"Sure." I reached for it, but at the same time, Sash took a sip of his water. His elbow bumped my arm, and I dropped the shaker right into the plate of sausages. One flew across the table onto the floor. Zorro was nearby, saw his opportunity, and was on it in a flash.

"Ooops." I shot Pop a nervous grin.

Sash put his glass down, coughing and sputtering.

"What's the matter with you two today?"

My eyes widened. "Us?"

Sash turned his attention back to the awning again, concentrating hard. Then he went back to his meal with exaggerated nonchalance.

Pop looked from me to Sash and back to me again. Then a light bulb switched on in his head.

"I'm guessing the two of you are an item now?"

Sash's fork froze in midair, and his mouth hung open as he shot a panicked glance my way.

I smiled and looked down at my plate; then I nodded.

AFTER LUNCH, SASH and I went to our local hardware store to pick up some supplies. We were in the paint and thinners aisle when he said, "My sister, Marcia, wants to meet you."

"Cool! When?"

"She's invited us over for dinner tomorrow night."

"How do you I know I haven't made other plans?" I teased. "I'm in real high demand these days, you know. You've got to book way in advance."

"If that's the case, can I book you in for next week as well?"

"Wow—another booking! What's the occasion?"

"It's Dad's birthday. Mum's throwing a party at the house. Want to be my date? They're dying to meet you."

"Your parents know I exist?"

"I've told them about you, but I'm not sure whether they believe me. They still make quotation marks with their fingers every time they mention the words 'Sash's girlfriend.'"

I laughed. "I think I like them already."

MARCIA LIVED IN a small apartment block just outside the city. After we were buzzed in, we walked up a short flight of steps to a dark blue door marked 201. Sash raised his hand to knock when the door was flung wide open. A pile of books came crashing down out of nowhere, falling around our feet. "Damn it, Georgie." A young woman scowled at a furry orange blur darting down the hall. She turned to us and grinned. "Hey, lil' bro." Next, she turned to me. "You must be Verity, the girl I've been hearing so much about. You're very pretty!"

"So are you," I blurted.

Her eyes crinkled in the corners. "She's funny!"

"I knew you'd like her."

I took a good look at Marcia. She had the same striking green eyes as Sash, and she was tall and willowy, dressed in jeans and an oversized white shirt. She had a quiet, calm way about her, and she seemed like the kind of person you'd turn to in a crisis.

We followed her down a short hall to the living room, sidestepping the litter of books scattered on the floor. It was cozy and warm, with overstuffed couches and colorful throws. A bookshelf took up an entire wall and was filled mostly with anything other than books—stuffed toys, framed photos, and other memorabilia. Books were stacked all along the walls and on the steps of a staircase. As I looked at their assorted covers, I couldn't help but notice they all had one thing in common; they were books about cats.

"Marcia collects cat books," Sash explained, following my line of vision.

"Which is just as well—they're easier to keep than cats," Marcia said cheerfully. "Luckily, we have only Georgie to worry about."

A strange yowling sound erupted as we walked past the staircase, and I looked up to see a Maine Coon with his head between the bannister struts, glaring down at me.

I stopped and waved. "Hello, Georgie!" He answered me with a sharp hiss, then skittered out of view, sending other books tumbling down the stairs.

Marcia put her arm around Sash's shoulder and squeezed. "I'm making your favorite—Bolognese. Stella's home. She's a bit down in the dumps since Charlie called it quits for the hundredth time. He needs space to finish his novel—yes, it's the same one he started back in his senior year." She rolled her eyes at Sash and turned to me. "Stella's my roommate, and Charlie's her good-for-nothing boyfriend. He lives in a trailer."

"Who is it, Mar?" a voice called.

A girl who was a dead ringer for Venus in Botticelli's painting appeared. She looked so ethereal I wanted to ask Marcia and Sash whether they could see her, too. She was deftly shuffling a deck of cards, but she threw her head back, sending fiery locks over her shoulders, and her wide, generous lips curved into a smile.

"Bashi!" she exclaimed. I assumed it was her nickname for Sash. She pinched his cheek.

"Ouch," I heard him whisper under his breath.

"Verity, meet Stella," said Marcia.

Stella grinned. "Hey, Verity. So you do exist! You owe me ten bucks, Marcia."

Sash raised his eyebrows. "You guys were betting on this, seriously?"

They nodded in unison.

"Your mum and dad are in on it too," Stella said.

Sash rolled his eyes.

"Aside from Penelope, you're the first girl he's introduced to the family," Marcia explained.

I looked at Sash, wide-eyed. "I am?"

"How adorable is she?" Stella declared. She made a move to pinch my cheek when Marcia tugged urgently at my arm. "Come with me, Verity; I need your help in the kitchen."

Stella plunked herself down on the couch with a satisfied sigh. She patted the seat next to her, eyes locking on Sash. "Come and tell me all about this gorgeous new girl of yours."

☆

IN THE KITCHEN, Marcia got me to help her with the salad. I cut up the tomatoes while she grated a wedge of pecorino cheese. "Sash loves this stuff."

"He is crazy about cheese."

She laughed. "It's his Achilles' heel."

I leaned in and gave her a conspiratorial wink. "What else have you got on him?"

"He doesn't like soda water because of how the bubbles tickle his nose. He won't wear socks that go past his ankles—he calls them 'clown socks.'"

I grinned. "This is good stuff! Tell me more."

"He's seen *Titanic* fifteen times."

"No!"

"I'm not kidding. There was a period where we used to tease him mercilessly by calling him Jack."

I clapped a hand over my mouth, giggling.

"I should probably stop sharing these embarrassing stories." She looked a little guilty as she sprinkled parsley over the bubbling pot. The aroma was tantalizing, and it filled the tiny kitchen with a warm, homey ambience.

"Well, Sash knows practically every embarrassing story about me, thanks to my friend Jess. Who can blame me for trying to even the score?"

In the short time they'd known each other, Sash and Jess had developed quite a bond, mainly thanks to the jokes they often made at my expense.

Marcia grinned. "Fair enough."

"Hey, isn't it weird how Sash mispronounces certain words?"

"You mean like, 'everythink'?"

"Yes! And how he blesses himself when he sneezes?"

We burst into a fit of giggles.

"I'm glad you appreciate what a dork he is. I'm not sure Penny was as keen on that side of him. Oops—sorry, Verity! I didn't mean to bring up his ex like that. How insensitive of me."

I waved my hand at her. "Don't worry—I don't mind at all. I know how important she is to Sash, and I'm OK with that."

"You're really kind. I think he still feels protective about her. Penny's parents weren't around much when she was growing up, and that's why she spent so much time with us. She was always being bounced between nannies, so Mum and Dad practically adopted her. You haven't met them yet, have you?"

I shook my head, sliding the chopped tomatoes into the salad bowl. "I will next week at your dad's birthday party."

"Oh, that's right! Gosh, is that next week already? I have no idea where the time has gone."

"Do I have anything to worry about?"

"Nah, Mum and Dad are chill. Dad's in construction, and Mum does a lot of charity stuff. She heads a big anti-drug organization." I heard the note of pride in her voice.

"That's good to know, but I'm still nervous as hell."

She put her hand on my shoulder and gave it a quick squeeze. "You'll be OK."

"Will Penelope be there?"

"Most likely," said Marcia. "Penny does a lot of charity work with Mum." She must have caught the look on my face because she said, "I know the two of you don't exactly get on. Sash told me about your dinner at Mechanical Mango."

"Yes, things got a bit heated between her and my best friend, Jess. Penelope ended up storming out. Over poetry, no less."

"Yikes, I know how touchy Penny can be about that! It must be a shock for her, seeing Sash with someone new, especially since you just so happen to be a poet! Just give her some time. I'm sure she'll come around."

She saw the doubtful look on my face and smiled.

"I know you don't believe me, but Penny does have a sweet side. She's got a trust fund bigger than Ben Hur, but she doesn't rest on her laurels. She does a lot of charity work—and I don't mean writing a check like most people in her position would. You'll find Penny cleaning out the litter trays at the local rescue or at a soup kitchen, ladle in hand. If you were cynical, you'd think she was doing it to score points. But I know for a fact that underneath the tough-girl act, Penny has a heart of gold. Mind you, it still doesn't excuse her behavior, but Sash has always been a sore spot for her.

And I guess you have it worse because this is probably the most serious he's ever been about a girl." She turned off the stove and drained the pasta.

"Really?"

"Oops! I've said too much again," she grinned. "Now, looks like we're all set. Let's go and rescue Sash from my nutty roomie."

☆

SASH WAS SETTING the table when I brought in the bowl of salad. I plonked it down, bumping my hip into his. He tucked his hand into the back pocket of my jeans. Stella approached with the deck of cards in her hands. On closer inspection, I could see they were tarot cards. She was doing some pretty cool moves, like a blackjack dealer.

Marcia set down the pasta. "Um, can't this wait until after dinner?" She nodded at the cards. Stella grinned, her eyes full of mischief. "It'll only take a second."

I gave Sash a questioning look.

"Stella's a fortune teller," he explained. "I was telling her the story of how we met, and she wants to do a reading for you."

"I'd love that! I've never had my fortune read before."

We sat on opposite sides of the table, and Stella kept shuffling the cards with amazing dexterity. She passed them to me. "Your turn, sweets." I worked them clumsily, one card, slipping free and falling to my feet. I made a grab for it, but she shook her head. "Leave it."

Then she arranged the cards on the table, and we all fell silent as we watched. "Well, well. Interesting . . ." She looked me in the eye. "I'm going to tell you three things. The first is something from your past, the second your present, the third your future."

I felt goose bumps all along my arms. I held my breath.

To my surprise, she burst out laughing. "Tell us about the boy on the bus."

Right away I knew what she was talking about and groaned. "Never."

"Oh, come on, Wolf." Sash nudged me with his elbow.

I shook my head, resolutely.

"Go on," said Marcia. "Now I really want to know."

I tried to weasel my way out, but I could see they weren't going to give up. "Back in the ninth grade, I had a major crush on a guy. He caught the same school bus as me, but I never plucked up the courage to speak to him. One day, I was gazing at him when he turned unexpectedly and caught me staring. My jaw dropped, which was bad enough. To make it worse, the gum I'd been chewing fell out of my mouth."

"No!" Marcia giggled.

"Word got around school, and for the rest of that year, I was gum girl."

"Can't believe I'm going out with gum girl," Sash grinned.

I swatted at him. "How could you have possibly known about that?" I asked Stella.

She shrugged. "A magician never reveals her tricks."

"I still can't figure out how she does it," said Marcia.

"I was terrified of her when I was a kid. She could always tell if I was lying," said Sash.

"Like the time you ate an entire packet of jelly beans and blamed it on your imaginary friend," Marcia joked.

"You had an imaginary friend, too?" I asked, delighted.

"Pipslet," Marcia and Stella said in unison.

"Pipslet?"

Sash groaned. "Guys, please. Verity doesn't need to know all this stuff."

"Mine was Posey Darling, but she left around the time I met Jess."

"Do you think that was a coincidence?" Sash teased.

"Pipslet and Posey," said Marcia, eyes twinkling. "Even your imaginary friends sound like they belong together."

"Now for the present." Stella's expression was suddenly serious. We all fell silent. She closed her eyes for a moment. When she opened them, they were looking straight into mine. "They are here with you. They've always been with you, and they love you, Verity—so much."

All of a sudden, I was crying, tears welling up so fast I couldn't hold them back.

"Hey." Sash put his arm around my shoulder.

"Stella, you're upsetting her!" Marcia cried.

"No, it's OK," I sobbed. "You're talking about my parents, aren't you?"

She nodded, her eyes moist and glistening. "I can feel their presence, even in this room. They're so proud of you, babe—of everything you've achieved and, most of all, the young lady you've become."

I nodded as Sash passed me a silk handkerchief monogrammed with his initials. I did a double take. "What the hell is this?" I started laughing.

He grinned. "Creature of habit."

"A bit of a fancy boy, isn't he?" Stella whispered to me.

This made me laugh even harder. "I'm keeping this for luck," I said to Sash, tucking it into my pocket.

"Stella, the food's getting cold."

Stella waved Marcia off. "We're almost done." She reached across the table and took both my hands in hers. "Now for the future."

I took a deep breath, steeling myself.

"Oh," she breathed, "sweetie, you are destined for great things. I can see you surrounded by people who love you. Crowds and crowds of people. Your wish will come true, but it will come at a cost."

At those words, a charge swept through my body. I shivered.

"What does that mean?" I asked in a hushed voice.

"She's being overly dramatic, Verity. It's just theatrics, that's all. Now, I think that's enough for tonight. Stella, why don't we pack away the cards?"

Stella still had my hands in hers, and she gave them a quick squeeze before letting go. "Marcia's right. Don't let it worry you." But there was an unsettling glint in her eyes.

Marcia set down four wine glasses and opened up a bottle of Pinot.

"How about a toast?" she said, looking from me to Sash, her eyes shining. "Here's to those who wish us well, and all the rest can go to hell!"

AFTER WE LEFT Marcia's, Sash took me home. As he pulled up into the alley beside the store, I saw the hallway light Pop always left on for me, and a lump rose in my throat.

"You were a hit with the girls tonight."

"Your sister is so cool, and Stella, well, Stella is amazing! It was freaky when she brought up my parents."

"Do you still remember them?"

"Just flashes here and there. The images are fuzzy at best. Sometimes when I look at old photographs, it's as though I'm staring at two strangers. But the feelings haven't changed at all. I remember the warmth of my mother's arms and my dad's scratchy beard against my cheek. Little things like that. With Nan, it's different because I can remember whole conversations. I don't know if that makes it better or worse."

"I'm so sad you had to go through all that. No one should have that much tragedy so early on."

I smiled to reassure him. "I've had some really great things too."

We were silent for a while.

"Sash, do you think your parents will like me?"

"Of course. How could anyone possibly not like you?"

"Um, have you met this girl named Penelope?"

"Who?"

I punched him lightly on the arm.

"Look," he said, "you've already met Marcia, and she likes you. My parents are cool. I'm cool, too. We're all cool. So the only one you'll have to charm is our dog, Little Lord Fauntleroy. We call him Fonty, or Monty, or Fontman—"

"OK, I get the picture."

"It won't be easy. He's the crankiest Chihuahua known to man, but in time he'll grow to love you as much as I do."

My mouth fell open. We'd never said that word before. "Sash. Did you just . . . did you just say you love me?"

He bit his lip and grinned. "Ah, man. I was trying to keep that a secret for now."

"Why?"

"I was planning on telling you at the airport, literally the second you were about to leave. I thought it would be more poignant. Since you're a poet, I thought that would impress you."

"Aw, Sash. That's sweet, but you can impress me in other ways."

"Such as?"

"You know the other day when you ate two sandwiches at the same time?'"

"A double-decker sandwich counts as one sandwich."

"Whatever that monstrosity was, I sure was impressed with how well you handled it."

"I could probably do three at once—"

I put my finger on his lips. "Shhhh."

He mumbled something incoherent.

"I love you, too, you know."

"I kind of suspected."

We held each other tightly, and I felt that warm, tingly sensation all over. Regretfully, I glanced at the clock on the dash and sighed. "It's late; I'd better go in. I don't want Pop worrying." I leaned in for one last kiss.

He took my hand. "Do you think we could stay here just a little while longer?"

We climbed into the back seat and were barely settled when his lips were suddenly on mine. I shivered as his hands moved under my sweater and into my bra.

We were breathing hard, our kisses switching from slow and lingering to frenzied and rough. His tongue traced the line of my collarbone, and I was losing it. I felt hot and sticky, like I was melting.

I'm not sure how we got our clothes off, wrapped in each other as we were, but somehow we managed. I felt a little self-conscious when he ran his eyes over my body. "You're beautiful, Wolf," he murmured.

His body was lean and muscular, arms taut like a swimmer's. I felt squishy in comparison.

"You're not so bad yourself."

Without breaking eye contact, I climbed onto his lap, wrapping my legs around his hips.

"Are we really doing this, Wolf?"

I nodded, cupping his face in my hands. "Put your hands on me, Jack."

He rolled his eyes skyward. "Is there nothing sacred?"

"You watched *Titanic* fifteen times. I'm impressed."

"Want to make it sixteen tomorrow?" he teased.

My eyes held his. "As many times as you want."

"Mmm," he kissed me warmly, "you drive me crazy, you know."

I moved my hips against his in response, and he let out a sigh.

"Have you got protection on you?"

His grin was lopsided. "I've had one on standby— you know, just in case."

And then it was happening. His hands gripped the small of my back, pulling me in, hard against him.

It felt exquisite with him inside me. As we rocked, skin on skin, my back arched against his palm. I whispered things I'd never said to anyone else before, held on to him like I was drowning. Condensation fogged the windows and ran in rivulets down the glass. The sounds coming from the street outside felt as if they were a world away. This wasn't how I imagined it would be, but it was perfect, and when it was over, I already was thinking about the next time.

"WHY DO YOU have that look on your face?" Jess squinted at me from across our table at Last Chance.

"What look?"

"Like you got lucky."

A grin broke across my face. "That's because I did!"

She clapped her hands together with obvious glee. "Where did this momentous occasion take place?"

I had discussed the big moment with Jess before, and of course, geography was a factor. Sash still lived at his parents' house, which made it tricky. And Pop hardly went out these days, so there weren't a lot of options on the table.

"We did it in his car."

"That's original—especially for you," Jess teased. She was referring to my first and only other sexual encounter. Guy was my prom date, and it happened in his parents'

Range Rover, in an empty parking lot. Halfway through, we were interrupted by a female police officer who proceeded to give us a lecture on safe sex.

Across the table, Jess had her eyes shut and was making kissing motions with her lips.

I threw a french fry at her. It missed and fell on the floor at Jonesy's feet.

"Girls," he shot us a look of disapproval, "we don't want a repeat of last week, do we?"

"Sorry, Jonesy," we said in unison, looking down at our plates. The week before, Jess and I inadvertently had started a food fight in the café. She threw a ketchup packet at me for teasing her about Haden, the hot professor whom she was still weirdly tight-lipped about. To retaliate, I threw a cherry tomato at her. She ducked, and the tomato sailed across to the next table, striking a little old lady right between the eyes. She flew into a rage, pitching her half-eaten tart in my direction. Her aim was terrible, and it hit the guy behind me. Then it was pandemonium, with everyone flinging food at each other. In the ensuing chaos, we tried to sneak out, but Jonesy grabbed us. "Oh no you don't. You've done the crime; now you do the time." We spent the rest of the day scrubbing dishes, floors, walls—everything. The place had never looked so spotless.

"We were just talking about Verity's new boyfriend," said Jess.

"I see. Who's the lucky guy?"

"Sebastian, but we call him Sash. He's really nice. You'd like him."

Jonesy dramatically gripped his chest. "I think my heart just broke."

"Aw, Jonesy. You know Jess is still available."

"That's right," Jess winked at him. "Not all is lost."

He grinned. "By the way, I have something for you." He took a notepad out of his back pocket and put it down on the table.

"Is that your diary, Jonesy?"

"It's the notepad I used when I was in New York years back, before I opened up Last Chance. I wrote little notes about the places I went to—thought it could come in handy since you guys are going there." Jonesy looked like he was already regretting his decision.

I flipped through the notepad, and my eyes lit up. "Jonesy, this is fantastic!"

"You are such a sweetheart," Jess agreed.

He beamed at us, then went to serve a group of exchange students.

"Wow, look, he's even drawn little maps."

"And reviewed every place he's been to."

"He uses carrots instead of stars! That is so Jonesy."

"Egg & Yolk got five carrots—let's have brunch there!"

At the back of the notebook, I caught sight of the words LAST CHANCE CAFÉ - RENT with figures scrawled beside it in blue and red pen. There was a lot more red than blue.

"Looks like poor Jonesy is struggling to keep this place afloat." I felt sad.

"Greedy landlords! Mum looked into it for him, but there's nothing he can do."

"If this place goes bust, I am going to cry."

"Same! There's nowhere else to go around here."

Jess reached across the table, grabbing a handful of fries from my plate. "How was dinner at Marcia's?"

"Oh, it was great! Marcia's really nice and easygoing. Her roommate is so cool. Get this—she's a fortune teller!"

"No kidding? Did she give you a reading?"

I nodded and gave Jess a quick summary. "She said I was going to be famous. She saw me surrounded by crowds of people."

"Didn't I tell you that was going to happen? It's written in the stars!"

I grinned. "You sure did, my friend. Oh, also, Marcia and I had an interesting chat about Penelope."

Jess made a face. "My favorite person."

"How are things between you two at Deep Sea Diver?"

"Well"—Jess crinkled her brow—"to be honest, I'm not sure what to make of Penelope. The other day she brought in cupcakes—you've never seen cupcakes like these." She cast a furtive glance at Jonesy and lowered her voice. "I mean, Jonesy's cupcakes are divine, but the ones Penelope had were on a whole other level."

Jess continued. "They looked like they were made by angels—each one a masterpiece. She was handing them out around the office, and I thought, no way in hell would I get one. We haven't been on speaking terms since the blowup at Mechanical Mango. But she popped one on my desk."

"That was nice of her," I admitted.

"Everyone adores her at Deep Sea Diver—apparently she's Mother Teresa. From the stories I've heard anyway."

"You mean all that volunteer stuff?"

"Exactly. How can anyone who saves the lives of innocent kittens be evil? Maybe she's just blinded by her jealousy when it comes to Sash, and that's the reason for her bad behavior."

"Marcia thinks she needs time to get used to the idea that she's no longer the center of his world." I shrugged. "So maybe the jury's still out when it comes to Penelope."

"Well, she can't be all that bad if Sash still cares about her—right?"

"They practically grew up together. Childhood sweethearts. Marcia said there's a lot of history there."

She sighed. "The boys said as much. Teddy told me the two have this special bond. Apparently, Sash was really into her, but she was a bit wishy-washy. I think she was waiting for someone better to come along. Like a safety-net guy."

"What's that?"

"You know, when you like someone but not enough to commit to them. You want to keep them on the back burner in case no one else comes along."

I looked at her aghast. "How dare she! Sash is no safety-net guy—he's way too sexy to be safe!"

"He's a great catch for sure, Vare. Now she's come to her senses, and it's too late because he's with you."

"I'm not going to let her get to me, no matter what. But I just wish—" I sighed. "Soon I'll be halfway across the world, and God knows what she'll do."

"Oh—I totally forgot to tell you. When I was in the office, she was flipping through her notepad, and I think I caught sight of your name."

"Really?"

"I'm pretty sure! I think she's planning something, so just be prepared."

"I bet she's going to review my book on Reader!"

"God, I hope not. The last thing you need before New York is Penelope poisoning the well. Speaking of which, I overheard her telling Teddy she thinks Sash has changed since he met you."

"Of course he has. Doesn't love change us all?" I said smugly.

"Anyway, don't worry about her, Vare. Sash is crazy about you, and it's not your fault she can't stand it. She had her chance!"

"Marcia told me it's the first time he's been this serious about a girl. Can you believe it?"

"Um, Verity? News flash! This is the first time you've been this serious about a boy."

"Wow." I sat back and shook my head. "Holy shit, Jess, you're right."

She rolled her eyes. "What would you do without me?"

"Um, curl myself into a ball and cry myself to sleep every night for the rest of my life?"

"Damn right!"

☆

POP WAS BEHIND the counter when I walked through the door. "Guess what came today?" He waved at a large cardboard box.

"Uh, more books?"

"They're your books, Verity! Advance copies."

I let out a whoop, raced over to the counter, and tore open the box. Then I was holding a precious copy in my hands. When Carry Way had sent me the cover design, it didn't feel right to me. They went back and forth with Mei Lyn and finally agreed to keep the original cover Jess had designed. I ran my fingers across her name printed on the dust jacket and grinned. She'd be over the moon.

"These are something, aren't they?" Pop said.

Zorro jumped onto the counter and rubbed up against the box. I held my book out to him, and he butted it lightly with his head. Almost like he approved.

"My book," I sighed, clutching it to my chest.

Pop handed me a pen. "Excuse me, madam, could you please autograph a copy for me?"

I laughed. "Certainly, young man."

"Now—you know where this is going, don't you?"

In dramatic fashion, he unlocked the glass cabinet behind us and placed my book right in the center. "A Verity Wolf first edition, signed and inscribed by the author herself."

I did a little curtsy.

"I'm so proud of you, little one." I saw a tear at the corner of his eye.

"Thanks, Pop."

He took one long look at me and shook his head. "You know, it's uncanny, but you look exactly like your mother did the day we met her. She came into the store looking for a copy of *Anna Karenina*. I was poring through the classics when your dad came down the stairs. It was love at first sight."

"Really?"

"For him, at least. She might have needed some convincing." Pop smiled at the memory.

"So how did they start talking?"

"I made some excuse and got your dad to help her out. Right away I could sense a certain magic in the air, between them. He didn't have much luck finding her *Anna* either. As it turns out, Nan always used the bookstore as her personal library, and she had it on her bedside table. That was just as well because if I had found it right away, she might have left before meeting your dad."

"It was fate."

"Certainly was. Come to think of it, that's similar to how you met Sash—isn't it?"

"Yes," I breathed. The thought of it filled me with wonder. I was desperate for anything that made me feel closer to my parents. "Pop? Could you tell me something about Mum?" I could hardly remember much about her, but there was one memory I kept, sharp as a tack. I had once spotted a bright yellow butterfly trapped on the inside of our window and pointed it out to her. We watched its panicked wings beat helplessly against the glass. Without a word, she slid open the window to let the butterfly out. Then I was overcome with an inexplicable sadness as we watched it soar far away into the blue sky. To cheer me up, Mum folded her hands into butterfly wings, dancing them in front of me. I remember how delighted I was, watching her hands and hearing the music of her laughter. Every time I saw a butterfly, I thought of her.

"Well, Katiya was a free spirit—fiercely intelligent, artistic, and funny. She was so light on her feet—your dad used to say that in another life, she must have been a sparrow. A happy little singing sparrow. She loved the world so much, wanted to see every inch of it. More than that, she loved you, Verity, with every ounce of her heart. You meant the world to her."

Zorro bounced up from the counter and placed one paw on my cheek with surprising lightness. I hadn't even realized I was crying.

"She was like a burst of sunshine in our lives. We were lucky to have her, even though it was for such a short time."

I was sobbing now. Pop reached over and pulled me into his arms.

"Come on—it's a day of celebration."

"I so wish I could remember her better."

"I know, sweetheart. Sometimes my memories get a little fuzzy, too, but then all I have to do is look at you." He cupped my face in his hands. "And it's like she's here again."

Ten

SASH'S FAMILY HOME reminded me of the house in the movie *Ex Machina*. Perched on a cliff edge, the room where the party was held had floor-to-ceiling glass and jaw-dropping views of Sydney Harbour. In the distance, the Opera House glowed surreally like a ghostship, and the bridge behind glittered against the city skyline. The place was already buzzing when we arrived. Men in suits and women in pretty dresses talked and laughed, fluted champagne glasses in hand, and waiters skittered around with bottles of Moët at the ready.

Marcia greeted us in the hall. "Hey, dorks," she said fondly. "Verity, let me take your coat."

"Looks like you're on coat duty tonight!" Sash said with a certain glee.

She glared at him. "Don't rub it in."

I looked from one to the other. "What's coat duty?"

"Well, it's a job that involves more than just greeting guests and taking their coats. When you're on coat duty, it's your job to make sure everything runs smoothly. You're like the maître d', hostess, and butler all rolled into one."

"Mum and Dad always assigned coat duty to one of us when they put on a party. Sash did the last one, so now it's my turn."

"Remember when you went abroad for a year and I had to be coat boy for three consecutive parties?"

Marcia laughed. "I bet Mum and Dad were pleased—you're so much better at it than me."

The doorbell rang, and Marcia groaned. "Coat girl's been summoned. Why don't you guys go and mingle? By the way, Verity, nice dress!"

"Thanks," I grinned, as Sash led me into the throng.

Just hours ago, I'd been in a panic about what to wear, but Jess came over to help. I must have tried on everything in my wardrobe, and in the end, I settled on an emerald-green halter dress that had belonged to my mother—a cherished belonging put aside for me by Nan. When Sash picked me up, he looked me up and down and whistled. He was so handsome in his tuxedo I even did a pretend swoon. Jess got a snap of us before we left, and I uploaded it to my Instagram. The comments that flooded in ranged from "couple goals" to "lol why is that dude wearing a bow tie?"

A scurrying sound accompanied by a flash of white caught my attention. I looked down to see a little

Chihuahua pawing furiously at Sash's feet, tail wagging. "Hey, little guy!" he cooed and picked him up. "This is Lil' Lord Fauntleroy."

"Hey!" I stretched my hand out to pat him, but midway I stopped when his sharp growl erupted.

"Come on, Monty. Where are your manners?" Sash set him down, and the dog still eyed me suspiciously.

"Monty!" I heard someone call. When I spotted Penelope making a beeline toward us, I groaned inwardly. As usual, she looked perfect in a little black dress and pearl earrings. She scooped up the Chihuahua, and he looked over the moon, panting and licking at her face.

"Hey, Verity!" To my surprise, she smiled warmly at me.

"Hi, Penelope," I answered warily.

"Any chance you know where I can find Mum and Dad?" Sash asked her.

"They're in the kitchen. Your mother's having a showdown with Jenny about the canapés, and your dad is playing diplomat."

"Great, I want to introduce them to Verity."

Penelope turned to me. "I love your dress! Is it vintage?"

"Yes, it was my mother's."

"It's stunning, great taste!"

I wasn't sure if her compliment was genuine, but then I recalled the story Jess told me about the cupcake. Maybe Penelope wasn't as bad as I thought after all.

I decided to give her the benefit of the doubt. "Thanks."
I smiled.

☆

IN THE KITCHEN, a tall, svelte lady was berating a woman
in a chef's uniform. The man next to them had salt-and-
pepper hair, and he watched the terse exchange with a
bemused expression. All three turned when we walked
in, and the chef used this distraction to quietly slip away.

"Mum, Dad, this is my girlfriend, Verity."

Sash's parents looked like a couple who modeled
for wedding cake toppers. Everything about them
was perfect—their clothes, posture, and hair. Sash's
dad wore a navy-blue suit, and his mother had on a
cream boatneck dress with a glittering tennis bracelet
on her wrist.

"Happy birthday, Sir," I blurted.

He walked over to give me a surprise hug. "Call
me Graham!"

"And you can call me Dotty." Sash's mother gave me
a quick peck on the cheek.

"We're so pleased to meet you," said Graham. "Sash
won't shut up about you."

"All we've been hearing lately is Verity this and
Verity that!" Dotty smiled at me.

"Mum," Sash groaned.

"Your house is stunning," I gushed.

Dotty beamed. "Has Sash given you the grand tour yet?"

"I was thinking of doing just that."

"Don't forget the library." Graham winked.

Dotty's eyes lit up. "Yes! Sash told us you grew up in a bookstore, so I'm sure you'd feel right at home."

A waitress came in to drop off a handful of trays. Dotty snapped to attention. "Beatrice, do you know where Jenny is?" She shook her head. "Sorry, Mrs. David."

Dotty rolled her eyes. "You must excuse me, Verity. I have to chase her down. Our chef was instructed not to put shellfish in the canapés. At least a dozen of our guests are allergic! And you, birthday boy"—she pointed at her husband—"you get out there and mingle."

Graham touched my arm, eyes twinkling. "Dotty's right. I can't hide in here all night, as tempting as that is. I'm sure we'll have plenty of time to talk later."

"They're nice," I said to Sash when his parents left.

"See, told you there was nothing to worry about. I'm your PR man, and the name Verity Wolf is on the up and up."

"Is that so?"

"Yes, the reports are flooding in, and word is you're on fire, baby." He kissed the tip of my nose.

"So did you manage to catch them?" Penelope walked in and strolled over to the fridge. She pulled out a bottle of Evian and uncapped it before pouring the contents into a glass. I felt a twinge of jealousy at how familiar she was with Sash's kitchen.

"We did," said Sash.

"How did it go?"

"Great. They're really nice."

"Aren't they? I wish they were my parents." She let out a little laugh. "Well, they practically are, aren't they?"

There was an awkward pause.

"So I promised Verity I'd give her the grand tour," said Sash.

"Make sure you show her the fortress."

"The fortress?"

"It's actually a panic room, but we call it the fortress. It's behind a secret door in the library. When we were kids, Sash and I used to play in there all the time. Didn't we, Sash?"

"Uh, yeah." He cleared his throat, then turned to me. "Ready?"

SASH TOOK ME straight to his bedroom and shut the door behind him. He flipped the lock and grinned.

"So this is you," I said with a wink.

"This is me." He winked back.

The layout was similar to the room downstairs, stark and modern with views of the harbor. It was spotless, with the exception of his desk—a long, dark wood panel that stretched down the length of the room. On it, a tangle of cables bunched around an iMac, and beside it there was a mountain of graphic design equipment. I recognized the drawing tablet that Jess had been ogling for ages. A framed picture of Sash with Teddy, Tom, and Penelope was propped between a pile of Lego bricks and a stack of tattered paperbacks.

"My parents are kind of neat freaks, but I'm allowed my one island of chaos. Our housekeeper has given up trying to keep my desk tidy."

"In the art world, we call it juxtaposition."

"Wow, you are so full of knowledge."

"I know so many things."

When I ventured closer, I saw bits of paper scattered around the table, drawings of buildings and architectural details. Then something caught my eye. On the top page of a spiral notebook there was a sketch of me chewing on the tip of a pen.

"I didn't know you were such an artist, Sash. When did you do this?"

"It was the morning you got that email from Carry Way."

"If I'd known, I would have posed for you."

He wrapped his arms around my waist from behind; his warm, sweet mouth inched its way along my neck. "How about you pose for me now?" His voice had grown husky and was doing all kinds of things to me. I closed my eyes, leaning my body into his.

He combed my hair to the side with his fingers, then undid the knot that held up my dress. It slipped off my shoulders, exposing my breasts. He ran his hands over them, thumbs circling my nipples. A sigh escaped from my lips.

I turned to face him, meeting his mouth with mine. In one smooth motion, he lifted me onto the desk, his hands on either side of my hips.

"Do you have any idea, Wolf, how many nights I've spent in this room lusting for you? Now here you are on my desk practically naked. You're like a wet dream. Only I'm awake, so you're a wet dream come true."

"You really know how to compliment a girl."

He laughed as I wrapped my arms around his neck, dragging my tongue across his earlobe. He took off his jacket and dropped it to the floor. My fingers went to work undoing his trousers, and I slid my hand in. He bit down on his bottom lip and let out a breath. "Jesus . . . "

Blood pulsed in my ears. My body hummed. "Do you want me to stop?" I teased.

He was breathing hard, his eyes holding mine. "No, keep doing what you're doing."

"Like this?"

He groaned in response, dropping his head down on my shoulder.

"Wolf—"

"Mmmmm?"

"Take off your underwear."

WE LEFT SASH'S room trying not to look too conspicuous. My face was flushed, and I hoped no one would guess what we'd been up to. Marcia was coming down the hall toward us.

"Hey, you two! Where have you been? You're missing out on all the fun."

"What's going on?" asked Sash.

"Mum's just started a game of Sardines."

"Sardines?"

"It's similar to hide-and-seek, but in reverse. You hide while everyone else looks for you. When someone finds you, they join you in your hiding spot. And the person to hide in this game happens to be my dear mother," Marcia explained.

"Oh! I think I've heard of this game. You pack yourself into a closet or whatever, and it starts to get crowded, like a can of sardines."

"Exactly! Anyway, it's coat girl's job to wrangle all the guests and let them know the rules. I'll see you two later."

"See you," Sash called after her.

"I hope Dotty wasn't hiding in your bedroom," I joked.

Sash laughed. "Actually, I think I know exactly where she is. Follow me!"

I WENT WEAK at the knees when we walked into the family library. There was shelving that took up an entire wall, with a ladder propped against it. Armchairs, rugs, and lamps were arranged artfully around a fireplace. The ceiling that soared above us was made almost entirely of glass, like an atrium. I made a noise in my throat that was halfway between a gasp and a moan. "I didn't know places like this existed in real life."

"It gets better!" Sash walked over to the bookshelf and pressed his palm against a row of books. To my surprise, the books slid back, and the entire shelf clicked open like a door. This must be the panic room Penelope told us about earlier. We walked in, and sure enough, there was Dotty sitting on a couch with a glass of wine in her hand.

"Quick, shut the door," she whispered.

"A bit unfair, Mum, considering most of the guests have no idea this room exists."

She gave us a cheeky smile. "Good! It gives me an excuse to take a break. Parties are exhausting, aren't they? I can't wait to get out of these shoes."

The door clicked open again, and Penelope appeared. "Thought I might find you here!"

Dotty took a sip of her wine. "We might as well get comfortable. We'll probably be here awhile."

We joined her on the couch, and I took in the room. It wasn't how I imagined a panic room would look. In fact, aside from a panel of screens on one wall, it looked like an extension of the library.

"This is cozy," I said.

Penelope looked at Sash. "Isn't this where we had our first kiss?"

Clearly, he was taken aback. "Uh, yeah, I think it could be."

I felt that now-familiar clench in my stomach—the one that happened when Penelope flaunted their history in front of me.

Dotty must have sensed the sudden change in atmosphere because she turned to me and asked, "Verity, what's it like being a published poet?"

"I suppose I'm still getting used to the idea."

"Well, you're a rare breed!" She tipped her wine glass at me. "Then again, you grew up in a bookstore, so your fate was probably set. You know, I've been to Wolf Books a few times. Found a gorgeous edition of *The Little Prince*. The store has so much character. It's a real treasure trove if you're looking for something rare. Have you been, Penny?"

She shook her head. "Not yet."

"Oh, you would love it. It's just your thing." Dotty turned her attention back to me. "By the way, my daughter sent me some of your poems. I just have to say that the insights you have are quite remarkable for someone your age. I'm impressed."

"Thank you," I beamed. I glanced at Penelope in time to catch a brief flash of anger in her eyes.

"Oh, I almost forgot, Verity, you dropped this." She extended her hand.

"Thanks," I said, thinking she'd found my keys. I had a terrible habit of losing them. But it wasn't keys Penelope had pushed into my hand. I looked down, confused. It was a joint.

I let out a short laugh. "Penelope, this isn't mine."

"You left it on the kitchen counter earlier."

I felt everyone's eyes on me, and my face reddened.

Dotty looked at my hand, eyebrows furrowed. "Is that a joint?" She plucked it from me and held it up to her nose, taking a couple of sniffs, nodding as if to confirm her suspicions.

"It's not mine," I repeated.

"Yes, it is," Penelope insisted.

Dotty looked from Penelope to me. She cleared her throat. "Verity, under no circumstances do we tolerate drugs in this family. I don't know if Sash has mentioned it, but I head up a major antidrug organization. To be quite frank, this is the last thing I need." Her voice was tense and sounded just the way she had spoken to the cook earlier. Only now it was directed at me.

Sash looked from me to Penelope, and I could see that once again, he was torn. When he finally came to my defense, it was weak. "Maybe another party guest left it?"

"Oh, it definitely belongs to Verity. I saw her drop it."

"You're lying!" I cried.

Dotty winced and turned to Sash. "You know we're just about to launch a massive campaign, and I can't have this anywhere near the media. They would have a field day!"

Penelope was nodding furiously, and I suddenly recalled how Marcia said they often worked together. "It would be a disaster for sure! If this ever got out, the public would crucify you, Dotty. You'd have no other choice than to step down."

Dotty's hand flew to her brow, as if the thought had only just occurred to her. "Oh, you're absolutely right, Penny, and that would be unthinkable. All my years of hard work down the drain." When her eyes met mine, they were flashing anger. "Look, I don't know what you are up to, young lady, but I don't like this one bit."

"Verity says it isn't hers!" Sash insisted.

"You're suggesting that Penny is lying? One of them must be."

Penelope crossed her arms. "Well, it's not me."

I took a deep breath, feeling panic rise up in my chest. It was obvious whose side Dotty was on. As for Sash, it hurt that I wasn't quite sure.

"Come on, Pen, just tell the truth," he pressed. The pleading tone in his voice infuriated me.

"You leave Penny alone!" snapped Dotty. "You've known her all your life. And this girl? You've known her five minutes. It's no coincidence that since you've met her, your career is going down the drain. You turned down the job offer with Das Haus—the one your dad jumped through hoops to get for you."

I gaped at them. Sash had mentioned the offer once, but he hadn't brought it up since. I had no idea how strongly his parents felt about it.

"Verity has nothing to do with that, Mum. That was my decision."

"Well, Penny did warn me that Verity might be a bad influence on you, and I'm starting to wish I had listened to her."

Suddenly, it made perfect sense why Penelope had been so nice to me all night. It was part of her plan to show me up in front of Sash's mother. Jess was right: Penelope had been plotting against me. She would have worked on Dotty weeks in advance, planting seeds of doubt about me. Tonight, I walked right into her trap.

I stood up. "Look, I think I should go."

"Good idea," said Penelope.

"Verity, wait!" Sash got to his feet.

"No, you stay here, Sash. I'll talk to you tomorrow."

"But—"

"Let her go," Dotty barked. "It's your father's birthday, and we're celebrating as a family." The way she put the emphasis on the word "family" told me Penelope was part of that and I wasn't. I'd never felt more like an outsider.

I glanced at her and caught the hint of a smirk at the corners of her mouth. I had never disliked another human being so much in my life. Hot tears springing to my eyes, I turned and pushed my way out of the room, then out of the house.

The cool air hit me when I stepped outside, reminding me I'd forgotten my coat. But I didn't want to go back inside and risk running into Marcia. I didn't want to have to explain myself while I was choking back tears. I crossed my arms over my chest and shivered. How could I go from being so blissfully happy to feeling this low? I pulled my phone out to call myself an Uber and heard footsteps pounding the path behind.

"Wolf!"

I turned to see Sash running toward me, my coat in his hands. He wrapped it around my shoulders, rubbing the sides of my arms. "You're shivering."

I stared down at my feet, wiping away tears. I felt utterly humiliated and knew that if I looked at him, I'd fall apart. "It wasn't mine," I said, in a small voice, and I hated the fact that I had to defend myself. It meant no one else was on my side.

"I believe you," he said earnestly.

"I don't know, Sash," I said sadly. "It didn't look as if you were all that sure back there. When it comes to Penelope, you seem to have a blind spot." Finally, I raised my eyes to meet his, and it felt as though what either one of us said next could change everything.

Sash went first. "I want to make something clear. If you thought there was any doubt in my mind whose side I was on, you're wrong. I'm on yours, Wolf. The way

I acted was out of loyalty to an old friend, not because I still have feelings for Pen."

I shook my head. "Sorry, Sash, I'm not sure if I believe you. To be honest, it didn't look that way to me. Your friends keep telling me you and Penelope are unfinished business. Maybe you need to finish it once and for all, before you start again with me." It broke my heart to say those words, knowing this could be the end for us.

"No." He said the word with such force it took me by surprise. I wished he had been that certain back in the panic room when it mattered.

"Look," he continued, running a hand through his hair, "I'm so scared I'll say the wrong thing because I feel deeply that this is the one time I shouldn't screw up. You came bursting into my life carrying bucketloads of sunshine, saying every last thing that pops into your head. Suddenly, I couldn't get you out of mine."

"Sash—" I felt myself waver.

He was talking fast now, as if I could vanish at any moment. "I can't bear the thought of going back to the cardboard-cutout life I had before I knew you—before you showed me what it was like to laugh out loud and not care what anyone thinks. You are unapologetically yourself, and you have no idea how refreshing that is. You won't believe how glad I am to have met you, and I love you, Wolf. I love everything that comes with that. I love the shop and its loud clanging bell, and I love Zorro, even if he keeps trying to kill me.

I love Pop and our crazy debates, and I love Jess because of how much she loves you. I love all of it because I don't think I've ever belonged anywhere as much as I do with you. Before I even knew what I wanted, it was this."

Tears coursed their way down my cheeks, and I felt the knot of anger in my chest gradually melt away.

"I love you too, Sash—we all do," I whispered, and his shoulders sagged with relief.

"Are we OK?" His eyes searched mine.

I nodded. "I think so."

He let out a long sigh, kissing my face over and over. We whispered words of how much we loved each other, and all my doubts about Penelope faded into the background.

"You're right; we deserve a fresh start. From now on, it's just you and me. I'll talk to Mum tomorrow and explain what's been going on. I'm sure she'll understand."

"Your spin doctors are gonna have to work overtime."

"That's right—I'm your PR man; remember?"

"You put the D in damage control."

A smile lit up his face. "How did I ever find someone as amazing as you?" He drew me into his arms and held me tightly. I pushed my head into the warmth of his neck and felt wave after wave of happiness engulf me.

A little ruffling noise caught my attention, and I broke away.

"Uh-oh, looks like we've got company."

Standing by Sash's feet and looking up was Little Lord Fauntleroy, tail wagging.

"Hey, Monty." I crouched down and, with great apprehension, went to stroke him. He froze for a moment, then he gingerly stuck out his tongue and licked my fingers. I scratched under his chin, and he closed his eyes, tipping back his head.

"How about that," Sash beamed. "Looks like our spin doctors are already making headway. Public opinion has shifted dramatically in the last thirty seconds."

"I knew I could count on you!"

We laughed as Monty rolled onto his back, legs stuck in the air, making strange, raspy noises.

"He likes it when you scratch his belly."

"Sounds like someone I know," I teased.

"But it's so soothing!" he protested.

I scooped Monty up and popped him onto my shoulder. I could tell by the way he was chewing on my hair that this was the start of a beautiful friendship.

Sash shook his head. "Can't believe you're going so soon."

"Only for a couple of weeks."

"God, I'm going to miss you, Wolf."

"You'll take care of Pop for me, won't you?"

"You know I will."

PART TWO

Eleven
(New York)

"On the count of three," I said.

Jess's eyes twinkled. "One."

"Two." I grinned.

"Three!" she finished.

At the exact same time, we bit into our first official meal in New York City—two hot dogs slathered in ketchup, pickles, and mustard that we bought at a street cart on Lexington Avenue from a guy named Lorenzo. When we mentioned it was our first time in the city, he gave us a couple of Diet Cokes and said they were on him.

"Oh my God, this hot dog is amazing!" I moaned.

"Mmmmm." Jess turned and gave Lorenzo the thumbs-up sign.

We had arrived at Newark that morning on a flight I thought would never end. I felt lightheaded and giddy as I stepped off the plane, despite looking like hell, my hair oily and matted against my forehead and a blemish forming on my chin. Meanwhile, Jess looked like she'd been at a spa. Typical.

At arrivals we were greeted by Tara, a twenty-something rep from Carry Way. She was in sky-high stiletto boots and skinny jeans, holding a placard with my name on it. When she caught sight of us, she waved enthusiastically, bounding over to greet us. Jess couldn't stop gushing about Tara's shoes, and I was smitten with her accent. On the drive to the hotel, we bombarded her with questions about the subway, Central Park, and Times Square. Looking through the windows of our Uber, we were overwhelmed by the sheer size of the city, the wailing sirens, the rush of traffic, and the chorus of honking. I cocked my head to see all the way up the tall buildings.

Tara checked us into a small, red brick hotel with cute flowerpots on windowsills and left us to settle in. The room was impossibly tiny; twin beds with barely a handspan between them were placed side by side. I found a welcome pack with my schedule and an envelope labeled "stipend" filled with twenty-dollar bills. Jess and I spilled the money onto the bed and took turns rolling around in it.

Now we were on a street corner, jet-lagged but wired, running on adrenalin, half-eaten hot dogs in our hands.

"Let's record our first big milestone!"

I whipped out my phone and started an Instagram story.

"Hi, it's Verity Wolf, and I'm in New York City with my best friend, Jess!"

Jess waved. "Hi, everyone! We're just enjoying our first-ever meal—"

"Our first in New York, not our first meal ever."

"Yes, we want to make it clear that we have had meals prior to this."

"Just not in New York City."

We giggled.

I waved my hot dog at the camera. "I'll be at the Sojourn Theatre Friday night. Event details are in my profile. Oh, and no big deal or anything, but my idol, Mena Rhodes, will be chairing my event. See you there!"

I uploaded the story, and my inbox flooded with messages.

NYC???? OMG I kerrnot I KERNOT

C U babbbbbyyyy gurl

Upload a vid of you eating in slow mo

My 2 faves what is life

I have something else to do SOZ

Your friend is hot Verity LOL

We giggled as we continued reading. I never got tired of the weird and wonderful messages and comments I was sent.

A hot dog emoji and wink appeared from Sash.

"Awww, I've been gone a day, and he's already trying to sext me."

"Vare, I don't need to know stuff like that."

I sent Sash a string of kisses, and we continued scrolling through the comments. Suddenly, Jess and I gasped in unison.

"Is that—"

"It's her," Jess confirmed.

"Her real account?"

"Yes! It's verified."

We looked at each other and shrieked.

"Oh my God! Mena just messaged you! Mena Rhodes!"

I scanned the message with eager eyes.

> Hey Verity It's Mena. Sooooo excited to be chairing your show this Friday. Are you free tomorrow? Want to catch up for a coffee?

Jess grabbed my arm, and we let out another shriek. Lorenzo smiled over at us from his cart. "Good news?"

Jess grinned at him. "The best news ever!"

I CAUGHT SIGHT of Mena outside Starbucks on Fifth Avenue, eyes glued to her phone. I stopped and took a deep breath, steeling myself. It was surreal seeing her in the flesh. Taller than I imagined, dressed in a white collared shirt tucked into a pair of tan trousers. A large black belt cinched her impossibly tiny waist. She had smooth, tawny skin and a light sprinkling of freckles across her nose. Her dark shoulder-length hair was stylishly cut and swished against her striking high cheekbones. I tentatively approached her.

"Mena?" Her eyes flickered up to meet mine. Up close, they were extraordinary. A light shade of brown, with flecks of gold and amber.

"Verity!" she exclaimed, pulling me into a warm hug. "Welcome to New York!" Her voice was soft and lilting, but there was power in it. A dreamlike quality, like you were hearing it underwater, yet every word was crystal clear.

"Thanks, Mena." I was trying my best to play it cool, but my heart was hammering loudly in my chest.

She slid her phone into a back pocket. "Gosh, your accent's adorable! Australian?"

"Uh-huh."

"So I thought we'd get our coffees to go. You don't mind walking, do you?"

"I totally love walking!"

"Great! It's such a beautiful day. I love it when the air's like this—when we're right on the cusp of fall. We can leg it down Fifth Avenue. What do you say?"

I nodded enthusiastically. At that point, she could have suggested we walk off a cliff and I wouldn't have objected. I'd never met anyone famous before and was starstruck.

"Is it your first time here?"

"Sure is!"

"Well, there's plenty to show you. I hope you haven't made plans for the rest of the day."

We walked down Fifth Avenue, Styrofoam cups in hand. The morning light bounced off the buildings, casting blocks of sun and shade on the bustling pavement. I took a sip of my mocha with an extra shot of espresso.

"How are you finding New York so far?"

"I love it!" I gushed. "I grew up watching American shows, so it's like walking onto a movie set. The vibe here is like a current—you can't help but get swept up in it."

"Spoken like a true poet!" She grinned.

A girl in white sneakers and cropped T-shirt stopped us. "Oh my God, Mena? Mena! Can I get a selfie with you?"

"Sure." Mena smiled and posed with the girl.

"Do you ever get used to that?" I asked when the girl left, thumbing furiously on her phone, no doubt sharing her fortuitous encounter on social media. I'd be doing exactly the same if I were her.

"Not really," she laughed. "You'll see what I mean when it starts happening to you! By the way, if you didn't already know, I am a huge fan of your work. When Carry Way sent me your book, I read it all in one sitting. I was in the bath and was practically a prune when I finished. I just didn't want to put it down."

"Really? You actually liked it?"

"Verity, I loved it! But I already knew I would from the pieces on your Instagram. Speaking of which, I couldn't find the one Karla posted." Mena put her hand to her chest. "When I first read that poem, it stopped me in my tracks. It's been ages since a poem has done that to me. Why wasn't it in your book?"

I bit my lip. "Um, the thing is it's not my poem. I think Karla assumed I wrote it because it was on my Instagram. But I found it in an old book, *Poemsia*."

"*Poemsia*?" She repeated.

I nodded.

"You know the same thing happens to me all the time. I get stuff attributed to me that I didn't write. Some I wish I had written, and others are just insulting. There's literally nothing you can do about it. If you try to set the record straight, you end up adding to the confusion."

"That's what I'm starting to figure out. It's like shouting into the void."

She laughed—a deep, rumbling sound so different from the musical quality of her voice. "That's the Internet, all right."

We were silent for a time as we walked. I had so much I wanted to ask her. In my head I had rehearsed this conversation over and over, and now my mind was blank.

"Are you nervous about your first event?" Mena broke into my thoughts.

"God, yes! What was yours like?"

She grinned. "It was at an indie bookstore over in Brooklyn. Only a handful of people, so it was no big deal. Luckily for me, I wasn't thrown straight into the deep end like you'll be on Friday."

I gulped. "Thanks—that makes me feel better."

She chuckled. "You'll be fine! Besides, I'll be on stage with you. It'll be a breeze."

"The thought of all those eyes on me is terrifying."

"No, no. It's more the idea of it, I think. When you're up there, it's like someone else takes over."

I thought back to that day in the park when I performed my poems. It had felt that way for me, like some other person had momentarily taken over. Even though a part of me knew I'd probably be fine, I couldn't stop feeling waves of anxiety every time I thought about being on stage.

Mena must have read my mind because she gave me a reassuring look. "After a while, it doesn't really matter if you're speaking in front of an audience of ten or ten thousand. It'll just feel like another day at the office. But, like, a really cool office where you're kind of the boss and everyone gets you snacks and stuff." She winked at me.

"What if something goes wrong? Like someone asks me a question I can't answer and I freeze up and look like an idiot?"

"I have all sorts of tricks for situations like this. I've done it a million times, so you're in good hands."

"What if hecklers come out?"

Mena snorted. "Never happens! The hecklers prefer to lurk behind their computer screens."

"Haters, you mean?"

She nodded. "Have they been bothering you?"

"Actually, I don't think I've ever had any hate."

"Never?"

I shook my head. "So far people have said only nice things. Sometimes a bit weird, but generally nice."

A soft smile played on her lips. "I remember those early days. Only people who love your work bother to interact with you. The rest kind of leave you alone. As you get more popular, that starts to change. I don't want to be the bearer of bad news, but the haters are coming, Verity. It's inevitable. They are packing up their little backpacks, and sooner or later, they'll be heading your way."

"Then so what's your advice on how to deal with them?"

"Well, you'll find three kinds of haters. You have the Pseudo Intellectuals, the Fake Haters, and the Hate Readers."

"This is weirdly fascinating. Tell me more!"

She drained her coffee before tossing the cup into a nearby bin. "OK. First are the Pseudo Intellectuals. They put out this image of being well read and intelligent, but no critical thought actually passes through their heads— just shit they memorize and regurgitate to spin their own delusions of grandeur. The crazy thing is they often get away with it. They just convince people who are dumber than they are. One guy like that wrote a dissertation on a poem he thought was mine. You should have read it, Verity. It was all over the place and went into weird territory. Halfway through, he was droning on and on about the evolution of language, using Darwin to point out the inconsistencies between the first and third stanzas of my poem. And his dick got a mention, like every other male would-be critic. No clue what he was talking about, of course, just stringing together a bunch of rubbish. It's sad that people are impressed with things they don't understand, so some got behind it, parroting lines from his paper. It was all over Twitter, and you know what? It wasn't even my poem. It was Plath."

I grabbed her arm. "No way!"

She nodded gleefully. "It was, no pun intended, poetic."

"Which poem was it?"

"'Mad Girl's Love Song.'"

I snorted. "OK, but that's just ridiculous. It's, like, her most well-known poem. Besides, her style is completely different from yours."

Mena shrugged. "Like I said, anyone with the most basic knowledge of poetry could tell you that, but he must have found it on Pinterest and assumed it was mine. As you found out, things are always getting misattributed."

"Did you call him out?"

"I almost never do. Why give trolls a voice? But this one was too good to ignore! I simply tweeted, 'Dude, are you sure that's even my poem?'"

"What happened?"

"Within minutes, he'd become a laughing stock. You could see a time line of the idiot imploding. First, he tried to defend himself; then he made out that he knew all along and tried to spin it as satire. But he wasn't fooling anyone, so he took it down. After that, he deleted his Twitter."

"I can't believe I missed this!"

Mena grinned and shrugged. "So that sums up the Pseudo Intellectuals. Next up, we have the Fake Haters. These guys aren't too bad. Truth is they don't actually hate your work. They send hate your way because they're bored and looking for someone to pick on. So no need to take it personally. They're like lemmings—pretty much harmless. That's more than I can say for the Hate Readers." She gave me a meaningful look. "Those guys are the real deal."

"Uh-oh."

She nodded and explained, counting on her fingers. "Your typical Hate Reader, one, is intelligent; two, comes with a small but vicious following; and three, is digitally savvy. These guys are on a whole new level of hate. They know the system and how to twist it to their advantage. They use platforms like Reader to pass as legitimate reviewers—some even write for big publications. They have no qualms about reading an entire book for no other reason than to trash it. That takes dedication—not to mention books are expensive! Which means the hatred runs deep. It's organized hate."

As Mena spoke, one person who seemed to fit that popped into my mind. "I actually know someone like that—in real life, I mean. Her name's Penelope, and she's a top reviewer on Reader."

Her eyes widened. "You're not talking about the one who also writes for Billy?"

"Yes! That's her."

Mena stopped walking and shook her head in disbelief. "Jesus Christ! That bitch practically invented Hate Reading. How the hell do you know her?"

I gave Mena a brief summary, and her face remained frozen with incredulity. I started from the night at Fidelio and went through to the blowup at Mechanical Mango. She interrupted me. "Her favorite poet is Calmine Verdue? Figures! So she's just as bitter and twisted in real life as she is online."

"She's pure evil, no question."

"And she's hanging around your boyfriend?" She gave me a wry smile.

I sighed heavily. "She's his childhood sweetheart, and, yes, they're still good friends."

"Oh shit, that sucks."

"It gets worse! She's trying desperately to get him back." Then I told her about the stunt Penelope pulled at Sash's house when she showed me up in front of his mother.

Mena let out a low whistle. "She's really got it in for you, doesn't she?"

"It looks that way."

"I don't envy you. All us pop poets are way too familiar with Penelope and her gang of Hate Readers. When you see her next, tell her to go to hell from all of us, OK?"

"I'll pass the message on," I laughed, as we continued strolling up Fifth Avenue. I noticed the shop fronts got flashier as we went.

"Anyway, we shouldn't worry about her. It's the Penelopes of the world who are the architects of our success."

"But . . . how?"

"I'm going to let you in on a secret." She stopped and gave me a mysterious smile. "Hate is bad for the ego, good for book sales."

"I don't get it. Why would that be?"

"When I first got hate, it felt soul destroying. I thought for sure that the haters would convince everyone what a bad writer I was—one who didn't deserve to be published. It's weird how skewed my perception was, but I'm older and wiser now."

"Well, in your case they obviously failed miserably. You're one of the most universally loved authors in the world. I mean, Sal Dollinger is a fan of your work."

She shrugged and grinned. "Sal is a sweetheart. He's kind of like my mentor."

"Oh my God, I'm so jealous. My granddad is such a huge fan. How on earth could anyone doubt your ability if Sal endorses your work? He's only, like, one of the greatest living poets of all time."

"That kind of stuff gets overlooked, Verity. People see only what they want to."

"It's such a shame, isn't it? People put so much time and energy into tearing others down. It seems pointless to me."

"Sometimes when it's happening, you can lose perspective. The truth is it's never as bad as you think.

Picture a stream of rushing water. That's the people who adore you. The haters are the little fish trying to swim against the stream."

I nodded. "That makes a lot of sense."

"Once I picked a fight with Toby White—you know, that god-awful YouTuber? The one who does those shitty pranks? He put on a wig and read some of my poems in a whiny, high-pitched voice. I called him out, and his fans descended on me like a swarm of locusts. You should have seen the backlash. My mentions were going nuts. People were telling me to shut up, that I was being overly sensitive, that I can't take a joke, or I must be on my period. It kept escalating, and the tweets got increasingly sadistic. I had to log off Twitter for, like, three days. It was horrible! I couldn't bear to look at another tweet describing my rape and murder in horrific detail. Anyway, it all died down pretty quickly, and to my surprise, I made record sales that week. The fact is people love drama! They can't resist it. Now when there's something controversial, I just take a few days off social media and wait for the money to roll in." We were walking past Tiffany's, and she stopped to admire a diamond cuff bracelet in the window. "Hey," she said, a wicked look on her face. She whipped out her phone. "I really want that bracelet! Want to help me stir up shit to fund it?"

Before I knew it, we were walking along the tree-lined pavement that ran by Central Park.

"Do you want to see my favorite thing ever?" Mena asked.

"Sure."

We walked along farther until we reached an entrance into the park. We went a few steps in, and it felt as if I was being transported to another world. I stared at the grand trees that edged the park, their sprawling limbs spread out as though they were trying to keep the advancing metropolis at bay. We passed an old-style lamppost that reminded me of Narnia.

"Oh my God! I can't believe I'm actually here!" I exclaimed.

Mena smiled. "I'm from Sacramento originally, so I know what it's like, seeing Central Park for the first time. It's a rite of passage."

Suddenly, I stopped. Jess and I had talked about visiting Central Park since we were kids, and here I was, without her. It didn't feel right.

"Are you OK?"

"Just thinking about my best friend, Jess. We've dreamed about coming here for so long; I wish she was with me. That's all."

Mena reached out and gave me a quick hug. "How old are you, Verity?"

"Nineteen."

She gave my cheeks a soft squeeze. "You're a baby!"

"How old are you?"

"Twenty-five, an old lady compared to you." She linked my arm with hers, and we continued walking. "You know, you totally remind me of myself at your age. That's when things started to happen for me, too."

"What was it like?"

"It was thrilling, intoxicating—and so ridiculously hard. It was really tough when I started touring, and I was away from home a lot. So I took the plunge and moved here. It was the best decision I ever made."

"You must pinch yourself all the time."

"I do. I mean, this is my dream. How many people get to live their dream? But fame doesn't come without setbacks. You were just talking about your friend Jess, and that reminds me of all the great people I've had to leave behind."

"That would never happen to me and Jess. Not in a million years."

"Well, that's what I thought about my best friend, June. We grew up together and shared everything—even boyfriends! We were that close. She knew everything about me, and I knew everything about her. Now we don't even keep in touch. Sometimes I so miss her, and I wish we could pick up where we left off, but it's just not the same. They say all this fame stuff changes you, but it doesn't. You're still the same person. It's just that everyone around you changes. The people you thought would always be in your life start to drift. It's as if, deep down, they've lost the ability to relate to you."

"That's so sad," I said. I couldn't imagine not having Jess in my life. The thought was so alien I couldn't even begin to conceive it.

Mena shrugged. "You get used to it, and you make new friends—ones you have more in common with. I guess that's part of growing up. I think you can't really get anywhere in life if you let sentimentality hold you back. That's what I've learned, anyway."

"I think for me, all that stuff is a long way off."

Mena shook her head. "You don't realize just how close you are, do you? I've been tracking your socials, and you're growing at a faster rate than any poet I've seen—myself included. Your numbers are going through the roof."

"You really think so?" Sometimes when I posted a new poem, I would watch awestruck as the counter ticked up and up. But for some reason, I'd always found it hard to attach those numbers to real live people.

"It won't fully sink in until you get up on stage." Once again, Mena had read my mind. "After Friday night, you'll see what I mean. When the fame comes, it will swallow you up like a tsunami. You won't see it coming until it's already here."

I looked into her honey-brown eyes, and suddenly, I was reminded of what Stella had said. "Your wish will come true, but it will come at a cost." I shivered, thinking of what I wanted more than anything else. Underneath layers of that dream, I felt a tiny creeping ball of dread, much like the princess and the pea.

"Is your boyfriend the cute guy who keeps popping up on your Instagram?"

"Yes," I said, a bit giddily.

"First love?"

I grinned and nodded.

"I remember my first—Josh. Back then I thought the world of him, but do you know what that asshole did? He went to the media with personal stuff about me. Like really intimate stuff. I could kill him."

"I can't imagine Sash ever doing that."

"You can never be too sure. Boys have egos the size of houses. They think with their dicks. It's been like that throughout history. That's why there's such a thing as locker room talk. Only now, the Internet is their locker room. It's pathetic."

"I don't think all guys are like that, and Sash definitely isn't. My grandad owns a bookshop, and it's been falling apart around us, but Sash has been fixing it up. It's really sweet of him."

"You'd be amazed what a guy would do to get into your pants."

"Oh no, it's not like that at all! I was the one who was trying to get into his."

She tittered. "You're so cute. We should have this conversation again when you're my age. You'll have learned by then that the world isn't all roses and everyone has a motive. How long have you known Sash?"

"We met a few months ago."

"Verity, you can't possibly get to know someone that quickly."

"But we just click, you know? I've never felt that way about anyone else—almost like we're—"

"Soul mates?" Mena interrupted. "Look, don't get me wrong. I've been there, and it's easy to get carried away with all that stuff in the beginning. But half a dozen guys later . . . well, your perspective might change a little."

I had to wonder whether there was truth to what she was saying. I loved Sash with all my heart, but what if it was because I had no one else to compare him with? Hadn't the past few months shown me how unpredictable life could be?

Mena went on, "And while you're away, he's got Penelope hanging around him. Do you really trust him, Verity?"

"Yes, of course! Sash is a great guy. I'm so lucky he came into my life when he did."

"You mean because you've got a maintenance guy around? You do know you can hire them?"

"No, no—Sash is so much more than that!" I felt like I was getting tangled up in my words and everything was coming out wrong. "Besides, we can't afford to hire anyone."

She put both hands on my shoulders and peered down at me, eyes laughing. "Verity, soon you'll be able to buy a whole new bookshop."

"But—it's where I grew up. It's my home. I don't want another one."

She stood back and shook her head; a knowing smile crossed her face. "You know what? I used to think exactly like you, but remember what I said about fame? You're going to have so much choice. You'll have the whole world right before you. The last thing you want is some guy holding you back."

"Sash isn't holding me back; he's really supportive and—"

"What will he do when you move to New York?"

All at once, I felt like I'd been hit with motion sickness. "Move?" I gulped.

"Don't tell me you haven't thought about it."

"Um, I—"

"It might sound crazy, but you have to think about your future. I know you're only nineteen, but the next few years will go by in a flash." She clicked her fingers. "This poetry game—it's all about youth, right? You've only got a handful of years to make it big, then someone younger will come along and replace you. That's the way it is in the music biz, and poetry is the same. Look at Sara Woo. She moved here all the way from Singapore, and her career is going from peak to peak. She started touring bookstores, and now she's just sold out a show at The Town Hall. You've had a massive break, Verity, but you can't coast on it forever. You need to be where the action is, or it will pass you by."

I was struggling to come to terms with what she was saying, grappling with the idea of moving all the way here. To be honest, the thought had never crossed my mind. How on earth could I leave Pop? I was the only family he had. And Sash and Jess. But perhaps Mena knew better. This was my dream, and a chance like this might never come again. If I didn't grab it with both hands, I might regret it for the rest of my life. I felt a strange sensation in my stomach that tugged in both directions.

"We're here! This is what I wanted to show you," said Mena, cutting into my thoughts. I immediately recognized the Alice in Wonderland sculpture from all the pictures I'd seen, but I wasn't prepared for how grand and detailed it was. My eyes eagerly took in Alice, the Cheshire cat, the Dormouse, the Mad Hatter, and my favorite—the White Rabbit. A shiver went down my spine, and I recognized an affinity with the story that I'd never felt before.

"You feel kind of like Alice, don't you?" Once again, Mena seemed to have an uncanny knack for reading my thoughts. It was as though she knew me better than I knew myself—perhaps because she'd gone down this road before.

I nodded. "Was it like that for you?"

"Like falling down the rabbit hole, you mean?" She answered her own question. "Without a doubt."

"Everything feels so surreal, you know? Like I'm in a dream."

She grinned. "Welcome to Wonderland, sweetie!"

☆

IT WAS SUNSET when I got back to the hotel. Jess sprang up from the bed, standing on her tiptoes like she did whenever she was excited.

"Well?" she said, anxiously.

"It was awesome!" I blurted, and she let out a whoop.

"You have to tell me everything!" she cried, grabbing both my hands and swinging them side to side.

"I don't know where to start. Oh my God, I'm still shaking a bit."

"I don't blame you! You just spent a whole day with Mena"—she paused for emphasis—"Rhodes!"

"Sorry I didn't call—totally lost track of time."

"That's a good thing, right? I had a feeling the two of you got on since you were away so long."

"How was Aunty Hoy?"

Jess had gone to visit her aunt, a pediatrician who lived out in Brooklyn, with her husband, Gerry, and their three-year-old, Pei Pei. I met Aunty Hoy once before, when she visited Jess in Sydney. She took us to Luna Park and seemed to enjoy the rides more than we did.

"Aunty Hoy was really good! She was bawling her eyes out and hugged me so tight I started to go blue in the face. Then she gave me a pile of the red envelopes she set aside for me every Chinese New Year. It's been quite a few years, so now I'm officially rich! Anthropologie, here I come!"

"Good for you!"

"Uncle Gerry took the day off, and we all went out to Yum Cha. My cousin Pei Pei is so cute—she has the chubbiest cheeks in the world and likes to remind us every two seconds that she's just turned 'thwee.' After lunch, we went to their place—a sweet townhouse with climbing red roses down one wall. And get this: they have five Pomeranians!"

"Five?" I held up my hand, fingers splayed.

Jess nodded. "Why would anyone need five? Especially since Uncle Gerry is allergic, poor thing. Aunty Hoy says he's allergic to everything, even though Uncle Gerry assures me he's not."

"I wish I could have seen them!"

"The Pommies?"

"No, your family, silly!"

"Oh, they'd love to see you, too, but they know what a busy girl you are. We'll catch up with them if we get a chance. You'll love the Pommies, but my advice is don't wear open shoes. I wore my sandals, and let's put it this way: I'm lucky I still have toes."

"Noted!"

"Enough about me! Tell me about your day with Mena! What was she like?"

"She's so pretty," I gushed. "The pictures don't do her justice at all. She's really nice and down-to-earth. We talked about literally everything!"

"Wow, this is so surreal!"

"You're telling me! I was so nervous at first, but once we got talking, the conversation just flowed. You know, she's got so much wisdom because she's been part of this scene for ages. She was the first poet really to break through—"

"Wait! How does Mena like her coffee?" Jess interrupted.

"Black."

"That's so gangsta!"

I laughed and continued, "We talked about poetry—she loved my book."

Jess squealed, and I giggled.

"We talked about what it was like for her in the beginning, what to expect for my event Friday night. Um . . . what else? Oh, we went to see the Alice in Wonderland statue in Central Park—"

"You went to Central Park?" Jess cut in. I caught a flicker of something in her eyes. For a second, it looked as though she was hurt.

"Well, we kind of just wandered in. I mean, I wish I had gone with you first . . ."

She shook her head. "Don't be silly, Vare! We can go anytime we want. What was it like?"

"You're going to love it! Why don't we go tomorrow? We can get one of those rowboats at the lake."

She clapped her hands together. "One more thing we can check off our list!"

"And afterward we can get some sandwiches and have a little picnic."

"Speaking of food, I'm literally starving! Since we've been out all day, why don't we have a night in? Order room service, watch reruns of *Friends* . . ."

"Yes! Sounds perfect."

"Tomorrow, we can go to Egg & Yolk for breakfast—that place Jonesy awarded five carrots."

"Or if you want, there's a place near Central Park that Mena says makes the best omelettes."

"Um, sure. OK," said Jess, but then there was an awkward pause.

"Actually, no. Let's go to Egg & Yolk. If Jonesy gave it five carrots, it must be good!"

"Don't be silly! We should go the place Mena recommended. It's right by Central Park, and that's our first stop tomorrow, right?"

"Are you sure? I just thought, you know, Mena's a local, and she was raving about this place. She even wrote down the address for me . . ." I trailed off.

"Vare, it's fine. We'll go to the place Mena recommended. Decision made, OK?"

"Sure," I said, even though a part of me now wished I hadn't brought it up.

"Now that's settled." She picked up the room service menu and put on her best posh sounding voice. "Now, what will madam be having this evening?"

LATER THAT NIGHT, I lay awake in my hotel bed. I could tell by the way Jess was breathing that she'd fallen asleep. Our room was on the third floor, and that meant we got the omnipresent sound of traffic punctuated by the high-pitched wailing of sirens. Every so often, there was a loud crashing sound nearby, like a pile of rocks being emptied into a garbage bin.

My mind sifted through the things Mena had said. Some parts were exciting, and others made me uneasy, especially what she had said about Sash. What if she was right? Could I really trust him around Penelope when I was halfway across the world? After all, I knew she would always be a huge part of his life. Didn't he tell me so himself? I grabbed my phone from the bedside table and tiptoed into the bathroom. I sent a text to Sash.

Skype?

He appeared on the screen moments later, face grinning and hair disheveled. He looked so sexy I wanted to press my face against the screen. My heart welled up, and any shred of doubt Mena had planted in me vanished in an instant.

"I miss you." I sat down on the cold tiles, my back against the door and knees tucked under my chin.

"I miss you too, Wolf."

"How's Pop?"

"He's good. I was over yesterday, putting up the new awning in the courtyard. He made me a sandwich."

"What kind?"

"Cheese and onion. It was delicious! The cheese was, like, bright orange—a hard cheddar so full of flavor. He won't tell me where he got it. I looked in the fridge for clues, but he'd gotten rid of all the evidence."

"I swear, in your last life you were probably a mouse."

"So that explains why your cat keeps trying to kill me."

"How is Zorro, by the way?"

"He's keeping it real."

I felt a lump in my throat. A feeling of despair swept over me, and I didn't know why.

Sash frowned. "Are you OK?"

Tears spilled down my cheeks.

"Hey, Wolf, what's wrong? Why are you crying?"

I cried even harder.

"Wolf? What's going on?"

"It sucks, you know," I sobbed. "I'm so lucky to be here, but inside I'm going haywire. I think maybe I'm homesick or something, but I keep getting hit with these waves of sadness. The second I feel anything negative, I get angry at myself because I'm in New York, and this is my dream—I'm literally not allowed to feel bad about anything. It's so overwhelming, getting hijacked by my feelings all the damn time, but I can't help it."

"Do you know what? Whatever it is you're feeling, go ahead and feel it. Even if it's negative. I hereby give you permission."

"You do?"

"Yes, I've just lifted the embargo on feelings. You can now enjoy them guilt free."

I wiped at the tears in my eyes. "I love you, Sash."

"The feeling is mutual, Wolf. I'm there with you, OK? Remember that."

"I still have your silk handkerchief—the one you gave me at Marcia's."

"There we go. I'm your lucky charm."

I sniffed. "What time is it over there?"

He angled his camera to where a miserable-looking Monty was standing in a bathtub, big, woeful eyes aimed squarely at me as though I could rescue him.

Sash ducked his head back into the frame, grinning. "It's bath time!"

"Now THIS IS more like it!" Jess said happily as we glided across the lake in our little boat at Central Park.

She was naturally good at almost anything, and despite never having rowed before, she mastered it in the first few minutes. Now we were bobbing along the water, enjoying the sunshine and views of the Manhattan sky-line that peeked out behind the clusters of trees.

"This is more like *us*, isn't it?" I said, grinning sheepishly.

I was referring to breakfast that morning. The moment we stepped into Pony, Mena's recommendation, we regretted it. We looked so out of place among the other diners. Even though most were dressed casually, they all seemed to have that glow, an indescribable look that distinguished them from ordinary people like us.

Then, after the shock of seeing the menu prices, we decided to split a single omelette, and instead of Pellegrino, we asked for tap. Our waiter was not impressed, and I swear I caught an eye roll.

To add insult to injury, the omelette was mediocre—Jess and I both gave it two and half carrots—even though it was served on the prettiest plate I had ever seen. This entire experience was excruciating, and I couldn't wait for it to be over. Now, here we were in the sunshine, relaxed and happy, listening to the chittering of birds and the gentle swooshing sounds of the oars sweeping the water.

"I still can't get over that we're actually here," said Jess dreamily.

"Don't you just love New York?"

"I adore New York! We should move out here someday, don't you think? We could get one of those loft apartments in SoHo. You could write poetry; I could draw and paint. We'd go gallery hopping, have long lunches, go see a show on Broadway. Can you imagine how much fun we'd have?"

"Funny you should say that. Mena totally thinks I should move here."

Jess smiled. "I'm sure one day, Vare—"

"No, no—she means now. I know it sounds crazy, but she made some good points. She said the poetry scene is all about youth, and I only have a handful of years to make it here."

Jess stopped rowing and gaped at me. "Are you insane?"

"But you just said you'd love to move here."

"Vare, I wasn't actually serious. I mean, what about Pop? Are you just going to leave him? You know he hasn't been well—who's going to take care of him? And what about Wolf Books?"

"I just thought that if things go well for me here, I'd be able to get the best treatment for Pop. And you know how many times Wolf Books has been close to shutting down. We keep thinking up all these schemes to save it, and Jess, what if this is the way? What if I am successful, like Mena or Sara? Then I'll have more than enough money to keep Wolf Books open."

"Oh my God, you're actually thinking about this, aren't you?"

"I don't know—it's just an idea. OK, let's forget about it."

"You can't just drop a bombshell like this and then brush it off. God, we're not living in a fairy tale. What about Sash?"

"I love Sash—you know that! But it's not like we're married or anything! Mena says the worst thing I could do is let a guy hold me back."

She gave me a wide-eyed look. "Sash isn't just some guy. He's special, OK? One in a million—take it from someone who's known you all your life. To be honest, something about Mena doesn't feel right to me. I know how impressionable you are, but you can't let her get into your head like that."

"Jess, stop treating me like a child. I can damn well think for myself. Any idiot can see this is a huge opportunity and I'd be crazy not to at least consider it. That's all I'm doing."

"Vare, you know I only want the best for you, right? If I thought even for a second that moving here would be a good idea for you, I'd be the first one to tell you."

"Well, Mena moved out here from Sacramento when she was my age and look where it's gotten her!"

Jess had a troubled look. "Mena is on a different planet. I thought the breakfast place she recommended would tell you that. It was beautiful, but it had no soul. All surface and nothing but empty space underneath." She sighed. "I don't know, maybe I'm wrong and I'm just being selfish because it would kill me to lose you."

"You could come with me, Jess."

She shook her head. "I've just started a new course that I love, and I don't want to give that up."

"You mean not give up your professor, Hayden," I shot, but I did not mean for it to come out the way it did.

Her face darkened. "What's that supposed to mean?"

"There is something going on there, and for some reason you won't tell me what it is. I thought you were my best friend!"

"Only because there's nothing to tell you. I might have a crush on him, and he might have a crush on me. But he's my professor, so it's a no-go. You're making something out of nothing, and I have no idea why. What has this got to do with anything anyway?" She shook her head in frustration.

Now I wasn't even sure what we were arguing about. I hated it when we argued, and I only wanted things to be normal again.

"I'm sorry," I said quietly.

"It's OK."

An uncomfortable silence hung on as Jess continued rowing. We passed under a bridge for a moment, and it blocked out the sun.

"I hate this—us fighting, I mean."

"Me too," Jess agreed.

She was on the verge of tears, and it made me want to cry.

All of a sudden, I came to my senses. "Hey, you are dead right, Jess. I don't know what came over me. I mean, seriously, it is a crazy idea!"

"Yeah, I'm usually the one with the crazy ideas—remember?" Even though I knew she was hurt, she managed a smile, and it lightened the mood.

"Besides, I can't leave Zorro, can I? I'd have to take him with me, and that cat would hate New York. I mean, he hates pretty much everything, but he would hate New York big-time."

FOR THE NEXT few days, Mena was an absolute angel. She took time out of her busy schedule to show me parts of the city she loved—things tucked away that felt like secrets, like the tiny bookshop in Brooklyn. You had to go through a long, dark alley to get to it, and it was so charming and quaint. The selection of books was curated by a little Russian lady who I swear is my literary soul mate.

I felt like Mena and I really bonded over our shared passion for poetry. We had so much in common it was freaky. Like me, she was a Pisces and loved the color green. She was crazy about sweaters, and autumn was her favorite season. She always played the thumbtack in Monopoly and was a sucker for knock-knock jokes. Even though we'd known each other only a short time, she was like a kindred spirit. We laughed a lot, and I felt as if I could tell her anything. On the downside, I didn't get to spend as much time with Jess as I wanted, but Mena said it was a work trip and that should be my main priority. Jess swore she didn't mind at all, and it gave her a chance to hang out with Aunty Hoy and little Pei Pei.

The day before my event was set aside for media interviews, and I was glad Mena was with me. The session was held in the lobby of the Mark, a flashy hotel on Madison Avenue. Doing back-to-back interviews was a lot tougher than I imagined, and I was so grateful to Mena for her guidance.

"You're doing so great, Verity!" she assured me. Finally, I was done with the bulk of my meetings and waiting for the last journalist to arrive.

"Do you think so? I kind of tripped up when the guy from *Lipstick* asked me whether I thought Instagram had democratized poetry or dumbed it down."

"Oh, you'll get asked that a lot. I thought you answered it really well. Like you said, we have to stop thinking our readers need to be spoon-fed. They are perfectly capable of deciding for themselves what they want to read."

I shrugged. "Just going by personal experience. I gravitate to authors I like and don't put too much thought into it."

"It's the same with most people, and that's the way it should be. You should just read whatever resonates with you. What's the point of suffering through a book just because the author is a literary star?"

"Exactly," I nodded, and once again, we were on the same page.

Mena took a sip of her tea. "You talked to an interesting mix of journalists today."

"They were kind of intimidating. I mean, hardly anyone smiled."

"That's not always a bad thing. It's the gushy ones you have to look out for. One time, a journalist posing as a fangirl interviewed me. She asked for my autograph and wanted loads of selfies. Afterward, she wrote a hit piece."

"Oh my God!"

Mena rolled her eyes. "Look, as an author you will occasionally get bashed by the media. It happens to the best of us. What I can't stand is when someone is duplicitous—and presents themselves a certain way that is contrary to what they are. It's so unethical."

"That's pretty low," I agreed, thinking back to Penelope and the way she acted at the party. She was nice to me right up until the moment she stuck the knife in my back.

"Sometimes you do get lucky. There are some journalists who are just decent, and they don't harbor a shred of resentment about your success. They tell the story like it is, without a trace of bitterness. Admittedly, those ones are rare, but they remind you there are still some good ones left."

"Fingers crossed for the next one. What's the publication?"

"BuzzFeed."

I recognized Sierra the moment she walked in. She had interviewed me via FaceTime when Karla first shared my poem. It was like seeing an old friend.

"Verity! Welcome to New York."

"Thanks!"

"Ready?" Mena asked.

I nodded, and we settled in. Mena shot me a wink.

"Verity Wolf," Sierra grinned, "tomorrow is your big event, right? Tell me—are you excited?"

Twelve

"YOU READY?" MENA asked. She was standing behind me, hands covering my eyes.

"Ready!" I crowed.

She lifted her hands, and my eyes flew open. "Holy shit!"

We were on our way to the Sojourn Theatre when Mena told me we'd be making a pit stop. At Barnes & Noble in Union Square, we were standing in front of a shelf display, near the entrance. One entire side was dedicated to Mena's new book and the other to mine—shelves and shelves of our books from floor to ceiling. Nearby, a large easel held a poster advertising my show. On a plain black background in a large, elegant font, it announced:

An Intimate Evening with Verity Wolf,
in conversation with Mena Rhodes
at the Sojourn Theatre.
Hosted by Carry Way Press
with Barnes & Noble.
Purchase tickets at counter.
$15 per person. $35 for book + ticket.

I reached out and stroked the cover of my book, touching it gingerly as if to convince myself it was real. Goose bumps rose on my arms.

"Pretty neat, huh?" Mena said.

I gulped and nodded, at a loss for words. I felt overcome as I remembered the day Jess had taken me to Berkelouw and put my book on the shelf. I could hear her voice clearly in my mind. "Imagine, Vare, your book on the shelf next to Mena's." Now it had actually happened, and it felt bittersweet because Jess wasn't here to see it.

"Hi, girls!" I turned to see a woman in her late thirties wearing faded jeans and a leather jacket.

"Kerry!" Mena reached out and gave her a hug. "Verity, this is our publisher, Kerry Ray."

"Oh!" I stuck out my hand, but she pulled me into a hug, too.

"It is so lovely to finally meet you! I hear Mena's taken you on as her protégé." She waggled her index finger at us. "I'm glad the two of you are getting on so well!"

"Mena's been wonderful," I gushed. "Thank you for setting all this up for me, Kerry."

"This woman is a rock star," said Mena, reaching over to massage Kerry's shoulders. "She had the top job at Geidt & Ekstrom, but they weren't interested in modern poetry, and she couldn't convince them otherwise. So she left and took a chunk of the team with her. They founded Carry Way."

"'Carry Way' is how my daughter pronounced my name when she was six," Kerry explained.

"That's so cute!"

"And the rest is history," Mena gestured to our books.

Kerry grinned. "I don't think we've spoken directly, Verity, but I've had lots of interesting conversations with your agent, Mei Lyn."

I smiled to myself.

"Are you excited about your show?" she continued.

"Excited and shit scared."

Mena cackled. "Isn't she a doll?"

"She reminds me of you at her age," Kerry smiled, a look of nostalgia on her face.

Mena draped her arm around my shoulders. "Mini me," she said fondly.

"Let me get a picture of you both for our Instagram."

Kerry pulled out her phone, and we posed. "By the way, I was just talking to Anya, the events coordinator here, and she said the show sold out yesterday."

"Your first sellout show! Congratulations, Verity!" said Mena.

"I'm sure it didn't hurt to have you chairing the event."

"No, no. They're mainly here to see you—remember that!"

"But you are very lucky Mena put her hand up for this. She's picky about whom she supports," explained Kerry. "Look at what she did for Sara Woo."

"I'm happy to do it any time! And this won't be the last, since Verity is thinking of moving to New York."

Kerry's eyes lit up. "Oh, that would be amazing! We can do so much for you here—get our little PR engine running. We'll make you a star!"

"Oh, I—I'm not sure if it's something I can consider right now," I faltered.

"You'd be crazy not to!" Kerry exclaimed. "We'd look after you, like we did with Mena. Our office is over in Chelsea, so feel free to pop by."

"That's a great idea," Mena agreed. "Why don't we drop by tomorrow, and we can all sit down and discuss Verity's future. We'll make a plan."

"Wonderful! I'll clear my morning schedule, and we'll work things out for you, Verity. I know it might seem scary, but we're like a little family—you'll be in good hands. You are going to love New York." She patted my arm, as though the decision had already been made. My stomach tightened, and I felt like I was locked onto a rollercoaster.

"What are we discussing, ladies?" A tall girl with glasses and braids suddenly appeared.

"We're talking about our star, Verity," announced Mena. "We see big things for her!"

"Verity!" exclaimed the girl, throwing up her hands. "It's an honor to meet you—I'm such a huge fan! I'm Anya, and I'm organizing your event."

Kerry beamed at her. "Anya does all the big ones! She put one on for Hillary recently."

"Wow," I gulped, almost breathless.

"She's my hero," Anya gushed. "But tonight, it's all about you. We're so excited to be hosting you at the Sojourn. It's a sweet little theater, and you're going to love it. Now!" She clapped her hands. "Do you have any preferences for the greenroom?"

"The greenroom?"

"It's the room we put you in before we take you out on stage. Just checking to see if you have any pre-show requests, any snacks or drinks you'd like? For example, mineral or still water?"

"Um . . . I don't really have a preference."

"That just makes my job easier. You can't imagine some of the demands I get."

"Guilty!" said Mena, with a sheepish grin.

"Oh, you're not so bad, Princess. Anyway, I have some last-minute things to do. I'll see you ladies later at the Sojourn."

Thirteen

WHEN WE WERE kids, Jess and I stumbled on a broken video recorder in Pop's junk closet. We played with it for days, Jess in front of the camera while I stayed firmly behind it. She would light up whenever it was pointed at her—so comfortable taking her place center stage. I loved watching her perform in front of an imaginary audience, whether she was singing, tap dancing, or acting out a scene from *Othello*. She was so natural that I was convinced she was born to be a star. As I sat in the greenroom at the Sojourn, I had to wonder why I was here instead of her.

It was a fair-sized room, with the couch I was sitting on at one end and a black upright piano at the other. It also had a row of vanities adorned with flower-filled vases and light bulbs dotted around the mirrors. Adjacent to the vanities was a mirrored wall that made the room seem far bigger than it was. Cupcakes and a variety of snacks along with tea, coffee, and biscuits were set up on a trestle table. A pitcher of water with lemon slices sat beside some glass tumblers.

Mena came waltzing in with a guy I didn't recognize. He had short, spiky hair and gold rings on his fingers. One arm held a clothing bag, and he dragged a large silver case behind him. He flashed me a quick smile that looked insincere.

"There's our twinkle, twinkle little star!" Mena sang. "Verity, you are in the presence of greatness. Meet Raphael!"

"Hi," I said, bemused.

"He is here to transform you."

"Stand up," Raphael barked. He had a French accent.

"Transform me?" I wondered, but I did snap to my feet. Raphael made a twirling motion with his finger, and I spun around in a slow, clumsy circle.

"Hmmmm . . ." He set down the clothing and directed me to sit at one of the vanities. "How much time do we have?"

Mena checked her watch. "Just over an hour."

Raphael sighed a loud, dramatic sigh.

"Don't expect miracles," he warned.

I STARED INTO the mirror and saw a stranger looking back. My tumble of dark locks was now shoulder length, hanging straight and glossy. I turned my head from side to side, and my hair swished, just like Mena's. In fact, we looked almost alike, although I was squatter and rounder. My eyes looked like they had doubled in size, due to the false eyelashes and eyeliner.

"Raphael, you've done it again!" Mena gushed.

"I look like I have cheekbones." I reached up to pat my face.

Raphael intervened, slapping my hand away. "It's called contouring, darling. Now, let's get you out of that godawful thing you're wearing."

He glared at my light blue pinstriped dress. It had a low-cut neckline trimmed with lace and puffy sleeves. Back in Sydney, Jess and I had spent an entire day shopping for a dress to wear on my big night, and this one was the most expensive dress I had ever owned.

Raphael started pulling at the clothing bags and came back with a stunning black dress with a Gucci label. He handed it to me without a word—my cue to put it on—and I made a beeline for the bathroom.

A few minutes later, I came out with the dress on, and it was short and too tight. It felt as if it was restricting my circulation, and I tugged at the hem self-consciously.

He looked me up and down.

"Back straight, like you've been shot with an arrow, and suck your stomach in!"

I did as told.

"Much better." Mena nodded.

"Oh God, those shoes," he moaned with a pained look.

I glanced down at the strappy heels I'd found on eBay for a steal. They were cute, with a diamante motif by the toe, but the straps did look a little worn. I probably should have bought a new pair for the trip, but I couldn't justify the expense.

Mena sighed. "Damn, I can't believe I didn't think of that! Oh well, they'll have to do. The shoes might look OK seen from the audience."

He threw up his hands and glared at me. "OK, not much to work with, but I did my best."

"Oh, I almost forgot!" Mena ruffled through her bag and pulled out the diamond cuff bracelet we saw in the window at Tiffany's. "For luck," she said, strapping it onto my wrist.

Raphael mumbled something under his breath that sounded like "Pearls before swine."

I stared at the bracelet on my wrist, moving it so the stones glittered under the light. I was mesmerized. It must have cost a fortune.

"It's on loan, of course!" Mena added with a short laugh.

She walked me to the walled mirror and stood me in front of it. I sucked in a breath. The dress, hair, and makeup had turned me into someone I didn't recognize. Yes, I looked better than I ever had before—I just didn't look like myself.

"OK, I'm going now," Raphael declared, packing up his things. Without another word, he picked up a cupcake from the table and headed for the door.

Mena blew him a kiss. "Thank you, sweetheart."

He answered with a dismissive wave and disappeared.

"Thanks, Raphael," I called softly after him, a beat too late.

"Is that you, Verity?" I turned to see Anya striding in. "You look like a million dollars!"

"I got Raphael to come out on short notice. Isn't he a darling?"

"Wow, that's some serious pull you've got." Anya winked at Mena. She glanced at the clipboard in her hand. "You girls are on in ten. I'm going to introduce you both. Then you'll walk onto the stage and take your seats. Verity, do you have a preference about what side you'd like to sit?"

I shook my head.

"OK, great. Your fans are so excited to see you! Oh, and your friend Jess is here, and we gave her the best seat—front row center. She's sitting right next to Kerry, so she's being well looked after. When the show's over, we'll fetch her for you and bring her backstage. Ready to go?"

"Wait!" I grabbed Sash's silk handkerchief from my purse, and because it wouldn't fit anywhere else, I hurriedly stuffed it into my bra.

Anya raised her eyebrows.

"My lucky charm," I explained.

We followed Anya through winding corridors and up some steps. I could hear the murmuring of the audience, and it immediately triggered my fight-or-flight response.

Anya then walked up the two steps that led onto the stage, and a hush fell over the crowd. "Thank you all for coming tonight." She went on to recap how I was discovered by a fateful post Karla Swann had made on her Instagram, sending my poetry viral. "Now here she is, all the way from Sydney, Australia! Please put your hands together for . . . Verity Wolf!"

All of a sudden, a microphone was pushed into my hand, and I put one foot after another, propelling myself forward to the tune of the chanting crowd. Then I was on the stage.

Fourteen

As I LOOKED at the sea of people, a roar of applause broke out; they were clapping and calling out my name. All at once, I knew Mena was right. I had crossed over into another world. Somewhere between the steps and the stage, I'd left my old self behind.

Mena grinned, waving at the crowd. "Are we all excited?"

"Yes!" they chorused.

My heart was pounding. I tried to make out some of the faces, but the bright lights disoriented me, so I put my hand up and waved. To my surprise, that seemed to send shockwaves through the audience. "Hello, New York!" I called, in a voice that rang with more confidence than I felt, and a roar went up. I scanned the front row and spotted Jess, sitting proud. She grinned and gave me the thumbs-up sign. Mena and I then took our seats, and I sat up as straight as I could.

The show was on.

☆

A FEW MINUTES into my show, Mena asked. "Verity, how are you finding your newfound fame?"

I ducked my head shyly. "Well, I don't know if I'm really all that famous . . ."

"Wow—humble and talented!" Mena addressed the audience. "Do you think Verity's famous?"

A resounding yes came back from the crowd.

She cupped her hand over one ear. "What was that? I don't think Verity heard you!"

"Yes!" came the collective cry, followed by loud clapping. I marveled at how Mena seemed so comfortable on stage. Even though this was my show, there was no question who was in charge. She handled the audience like a conductor in front of an orchestra.

With a gesture outward, she said, "This is it, Verity— your big moment! Look at all the people who are here for you! Who love and support your work because it's made a difference in their lives. How does that make you feel?"

I answered honestly. "Like a princess in a fairy tale."

"You've definitely lived my definition of that— growing up in a bookstore. Can you tell us more about that?"

"Wolf Books is my grandad's bookshop, where I've lived since I was a little girl. It's so old and practically dilapidated—but to me, it's home. Books have always felt like home to me."

"Oh my God, I've got goose bumps. You've just put into words what most people feel but can't describe. I'm sure everyone here knows what it's like to be nostalgic for books. It's like that poem you posted on your Instagram—the one from that book, *Poemsia*. Sometimes fiction is more real to us than reality."

I thought back to when I discussed *Poemsia* with Mena. "Yes, and these days the lines feel even more blurred. It's getting harder to tell what's real and what isn't."

"Tell me about it! I know from personal experience how tough female authors have it in our post-truth world. But let's not focus on the negatives! We're lucky to have so many strong, powerful women lighting the way."

"That's exactly what you've done for me, Mena! You're my trailblazer. Before I picked up *Cult of Two,* I didn't know I could be a poet. You've shown me what was possible, and I owe it all to you."

Light clapping and murmurs of agreement followed.

"Aw, you're a sweetheart. I'm just pleased that the world is reading poetry again! And I'm sure there are people in the audience who are just dying to ask you about your amazing work. Does anyone have a question for Verity?"

Hands shot in the air.

Mena pointed at a geeky, teenage boy with braces. Someone passed him a microphone, and he cleared his throat. "Do you write your poems by hand or do you use an app?"

"Actually," I laughed, "I usually write my poems in an old receipt book. My granddad keeps a box of them behind the counter of his bookshop."

An appreciative murmur went through the audience, as though this small, mundane detail about my writing was something precious—though I was no different these past few days, hanging on to Mena's every word.

A girl wearing a Ramones t-shirt and denim jacket stood up and gushed. "Verity, I'm such a huge fan! I'd love to know how you got up the courage to share your work. Were you afraid people might steal it?"

"Of course, I was! But my fear was just an excuse, and I allowed it to hold me back. For a long time, the thought of sharing my work terrified me. I wanted to stay in a cocoon where I could dream about being a poet, without ever having to put myself out there. Then one day, I confided in my best friend about my fears and she said something that struck me." I stopped, as I caught Jess's eye in the front row and pointed her out. "There she is—my best friend, Jess." She turned and waved, eliciting cheers and whistles from the crowd. I asked the audience, "Do you want to know what Jess said?"

"Yes!" they chorused back.

"When I told her I was afraid someone would steal my work, Jess said, 'So what if someone does? You'll just keep writing better stuff.' And she was right. The truth is, those who lack authenticity, and write for all the wrong reasons, are building their future on shaky ground. If you have to steal from others to win, then you have already lost. Anything you gain, any sense of victory you feel, will be hollow because you know you haven't really earned it. You can convince the whole world, but the one person you'll never convince is yourself."

Mena nodded. "You're absolutely right, Verity! They say imitation is the sincerest form of flattery, and if you have work that is worth stealing, that just proves how talented you really are."

Question after question came from the audience, each more thought provoking than the next. I felt such joy sharing my inner world with a roomful of strangers, knowing they had experienced many of the same things I did. It thrilled me to imagine that there were writers and poets in the crowd who would one day be sitting where I was.

"One last question for Verity," Mena nodded at me.

A pretty brunette with a pixie cut asked me in a shaky voice, "Verity, I'm an aspiring poet. Do you have any advice on how I could be a famous poet just like you?"

For a moment I wasn't sure how to answer. Doubt began to creep into my mind. Am I really a famous poet? Did I deserve to be here? Have I earned this? As these thoughts raced through my mind, a cold panic held me in its grip. I looked out at the audience and gulped. Then I caught sight of Jess again, and suddenly, I saw myself through her eyes and knew she would never question my place on this stage for a second.

The brunette girl fidgeted, and the audience seemed to hold their breath in anticipation. I opened my mouth, and the answer came to me the way a poem sometimes did—from a place that centuries of writers before me have attributed to the mysterious and divine. "There's no way to be a poet. You can't choose it because it chooses you. Maybe your soul refracts the universe in all its complex beauty and you are a shard of light in its great hallway of mirrors. The universe calls and compels you to write poetry because with every ounce of its being, it yearns to know itself through you."

"Verity, that was insane—congratulations!" Anya kissed me warmly on the cheek. "You are a star!" The curtain had just dropped, and I knew my show had been a raging success.

"Thank you," I beamed, and I couldn't believe it was over.

"The way you handled that last question . . ." she shook her head. "You're frickin' nineteen! Where the hell does that wisdom come from?"

I shrugged and laughed. "I have no idea."

"Look who I have here!" Kerry appeared with Jess in tow.

I threw my arms around her, and she hugged me tightly.

"You were amazing! Seriously, who are you, and what have you done with my best friend?"

We giggled.

"What do you think of the hair?" I patted the sides of my head.

"I love it. And your dress—do you get to keep it?"

"It's Gucci, so I doubt it!"

Mena ambled up. "Verity, I organized a little get-together for you at my house—just a few close friends. You're coming, right?"

"Of course! Can Jess come?" Mena's eyes darted to Jess, then back to me. She sighed. "Look, normally, I would say yes." She was talking as though Jess wasn't even there. "But, well, I've had complaints recently from the tenants in my building. A bunch of stuffy retirees. So I'm kind of trying to limit my guests."

"It's cool," said Jess. "You go ahead, Verity. Uncle Gerry wants to take us to this new Italian place anyway. I'll see you at the hotel when you get back."

"But . . ." I looked from Mena to Jess, conflicted. I didn't want to celebrate my big night without my best friend.

Mena wove her arm through mine. "Guess who's coming? Sal Dollinger. Didn't you say he was your grandad's favorite poet? I told him to bring a couple of his books for you."

I glanced at Jess again, and she smiled. "Pop would love that so much, Vare."

"Um, OK." I still had an anxious feeling in the pit of my stomach.

Kerry tapped my shoulder. "Sorry to interrupt you Verity—Helen from the *New York Times* is keen to speak with you. Do you have a few moments?"

"Verity, over here, big smile!" A photographer began firing shot after shot.

A woman then appeared out of nowhere and grabbed my hand, "Oh my God, you were amazing, Verity! I'm Stacey, the manager here at Sojourn. My daughter is one of your biggest fans—can you autograph this for her?" She thrust a pen and my event poster at me.

"Verity, I'm Jimmy—an agent from Stabscotch, public relations. Here's my card! Maybe we can have a chat sometime—"

"Verity . . . over here . . ."

Suddenly, I was aware of the people around me jostling for my attention. I felt like I was spinning out of control. Out of the corner of my eye, I saw Jess leaving. I opened my mouth to stop her, but someone grabbed my arm, and I was being led somewhere. It was like the tsunami Mena had predicted, and I let myself get swept up.

Fifteen

MENA'S PLACE WAS thumping with loud dance music when we arrived. Her apartment on the thirty-first floor of a high-rise in Midtown Manhattan was filled with beautiful people laughing and dancing. I had expected a small get-together and was surprised. It did not look like an intimate affair. No one batted an eyelid when we walked in, suggesting the party wasn't actually thrown in my honor, as Mena had said.

"Let me give you the grand tour!" she declared, tossing her handbag on a buffet table in the hall.

The place was impressive, with high ceilings and wide, sweeping views of the city skyline. Pinpricks of light twinkled everywhere as though the night sky had been turned upside down. I noted a small gathering smoking and drinking outside on the balcony, lost in conversation. At the edge of the balcony grew a row of hedge trees pruned into tiny woodland creatures like elks, owls, and foxes.

"Your place is gorgeous," I exclaimed.

"I bought it a couple months back."

"You bought this?" I was incredulous. The idea of actually owning a place seemed so impossible to me, like winning the lottery.

"It cost a fortune," she moaned. "I'm literally broke now!"

Then I glanced at the diamond cuff bracelet she'd loaned me, and she followed my gaze.

"Maxed out my credit card," she explained with a shrug. "But I'm expecting my next royalty check later this month."

"So how is French Fry liking your new place?" I asked looking around the apartment, hoping to spot her famous French bulldog.

"Oh, I had to give him away. I can't manage a dog in this building. Don't judge me."

"Mena!" A guy in a white short-sleeve shirt tapped her on the shoulder. She turned and threw her arms around his neck.

"André!" She cried, with delight. "Verity, meet my special friend." Her voice was full of pride as she ran her hands over his bulging muscles. "Flex for me, baby," she cooed before turning to me. "Isn't he hot? Do you want to borrow him?"

"Um, I have a boyfriend."

Mena burst into laughter. "She's such an innocent— we have to find a way to corrupt her."

He leered at me. "Maybe I can help with that."

All of a sudden, I felt totally uncomfortable and wished I had been insistent that Jess come along. An extra person would not have made a difference to Mena, but it would have meant the world to me. I hated not knowing anyone here.

Mena must have caught my look. "Relax, we're just fucking with you. Jesus Christ, go have a drink." She seemed like a completely different person, and I wondered if I had said something to upset her.

"Oh, um, I—"

She cut me off. "I always like to blow off a little steam post-show, so I'm going to take this hunk into my bedroom and do some very bad things to him. Why don't you hang out and enjoy yourself? It's your party, for Chrissake!"

"It is?" André said, brow furrowed.

"Babe, of course it is! She's Verity Wolf—don't you know who she is?"

He shook his head stupidly.

"She's me, of course. Just five years behind."

AFTER MENA DISAPPEARED, I made my way to the dining table laden with finger food. I hadn't eaten since morning and suddenly realized how hungry I was. In the center of the table was a silver bowl filled with ice that held a small gold tin of caviar. I'd never had it before and always wondered what it was like.

"Are you Verity?" I looked up to see a girl with short cropped hair and bright red lipstick. "Were you at the Sojourn tonight with Mena?"

"Yes," I said, thinking back to my show. My mind lingered on the bright lights, and the deafening crowd— the sheer magic of it all. My heart swelled.

"Mena told me about you. You're the one-hit wonder poet."

My stomach seized. "One-hit wonder?"

"You know, the poem Karla Swann shared on her Instagram. Mena said it's the only decent thing on your page. She thinks the rest of your stuff is juvenile, and I have to agree."

"Mena said that?" I found it hard to breathe.

"Not that it matters. It's not as if quality counts for anything, does it? As long as they can turn you into a commodity, right?"

I blinked and drew back, affronted.

"Mena's a partner in Carry Way Press. Don't tell me you didn't know."

I shook my head. "I had no idea."

"Did you think she was helping you out of the kindness of her heart? Because she's passionate about supporting young poets?" The girl let out a bitter laugh. "Her passion is purely financial. She's a smart girl, and she knows she can't be the star forever. That's why she needs other poets to siphon from. She'll turn on the charm as long as you're hauling in the cash, like her pet poet Sara Woo. It was the same with me in the beginning. Mena promised me the world, but when my poetry never took off, she dropped me like a hot potato. Don't think the same won't happen to you."

I wasn't sure what to say to this. Was I really just a means to an end for Mena? My mind went over the past few days, when we seemed so in tune. I'd come to think of us as friends, but was I wrong?

The girl waved at the spread on the table. "Aren't you going to eat anything?"

Awkwardly, I piled the caviar onto a cracker.

"Whoa! Go easy on that—it's Beluga!"

"Oh." I slid some of it off. I had no idea what Beluga meant.

"No! Don't put it back!" She looked horrified. "Haven't you had caviar before?"

I shook my head.

She rolled her eyes. "That's like a hundred bucks you just put on that cracker. People are starving, you know."

"I'm sorry," I said, confused.

"Well, aren't you going to eat it?"

I popped the cracker in my mouth. It was so salty I almost gagged. It was like swallowing a mouthful of the sea. She continued to watch me like a hawk.

"Mmmm," I said, nodding, as my eyes began to water. "It's delicious."

She rolled her eyes and left.

"My favorite!" I turned sharply to see a paunchy middle-aged man with salt-and-pepper hair digging into the caviar. I did a double take.

"You're Sal Dollinger!" I blurted.

"And I'm guessing you're Verity. Mena's told me all about you."

"Oh my God, I am such a huge fan! And my granddad—he's an even bigger one. He's been trying to hunt down an autographed book for years, but they're hard to come by."

He grinned widely, and I couldn't help grinning back. He had bright, laughing eyes, and I felt immediately at ease.

"Well, you're in luck. I promised Mena I'd bring a couple of books along. Let's get them signed for you."

I followed Sal into a room that seemed to be Mena's study. Like the rest of her apartment, it looked like a page torn from a decorating magazine. A large desk sat by a wall of books; some I recognized as first editions. Framed pictures of Mena posing with her celebrity friends at red-carpet events were arranged on a designer buffet. A couple of Sal's books lay on the desk next to a crystal paperweight. I picked up Pop's favorite, *Grape*.

"My grandad can practically recite every poem in this book by heart."

"I'm flattered. He sounds like an interesting guy."

"He's the proud owner of a bookshop—Wolf Books."
I gave Sal a short history of our store, starting from
when Pop opened it in the early seventies to its glory
days when Stephen Fry stopped by on his world literary
pilgrimage. "It's an old establishment that's probably
seen its best days, but it's Pop's legacy. I'm desperately
trying to save it."

"I'd love to see it one day."

"You're welcome anytime."

"You know, you remind me of Mena when she was
your age."

"I get that a lot for some reason."

"Something about the way you hold yourself, I
think. I remember Mena when she was a doe-eyed,
fresh-faced girl from Sacramento. Now look at her—
she's a firecracker!"

I half smiled. I still felt hurt and confused by the
way Mena had spoken to me earlier. It was such a
sudden and dramatic turnaround. I thought over what
the girl at the buffet had said. Was she telling me the
truth about Mena?

Sal continued, "The industry isn't the way it was.
Back in my time, it was all about the craft of writing.
No social media. Whether you got published wasn't
up to the masses, like now. That means a lot of shit
that should never see the light of day gets through. On
the flip side, we get to discover hidden jewels that we
might have missed under the old system. The critics are

notorious for getting it wrong. Take Mena. She's a talent, no doubt. But between you and me, there's something lacking in her work. She has the technical ability, for sure." Sal paused and scratched his chin, a thoughtful look on his face. "What's missing from Mena's work is a certain quality—one you can't exactly describe. You either have it or you don't. Look at Mozart. He could compose an entire symphony in his head when most musicians follow a process of trial and error, correcting as they go. Mozart only had to find the first note, then the rest followed, each as flawless as the next. It was as though he were less of a creator and more of a transcriber. His music came from a place not of this world—that's what separates talent from genius. I don't believe Mena belongs to the latter. That's why she papers over it by dazzling people. But you, Verity, you belong to the old world of poetry. You were born with that quality. I don't think you're aware of the power you possess yet, but in time you will learn how to harness it. Then you'll be unstoppable. You won't need any of this." He waved his arm around Mena's extravagantly decorated study.

I hadn't realized I had been holding my breath until I let it out. "You really think that?"

His eyes held mine. "I know it."

Sal then settled into Mena's desk and uncapped a silver fountain pen. "What's your grandad's name?"

"Eilhard Wolf."

"Fantastic name."

"My parents were killed in an accident when I was seven. Pop and Nan took me in. We live above the bookshop. Nan passed away just over a year ago, and now Pop is all I have left. Only his health isn't so good, and—" Tears filled my eyes, and I couldn't finish the sentence. Sal paused and looked up, and I sensed he knew what I was about to say.

He nodded. "That makes sense. You've known far too much sadness for someone so young. I believe that's why your writing is so mature. Your work feels like it's written by someone who has lived several lifetimes. In a way, you have."

He finished signing the books and handed them to me. I tucked them away in my bag for safety.

"Thank you."

"You're more than welcome, Verity Wolf."

We exchanged a smile across the table.

"Sal, I'd like to ask you something. Mena thinks I should move here—to New York. She said I only have so much time to make it in this industry."

"And what do you feel?"

"I don't want to leave Pop or the bookshop. At the same time, I don't want to spend my life wishing I had the courage to follow my dream."

"Do you know what that dream is?"

"I want to be like you."

"I wasn't published until I was well into my thirties, and a decade later I won my Pulitzer. So like I said earlier, you belong to the old world of poetry. In the words of Jean de La Fontaine, 'A person often meets his destiny on the road he took to avoid it.' As a poet, this is something you inherently know. Whatever path you choose will take you to the same destination. The only thing that should guide you is your intuition. Trust that. And don't worry—time is most certainly on your side."

"There you are!" Mena's voice cut through our conversation as she swept into the room. Her cheeks were rosy, and her eyes a little glazed. "I'm sorry, Sal, but I have to steal Verity away. There are people who want to meet our little star."

MENA PULLED ME into the main lounge to the white chesterfield couch where three girls sat. One of them was Sara Woo.

"Girls, this is Verity, my little protégé. As you know, she's in town this week, and I've been showing her the ropes. Verity—" she gestured to the group who had their eyes fixed on me. They all looked like clones of Mena, immaculately dressed and bejeweled, not a hair out of place. "These girls are my posse, my confidantes. Saba is my sister. Pixie—she's just starting out, like you. And I'm sure you've heard of Sara."

"Hi, everyone."

"Hi," they chorused back.

"What do you think, girls?" Mena asked.

Three sets of eyes bored into me, and I felt exposed, like I was a specimen Mena had wheeled out to be poked and prodded.

"She kind of looks like you," said Saba.

"But not as pretty," Pixie added quickly.

"Sara?" Mena asked.

Sara shrugged. "There's potential there, I guess."

Saba nodded. "She just needs to lose a few pounds."

"Her skin is breaking out. Girl could do with a decent facial," Sara suggested.

Saba snickered. "Love the dress and bracelet, but those shoes—ew . . . tacky! Especially paired with a dress like that."

I opened my mouth to explain that I'd wanted to buy new shoes—of course I did. They weren't exactly on my priority list next to bills and the mounting cost of Pop's meds. Suddenly, I missed him so much I couldn't breathe. I missed our shop, and the rooftop, and the whole saga of Paul, Margo, and Sandra. I missed Centennial Park, where Jess had convinced me to recite my poetry to a bunch of strangers. And Berkelouw, where Jess put my book on the shelf next to Mena's. And Last Chance, where we flirted and bantered with Jonesy. All at once, my heart swelled with love for Jess because she never cared what shoes I wore. She didn't give a damn about diamond bracelets, and she thought the world of Sash, just like I did. Without a word, I turned and headed for the door.

Mena caught up with me as I got to the hallway. She tugged at my arm. "Verity, wait!"

I took off the diamond bracelet and handed it to her. "I'm leaving."

"But it's your party. You can't go."

For the first time, I looked at her without that halo of celebrity. It occurred to me that perhaps her hair wasn't as shiny as I thought or her eyes nearly as spectacular as when I first met her.

She gave me a wry smile. "Come on, the girls were just kidding. They're really nice once you to get to know them."

"I doubt it," I said, and she flinched.

"What's wrong with you? I've gone out of my way to help you, and this is the thanks I get?"

I took a deep breath and channeled Jess. My back straightened, and I looked Mena dead in the eye. "I'm sorry, but I didn't know that your help came with strings attached."

She looked taken aback but quickly recovered. Her voice softened. "Verity, I'll tell you what. Let me make it up to you. We'll go out shopping for some new shoes tomorrow. I'll get you into your first pair of Loubies. My treat, OK?"

"I like my shoes."

"I don't mean to preach. God knows I hate that shit. But you're a star now, babe. I thought tonight would have shown you that. You're a pretty girl, and with the right clothes, makeup, and diet, you could be beautiful. Do you have any idea how lucky you are, how many girls would kill to be standing where you are now? The world is waiting—so what are you going to do?"

I pictured my future self, the version of me that stays here and lives out the same path as Mena. I caught a glimpse of myself in the hallway mirror, at the new me, the one I thought I'd always wanted to be. I decided then and there that I liked my old self a whole lot better.

☆

"YOU'RE BACK EARLY," said Jess. She was sitting on the bed, paperback in her hand. I sat down next to her.

"What are you reading?"

She held up the cover. "*A Snowflake in a Snowfield.*"

"Is it any good?"

"It's great. It's about a woodcutter's daughter. Kind of like a fairy tale, but really messed up."

My phone rang, but I let it go.

"Aren't you going to get that?" Jess asked.

I glanced at the screen. "It's Sash, probably calling to hear how tonight went. I'll call him back in a minute."

"OK," she said and went back to her book.

I put my hand on her arm. "Jess."

When she looked up at me, I saw tears in her eyes.

"Vare, I'm so sorry. I know I've been kind of weird lately. It's unfair to you. You've got so much going on, and I don't know if I've been the greatest friend. I feel bad about how I reacted when you talked about moving to New York. Of course it's something you should consider, especially after the success of your show tonight—God, you'd be crazy not to! And I guess this whole time I was jealous of Mena. It's always been me and you, and it felt like she was taking my place. Like I was losing my best friend. I know it's wrong of me to hold you back for my own selfish reasons."

I shook my head. "No, you've got it all backward. I'm the one who should be sorry. I let myself get swept up in all of this. It went to my head because, well, Mena just dazzled me. Now I've seen another side of her—the one you've been trying to warn me about. You were right, Jess; Mena is just like that breakfast place Pony—all surface and nothing much underneath. Her friends are like that, too."

Jess nodded. "That's the opposite of who you are."

We hugged, and everything suddenly felt lighter.

"So what was the party like?"

I clapped my hand over my mouth. "Oh my God, where do I start?"

I gave Jess a recap, describing Mena's apartment, the incident with the caviar, hanging out with Sal Dollinger, and Mena's posse of superficial clones. Jess listened raptly, relishing every detail.

"You were amazing tonight, Vare. I can't put into words how proud of you I am."

"From Centennial Park in Sydney all the way to the Sojourn in New York," I said in a dramatic voice. She swatted my arm. "Hey, can you believe we haven't been to Egg & Yolk yet?"

"Tomorrow is as good a day as any," said Jess.

"I'm meant to meet up with Mena tomorrow, but you know what?" I grinned. "I think I'm coming down with something." I did a little cough. "I think I might have to cancel."

"You're skipping a day out with Mena Rhodes for me? Who would have thought?"

I grabbed my phone, and we started crafting a text. "Hey, Mena, sorry I can't make it tomorrow. Not feeling great."

"Hmmm, that seems open to interpretation. What about 'feeling well' instead? That makes you sound contagious."

"Good call."

My thumbs went to work. "Mena, sorry I can't make it tomorrow. Not feeling well."

"Stomach bug?" Jess suggested with a wink.

"Or maybe food poisoning?"

"The caviar," laughed Jess.

We giggled as I finished typing. I showed it to Jess, and she nodded her approval. It read, "Hey, Mena. Sorry I can't make it tomorrow. Not feeling well. Bad stomach cramps, possibly due to an infectious tummy bug or too much caviar."

"Send it!" Jess said gleefully.

We smirked at each other, and I pressed send, then dropped the phone. My heart was full to the brim, and I thought back to what Sal had said to me about following my intuition. For me, intuition is kind of like a bell that's inside your chest. It rings when you know unequivocally that you've made the right choice. Now I could hear it ringing away, and its music was almost like laughter.

My phone pinged with a text.

"Jeeez, that was quick," I said.

"How did Mena take it?"

I looked at my phone, suddenly frowning.

"Vare? What's wrong. You've gone all pale."

"It isn't from Mena; it's from Sash." My voice dropped to a whisper, trying to process what I was seeing.

"Is everything OK?" she asked anxiously. "It's not Pop, is it?"

I shook my head. "It's not Pop. Sash just sent me a link to an article about me." I was shaking. "Penelope wrote it for Billy."

Jess grabbed the phone, and I watched her skim over the words I'd just read. She slammed down the phone, eyes shooting venom. "That. Fucking. Bitch!"

Sixteen

"Verity Wolf plagiarizes from 18th-century master-piece *Poemsia*" read the headline. The article was posted three hours ago right to the minute when my show started. And it already had hundreds of shares next to the Twitter tab.

"But she must know that I've—"

"Of course she does," Jess said through gritted teeth. "You made it perfectly clear in your post—it's not your fault no one checks anything these days. And there's the BuzzFeed article where you mention *Poemsia*! A quick Google search would show you that, and she's supposed to be a journalist, for Chrissake. This isn't an article; it's a hit job."

I got Sash on the phone. "I just saw the article."

"I'm sorry, Wolf—I tried to call you." He sounded livid. "Pen's not answering her phone, so I'm driving to her house now to see if I can get her to take it down."

"Keep us posted, OK?" I hung up.

Meanwhile, Jess was already on the phone to Mei Lyn.

"Can't we sue? Defamation? Oh, OK. It sounds complicated . . . Mum, can you look into it? Thanks, love you, too. Bye." Jess turned to me. "Mum's going to see what she can do, but she said not to get our hopes up. The Internet is one big gray area."

My heart sank. "But it's an outright lie! Doesn't Penelope have a shred of decency?"

"Guess not," Jess murmured, thumbing angrily on her phone. Then her expression froze.

"What is it?"

"Nothing," she said quickly.

"Jess, come on." I grabbed at her phone and saw she was on Twitter.

"Don't," she said to me.

I logged onto my Twitter and immediately regretted it. My mentions were insane.

 Fake ass bitch

 saw her tonight at the Sojourn, can't believe she's a FAKE

 Verity wolf how could you? I was a fan. Unfollowing

 Can I get a refund for the book I bought tonight? @bnbuzz

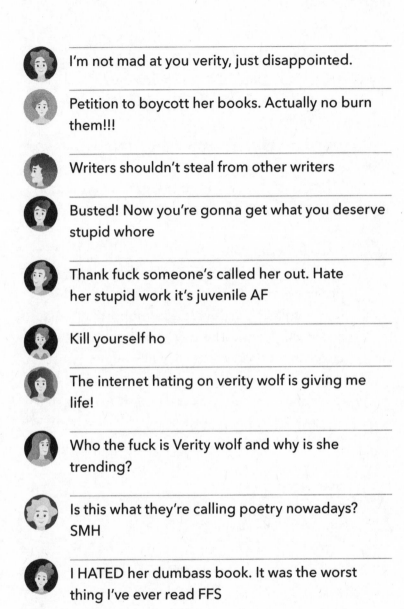

I'm not mad at you verity, just disappointed.

Petition to boycott her books. Actually no burn them!!!

Writers shouldn't steal from other writers

Busted! Now you're gonna get what you deserve stupid whore

Thank fuck someone's called her out. Hate her stupid work it's juvenile AF

Kill yourself ho

The internet hating on verity wolf is giving me life!

Who the fuck is Verity wolf and why is she trending?

Is this what they're calling poetry nowadays? SMH

I HATED her dumbass book. It was the worst thing I've ever read FFS

Ooops! Looks like your career's over bitch

Every single comment hit like a hammer squarely in my stomach, but I couldn't tear myself away.

"Vare, give me your phone. You have to ignore what they're saying."

I chewed at my fingernails. "Jess, someone's tagged Karla Swann in the article!"

I felt like everything was disintegrating around me. Karla almost immediately posted her response.

 KarlaSwann ✔ @karlaswann
I didn't know Verity Wolf had plagiarized the poem I shared. I am so sorry to have misled my fans. I believe passionately in supporting artists and giving credit where due. In the future, I will check my sources more carefully before I post.

Jess gave me a pained look, and my heart dropped.

 Karla's just confirmed it . . . Verity is a plagiarist!

 queen has spoken

 Haha, did I just witness a murder?

"Mena," I said suddenly. "She knows I didn't plagiarize that poem. She has millions of followers. She can set the record straight."

"Good idea! She even mentioned *Poemsia* at your show tonight."

I dialed Mena's number, but it went straight to voicemail. Then a tweet appeared that sent chills down my spine.

MenaRhodes ✔️ @menarhodes
Tonight, I chaired a show for Verity Wolf. She's such a lovely person, which is why I am shocked at the allegations of plagiarism. I want to make it clear that it is something I would never condone.

Then the responses came thick and fast.

Mena just unfollowed Verity . . . lol, she's finished

You're an angel @menarhodes Sorry you had to waste your time with that piece of trash

Verity is officially canceled boys and girls

Verity is dead yay

"I can't believe she would just throw you under the bus like that," Jess cried.

I was shaking. "Everyone hates me."

"Well, why don't we tell our side of the story?"

"OK," I said, and my fingers worked furiously. "What do you think?"

Jess looked at what I had typed and nodded. I posted it.

VerityWolf @veritywolf
Hi everyone. Just letting you know this is a case of misattribution, not plagiarism. I clearly tagged the post as #notmine and mentioned Poemsia in this BuzzFeed interview.

I linked my tweet to Sierra's BuzzFeed article. Then I held my breath. The first response made my stomach turn.

Well you still got famous from someone else's work, so fuck you anyway

is it just me or does that post look edited

haha what a shady bitch

A pornographic picture appeared where my face was photoshopped onto someone else's body.

Misattribute this, bitch!

"Yuck!" I said, disgusted.

 Don't need an article to know ur a ho

Then came a surprise tweet from Sierra.

 SierraRadić ✔ @ilovebubblewrap
I interviewed Verity months ago and she CLEARLY said it WASN'T her poem. Get your facts straight people!

To my dismay, she was immediately attacked for jumping to my defense.

 FAKE NEWS

 How much did Verity pay you to say that?

 SierraRadić ✔ @ilovebubblewrap
Wtf, I wrote that article MONTHS ago?

 Whatevs, you could have just posted it now.

 What the world needs, another journalist who sympathizes with plagiarists

Others joined Sierra, and my heart leapt with hope.

SHUT UP everyone I STAN Verity Wolf to the day I DIE. Her poems are LIFE.

Remember when journalists actually checked their sources?

Who the fuck wrote this travesty of an article? Do your research, you amateur!!!

Someone replied to the comment with a picture of Penelope.

This is the hate reader choking on her DUMB BITCH JUICE bc she's so jelous of Verity Wolf

Verity is the only decent pop poet, rest are trash. Mena included! Sorry not sorry.

Um guys? I was at Verity's show tonight and Mena literally talked about Poemsia????

I gave Jess a hopeful look. "Maybe they're starting to see the truth?"

Uh, Verity stop making fake accounts and talking to yourself

"Then again, maybe not," I muttered.

I would take Penelope's poetry over that trash writer Verity ANY DAY

Holy shit, Penelope's a babe

OMG you guys are blind, Penelope's shady as fuck!! She's just jealous of verity! Like it's so ob???

"The truth is right in front of them! Why can't they see it?" I stammered.

Jess shook her head. "I guess this is what Penelope was counting on."

"I wish there was a way we could get her to publicly admit I didn't plagiarize that poem."

"I think hell would freeze over before that happens."

I went back to my Twitter and sighed, realizing how pointless it was to defend myself.

Everyone chill for a second and tell me what's going on what did I miss

Verity Wolf got canceled

wth why

she's a plagiarist

OMG what a skank hope she gets what she deserves

"I give up," I said under my breath. With that, I switched off my phone and dropped it onto the bed. We both sat there feeling like the whole world had gone deathly silent.

Seventeen

"WE FINALLY MADE it, huh?" I grinned at Jess.

It was our last day in New York, and we were sitting in a booth at Egg & Yolk, an old-style diner with a retro feel—quaint and light with a jukebox playing fifties rockabilly. Across the table sat Aunty Hoy, tucking a paper serviette into Pei Pei's collar.

"Last time I saw you, Verity, you were this tall!" She pinched her thumb and forefinger together.

Pei Pei's mouth fell open. "Wewity was that wittle?"

We burst into laughter.

Our breakfast came soon after, and Aunty Hoy took a sip of her coffee and declared, "Hands down the best coffee I've ever had in New York."

"Mmmm . . . best coffee in the world!" I said, after sampling my mocha.

Jess winked at me. "Other than Last Chance, of course."

I spooned some scrambled eggs into my mouth and moaned. "These eggs are to die for."

"Try this!" Aunty Hoy tore her cinnamon toast and popped a piece on my plate.

The whipped butter was smooth and silky on my tongue, and the toast was heaven. "Oh my God!"

Between mouthfuls of her bagel, Jess said, "Everything is so worthy of the five carrots awarded by Jonesy."

We took turns sampling each other's meals, but when Jess tried to get a forkful of Pei Pei's butterscotch pancakes, the chubby toddler threw her head back and howled.

Aunty Hoy and I exchanged a knowing look.

"Well, we know who she takes after!" I grinned, nudging Jess with my elbow.

We all chatted and laughed through our meal, until we were down to crumbs.

"Hate to leave you girls, but this little one has a playdate to get to," said Aunty Hoy. We hugged and said our goodbyes, promising we'd come back again soon. It seemed a little less sunny when they left, and I wished I had spent less time with Mena and more with Jess's family. Jess must have been thinking the same thing because a sad look crossed her face. I reached over and gave her a hug. "Want to get another cup of coffee?"

"Sure," she said.

We opened Jonesy's notebook and added our own little notes and scribbles. Jess drew in tiny cute sketches in the corners.

"Hasn't this trip turned out to be a mess?" I sighed.

Sash had managed to track down Penelope, but when he asked her to take down the article, she flat-out refused. Teddy and Tom had also tried their best to convince her, but she wouldn't budge.

I wrote to Sierra to thank her for sticking up for me, and we wrote back and forth about the madness of social media and how horribly corrupt it could be. Talking about it didn't do much to dissolve the knot of frustration in my chest, so I decided to take a hiatus from the digital world. It worked, and now I felt myself slowly coming back to the real one.

All of a sudden, my phone buzzed from an unknown number.

"Verity? It's Kerry here. Have you heard the good news?"

"Good news?" I asked cautiously.

"Your book's just hit the *New York Times* best-seller list! It's racing up the charts."

"What? But how could that be?"

My mind shot back to what Mena had said—hate is bad for the ego, good for book sales.

"What was that about?" Jess asked when I hung up.

Deadpan, I delivered the news to her. "That was Kerry. She wanted me to know my book's now officially a *New York Times* best seller."

Her eyes grew wide. "Are you serious? Don't you have to sell a ton of books to get on that?"

"I guess I did."

"Vare . . ." she breathed.

"Jess," I echoed.

"OK, this is not the place," she squeaked.

"The *New York Times*," I mouthed at her.

Her hand flew to her mouth, and my hand clamped tightly over mine, our eyes laughing at each other.

It took every ounce of self-control to remain perfectly quiet, to sit perfectly still, when on the inside we were squealing at the top of our lungs.

Eighteen

My heart leapt with joy at the arrival terminal when I spotted Pop with Sash in tow. I wondered how I had considered moving to New York even for a second. I dropped my bags and ran over, throwing my arms around Pop's neck.

He smiled down at me. "I've missed you, little one."

"I've missed you too!"

I turned to Sash, who was looking at me with a lopsided grin. All of a sudden, I felt kind of shy. "Hey," I said, punching him lightly on the arm, even though I was ready to throw myself at him. I felt self-conscious in public, especially with Pop there.

"What's up, Wolf?" he said, with feigned nonchalance.

It was ridiculous how happy I was to see them both. It felt as if I'd been away for an eternity, and I was so glad to be back.

"You will never guess what I got you, Pop!" I was bursting with excitement.

"I think all your Christmases have come at once." Jess had now caught up with me.

Pop looked from me to Jess. "What is it, girls?"

I reached into my knapsack and pulled out a signed copy of *Grape*, passing it to Pop.

He held it like it was something delicate, turning it over in his hands. Slowly, he turned to the autographed page, and his bottom lip trembled. "You got it signed?" he said in wonder. "But how?"

I winked. "I had to pull a few strings."

"Oh, Verity, this is so special . . ." His voice was heavy with emotion.

"Verity actually met Sal!" Jess blurted. "And you know what he said about Verity's work? He said she belongs to the old world of poetry."

"Whoa," said Sash, impressed.

Jess nodded. "It's like a Jedi Master telling someone they have the Force."

I looked up at Pop, and his face was shining with such pride and happiness that it filled my heart right up. Then, his expression suddenly changed, his face twisting into a pained grimace. His hand rose up to clutch at his chest, and his breathing became ragged.

"Pop!" I cried, panicked.

"Oh my God," gasped Jess.

When Sash grabbed him around the waist, he was on the verge of collapse.

I heard my own voice roar with a fierce urgency. "Somebody! Help!"

Nineteen

I SAT IN the hospital waiting room, my mind racing with every possibility. There were a handful of strangers around me, people just like me, sitting on hard plastic chairs and trying not to think the worst thoughts. Faces stone-cold and lined with worry under the harsh fluorescent lights.

Every time I heard footsteps, my head snapped up, hoping it was someone with news about Pop. The only thing worse than saying goodbye, I thought, is not getting the chance to say it. I couldn't help my mind drifting back to the year before, when I saw Nan from my window, collapsed in her garden. We had only just been laughing at a YouTube clip, minutes before. It still hurt me to recall the terror in Pop's eyes when I had raced into his office. When everything changed for us in an instant.

That day, we lost Nan, but we also each lost a huge part of ourselves. It took such a long time before we could feel anything close to normal. And now here I was, facing the possibility of going through it all over again. The thought was too much to bear.

I bit my lip and blinked back tears, desperate to believe that my last memory of Pop wouldn't be the sight of him strapped into a gurney as paramedics attached him to tubes and wires. Or the journey here in the screaming ambulance, his clammy hand in mine as he lay so still that I wanted to beat his chest, yell at him to wake up.

"Verity Wolf?" I stood up as a doctor came striding toward me. He had a thick beard and kind eyes, stethoscope hanging slightly crooked around his neck against his light blue scrubs. "I'm Ahmed, the doctor treating your grandfather."

"Is he OK?"

Dr. Ahmed nodded. "He's OK."

My entire body crumpled with relief.

"What happened?"

"He had a mild heart attack, Verity. I looked at his history, and apparently, he's been warned this could happen."

"I know. Pop's had a bad run. Lost the love of his life not long ago. On top of that, his business has been failing. All this had to be weighing on him."

Dr. Ahmed nodded. "I fully understand. But now he does need to take it easy. He was lucky this time, but he might not be the next."

A cold chill went down my spine.

"We'll need to keep him a few days, just to be on the safe side. Then I would suggest you take him to see a specialist. I'll put together a list of names for you. Do you have insurance?"

I shook my head no, a sinking feeling in my stomach.

He gave me a sympathetic look. "No need to worry; the public system is more than adequate."

"Verity!"

Jess and Sash arrived and were rushing toward us.

"Any news?" Jess asked, out of breath, looking from me to Dr. Ahmed and back again.

I nodded, barely able to hold back tears. "He's going to be OK."

Her face dissolved in front of me. "Oh, thank God."

"Is he awake?" I asked the doctor.

"I'll walk you to his room."

I entered Pop's room and sat on his bed. All my life, I'd seen him as Goliath, my infallible protector, the person who loved me more than anyone else. Now he looked so woefully frail. It broke my heart to see him like that. His eyes opened just a fraction, and his voice was hoarse when he spoke. "Tell me something good, Verity."

I said the first thing that came to mind. "My book made the *New York Times* best seller list, Pop."

The smile that broke out on his face was so radiant it lifted the heaviness in my chest. I buried my head on his shoulder and felt his hand against my head. Tears swam, blurring everything.

"That's my girl."

Twenty

"HOW ARE YOU holding up, Verity?" asked Jonesy. I was waiting for Jess at Last Chance when he slid into the empty seat opposite me. "How's Pop?"

"He's doing OK. He says hi and thanks for the macarons."

A few days had passed since Pop's collapse, and now I had him at home ensconced in bed. He was a huge part of our community, and his hospital room had been flooded with flowers, gift baskets, and cards—so many that Jess had handed them around to other patients on the floor.

"I thought my macarons would have gotten lost in the sea of gifts," said Jonesy, reading my mind.

"Actually, Pop ate one, and Jess and I kind of split the rest."

"Predictable," he said, with a wry grin.

"Speaking of gifts—I've got something for you! Jess and I saw it in a shop next to Egg & Yolk when we were in New York." I reached into my bag for a little purple box and slid it across the table.

He opened it and burst out laughing. It was a fridge magnet displaying the phrase "I kiss better than I cook."

"It's for the magnet wall."

A sad look came over his face, and his eyes darted to the Altar. "Thanks, but it looks like I'll be shutting this place down."

My heart sank. "But there must be something you can do! Jess and I can help out here, especially on weekends when it gets really busy. You can pay us in cupcakes."

He sighed. "I wish it were that simple. My landlord just raised the rent up again, and this time it's pretty much the last straw. I've burned through all my savings—nothing left. That's why I called this place Last Chance. Literally my last chance to follow my dream."

"You should have called it Thanks for Muffin."

He laughed. "I guess you saw that in my notebook, huh?"

"I also liked the name Good in Bread. But that really sucks, Jonesy. Everyone loves it here! There will be an uprising, for sure. Possibly led by us."

"I don't doubt it."

"What are you going to do next?"

"I'll figure something out."

Jess turned up and stood behind Jonesy, clearing her throat.

He hastily got up, chair scraping loudly against the floor. "Hey, Jess, thanks for the magnet."

She blew him a kiss as he hurried off to the till, where a couple stood waiting.

"Oh my God, do I have news!" she said, waving her arms dramatically.

"What is it?"

"OK, so get this. I was at Deep Sea Diver HQ, and I bumped into Penelope. Of course, we got into a huge argument. It was pretty heated, and Teddy physically had to separate us. First time I've seen her since we got back from New York, so as you can imagine, I had a few things to get off my chest."

A smile crept across my face. Even though the boys regularly complained about the tension between the two girls, I thought that secretly they thrived on the drama.

Jess continued. "Anyway, Penelope stormed out in a huff—so predictable. That bitch can dish it out, but she can't take it. She was in such a hurry to escape the argument she was definitely losing that she left her phone behind."

I was all too familiar with the triumphant look on Jess's face, and I groaned. "Jess, tell me you didn't."

She ignored me. "I remember one time when Teddy was teasing Penelope about using her birthdate as her pin code. The idiot apparently uses it for everything, even her debit card. I literally could rob her blind if I wanted. Anyway, it took me all of five seconds to work out her DOB, and as soon as Teddy had his back turned, I was in."

I buried my face in my hands. "Oh, Jess."

"The first thing I did was click on her Reader account." Jess pinched her thumb and forefinger. "I was this close to deleting it."

I gasped. "Jess! No!"

Jess cut me off. "No one comes after my best friend and gets away with it."

"Easy there, Corleone."

"Then something caught my eye. It was a tab for secret groups. I thought, what the hell—she didn't think twice about screwing you over, so I went in. And bingo! There it was: a salacious and incriminating thread where she brags about her evil plot to destroy you."

My jaw dropped. "Serious?"

"I took some screen grabs and AirDropped them straight to my phone. Here, take a look!"

She handed over her phone, and I scrolled through. It was a private conversation between Penelope and two other users—Sean-of-the-read and Bookbabe94.

PENELOPE: Here's the article I wrote about Verity Wolf and that poem she stuck up from Poemsia. What do you think ppls?

BOOKBABE94: Reading now

SEAN-OF-THE-READ: Isn't she that pop poet who got famous bc of Karla Swann?

PENELOPE: Uh huh. B&N are hosting her at the Sojourn tonight. Can you fucking believe it?

BOOKBABE94: OMG busted!

BOOKBABE94: Wait just did a quick google. There's a BuzzFeed article where she says she didn't write that poem????? That it was just a misattribution and she tried to tell Poetry Seen? Here's a link.

SEAN-OF-THE-READ: So what if she isn't a plagiarist? Who gives a shit?

BOOKBABE94: Ahhahah, ur right. Hang the bitch anyway.

SEAN-OF-THE-READ: This pop poetry shit is killing literature. You're doing the world a favor.

BOOKBABE94: Do it Pen. Destroy her!

SEAN-OF-THE-READ: Yaaas queen, publish! Do it! Tear that bitch down

PENELOPE: OK, omg. I just hit the upload button. It's live guys.

BOOKBABE94: Omg shit's gonna hit the fan

SEAN-OF-THE-READ: Gonna make some popcorn. BRB

"Unbelievable," I said, shaking my head.

"You see? Now we have proof that she knew you're not a plagiarist. You know what I think?" Jess's eyes shone with glee. "I think we should go public with it."

"You're crazy!"

She grinned, looking like the cat that got the cream. "So? Want to start working on the tweet and expose her for the monster she is?"

I considered it. Part of me wanted to out Penelope for the lying, evil rat that she was. But wouldn't that make me just as bad as she is?

"Well?" Jess gave me an expectant look.

"Let me talk to her first."

I CAUGHT PENELOPE as she was walking out of Deep Sea Diver. She looked mildly shocked to see me but quickly recovered.

"I have to talk to you," I said.

"Oh God. I've already had a showdown with your idiot friend this morning. I'm not taking it down, and that's final."

"That's your call, Penelope."

"I guess we're done here, then?"

She pushed past me as I reached out and grabbed her arm.

"Not so fast."

Without a word, I handed her my phone. I watched a myriad of emotions cross her face as she scrolled through the screen grabs Jess had taken. Her face went deathly pale.

"This—this is private," she sputtered. "How the hell did you get this?"

I narrowed my eyes. "We're watching you, Penelope. We're watching your every move."

"This is illegal! I'm calling Daddy."

She pulled her phone out of her bag, thumbs moving at lightning speed.

"Sure, Penelope. While you do that, I'll just upload these screen grabs, so the world can finally see the real you."

She froze. Slowly, she put her phone away and met my eyes. "Why haven't you exposed me yet? You have a huge social media following. What do you want? Is it money? Are you blackmailing me?"

"I just want you to write a retraction and full apology for Billy. Set the record straight."

She stared at me for a long time, then her lips quivered, eyes filling up. "OK. And what else?"

"That's all."

She was quiet for a few moments, and I almost felt sorry for her. When she finally spoke, her voice was very subdued. "Before you came along, Verity, I had all these plans. I was going to be a poet—not a pop poet like you," she added quickly. I rolled my eyes. "I mean, I'm not even sure if your work even belongs there. To be honest, anyone with a social media following gets lumped into that category, and in your case, it's probably not correct. The thing is I actually do appreciate your work, and I hate that I like it." She was blubbering now. I reached into my pocket and handed her Sash's handkerchief. "Thanks," she sniffed. When she saw his monogrammed initials, she started bawling even harder. "And to top it off, you stole Sash from me."

"He doesn't belong to you, Penelope."

She gave me a miserable look. "But I liked him first!" She must have realized how childish she sounded because she quickly changed her tone. "I know, I know—Sash is his own person, but I can't help it. I was going to marry him. I even picked out the names of our kids. Cortland and Patchouli."

"Of course those would be their names," I said, already feeling sorry for Penelope's future children.

"And I picked out the Vera Wang dress I was going to wear at our wedding. I even found a company that makes these life-like ice sculptures. I was going to have one made of me and Sash. I had it all planned out, and then you came along, and everything went to hell. The thought of losing him drove me crazy, and I just panicked. I know it's not your fault, and it was mean to treat you the way I did . . ." She trailed off. There she was, standing in the middle of the street with her usually perfect mascara running, and for the first time, Penelope seemed genuine.

Her voice trembled. "It's just so unfair, you know?"

"Unfair? You're young, beautiful, rich, and talented. I'd given anything to look like you."

"I suppose most girls would," she sniffed, and I raised my eyebrows at her. "But I know what I did was wrong. I wanted to hurt you, but now I realize how awful I was. I'm really sorry, Verity—I would take it all back if I could."

"OK," I said, still doubtful.

She continued. "I never thought I'd say this, but thanks, Verity. Thanks for giving me a chance to make this right. I mean, you could have outed me, and that could have destroyed my reputation. At least this way, I probably can salvage things."

Penelope sniffed a little and babbled, "You're really OK, Verity, and Jess isn't an idiot. She's doing a great job at Deep Sea Diver, and she lent me a tampon one time when I was out, even though we'd just been screaming at each other. That was big of her."

"I'll let her know you said that."

"Tell her I like *Finding Nemo*, too. In fact, I love it! I love that damn cartoon to pieces, but I've never admitted it to anyone. I don't know why. I've never had girlfriends because they're always so jealous of me. But I look at you and Jess, and sometimes I have to admit . . . I wish she was my friend."

I smiled, thinking how powerful the two of them would be if they ever managed to put their differences aside. "You never know. Stranger things have happened."

"Do you really think so?" She looked almost hopeful.

"The trick to winning Jess over is cupcakes. She often mentions the ones you brought into the office that one time."

She hiccupped and laughed. "Thanks for the tip."

We shared an awkward smile.

"I know I've been ghastly to you, Verity, and that's not really who I am. I'm going to make it up to you."

I breathed a sigh of relief. I had to admit it was exhausting to always be on guard around Penelope. I knew if the two of us could find a way to get along, it would mean the world to Sash. Then I thought back to the stunt she pulled that night at his house and immediately felt wary.

She must have read the look on my face because she continued. "I know you don't believe me, and I don't blame you after all the things I've done. But I will set things right; I promise. In fact, I'm going to start right now."

She dialed a number on her phone and put the call on speaker.

"Hi, Penny," answered Sash's mum.

Penelope looked at me and took a long, deep breath. "Dotty, about the joint I found at Graham's birthday party . . ."

A COUPLE OF days later, Jess and I found ourselves sitting in Mei Lyn's office.

"Verity, your book sales are going through the roof. Just got your first royalty check and it's a good thing you're sitting down."

She handed me the check, and on it was a number so long it actually took me a few moments to work out the figure. I'd never seen so much money in my life. "Is that for the rest of the year?"

"That's how much you've earned in the past month."

Jess was staring openmouthed and looked like she was going to faint. "You're buying me lunch tomorrow. And a new dress," she added quickly.

Mei Lyn tossed her a look.

"What? It's not like she can't afford it."

"So what happens now? Do I get all this money right away?" I immediately thought of Pop and how I could use some of the money to get him seen by a top specialist.

"Of course you don't get the money right away," said Mei Lyn matter-of-factly.

My face fell.

"It's an international check," she continued, "so it would take at least three days to clear—"

She couldn't finish her sentence because Jess and I started squealing at the top of our lungs.

She opened her mouth to tell us off but closed it again, her lips forming into a tiny smile.

Twenty-one

SPRING WAS IN the air when I sat with Pop in the courtyard. Nan's bonsai garden wasn't the same without her
love and care, even though Pop did his best to maintain
it. Sash had just started bonsai classes and was slowly
taking it over.

"Sash has been a real gem, hasn't he?" Pop
instinctively followed my train of thought.

"He's pretty special," I smiled and knew it was an
understatement.

We were quiet for a few moments, enjoying the
warmth and birdsong.

"I'm so proud of you." Pop looked at me with a
new intensity. "You've had a lot of tragedy in your life,
things that weren't your fault. Lost your parents when
you were only seven and then Nan, far too early. You've
known more sadness than anyone deserves, but despite
it all, you've managed to stay optimistic."

"I thought I was going to lose you, too, Pop." My voice cracked with emotion.

He nodded, and suddenly his expression was serious.

"Verity, there's something I want to discuss with you. Don't fret," he said, seeing the worried expression on my face. "It's not bad news. In fact, I'd say it's good."

I heard something in his tone that told me it would be a mixture of both. I took a deep breath and steeled myself.

Pop reached into his jacket pocket, pulled out an envelope, and handed it to me. "This is the title to Wolf Books. It's yours—if you want it. Mei Lyn has drawn up the papers."

I felt a jolt of panic. "But, Pop, I'm not ready—"

He held up his hand to stop me. "Yes, you are, Verity. You'll be fine. Mei Lyn and Jess have your back if you need it. I have a feeling you won't."

"But you'll be here, too, Pop. Why are you talking as if you won't be? The doctor said you're going to be OK as long as you take it easy. I mean, Pop—" I felt all choked up and was speaking so fast I tripped over my words.

"That's what I wanted to discuss with you. I've been thinking a lot about things, ever since I ended up on that gurney. When I married your Nan, we spent our honeymoon in Kyoto. We stayed in this little house and spent our days visiting shrines and bathing in hot springs. We slept when we were tired, woke up when we weren't. We ate simply—rice, fish, and pickled vegetables. I spent some time with master bookbinders, got to see some rare manuscripts. Nan developed her lifelong passion for bonsai. It was one of the happiest times in our lives. We'd planned to go back once your dad took over the store, but of course that never happened. So I'd like to do it now. I know it's something Nan would have wanted for me."

"For how long?"

"I'm going to get a one-way ticket and see how it goes. I figured if I sell my signed collection of books, I could live off that for a long time."

I felt a grim weight in my chest, thinking how much I would miss Pop, how untethered I'd feel without him. What if his heart gave out again and I wasn't there? I couldn't bear the thought of it. "What about your condition, Pop? Who will look after you?"

"I've spoken to my doctor, and he agrees it would be the best thing for me. They have excellent physicians in Kyoto. I will be in good hands—don't you worry."

By now my anxiety had reached fever pitch, and I opened my mouth to tell Pop he was making a mistake, that he should stay here where I could take care of him. Then I thought of the poem from *Poemsia,* and all at once I understood what the poet meant when she wrote about the certainty of endings—how each goodbye had its own destiny to fulfil. I realized Pop had already made up his mind and nothing I could do would convince him otherwise.

I let out a sigh of resignation. "I'm not going to talk you out of this, am I?"

"Not this time, my sweet."

"Will you check in with me? At least once a day."

"I promise."

"And if you feel like coming back, you come back, OK?" I choked on the last word, tears spilling down.

"Hey," he said, and his eyes began to water.

Then there were no more words to say. It was done.

After a few moments, Pop cleared his throat. "You know, I'll bet if you and Sash put your minds to it, you could turn this old place into something special."

Together we looked at the new awning Sash had put up while I was away. The yellow and white stripes reminded me of New York. Suddenly, I was transported back to the rooftop that first day with Sash when he confessed his dream of owning a bookstore. A shiver went down my spine, and I was overcome with a feeling of coming full circle. Goose bumps rose all along my arms as my mind conjured up images of what this place could be, the things we could dream up and do together.

I took a deep breath. "Pop?"

"Yes, my love?"

"You know your signed books? I know someone who would be interested in acquiring your entire collection."

Pop's eyes widened. "Who?"

"Me."

His eyes softened, and a proud smile lit up his face.

"What do you say?" I asked.

"Sold!" he beamed.

We fell into an easy silence, watching Zorro chase a bright yellow butterfly across the courtyard. I thought of my mother, and a bittersweet feeling welled up in me.

"Daverist is the brand of cheese Sash is wild about. You can find it in the deli on that quiet strip—the one with the fruit cart out front."

"Noted," I grinned. I thought about a picnic I could organize for the two of us and the surprised look on Sash's face when he bit into his sandwich and realized it was made with the cheese he loved. I thought about how the smallest things could make him so happy, how lucky I was to have found him. All at once, I saw our life play out before me like a movie, one happy moment after the next, and the future somehow felt as familiar as a memory.

Pop cleared his throat. "You know, a few weeks ago my story almost ended. By some miracle, I'm still here, and the story goes on. I'm ready for my next adventure."

"It's funny you should say that. A few moments ago, I was thinking about that poem, you know the one from that book *Poemsia*?"

"Remind me again—what was the poem about?"

"About coming to the end of a book and not wanting to say goodbye to your favorite character."

"Ah, yes, that's right, the struggle of parting ways, real and imaginary."

The sunshine warmed my skin, and a gentle breeze stirred the trees overhead. I loved the way the light streamed into the courtyard this time of day, arousing feelings of home and belonging.

I saw Zorro take one more lunge at the yellow butterfly as it flew by Nan's Japanese maple. It darted just out of his grasp, and I let out a sigh of relief. "Pop? If you were the author of this story, do you think this is where it ends?"

Pop reached out and took my hand across the table. Together we watched the butterfly swoop into the sky.

He shook his head and smiled. "For you, I think this is where it begins."

Epilogue

THE GRAND OPENING of Wolf Books far exceeded our expectations. A large crowd turned up to see yours truly cut the red ribbon with a pair of giant novelty scissors. I made a speech gratefully acknowledging Sash for the role he played in transforming the store from a shabby bookstore to a modern oasis for booklovers. I even thanked Penelope for dipping into her trust fund when the project went over budget.

For six months Sash and I worked hard—drawing and redrawing plans, knocking down walls, sanding, and rewiring. We spent the good part of a month waist-deep in paint and fabric swatches. Jess helped with all the signage, and even Penelope lent her many talents to the project. I was surprised, even suspicious at first, by her sudden turnaround. After a while, even I could see that her passion and enthusiasm for the project were genuine. And some of her ideas were absolute genius.

The best one involved splitting the store into two levels. The first floor was a mecca of new and out-of-print titles; the second held a treasure trove of secondhand books. The place was bright and airy now, with a feeling of newness and promise. We did make sure to keep the things that were important to Pop. The rusty old bell that had hung over the door remained exactly where it always had been, and of course, we kept the glass cabinet housing his cherished collection of signed books.

On opening day, I could feel the satisfaction of making a dream come true with hard work and passion, seeing it through the eyes of all the people who had come to support us. There was a celebratory feeling in the air; laughter and chatter sounded all around me. The place had come to life, and I took a moment to appreciate it.

Then the smell of freshly ground coffee hit me, and I turned to gaze proudly at the new home of Jonesy's Last Chance café, tucked away under the staircase. It had taken a lot to convince Penelope to keep Jonesy's eclectic décor, including the magnetic altar. I don't think she had ever seen a fridge magnet! In the end I was glad we managed it because Last Chance fit in so perfectly it was hard to believe Jonesy's café had ever been anywhere else.

When it came to the PR, Penelope had worked miracles, and the place was swimming with journalists and influencers. By midmorning, we had already racked up hundreds of our #wolfbooks tag on Instagram. Crowds had been pouring in, and the lines that snaked around the cash register showed no signs of slowing. Penelope herself was looking more relaxed than I had ever seen her, in a pair of denim cutoffs and a T-shirt, chatting with Jonesy, who obviously was smitten.

After Penelope wrote her retraction and apology in Billy, a slew of articles followed reporting on the fiasco. It sparked a healthy debate about misinformation and the danger of how quickly it can escalate. Now the dust had settled, and like Mena predicted, I still got hate from time to time. These days, I worried about it less.

I spotted Sash straightening the collage he had made for me that now hung by the fiction shelf.

"Hey," I said, lightly punching his arm.

"Hey," he grinned.

"How are you doing with the unpacking?"

Sash officially had moved in to the small apartment he and I built upstairs. As a surprise, he created a charming outdoor area on the roof where we could follow the Sandra, Margo, and Paul saga in comfort. Currently, things were looking up for Margo.

Sash also brought a member of the family with him—his cranky Chihuahua, Monty. He did it with a little trepidation, and as we feared, Zorro detested Monty on sight. After a brief altercation, the two kept their distance. But the other night, when he thought no one was looking, Zorro crept up to Monty and curled into his belly. Monty, who was madly in love with Zorro, hardly dared to breathe, but his tail twitched with barely contained joy.

"Marcia says hello." Sash's mother appeared out of nowhere and drew me into a tight embrace.

"Dotty! How is she doing over in Cebu?"

A week ago, Marcia went to the Philippines with a team of doctors to work on Operation Smile, a volunteer project that provided life-changing surgery to children born with cleft lips.

"She's making a real difference," Dotty said proudly.

"Runs in the family."

"The place looks wonderful, guys. I'm so proud! By the way, how's Little Lord Fauntleroy settling in?" In answer to her question, we heard Monty's trademark grunt as he appeared at her feet. "Hey, we've missed you, little buddy!" She scooped him up and put him on her shoulder. Predictably, he proceeded to chew on her hair.

After Penelope owned up to the stunt she pulled at Graham's party, Dotty apologized profusely for how she had treated me. We went out for a cup of coffee and had been the best of friends ever since.

Teddy and Tom came over to join us.

"Hey, gang! Love what you've done here!" Teddy sang.

"Glad you kept the old bell, even if it does remind me of Parker's gong," said Tom.

I grinned. "How are Penelope and Jess getting on at Deep Sea Diver?" After the success of their cider launch, the boys were now moving into potato crisps. Jess, of course, was tasked with designing all the packaging.

"Still fighting like cats, but the other day, we caught Jess breaking her subway sandwich in two and handing half to Penelope."

I couldn't help but smile. Knowing Jess as well as I do, that was a big deal.

A call came through on my FaceTime, and I left the group to take it. Pop's face beamed at me from somewhere in Kyoto. "What do you think, Pop?" I spun around slowly so he could get a better look.

"Thumbs up all the way!"

"I can't wait for you to see it in real life."

"Ticket's all booked for your birthday next month! I'll be there before you know it."

"The spare room's ready and waiting. We've set up your favorite armchair so it overlooks the courtyard." Sash had restored Nan's garden to its former glory, and I couldn't wait for Pop to see it. I blew him a kiss and put my phone away.

Someone tapped my shoulder. "Verity Wolf?"

I turned to see a petite lady with dark, wavy hair, her elfin-like face framed in tortoiseshell glasses.

"My name is Geraldine, and I've been following your career. It's been remarkable to see how well your book has done."

"Thank you!" My book was selling so well that Carry Way signed me up for a second one, and I couldn't wait to get started.

"I was actually in the crowd that day when you read your poetry in the park. I think I fell under your spell."

"Well, that was a really long time ago. I've improved since!" I gave her a sheepish smile.

"Don't sell yourself short. You were perfect. By the way, I'm one of the admins for Poetry Seen. I was the one who shared your post."

"You're kidding me!"

"Not at all! I'm so happy to have discovered you. Your talent deserves to be appreciated by the world."

In a single moment of clarity, I saw all the way back to that day in the park and then forward again to the present. I looked around at the transformation of Wolf Books. I had witnessed all my dreams come to fruition, and I knew without a shred of doubt there was one person who was responsible for making it happen.

I found Jess standing with a group of her college friends, animated and alive. My heart swelled with pride and happiness at the sight of my best friend. Impulsively, I threw my arms around her and hugged her tightly to me. "Thank you, Jess," I whispered.

She laughed. "For what?"

"For everything."

Acknowledgments

The story of *Poemsia* came to me when I was midway through writing an entirely different novel. The voice of Verity Wolf was so vivid and insistent, I wanted to immediately abandon my current project and start work on *Poemsia*. You can imagine my trepidation when I broached this with my agent, Al Zuckerman. But after sending him a few sample chapters of *Poemsia*, Al was well and truly on board. His enthusiasm, right from the beginning, helped spur this book into the novel I am immensely proud of today. Thank you, Al, for your faith in my vision. As always, it is a great privilege to work with you!

Samantha Wekstein, thank you for your valuable feedback. Your insight from the start greatly helped to shape *Poemsia*, and for that, I am truly grateful.

Thank you to Kirsty Melville, Patty Rice, Kathy Hilliard, and the team at Andrews McMeel for all your support. Kirsty, you were a fan of *Poemsia* back when it was just an idea in my head. Patty, this was our most exciting project to date, and I had so much fun working on this book with you! Kathy, I can't wait to send another one of our books into the world.

Chris Schillig, thank you for whipping my manuscript into shape. It wouldn't be the same book without you!

Cameron Stewart, thank you for lending your striking illustrations to the cover, and Diane Marsh for putting it all so beautifully together.

Oliver, who is always cheering me on. Proud of you, math boy!

To Michael, my love. My partner in life and work. Thank you for more than a decade of laughter, creativity, and magic.

Last but definitely not least, thank you to all my readers. My heart bursts with love for you.

The Practical Handbook of
TV REPAIRS

By Art Margolis

Fawcett Publications, Inc.
67 West 44th Street
New York, New York 10036

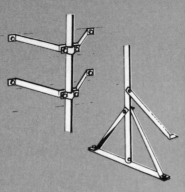

LARRY EISINGER: *Editor-in-Chief*

GEORGE TILTON: *Executive Editor*

SILVIO LEMBO: *Creative Director* • HAROLD E. PRICE: *Associate Director*

FRANK BOWERS: *Editor*

ELAINE E. SAPOFF: *Production Editor* • ALAINE TROW: *Production Assistant*

Editorial Staff: JOE PIAZZA, DAN BLUE, RAY GILL
ELLENE SAUNDERS, PAMELA RIDDLE, AMY MORRIS

Art Staff: MIKE GAYNOR, ALEX SANTIAGO, JOHN SELVAGGIO,
HERBERT JONAS, JOHN CERVASIO, JACK LA CERRA

Art by Henry Clark and Bruce Aldridge
Cover Color by Art Margolis

Printed in U.S.A. by
FAWCETT-HAYNES PRINTING CORPORATION
Rockville, Maryland

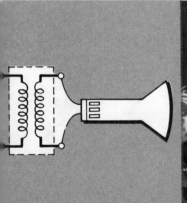

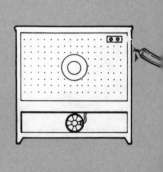

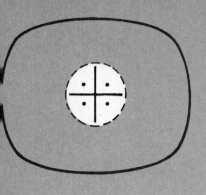

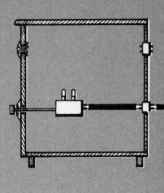

CONTENTS

Chapter

1 Getting the Jump on Repairs 4

2 When Your Set Goes Dead 16

3 Tips on Fixing High Voltage 24

4 Other Brightness Irregularities 30

5 Taking the Jitters Out of Your Picture 38

6 When Contrast's the Culprit 48

7 Repairing TV Sound 60

8 Properly Adjusting the Colors 64

9 How to Touch Up the Color 68

10 Curing Color Ills 80

11 Remedying Antenna Problems 86

12 The World of New Antennas 94

13 How to Tackle TV Interference 104

14 Let's Examine Your Picture Tube 110

15 Replacing Old Picture Tubes 116

16 UHF for Older Sets 122

17 Understanding Cable TV 126

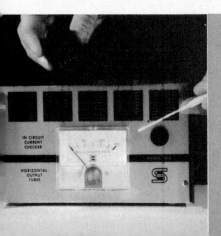
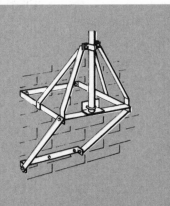

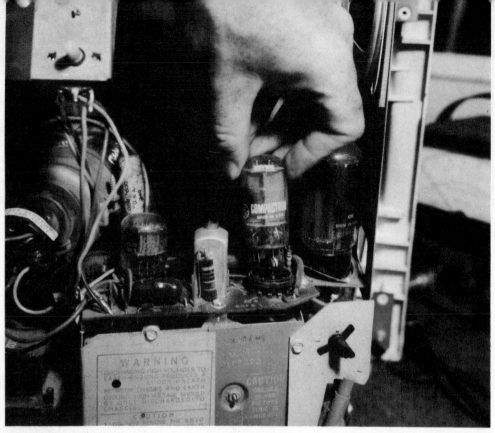

It's easy to physically pull and install tubes. The trick is knowing which tube to pull.

GETTING THE
JUMP ON REPAIRS

For the 55 troubles, use tube tester, hand tools and common sense

As many TV's as I've worked on, at least once a week I'll open up a chassis and find a repair situation that perplexes me. What do I do? I pull the service notes of that set out of my repair library and begin looking over the schematic. This primes the flow of my experience and I get underway again toward the completion of the repair.

This book, used correctly, will do the same thing for you. It will prime your activity, guide you to the troublesome circuit and most of the time to the actual defective part.

You can actually repair nine out of ten TV breakdowns with nothing more than your brains, eyes, ears, nose, a few special hand tools and drug store tube tester. That is, if you follow directions carefully.

A repair consists of four steps.

1.—Name the trouble. This means matching up the TV trouble with its counterpart in the IDENTIFICATION CENTER and giving your trouble a name.

2.—Locating the suspected circuit or circuits. In the IDENTIFICATION CENTER alongside each trouble is a list of chapters wherein the trouble is explained and the indicated circuits are listed in their order of probability.

3.—Locating the defective component in the suspect circuit. In the indicated chapter you'll find troubleshooting techniques and typical components that go bad and cause the troubles shown in the IDENTIFICATION CENTER.

4.—Once located, the bad component has to be replaced with an exact or substitute component. Once this is done the trouble is gone.

IDENTIFICATION CENTER

When I had chemistry in High School there were 92 elements, no more, no less. Today at latest count students are told there are 104 elements, maybe a few more unnamed.

By my latest count there are 55 TV troubles, no more, no less. As time goes by I'm sure more troubles will be discovered. At any rate I'm going to dwell on the 55 I know of.

They break down into six general types. They are:

1.—Dead Set troubles. (By definition this grouping comprises the troubles evidenced by the symptoms of no light on the screen and no sound issuing from the speaker. The pilot light might be lit or a glance in the back reveals the tubes might be lighting up. Even so, the sound and picture-making qualities of the TV is not operating and the trouble comes under the heading of "Dead Set.")

Adding a few spare tubes to your tool box enables you to test tubes by substitution.

Be careful taking back on and off. It can sometimes be more trouble than the repair.

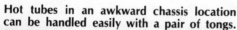

Hot tubes in an awkward chassis location can be handled easily with a pair of tongs.

While testing tubes, tap lightly, observe meter needle. It'll reveal loose elements.

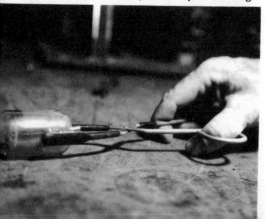

Tube tester found in many stores guides you to troublesome circuit and defective part.

Once defective part is located, replace it with exact or substitute replacement part.

Sets today are being built with space age-type components, which are more reliable.

There are now a few hundred different commercial tubes and 12 color picture tubes.

Almost all TV's have a tube location guide pasted somewhere in set. It's valuable aid.

Guide lays out pictorially tubes as they're placed in TV, plus other vital information.

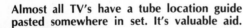

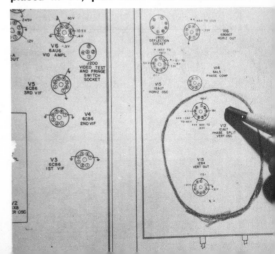

2. — **Brightness troubles.** (This grouping includes all variation from the normal picture brightness. It includes all shades of trouble from a black screen to an overly bright one. It is directly tied in to a brightness control that doesn't work correctly. Some of the troubles are obvious and others are subtle.)

3. — **Synchronization troubles.** (These are the troubles known as flopover, bends, lines, rolling, or just some jiggling. It has to do with keeping the picture locked solidly in place. Unless your picture is so locked, you have a sync problem. No compromise will do.)

4. — **Contrast troubles.** (These are the troubles that can be confused with brightness troubles. Your first step is to separate the two. Contrast troubles are no contrast, too much contrast, smeared blacks and whites and variations on this theme.)

5. — **Sound troubles.** (There is no difficulty diagnosing these.) It's quite obvious when the sound is dead, low, too high, muffled, garbled or squealing.

6. — **Color troubles.** (This group can be difficult to identify.) Keep in mind a color trouble is somehow tied in with the color controls. When you have no color, wrong colors, blurred colors, moving colors or what have you, and the color controls won't help, look for the trouble in the color group.

The newer TV's are being built with a lot more reliability than older models. The reliability is especially evident in the fixed components such as resistors, capacitors and coils. This makes for a higher completion of repairs for you the do-it-yourselfer.

However, there are hundreds of new type tubes. While there used to be in general just three kinds of tubes, seven pin miniatures, nine pin miniatures and octals, there are now many more. There are ten pin miniatures, twelve pin miniatures, novars, compactrons and others. Also instead of tubes, in some circuits you'll find diodes, dual diodes, transistors and other items.

While there used to be 70-degree and 90-degree picture tubes, all with a universal twelve pin base, there are now 110-degree, 114-degree, all sizes, shapes and different kinds of bases, plus many different color picture tubes containing many different kinds of bases.

With it all you can still score more repairs than you were able to with just the older type TV's. You'll have to adapt yourself to the changes and pay a little more attention than previously but the complications do not change the fact that tubes plug in and adjustments just need manipulation.

SERVICE INFORMATION

Just as you can't tell the players without a program you can't tell tube functions without service information. The first and most important service sheet for you is the tube location guide.

After you name the trouble, the IDENTIFICATION CENTER tells you the circuit under suspect. The only way you can find the suspected circuit among all that mumbo jumbo in the TV is to consult the tube location guide. You'll find it pasted somewhere inside the TV, either on the rear of the chassis or on the wall of the cabinet. Sometimes it's on the inside of the back cover.

The guide lays out the tubes pictorially as they actually exist in the TV. Near the tube is an abbreviation of the job the tube is doing.

While that is the most important piece of news you want, if you look close you can also find a pictorial view of the tubes' key way, where the chassis adjustments are, fuse sizes and location, heater circuit paths, signal paths, location of other plug-in units such as dual diodes and germanium diodes, and other common offender components such as power rectifiers and heater resistors.

The tube location guide differs from a schematic like a street guide differs from a map. The tube location guide provides you with all the service information for quick check repairs. The schematic package gives you all the information available for your TV. You use the guide for the nine out of ten easy repairs. The schematic is needed for the other ten percent, the really tough repairs.

7

There are hundreds of newer-type tubes of all sizes, and various transistors, diodes.

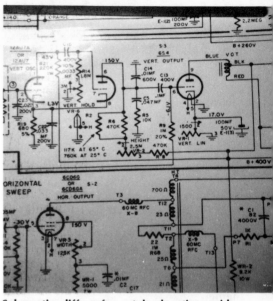

Schematic differs from tube location guide as good road map differs from street guide.

55 TV TROUBLES

CHAPTERS	TROUBLES & NUMBERS
2 Low Voltage	1. Dead set—no heaters
	2. Dead set—heaters lit
3 High Voltage	3. No brightness—sound okay
4 High Voltage	4. 2 Sided shrink
	5. 4 Sided shrink
	6. Blooming
	7. Defocused
	8. Keystone
	9. Arc Lines
	10. Corona
	11. Pie crust
	12. Barkhausen
5 Sync	13. Horizontal lines
	14. Christmas tree
	15. Horizontal split picture
	16. Bends
	17. Poor horizontal linearity
	18. Vertical roll
	19. No vertical sweep
	20. Top and bottom shrink
	21. Vertical foldover
	22. Vertical retrace at top
	23. Poor vertical linearity
	24. No sync
	25. Barber pole
	26. Light green picture

CHAPTERS	TROUBLES & NUMBERS
6 Contrast	27. Raster only, no sound or picture
	28. Raster, sound okay
	29. Weak contrast
	30. Too much contrast
	31. Smeary picture
	32. Negative picture
	33. Pulsating picture
	34. Hum bars
	35. Snow
	36. No high band
	37. Sound and picture won't tune
	38. No UHF
	39. No VHF
	40. Tunable ghosts
7 Sound	41. No sound
	42. Poor sound
	43. Sound bars
9 Color Adjustments	44. Tinted pix
	45. Poor purity
	46. Poor convergence
10 Color	47. No color
	48. No video, color okay
	49. Weak color
	50. Overly bright, 1 color pix
	51. Loss of one color
	52. Worms
	53. Color snow in B & W pix
14 Picture Tubes	54. Dim pix
	55. Fixed brightness

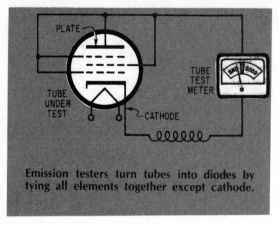

Emission testers turn tubes into diodes by tying all elements together except cathode.

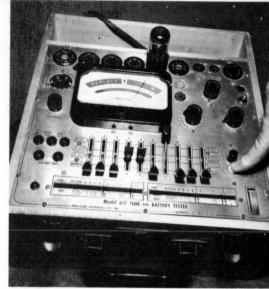

Tube tester provides good service information, but take its results with caution.

It wouldn't hurt to own the full service folder for your TV. You can get it by writing to the manufacturer of your TV and requesting it. They might charge you or might not. Another source is to buy the Sams Photofact holder containing your TV's schematic. Only thing is the folder contains a lot of other service information concerning other TV's that you have no interest in.

It's worth it though because the service folder contains the following valuable information. Step by step, take apart and put together instructions, servicing tips peculiar to your TV, detailed schematic, pictures of top and bottom of all vital sections of the TV with numbered callouts showing every part, detailed parts list with suitable replacements, two tube location guides top and bottom view, detailed tuner schematic and parts list, detailed alignment instruction for the tuner, IF strip, horizontal phase, AGC, color setups all step by step, other things.

TRUTH ABOUT TUBE TESTING

I use a tube tester under one set of circumstances. That is when I suspect a tube and do not have a new one in stock

If either of these two bulbs light up, tube is defective, no matter what meter reads.

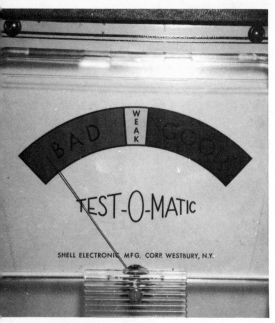

Double-check all bad tubes. If you make just one mistake in setting, it reads BAD.

to stick in its place. If I have the replacement for the suspect tube I do not use the tester, I put the replacement in and see what happens. If the trouble clears, the tube was bad. If the trouble stays, the tube was probably good.

You probably can't perform the direct substitution technique since you are not in the business and do not stock replacement tubes. You are in the position of having to use the tube tester most of the time.

The tube tester is useful. It provides the operator with a certain amount of service information. However, it is not a cure-all for TV troubles. It can tell you a tube is good when it's really bad. It can tell you a tube is bad when it's good. There can be mistakes on the tube chart that give you wrong settings and if you make one wrong move in the settings your reading will be inaccurate.

Fortunately, it's right the majority of times so as long as you are on the lookout and doublecheck all tubes that read

Use one of these hot tube pullers and spare yourself a nasty burn off a red hot tube.

If you own heater tester, you can check tubes, fuses and make easy ohmmeter tests.

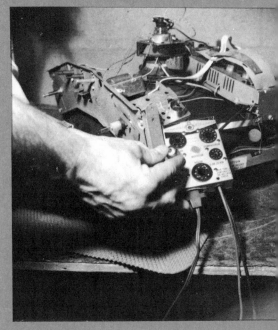

bad, the tube tester is a valuable aid.

All the tube testers you will come in contact with are emission checkers. There are lots of other characteristics in a tube too but emission — that is, the amount of electrons that flows in the tube — is a good indicator. It follows that as the emission goes so go the rest of the tubes' characteristics. Good emission usually but not always means the tube qualifies for TV duty.

The actual test makes all tubes act like a two-element diode. When you make your settings you are shorting all the elements except the cathode and heater together. Then as the tube heats up you press a button. This puts a positive voltage on the tied elements. Electrons flow from the cathode and heater to all the rest of the elements and the flow is measured on the meter where the GOOD — BAD is indicated.

In addition to emission tests there are usually a couple of neon bulbs labeled SHORTS and GAS. If either bulb lights,

the tube is defective no matter what the emission reads.

Be sure to leave the tube in the test position as short a time as possible. With all the elements tied together a tube can overheat and burn out as you stand and watch hoping for the needle to go higher.

Double check all bad tubes and then as a further check test the new tube you buy too. Besides the fact that the new tube can be bad you won't have to buy a tube because the tube tester is inaccurate or you made a mistake in your settings. Should the new tube also read bad that's probably the case.

On occasion the tester, even though you do everything perfect and the tester is fine, will not single out a bad tube. There are intermittent shorts that only occur after a tube is on awhile, tubes with loose elements that vibrate in action but read good on a tester, tubes that have severe interelectrode defects that alter other characteristics, etc. The main thing is to realize the tester has many limitations

In TV repair, first clean away dust so you can do your work in clean, efficient manner.

Spray can of quick-drying solution freezes component in seconds, reveals the defects.

and does not preach gospel.

TALKING ABOUT TOOLS

Your everyday tools will be needed in a TV repair. In addition, there are a few items that I would deem a must if you are a serious electronic do-it-yourselfer. They really don't come to too much money and you can use some of them for other home repairs besides TV and radio.

There are 17 of them. 1) Soldering gun with two speeds. 2) Roll of 60/40 solder. 3) Neon test lamp. 4) Hot tube puller. 5) Cheater cord for your TV. 6) Roll of high dielectric tape. 7) Plastic hex head alignment tool. 8) Phillips head screwdriver. 9) Set of nut drivers especially the ¼ inch. 10) Filament Continuity Checker that includes latest sockets. 11) Paint brush to loosen dust. 12) Wire strippers. 13) Diagonal cutters. 14) Long nose pliers. 15) Jumper cord with alligator clips on each end. 16) Spray can of tuner lubricant. 17) Spray can of freeze mist.

As you go through the book you'll see how the ownership of these items solves

a lot of problems. Of course there are many other items that can be useful but these are a must.

SAFETY FIRST

There are three potential types of danger that lie in wait when you attempt to repair your TV set, black and white or color. You can cut yourself on broken glass, you can accidently absorb some roentgens due to x-ray, and you can somehow become part of an electric circuit.

Cuts, x-rays and electric shocks can be avoided by following some simple safety rules.

Broken Glass: Quite often a small tube or the picture tube can overheat or get whacked enough to cause the glass to fracture. Sometimes the glass will fall apart and other times just crack. Then when you come along, reach into a darkened area and pull, you get cut.

Be sure to use plenty of light and look over any tubes before yanking them out. If you see any milky coating on the glass (caused by loss of vacuum) or cracks, use gloves to remove the glass.

This is the spot for a chest X-ray! Never assume this position while the set is on.

A hazard of repairing a TV set is accidentally cutting yourself on cracked glass.

TYPICAL FILTER CAPACITOR
80 TO 300 MICROFARADS

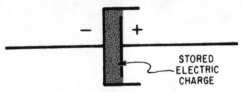

Even though set is off, stored-in capacitors near TV can get you if you're careless.

Don't operate a color TV with high voltage cage off; it's designed as an X-ray shield.

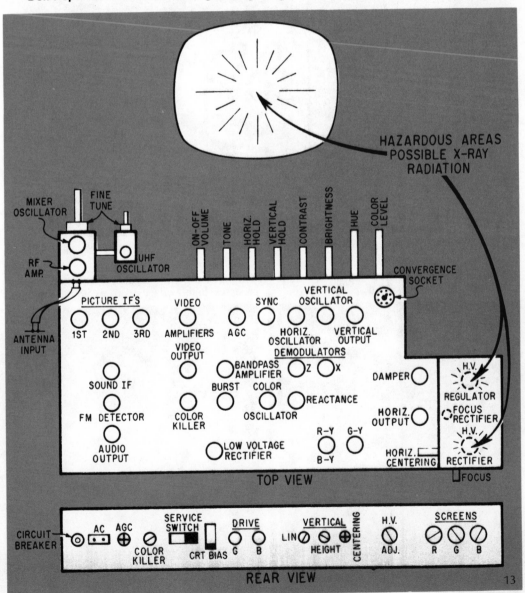

13

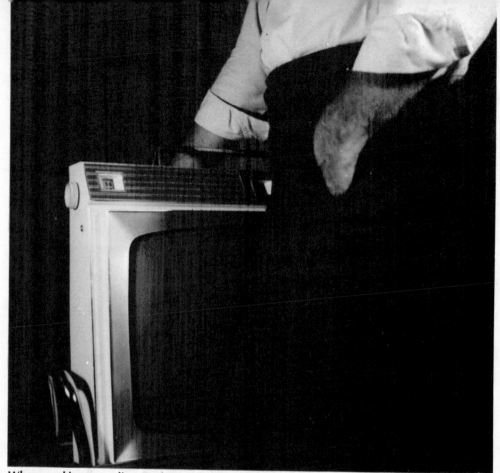

When working on a line TV keep your left hand in pocket so current can't pass near heart.

When a tube has a milky appearance, it is cracked. Be very careful pulling it out.

Jumper cord with insulated alligator clips releases high voltage well, avoiding shock.

If you see a broken tube, with the tube elements the only fingerholds, be sure to be careful. Not only can you cut yourself on the elements but they might lead into charged filter capacitor that will shock you too.

X-Rays: While most of the rumors about X-Rays emanating from color TV sets are exaggerated there is the possibility of some S-Ray activity taking place. If it is, the danger spots are around the high voltage regulator tube, the high voltage rectifier tube and the face of the picture tube. Needless to say avoid these areas while the TV is on. You would naturally avoid the tube areas since the high voltage exists there, but not so naturally avoid the picture tube face.

To sum up, do not get near the bottom of the TV on the high voltage side while the TV is on. Do not get near the high voltage cage side of the TV while it is on. Do not press up against the picture tube face while the TV is on. When the TV is off have no fear, there cannot be any X-ray radiation.

Electric Shock: You can get a shock from a TV whether it is on or off. When the TV is on you can get a shock from practically any area of the chassis. When the TV is off you can only get a shock from places where electricity is stored. They are the filter capacitors and the shell of the picture tube.

FILTER CAPACITORS

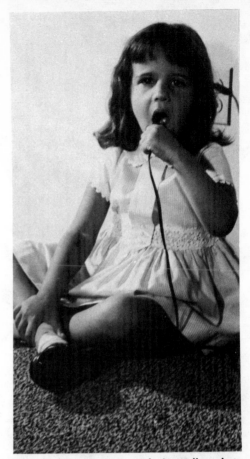

Never leave cheater cords in wall sockets, because children can get hurt eating them.

The filter capacitors are usually out of harm's way but be on the lookout for them. The shell of the picture tube unfortunately is usually quite accessible. Therefore, before working with the picture tube shell be sure to discharge it. This can be done easily with a jumper cord. Attach one end of the jumper to the TV chassis. Then touch the other end of the jumper to the anode button or high voltage well of the picture tube. A healthy spark will fly through the jumper. Better the jumper than you.

When working on the TV it's a good idea to wear rubber-bottomed shoes and keep your left hand in your pocket. That way if you do get a shock the current cannot pass near your heart or get a good path to ground. It will jar you but not hurt you.

When working on a TV be sure to move it far away from any radiators, air vents, lamps, etc. Should you accidentally touch both a grounded radiator and a TV that is on at the same time a severe electric shock could result.

Cheater Cords: A cheater cord is a necessary tool for the do-it-yourself repair, but follow one safety rule. Do not leave a cheater cord plugged into the wall after you are done. A pet or child can come along, place the cord in its mouth, short out the connections with saliva and get a bad burn. Be sure to put cheater cords back into your tool box when you are finished.

15

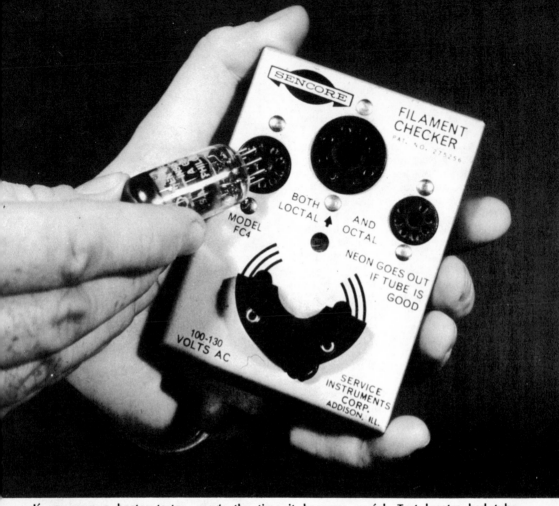

If you own a heater tester, now's the time it becomes useful. Test locates bad tube.

WHEN YOUR SET GOES DEAD

Whether tubes are lit or out cold, this is /most prevalent trouble

Out of the fifty-five varieties of TV trouble symptoms, two of them are worth devoting an entire chapter to. That's because one out of every two troubles I encounter is either a DEAD SET with tubes lit or a DEAD SET with tubes out cold.

This repair situation is different than it was a few years ago. That's because the power supplies you'll find in present day TV's use silicon rectifiers instead of the tube or selenium rectifiers that were once the standard.

Fortunately these power supplies, even though they break down the most, are the simplest circuits in the TV. They

DEAD SET

TROUBLE	REMEDY
Dead Set—Tubes Out— All Sets	Wall plug—line cord— Off On Switch—Circuit breaker—line fuse
Dead Set—Tubes Out— Parallel Wired Heaters	Heater fuse links
Dead Set—Tubes Out— Series Wired Heaters	Heater dropping resistor—Series heater choke—Bad tube—Tube in wrong socket
Dead Set—Some Tubes Lit Normally—Others Out— Parallel Wired Heaters	Loss of one of the heater fuse links
Dead Set—Some Tubes Lit Bright—Others Out— Series Wired Heaters	Shorted tube in heater string
Dead Set—All Tubes Lit Normally	Fusistor—Rectifier tube —Silicon rectifier—Input filter—Circuit breaker high voltage fuse

TUBE COMPLEMENT

RF—6EA8	AGC, Sync—8BA11
Osc. Mixer—3HA5	Vert.—10GK6
1st IF—4BZ6	(CRT—19GAP4—6 volts)
2nd IF—4BZ6	Hor. Osc.—6GH8
3rd IF—4BZ6	Horiz. Out.—17JN8
Audio, video—10GN8	Damper—22BW3
Audio—13Z10	Total Volts equal 113

Typical of newer type "Dead Set" troubles is open circuit breaker. Step one — reset.

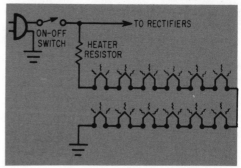

Latest type TV's employ solid state rectifiers like these instead of a larger tube.

Note that the simple heater string has few parts. Remember to test them one at a time.

only contain a few components and the heater string of the tubes.

The do-it-yourselfer can score high in the power supply. Let me brief you on the repair techniques on these latest circuits and then I'll review briefly, at the end, the older power supplies.

TROUBLE NO. 1— DEAD SET, TUBES OUT

After making sure your wall plug is working and the TV's circuit breaker is reset get ready to use two pieces of test gear. Your jumper wire with the alligator clips and your neon test lamp.

It is indicated that the heater string is in trouble. In the heater string there is 1) the line cord, 2) the off-on switch, 3) the circuit breaker or heater fuse, 4) the

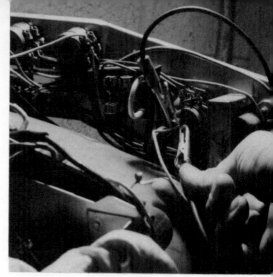

Quick check of incoming AC and cheater cord is to put your neon tester into the holes.

To check the OFF-ON switch, short it. That way it automatically is on the ON position.

heater dropping resistor, 5) the heaters in each tube.

The Line Cord: Unplug the line cord from the TV but not from the wall socket. Stick the test prongs of the neon bulb into the line cord holes and see if the neon lights. If it does the line cord is good. Another check is to substitute for the line cord with your cheater cord.

The Off-On Switch: Once the line cord is exonerated the next suspect is the off-on switch. As the name implies it is either on or off. The test is to short the switch so it is on. This is done by taking your jumper wire and attaching it across the two terminals with the TV unplugged. If there are four terminals, either locate the two that go to the line or short all four of them together. Then momentarily plug the TV on. Should the tubes start lighting, that's it! Unplug the TV immediately, you have a bad off-on switch. If nothing happens, the switch is probably good.

The Circuit Breaker: When the off-on switch is determined good the next suspect in line is the circuit breaker. Widespread use of the circuit breaker in TV sets has occurred in the last few years. It's a good item, more convenient than a fuse but it carries complications that a fuse avoids.

The common conception is that a short in the TV causes a breaker to open just

as a fuse pops. However, if a breaker keeps reopening it is not necessarily due to a short. In fact, it is only due to a short in about one out of four cases.

Most of the time when a breaker keeps opening it's a problem in the breaker itself. The circuit breaker has lost some of its current-carrying ability and cannot stay open during normal operation of the TV.

CHANGE BREAKER

There are two fixes. One, if there is a screw adjustment on the breaker, turn it in a turn or two. That increases its amperage.

If there is no screw adjustment change the breaker with a correct replacement. Should the fix not take, then it is possible a short circuit is causing the opening. (We'll cover the shorts you can fix in the rectifier section of this chapter.)

While the continual necessity of resetting the breaker is the main way the breaker fails, on occasion it just quits and won't be reset. It might feel broken or it might click into position five yet the TV still stays dead.

The quick check is easy like the off-on switch. A jumper wire is shorted across the two terminals and the TV is plugged

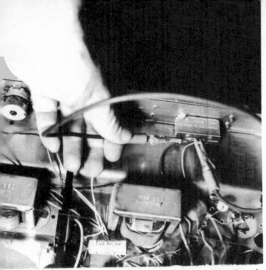

Check circuit breaker by simply shorting it. If the TV comes back on, the breaker is bad.

Some circuit breakers have a screw-type adjustment. Turning it in increases amperage.

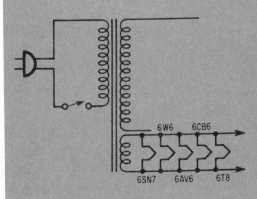

You can tell parallel-wired heater string by numbers on tube. Most lead off with a six.

Fine wire covered by insulation is actually a heater fuse found in parallel-wired TV's.

Series-wired heater strings might have any number on its tube — 12, 19, 21 or anything.

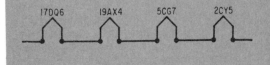

in. If the tubes start to light the breaker is bad and needs a new one.

A word of caution. During these quick checks on the breaker, the off-on switch, etc., be careful not to short the terminals to the wrong place or let the alligator clip accidentally touch the chassis or pow! Also do not leave the short in as a permanent fix. You must have the part replaced or you're flirting with electrical troubles.

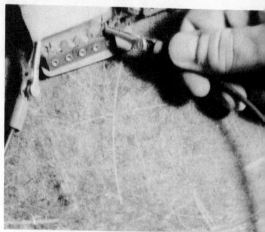

Large wire-wound resistor is in series with tube heaters; it's often cause of Dead Set.

To check resistor, clamp one end and touch down with other. If tubes light—get off!

If tubes light too brightly in series wired TV, a lit tube is shorted, causing trouble.

B plus line, part of power supply, contains a fusistor, rectifiers and an input filter.

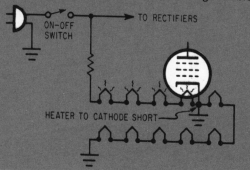

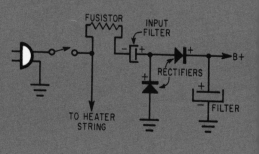

While the line cord, off-on switch circuit breaker and fuses are in all sets, heater fuses are only in parallel heater wired TV's and heater dropping resistors are only in series heater wired TV's. You must know which is which. This knowledge is also useful for the tube servicing.

Parallel Wired Heaters: This type heater circuit has a heater transformer. This is a separate transformer or a part of a power transformer that takes the 110 volts from the line and steps it down to 6.3 volts. You can tell a parallel heater setup by the numbers on the tubes. Look on the tube location guide. Parallel wired tubes all have a six leading off the numbers. There might be a couple of tubes

there with a twelve lead off number. There won't be any other numbers. Should you see any twos, threes, nineteens, etc., it's not a parallel job but a series string.

HIDDEN COMPONENT

The Heater Fuse: This particular component is one of the most hidden in the TV. It is nothing but a piece of fine wire contained in a sleeve of insulation linking the heater transformer to the parallel heater string. It might be shown on the tube location guide and it *is* displayed on schematic.

When it opens you can spot the break

visually if you remove the sleeve. Sometimes it breaks when there is a short in the TV, but most of the time it breaks just because it is a fine piece of wire. Replacing it is easy. Get the same gauge wire.

Series Wired Heaters: This type heater circuit is transformerless. This feat is accomplished by wiring all the heaters together like Christmas tree bulbs. Effectively, then, the two ends of the heater string is hooked into the AC line and the circuit is complete.

When the string is operating normally all the heaters light, not too bright, not too dull but with a normal healthy glow. The tubes are not just thrown in but are placed in line, each tube absorbing a certain amount of voltage. Two volt tubes (like a 2CY5) absorb two volts from the line, twenty-five volt tubes (like a 25CD6) absorb twenty-five volts from the line and so on. Exactly the right amount of tubes with exactly the right voltage dropping is placed in the line to drop the 117 volts from the wall plug.

The Heater Tube Test: In a parallel wired TV, when one tube loses its heater that tube goes out and is quite easily spotted. In a series wired TV when one tube loses its heater, all the tubes go out. You can't tell by looking that one is bad. Just as you would troubleshoot a Christmas tree light string—that is, look for a dead one—that's just the way you seek out a bad tube in a dead series string.

You could pull all the tubes out and head for the nearest do-it-yourself tube tester. However, if you have one of those heater testers I mentioned in Chapter 1, here is where it becomes useful.

Since you are only testing for a bad heater, you simply plug tube after tube into the little tester. The indicator will tell you when you have discovered the bad tube.

WHEN THE WIRE BREAKS

The Heater Dropping Resistor: There is one difference between a Christmas tree bulb line and a TV series string. That is the heater dropping resistor. For in actuality the TV tubes usually are designed to drop only about eighty or nine-ty volts. A large wattage resistor is then also placed into the series string to absorb the remainder of the voltage.

It dies by breaking open. It is wire wound and the wire breaks. When it conks out all the heaters in series with it also go out. Thus when you test all the tubes and they are good, chances are high that you've lost your heater resistor.

Once you locate it you'll find it is one of the largest resistors in the TV and has a value something around 50 ohms at 30 watts. You can quick-check it by shorting it out momentarily with your jumper wire. However, don't keep the wire on more than a second or two for as the tubes light, they will get overly bright since 117 volts is coming in, where only eighty or ninety should be. When you replace the resistor be sure to get one with the same ohmage and wattage. Otherwise you can burn up tubes in a wholesale fashion.

VARIATION OF TROUBLE NO. 1— DEAD SET, SOME TUBES LIT

This is a case of some tubes lit and some tubes out. This trouble clears the off-on switch, the circuit breaker and the heater resistor. If it is a parallel wired TV the trouble is usually a heater fuse link. In lots of these TV's there are two or more heater transformer windings, each one with its own fuse link. When one of the tube links open up it kills the light in that one string and the other tubes off the other windings stay lit. The tip-off that it is a fuse link is the fact that the tubes that stay on are lit normally.

On the other hand when you find this condition in a series wired TV the tubes that are lit will be overly bright. This is because the trouble is one of the tubes that is lit. It has shorted and stopped the normal heater voltage flow in itself. That puts the full 117 volts across the tubes that are lit and they light bright.

The heater tester won't show up this trouble since it only reveals open heaters and not shorted heaters. The drugstore tester is the one you'll have to use. However, you only have to test the tubes that are lighting. The ones that are out cold are probably OK.

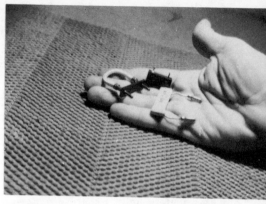

Fusistors vary in size, shape, color. They come in wire wound and also chemical state.

Common B plus symptom is blown fusistor. It usually opens itself or is caused by short.

TROUBLE NO. 2—
DEAD SET, TUBES ALL LIT

When you have a dead set but the tubes are lit, it's because you've lost use of the other part of the power supply, the B plus source. In the B plus line of the supply there is 1) the fusistor, 2) the rectifiers, 3) the input filter, 4) on occasion a circuit breaker.

The Fusistor: The fusistor is a plug-in resistor that is used instead of a fuse. They have become very common and their job is to burn up during a short circuit instead of the rest of the TV.

They do the job nicely; however, they have thrown a complication into TV service similar to the circuit breaker complication. The fusistors burn out during normal use without anything being wrong with the TV.

Therefore first step when you lose power and the tubes are still lit is to change the fusistor. Most of the time you have completed the repair.

If the new fusistor also burns up quickly then you know there is other trouble in the TV. Fusistors come in many sizes, shapes and colors. They come in wirewound and chemical states. You can usually find them easily and they are usually spotted on the tube location guides.

Most heater testers or tube testers will check them for you.

The Rectifiers: B plus voltage is the DC output from the rectifiers in a TV. The rectifier changes the line voltage AC to DC. Rectifiers come mostly in solid state form today; however, there are still plenty of tube rectifiers around. Typical tube numbers are 3DG4, 5U4, 5BC3, 5AS4, etc.

Rectifier tubes display their trouble lots of times. They get pink or purple or go out cold. Other times they won't tip you off that way and light normally even though they have died. The best test is to put another tube in its place. Restoration will be instantaneous when the tube is bad.

FIRST LOCATE THEM

Silicon solid state rectifiers are not so easily pinpointed as bad. You must first locate them. They are unbelievably tiny, in comparison to their tube counterparts, and come in many different types. Some look like top hats, others like little bullets, and others like small capacitors. They are all the same, however, and are all interchangeable as long as you use the same current rating. Typical values are

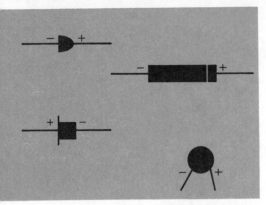

It's important to observe polarity when replacing rectifier, otherwise TV might smoke.

Usually, "Dead Set" is caused by open input filter. Observe polarity when replacing it.

500 MILS, 750 MILS or 1 AMP.

The big problem you will have is with their POLARITY. Like a battery, there is a plus and a minus. You must observe the correct polarity or the TV will start smoking.

Once you have located them and made provisions to observe polarity you can unsolder them from the TV. Now during the heating process no heat from the iron is allowed to get into the body of the rectifier or else the tiny one will be ruined. This is accomplished with a heat sink — that is, attach a clip lead, say from your jumper wire between the body of the rectifier and point of contact of the solder gun. That way the heat is siphoned off before it can run down the rectifier lead into the innards of the rectifier.

Rectifiers either short or open. You can test a silicon on the heater tester on the drugstore tester or on an ohmmeter. A good rectifier will show a short in one direction and an open in the other on the heater tester. All you have to do is attach the rectifier to the fuse test and then reverse it. In one instance the tester will read it like a good fuse, and in the other it will read like an open fuse.

With an ohmmeter perform the same test. In one direction the silicon will read a low resistance, and in the other a high resistance when it is good.

Should the rectifier read the same, either good or bad, it's bad. When it reads a low resistance both ways it's shorted. When it reads a high resistance both ways it's open.

The Input Filter: In series with the fusistor is a filter capacitor with a value around 200 MFD @ 200 WORKING VOLTS. It is also a common offender causing this DEAD SET — TUBES LIT trouble. After you have exhausted the fusistor and rectifiers as suspects, you stand a very good chance of fixing the trouble if you can locate and replace this filter. You needn't worry about heat sinks. You do have to concern yourself with POLARITY and making sure all the wires you remove from the old filter you put back onto the new replacement. I won't go into the details of location and replacement but this measure will cure this type trouble. If you feel it's over your head call for skilled help and at least you'll have a good idea what he's doing.

Circuit Breakers: On occasion a circuit breaker is installed into the B plus line, so when all else fails, before calling the doctor follow the same instructions as outlined in the beginning of this chapter.

The business end of a high voltage probe easily tests the number of volts in the danger area.

TIPS ON HIGH VOLTAGE

This is the problem when the brightness goes but the sound remains

The trouble of NO BRIGHTNESS— SOUND OK is the second commonest TV trouble after DEAD SET and is worth two complete chapters. Between the two symptoms about three out of four TV troubles are encompassed. While DEAD SET concerned itself with the low voltage power supply, NO BRIGHTNESS—SOUND OK indicates troubles in the high voltage power supply.

The low voltage supply produces heater and B plus voltage for all the tubes in the TV except the high voltage rectifier and the focus rectifier. The high voltage supply produces heater voltage for these two tubes, a sawtooth waveshape to drive the yoke and the very high voltage needed to power the picture tube; hence its name.

That's why when the high voltage quits, it shuts the light off the picture

NO BRIGHTNESS—SOUND OK

TEST RESULTS	REMEDY
Neon Bulb Lights Brightly	High voltage rectifier High voltage regulator Picture Tube Video Output Tube
Neon Bulb Lights Dimly Pull Rectifier & Regulator, Then Neon Lights Brightly	High voltage rectifier High voltage regulator
Neon Bulb Lights Dimly Pull Rectifier & Regulator, Neon Still Lights Dimly	Horizontal Output Damper Horizontal Oscillator High voltage fuse ckt. bkr.
If Horizontal Oscillator is bad	Replace horizontal output tube also
If High Voltage Fuse is bad	Replace damper tube also
If High Voltage Rectifier in Color TV is bad	Replace horizontal output tube also
Flyback Feels Hot to The Touch	Replace flyback
Width Coil Feels Hot to The Touch	Replace Width Coil
Neon Bulb Lights Dimly or Not At All, Pull Yoke Plug then Neon Lights Brighter	Replace Yoke

High voltage in a color TV must be set exactly in order for picture to come in clear.

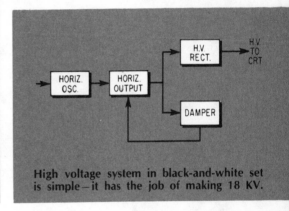

High voltage system in black-and-white set is simple—it has the job of making 18 KV.

tube face yet leaves the sound blaring merrily along.

Other symptoms such as TWO and FOUR SIDED SHRINK, DEFOCUSING, KEYSTONE, BLOOMING, ARC LINES, CORONA EFFECT, PIE CRUST AND VERTICAL RINGING BARS (See Chapter 4) occur when the high voltage gets weak or begins to leak. All these symptoms are common to color as well as black-and-white TV's.

The high voltage itself is produced for the sole purpose of being applied to the well of the picture tube. About twenty-six thousand volts are made for a color picture tube and about twenty thousand for a black and white.

Yoke is mounted around neck of picture tube, sweeping cathode ray and making high voltage.

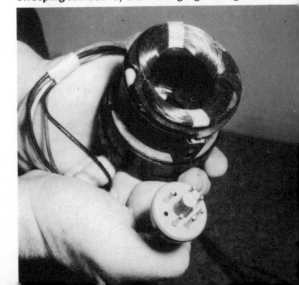

The high voltage production starts two circuits ahead of the actual power supply in the horizontal frequency network. Troubles in the horizontal network also can cause the classic NO BRIGHTNESS—SOUND OK symptom. In addition, the horizontal circuits can cause a few other symptoms such as HORIZONTAL SPLIT PICTURE, POOR HORIZONTAL LINEARITY and THE BENDS (See Chapter 5). Also keep in mind the fact that the horizontal circuits work so close with the high voltage power supply, all the listed symptoms can occur due to defect in either area although they are commoner in the circuits I've indicated them under.

FREE-RUNNING CIRCUIT

The high voltage has its beginnings in the HORIZONTAL OSCILLATOR. This is a free-running circuit that runs continually as long as the TV is turned on whether a TV program is on or not. It makes a sawtooth waveshape with a frequency of 15,750 cycles per second. The HORIZONTAL OUTPUT is the next circuit in line. It is fed the oscillator output and amplifies the sawtooth from about 400 volts to about 3000 volts. The 3000-volt output is fed in the horizontal winding of the YOKE.

The yoke then transfers the sawtooth to the FLYBACK or HIGH VOLT-

High voltage regulator tube is found only in color sets, keeps voltage at even level.

High voltage in color TV gets complicated, since it's much higher, needs regulation.

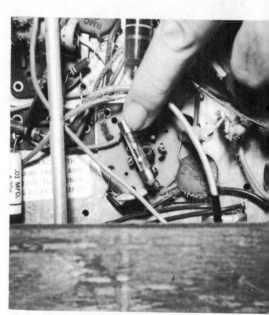

Blown high voltage fuse is common trouble. Always replace damper tube as insurance.

Screen goes black and sound stays on when voltage quits, knocking out cathode ray.

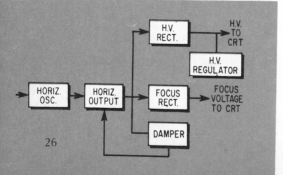

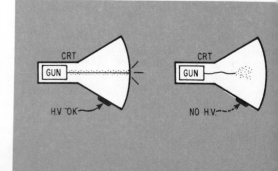

AGE transformer. In the transformer the 3000-volt sawtooth is stepped up to 20 kilovolts for black-and-white picture tubes and 26 KV for color.

As the sawtooth is thrown back and forth between the yoke and flyback it tends to take off into further oscillation. The DAMPER circuit dampens these oscillations. Without the DAMPER circuit standing guard there between the yoke and flyback these spurious oscillations would kill the high voltage.

From the flyback the high AC voltage is fed in the HIGH VOLTAGE RECTIFIER. There the AC is changed to DC and sent directly to the well of the picture tube.

In color TV's a FOCUS RECTIFIER might be found. It acts like the high voltage rectifier except its output (about 5000 volts) is sent to the neck of the picture tube for focusing purposes.

Also in color TV's a HIGH VOLTAGE REGULATOR might be found. It is located between the high voltage rectifier and the picture tube well. It keeps the picture tube input at a steady 26KV no matter how bright the picture might be. Bright pictures tend to lower the high voltage.

When you develop NO BRIGHTNESS—SOUND OK these eight circuits all become suspect. Let's go through the step-by-step approach that

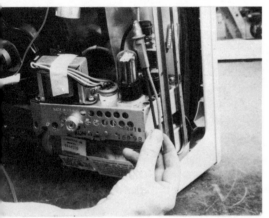

A quick, safe way to test for presence of high voltage is to place neon bulb in area.

Arc test for high voltage is dangerous. Always follow the manufacturer's instructions.

Sometimes a high voltage cage will vibrate or squeal. Tightening bolts usually helps.

Replacing pigtail fuse can be accomplished without soldering if you use these S clips.

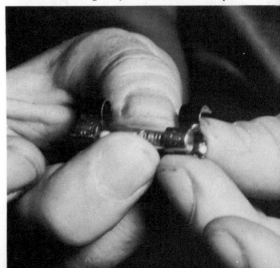

A common trouble in color TV is shorted H.V. rectifier; it also burns up horizontal output.

Cutaneous test for heat in flyback with TV turned off is useful. It can't run too warm.

will narrow down and then pinpoint the actual bad component.

TROUBLE NO 3 —
NO BRIGHTNESS, SOUND OK

Since there is such a vast circuit area to investigate when this symptom appears, you must make some tests to accumulate some service information so you can head for the right circuit.

Take your neon tester in hand and turn the TV on with your cheater cord. Place the neon near the cap of the horizontal output tube. The bulb will light bright, light dimly or not light at all. There is RF energy generated around the output tube when it's working, causing the neon to light brightly. The neon

lights dimly when the high voltage is weak, and doesn't light when there is no high voltage at all.

When the bulb lights bright it means the high voltage AC areas are cleared. The trouble is in the high voltage DC circuits. These are the HIGH VOLTAGE RECTIFIER and HIGH VOLTAGE REGULATOR. Test these two tubes. There are two other possibilities but they are not connected with the high voltage. One, a bad PICTURE TUBE (see Chapter 14 for further information) and two, a bad VIDEO OUTPUT tube in color sets. See Chapter 6 for further information on this.

When the bulb lights dimly or not at all disconnect the DC area by pulling the

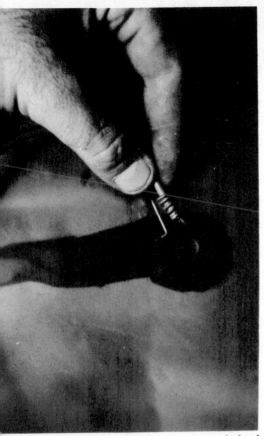

Be sure to always discharge both anode lead and well every time you place hands there.

Show care in removing caps from high voltage tubes. Male, female parts can crack.

high voltage rectifier and regulators out of the TV. Then try the neon test again. If it lights up now one of these two DC tubes is probably bad. Test them for the AC area is clear.

Should the bulb still light dimly or not at all the DC area is probably clear. Now it's time to test the HORIZONTAL OS-CILLATOR and the HIGH VOLT-AGE FUSE or CIRCUIT BREAKER.

If you do find a bad fuse change the damper tube as insurance. It is usually the cause of blown high voltage fuses.

Should you find the horizontal oscillator is bad, change the horizontal output as insurance. It usually burns up when the oscillator kills high voltage. If you find a bad high voltage rectifier tube in a color TV, replace the horizontal output as insurance. It's probably bad, too.

After running the TV for awhile, turn it off and feel the flyback and width coil. They must run cool. If either one is over-ly warm or hot it is the troublemaker.

Your last quick check can be made if your yoke is the plug in type. If so, pull out the plug and try the neon test again. Should the neon come on bright the yoke becomes a prime suspect. It is not neces-sarily bad but is worth a replacement try. You don't have to install the new yoke around the picture tube neck for a test. Simply plug the new yoke in and try the neon test again. If the neon still lights bright you can be sure the old yoke was bad.

Quickest, safest way to test for presence of high voltage is with ordinary neon bulb.

Shrink, blooming, keystone,

defocusing, yoke replacement

troubles can also befall set

OTHER

BRIGHTNESS

IRREGULARITIES

Besides no brightness there are nine other brightness symptoms that occur when troubles appear in the high voltage environs. Five are due to weakened high voltage and the other four happen with high voltage going full strength. Let's go through them.

TROUBLE NO. 4 —
TWO SIDED SHRINK

This is a common trouble that happens when the sweep is restricted on the two sides but there is enough output from the sweep circuits to keep the high voltage high enough to show light. The trouble has degrees from a slight space on either side to three or four inches on either side. If the shrink develops any further than that, the picture usually blacks out altogether.

A variation of this trouble happens like this. The picture comes on fine. After a minute or so, as the TV heats up, the picture begins to shrink from the sides. Suddenly the picture collapses into a white vertical line, then disappears altogether.

Invariably this trouble is caused by a weak HORIZONTAL OUTPUT tube. Other suspects are the HORIZONTAL OSCILLATOR and the DAMPER. On occasion the FLYBACK or YOKE can cause this condition.

TROUBLE NO. 5 —
FOUR SIDED SHRINK

Go back to Chapter 2 and read the rectifier section. The high voltage is being weakened because there is not enough low voltage. If the rectifier is a tube it's most likely weak and a new one will restore a full picture. If the set has silicons one of them is probably open. Should the low voltage troubleshooting not help the next suspects are the DAMPER and HORIZONTAL OUTPUT tubes.

TROUBLE NO. 6 — BLOOMING

The condition of blooming — that is, the picture puffs up as you advance the brightness control and shrinks as you turn the control back — is due to low high

CATHODE CURRENT CHART

Family of Tubes	Approximate Cathode Currents (MILS)
'AU5*	75
'AV5	75
'BG6	75
'CB5	170
'CD6	130
'CL5	170
'DN6	130
'DQ5	220
'FW5	125
'BQ6	75
'CU6	75
'DQ6	125
'GW6	125
'JY6	150
'GJ5	125
'GT5	125
'JB6	135
'JE6	220
'JF6	195
'JG6	190
'JT6	125
'KF6	195
'KM6	195
'GE5	125
'GF5	120
'GV5	125
'GY5	160
'HB5	160
'HD5	195
'HF5	220
'HJ5	195
'JM6	125
'JN6	125
'JS6	220
'JV6	160
'JZ6	160
'KD6	260
'KE6	220
'KN6	260

This list is far from complete. If the tube you are looking for is not listed check the TV service notes for the correct cathode current. A good rule of thumb for color TV's is a cathode current between 180 and 220 MILS.

*Apostrophe is used in lieu of actual prefix such as 6AV5, 12AV5, 25AV6, etc.

Horizontal output tube operates within certain limits. If it doesn't, it'll burn up.

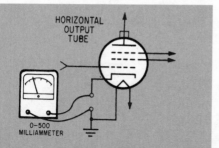

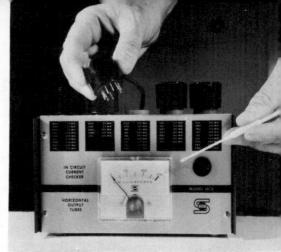

Service technicians use a special cathode current meter designed to test most tubes.

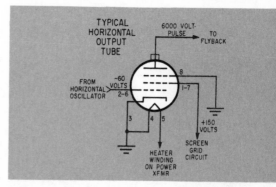

Whenever you replace the horizontal output tube, check its cathode current with meter.

Many degrees of two-sided shrink condition exist. As shrink increases, brightness dims.

Sometimes, horizontal shrinking looks like four-sided shrinking rather than just two.

Blooming is caused by low high voltage. Adjusting brightness reveals this condition.

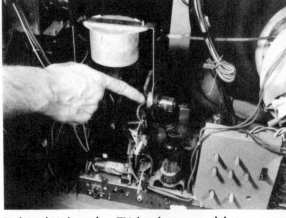

Defocusing isn't common monochrome trouble but it happens often in color high voltage.

Defocusing in color TV is often caused by small focus diode tube mounted by flyback.

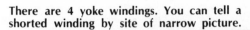

Classic symptom found mostly in black-and-white TV. It is generally caused by yoke.

There are 4 yoke windings. You can tell a shorted winding by site of narrow picture.

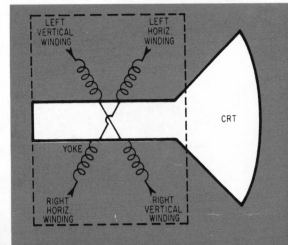

voltage. As the potential decreases the condition becomes more and more pronounced.

In black and white TV's whenever that condition occurred a fast replacement of the HIGH VOLTAGE RECTIFIER usually effected a cure. It gets a little more sticky with a color set. The rectifier is still a prime suspect, but the HORIZONTAL OUTPUT tube, the DAMPER, the HIGH VOLTAGE REGULATOR, and the FOCUS RECTIFIER are also consistent troublemakers. Anything that will lower the regulated 26 kilovolts just a little bit causes the blooming. The monochrome TV could become lowered a great deal before it would display blooming.

TROUBLE NO. 7 — DEFOCUSED

When you lose focus try the brightness control. If the picture blooms too, the blooming is the real symptom, with the defocusing a secondary result. If the picture doesn't bloom you have a true focus symptom. Turn the focus control in the back. On color TV's it usually sticks out of the high voltage cage. If the control has no effect, replace the FOCUS RECTIFIER. It can be a tube or a small skinny selenium rectifier. In most cases it will probably cure the trouble.

When the control does have some effect but won't quite bring the picture back into sharpness, first test the focus rectifier again, but chances are good the HIGH VOLTAGE RECTIFIER,

HIGH VOLTAGE REGULATOR or HORIZONTAL OUTPUT is at fault.

This particular service tip if not heeded can cause your flyback transformer to run too hot and in a short period of time burn up. Be on the lookout for it and if you note any signs of it occuring, remedy it or call for skilled help to do so.

The first step of this complication is your need to replace your horizontal output tube. This procedure could be useful in a black and white TV and is a must in a color TV.

Whenever you do replace the horizontal output tube, especially during troubles numbered 4, 5, 6, and 7, let the TV run for about five minutes, then turn it off, then open up the high voltage cage and feel the body and core of the flyback transformer.

FLYBACK TOO HOT?

There is a certain amount of ambient heat generated in the closed cage, so taking that into consideration, decide if the flyback is running too hot. If you can't keep your hand on it, it is definitely so. Should you be able to keep your hand on it but it still feels like heat is emanating from it, it probably is too warm. If it is just luke warm due to surrounding temperature it's probably OK.

When it is too hot, the following procedure must be performed in the effort to lower its fever. Whether you do it or a technician does is immaterial. It must be done.

If yoke is replaced and the picture looks as such, reverse leads in order to restore.

If these ringing bars appear after replacing yoke, install old network into the new yoke.

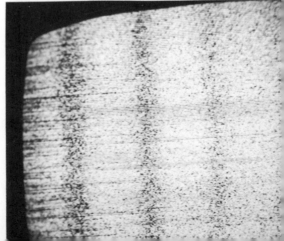

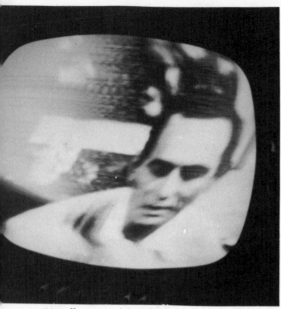

Usually caused by damper, arc lines across screen are common black-and-white trouble.

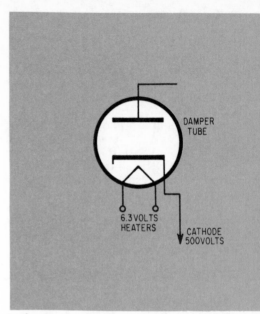

In the damper, potential between heater and cathode is high, causing constant breakdown.

Take the number of the tube and find it on the accompanying chart. (If the tube is not listed use the TV's service notes to find out the same information.) Find the cathode pin and disconnect the lead to that pin. Then attach an 0-500 milliammeter across the opening as shown in the hookup sketch. (Lots of color TV's provide removable links for this purpose.)

Next turn on the TV and read the circuit in mils. It should correspond with the reading on the chart. If it doesn't, adjust the efficiency coil or horizontal linearity coil (both names for the same component) till the correct reading is attained. It is permissible to be off 10 percent.

Should the current reading be way off and won't adjust in, that's a sign of serious trouble in the circuit and expert troubleshooting is in order. It doesn't matter whether it's too low or too high, the flyback will boil away in a period of time.

I adjust cathode current every time I replace a horizontal output tube. It is an important color TV procedure.

TROUBLE NO. 8 – KEYSTONE

This classic picture-book symptom

happens if one of the windings of the yoke shorts. There are four windings, two horizontal and two vertical. The horizontal has one winding for the left side and the other for the right side of the screen. The vertical has one for the top and one for the bottom. When one of these shorts, that side narrows and the picture develops a keystone look. The condition can be accompanied by blooming, defocusing and low brightness. However, forget these secondary symptoms. Whenever you see a keystone picture, change or repair the yoke.

The next two troubles are due to full strength high voltage that is leaking from the circuits.

Saying "change the yoke" and actually replacing it are not quite the same thing. Quite often I change a yoke, the keystone is cured but I find the TV now exhibits one or more of three post-yoke troubles.

They are MIRROR IMAGE – all writing on the screen reads backwards like it does in a mirror. UPSIDE DOWN – the picture shows heads at the bottom and feet at the top. VERTICAL RINGING BARS – the picture shows

Move lead and insulate to remedy insulation breakdown between anode lead, metal area.

High voltage can spew out if sharp points exist. Smooth parts with hot iron to cure.

four or five vertical white bars superimposed on the picture.

Mirror image occurs when the horizontal yoke leads are reversed. To cure, simply switch them.

Upside down happens when the vertical yoke leads are reversed. To cure switch them.

Vertical ringing bars show up when the new yoke has the wrong anti-ringing network inside the yoke. These are all the little capacitors and resistors you'll see as you peel off the yoke cover. Each component is on a numbered tie point. Make a sketch of their positions and install the old components on the new yoke. The ringing bars will disappear.

If all three conditions appear together proceed with all three repair measures.

TROUBLE NO. 9 —
ARCING LINES ACROSS SCREEN

The damper circuit has a rough voltage arrangement imposed on it: 600 volts is taken off at the cathode. The heaters run around six volts. This makes the potential between the cathode and heaters close to 600 volts.

The heaters physically touch the cathode with only a ceramic sleeve between them. The insulation sleeve is subject to breakdown. When it does break, the voltage leaks across to the heaters. This causes the arc lines on the screen. If the arcing continues or develops into a dead short, the high voltage fuse will blow.

To cure arcing, try replacing the DAMPER tube. Also, should the high voltage fuse blow out periodically, change the damper tube.

In rare cases, other tubes can cause similar troubles. Fortunately you can get a visual tipoff by looking for sparks in the tube. Look in all the tubes. Any such spark indication in any tube means the tube must be replaced.

TROUBLE NO. 10 —
CORONA EFFECT

This is caused by the high voltage spilling out of its circuit to the nearest ground point. When it happens you can hear the hissing, smell some ozone, and if you darken the room, see a blue trail of electricity somewhere in the high voltage or sweep circuits.

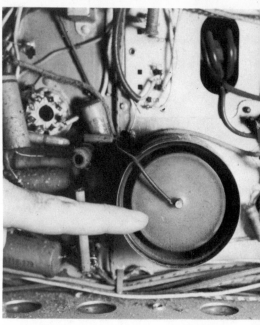

Clean off all dust near well, especially on color TV's, to prevent corona discharge.

Thick plastic covers are placed on rectifier bottoms to insulate it from chassis.

One cause of high voltage leaking is rectifier heater winding; one turn is easily replaced.

When circle looks like a piecrust, replace horizontal output tube or tighten flyback.

Output tube is cause of this set's trouble. It'll test GOOD in checker but still be bad.

Tamping few pieces of wood between core and winding tightens flyback, stops vibration.

This trouble is especially prevalent in hot humid weather and will occur around the picture tube well or cap of the high voltage rectifier. The cure is usually easy. Place a piece of high voltage insulation material like plastic, or fish paper, between the emitting surface and the ground point.

If the bottom of the high voltage rectifier socket is emitting to the chassis there are plastic cups made especially to be placed there.

If the picture tube well is emitting, clean the surrounding surface thoroughly and wipe it dry. That should cure it.

Should you cure one corona discharge and another one starts up, there is complication. There is a short some place else. It usually is in the anode lead from the rectifier to the picture tube well or in the rectifier heater winding in the flyback. Taping up the anode lead short usually cures the condition but the heater winding must be replaced.

There are two troubles that occur when the horizontal output tubes' internal structure gets loose and begins to vibrate mechanically as the sawtooth wave is processed through it. When that happens you'll see on the screen:

TROUBLE NO. 11— PIECRUST EFFECT

(It gets its name from the raggedy appearance of any circle that might show on the screen.)

TROUBLE NO. 12— BARKHAUSEN EFFECT

(This name comes from the man who first noticed the condition.)

A new HORIZONTAL OUTPUT tube will usually cure both conditions. If it doesn't, the FLYBACK transformer might have a loose core. You could try tamping little wooden sticks between the core and the metal frame to halt any physical vibration.

As a last resort before turning these troubles over to the TV man test the HORIZONTAL OSCILLATOR, HORIZONTAL PHASE DETECTOR and the DAMPER.

TAKING THE JITTERS OUT OF YOUR PICTURE

How best to counteract

horizontal, vertical and

color sync troubles

There are three different types of TV flopover, each with its own little family of troubles. There is horizontal sync trouble, vertical sync trouble and color sync trouble.

Horizontal sync trouble is most easily recognized as HORIZONTAL LINES. Its close relatives are CHRISTMAS TREE EFFECT, HORIZONTAL SPLIT PICTURE, THE BENDS and POOR HORIZONTAL LINEARITY.

Vertical sync trouble is most evident as VERTICAL ROLL. Its brothers and and sisters are NO VERTICAL SWEEP, TOP AND BOTTOM SHRINK, VERTICAL FOLDOVER AT BOTTOM, VERTICAL RETRACE AT TOP and POOR VERTICAL LINEARITY.

A variation of both horizontal and ver-

TV picture can slip down, roll up or whirl past. Either way, the trouble is a vertical one.

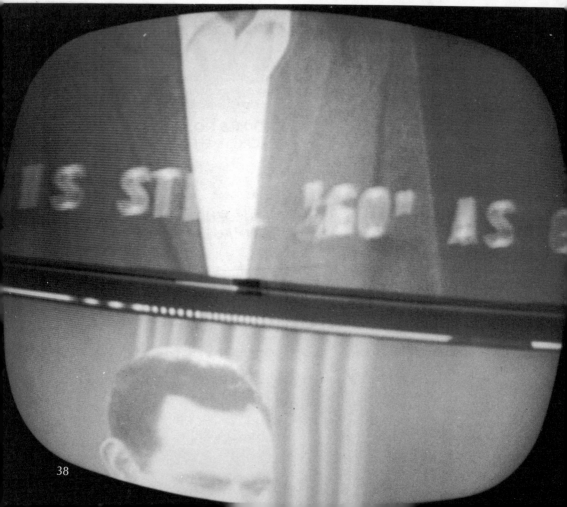

tical SYNC TROUBLE happens when the two of them are combined and the picture won't lock in either horizontally or vertically.

Color sync trouble becomes noticeable when your color picture displays a rainbow. The rainbow can be fixed onto the screen in three thick swaths of color or it can be rolling through the picture. It's named BARBER POLE EFFECT. It has only one close relative — and it is hard to recognize because there is no family resemblance. Its name is LIGHT GREEN SCREEN and when it's appearing it does so at all times whether a color or a black and white picture is supposed to be showing.

What the Oscillators Should Do: I mentioned the production of the sawtooth waveform (in Chapter 3) by the horizontal oscillator, its amplification by the horizontal oscillator, its amplification by the horizontal output and its transference into the yoke where it helps make the high voltage.

The sawtooth does a second job in the yoke, having nothing to do with high voltage. In fact, this second job is really what the sawtooth was designed for. The high voltage production is really just a by-product.

MAGNETIC INFLUENCE

The yoke is in effect around the picture tube neck and has a magnetic influence on the electron beam that is traveling from the electron gun to the phosphor. The sawtooth waveshape's job is to cause the beam to sweep side to side

Adjust vertical hold control to see if you can stop this movie film-type slipping action.

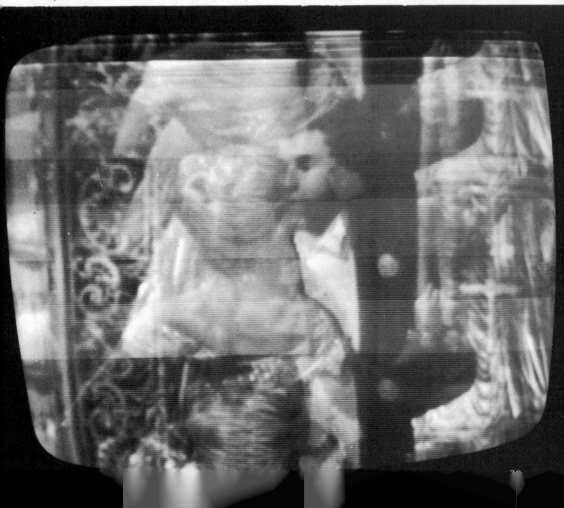

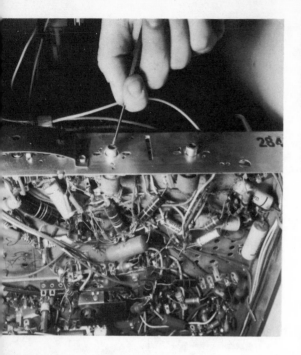

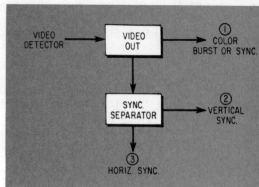

There are 3 types of flopover because there are 3 of sync: horizontal, vertical, and color.

At left, "Christmas tree" problem can be cured by backing off horizontal core a turn.

across the screen. The horizontal sweep causes 15,750 horizontal lines per second to appear on the picture tube face.

At the same time, the vertical oscillator is also making a sawtooth waveshape — that is, amplified in the vertical output and transferred to the vertical windings of the yoke. The vertical frequency is only 60 cycles per second and causes the horizontal lines to be pulled up and snapped back 60 times every second.

To be exact, there are 30 full picture frames drawn on your TV screen every second. First the odd number lines 1 through 525 are drawn. Next the even number lines are drawn 2 through 524. These two line fields make one picture frame. The result of the 60 fields is the 30 frames.

The two oscillators run free and produce this precise screen full of light as long as your TV is on, regardless of whether the TV transmitter is on or not.

Now that's what your horizontal and vertical circuits should be doing. Let's see what happens when they start doing what they're not supposed to.

TROUBLE NO. 13 — HORIZONTAL LINES

When the horizontal oscillator begins drifting away from the 15,750 CPS, instead of a picture your TV displays a screen full of horizontal lines. The further away from 15,750 the oscillator gets the more lines appear on your screen.

In older TV's this circuit was quite unstable and there were many components and horizontal frequency controls. In the past few years the TV's dispense with all that and the circuits are quite stable. If you have an old TV, refer to the old alignment notes for your particular set. However, if your TV is under six years old the following quick checks are applicable.

Replace the HORIZONTAL OSCILLATOR tube. Next major suspect is the HORIZONTAL PHASE DETECTOR. In some sets it's a tube but in most sets it's a silicon dual diode. Some of them plug in, others must be soldered in. Be sure to get the right type. There are three types and they all look physically the same. They are not interchangeable.

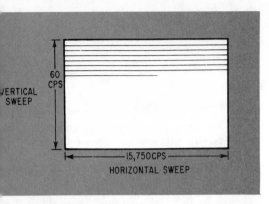

Raster is caused by two sweeps: 15,750 CPS horizontal line sweep and 60 CPS vertical.

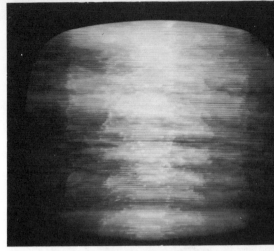

If horizontal oscillator drifts from 15,750 CPS or gets out of phase, this is the effect.

When horizontal sync is lost, the picture whirls off into horizontal lines like this.

When picture rolls sideways, the trouble is in the horizontal phase, not the oscillator.

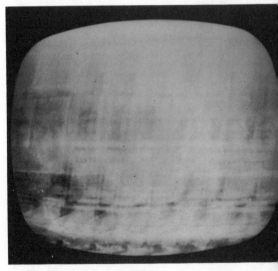

Next step is to try adjusting the HORIZONTAL FREQUENCY and HORIZONTAL PHASE coils. Be sure to use only the correct tool: a hex head neut stick for powered cores (otherwise you'll crumble them) and a screwdriver for metal adjustments.

Should none of these measures cause a fix you have one last chance and it's a good one. Take your spray can of FREEZE MIST, and with the TV on,

spray all the little components, one at a time, in the area of the horizontal oscillator and phase detector circuits.

Should your picture clear or change its appearance drastically as you freeze a component change that component. It's probably the troublemaker.

There are two variations of this same trouble. In older TV's they had a separate cure, but in more recent models use the same technique I just covered. These

41

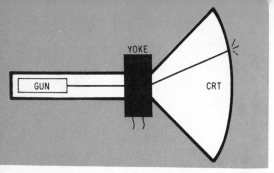

Yoke is contrivance that grabs the cathode ray and keeps it moving on the TV screen.

There are three kinds of diodes: common cathodes, common anodes, series cathodes.

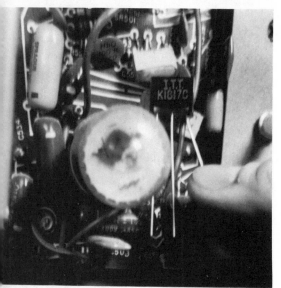

Diodes replace horizontal phase detector tube. Some plug in, most need soldering.

Never use metal screwdriver in horizontal phase coil. Electrical effects crumble coil.

If you freeze capacitor and it has a large effect on picture, it's probably the bad one.

When bends appear without heavy black hum bars, trouble may be in sync circuits.

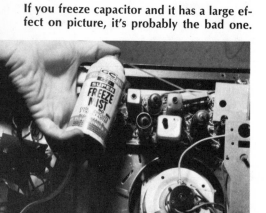

two troubles are **Trouble No. 14—Christmas Tree Effect** and **Trouble No. 15—Horizontal Split Picture.** The next trouble in line is called:

TROUBLE NO. 16—THE BENDS

When the TV performers get twisted faces or spinal curvatures it can be a horizontal circuit or sync circuit problem. Try replacing the HORIZONTAL OUTPUT, the HORIZONTAL OSCILLATOR, HORIZONTAL PHASE DETECTOR, SYNC SEPARATOR, NOISE CANCELLER and any other tubes with word SYNC in its nomenclature.

A heater to cathode short or change in any of these tubes causes this problem. Also try the freeze mist spray on associated components. This trouble sometimes responds to this technique.

TROUBLE NO. 17— POOR HORIZONTAL LINEARITY

The damper circuit, in addition to dampening spurious flyback oscillations, ends up with a rectified output like a power supply. Its output is higher than the low voltage supply and is called boost B-plus. It produces about 600 volts DC. This voltage is fed to output tubes such as the horizontal, vertical and audio.

When the damper circuit weakens, especially because of a weak DAMPER tube this boost B-plus lowers and one of the results is poor horizontal sweeping of the CRT screen. An extreme case is a picture that exhibits a shrink from one side and an oversweep on the other. A circle on the screen looks like a flat-headed egg lying on its side.

Also, white vertical lines can appear. A slightly weak damper just pulls the picture out of shape slightly. A TV performer will have one large shoulder and one narrow one.

You can attempt the cure by replacing the DAMPER and the HORIZONTAL OUTPUT. Also by adjusting the HORIZONTAL DRIVE CONTROLS, LINEARITY and WIDTH CONTROLS.

TROUBLE NO. 18— VERTICAL ROLL

The vertical problems can be a little less obvious than the horizontal. Analyze them a little further before you attack. Try adjusting the vertical hold control to see if you can stop this movie film type slipping action. If the picture can be stopped but won't lock in, test the

FLOPOVER

TROUBLE	REMEDY
Horizontal Lines	Replace horizontal oscillator
	Horizontal Phase detector tube or dual diode
Christmas Tree Effect	Adjust horizontal frequency phase coils with neut stick Freeze mist all associated components
Horizontal Split Picture	Replace those that cause extreme change or clear trouble
The Bends	Horizontal output, oscillator, phase detector, sync sep., noise cancellor, sync Freeze mist
Poor Horizontal Linearity	Damper—Horizontal output, adjust horizontal drive, linearity, width, pull width sleeve
Vertical Roll	Vertical oscillator out, sync tubes
No Vertical Sweep	Vertical oscillator out Vertical linearity pot
Top & Bottom Shrink Vertical Bottom Foldover Vertical Top Retrace Poor Vertical Linearity	Vertical Height pot, Yoke Freeze mist
Sync Trouble	Sync separator, noise inverter, horiz. phase detector, vertical integrator, vertical oscillator
Barberpole Effect Light Green Screen	Reactance tubes, burst amplifier, burst keyer 3.58 mc oscillator

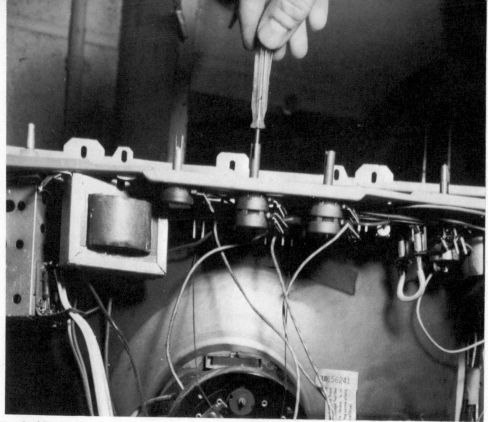

Vertical lin and height controls are usually hidden on chassis. This one's beneath horizontal.

SYNC tubes first and the VERTICAL OSCILLATOR-OUTPUT second. The oscillator is running at the right frequency but there is no lock-in action. When the picture is running and can't be slowed or stopped, check the VERTICAL OSCILLATOR OUTPUT first and the SYNC tubes next, for the oscillator is nowhere near 60 CPS.

TROUBLE NO. 19— NO VERTICAL SWEEP

The clear-cut trouble of one bright white horizontal line needs one immediate service move. Turn the brightness down! All the 525 lines of TV picture are being concentrated on one section of phosphor. Prolonged TV operation in this defective manner will burn a mark across your screen that can only be remedied with a new picture tube.

After that you can try restoring your vertical sweep. Test the VERTICAL

OSCILLATOR OUTPUT and try adjusting the VERTICAL LINEARITY and VERTICAL HEIGHT controls.

Lastly, you can try freezing the associated components. Should you freeze one and the sweep is returned, even slightly, replace that indicated component. It is probably the bad one.

If none of these measures restore, you can try a new YOKE, then call for skilled help.

There are four variations of this trouble, actually minor degrees of no vertical sweep. The exact same repair measures apply. They are **Trouble No. 20 – Top and Bottom Shrink, Trouble No. 21 – Vertical Foldover at Bottom, Trouble No. 22 – Vertical Retrace at Top,** and **Trouble No. 23 – Poor Vertical Linearity.**

There are three points about the LIN and HEIGHT controls to remember. 1) Lots of times adjusting these controls throws the vertical frequency off and you must continually readjust the vertical

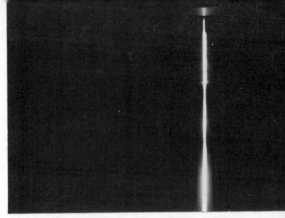

No vertical sweep requires you to turn down brightness so it won't burn trace on tube.

Small degrees of loss of vertical sweep are simply variations of complete loss of sweep.

hold control to see where you are. 2) The VERTICAL LINEARITY control tends to spread the top section of the picture. 3) The VERTICAL HEIGHT control tends to spread the bottom section of the picture.

TROUBLE NO. 24— SYNC TROUBLE

While the two oscillators run free and produce a fine screen full of light the TV transmitter sends a picture to be displayed on the lit screen. It's as if the TV is like a movie projector. The screen full of light is analogous to the bulb in the projector and the TV picture does the same job as the movie film. That is, it intercepts the light to produce different shades of gray on the screen.

The TV transmission also contains three special lock-in signals, one to lock the horizontal oscillator, two to lock the vertical oscillator and three to lock the color oscillator.

Should you lose the horizontal sync signal you'll lose horizontal sync causing all the aforementioned horizontal troubles. The same also applies for vertical and color sync.

There is a special hookup into the path the signal takes that siphons off a portion of the signal. This sampling is then sent into the SYNC SEPARATOR and its

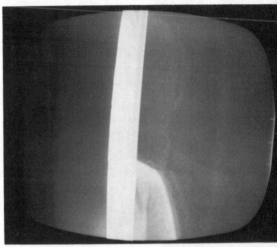

When picture scrunches up or exhibits poor horizontal linearity, first check is damper.

If vertical and horizontal aren't locked in, sync trouble results. Sync circuit's suspect.

Complete sync circuits except for tube are often found in one printed circuit unit.

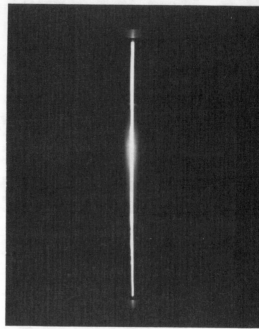

Turn brightness down when this occurs. Then you can go about trying to cure the trouble.

On some sets No Vertical Sweep will look like this rather than just a line of light.

For vertical trouble on set, try adjusting the vertical linearity and vertical size control.

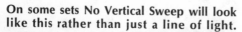

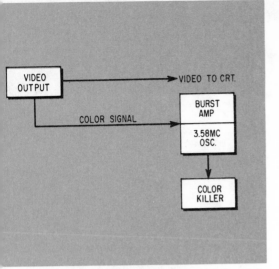

Color sync signal is called burst; it has job of turning on color and running oscillator.

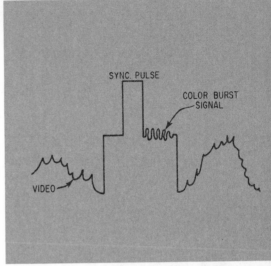

Color burst is found on back porch of composite signal near horizontal and vertical.

associate circuit the NOISE CANCELLER or NOISE INVERTER.

In these circuits the horizontal and vertical sync components are separated and the horizontal signal is sent to the HORIZONTAL PHASE DETECTOR as the vertical signal is sent to the VERTICAL INTEGRATOR and on to the VERTICAL OSCILLATOR.

Should your TV display sync trouble those are the tubes to change. The VERTICAL INTEGRATOR is not a tube or solid state diode. It is a little printed circuit component that contains a bunch of resistors and capacitors and is soldered into place between the separator and the vertical oscillator. It shapes and gives the proper voltage to the vertical sync pulse and then feeds it to the vertical oscillator.

TROUBLE NO. 25 —
BARBER POLE EFFECT

This trouble gets its name from one variation of the trouble. That is when the colors roll slowly through the picture. The barber pole is laying on its side, however, since the colors roll from a horizontal plane. Other forms of the

same thing are stationary stripes across the picture or quick intermittent shimmering of the rainbow from top to bottom.

Any of the color sync tubes will cause the condition. They are the REACTANCE tubes, BURST AMPLIFIER, BURST KEYER and 3.58 MC OSCILLATOR.

Loss of color sync occurs only while the black and white picture itself remains locked firmly in place. Should the horizontal and/or vertical sync also be out, you probably do not have a color sync problem but conventional sync trouble.

TROUBLE NO. 26 —
LIGHT GREEN SCREEN

This trouble does not in any respect look like loss of color sync. Yet it is caused by the loss of the burst signal (color sync). The barber pole occurs when the burst is weak, the light green screen by the burst being missing.

This light green screen problem is entirely different from the bright green screen trouble that will be covered in Chapter 10.

To cure a light green screen use exact measures as needed for barber pole.

Causes of weak contrast like this range from tuner input all the way to picture tube input.

WHEN CONTRAST'S THE CULPRIT

Don't confuse it with brightness:

Contrast has a faulty Y signal

Chapters 3 and 4 dealt with the brightness troubles in a TV set. This chapter is about the CONTRAST troubles that occur. There is much confusion in telling the difference between brightness and contrast. The old analogy comparing a TV set with a movie projector applies here. Just as a movie projector has a bulb causing brightness and film intercepting the brightness to cause contrast, so a TV set has a raster which is brightness and

TV transmitted signal called contrast which intercepts the raster.

You can further separate them by realizing that the brightness is affected by the brightness control and the contrast affected by the contrast control.

This brings us to the title of this chapter. When your brightness quits the TV picture blacks out. When the contrast quits the TV picture whites out leaving the raster.

The contrast enters your TV through the antenna terminals and is fed directly into the tuner. First circuit is the RF AMPLIFIER. Next it passes through the MIXER-OSCILLATOR. From there it leaves the tuner and is further amplified in the first, second and third IF's. From there it goes to a VIDEO DETECTOR and then on into the VIDEO AMPLIFIER and VIDEO OUTPUT. Then it is injected into the cathode of the picture tube. This is true in both black and white and color TV's. In a color TV the contrast is called the Y signal.

Right, many new sets use transistorized tuners and IF stages. Let repairmen do it.

Common cause of contrast loss is this tiny solid state diode. Some simply plug in.

As film is able to intercept a projector's light beam, TV signal can block cathode ray.

Below, route of signal. Contrast control adjusts its strength. Brightness is in the CRT.

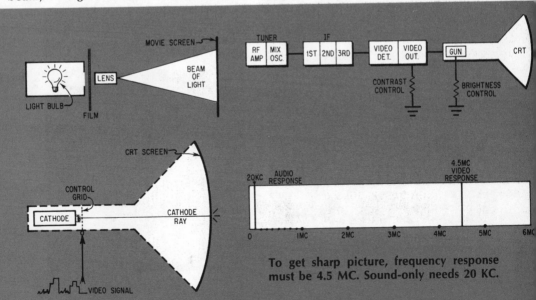

To get sharp picture, frequency response must be 4.5 MC. Sound-only needs 20 KC.

When picture whites out — i.e., only leaves brightness — first check is to test for audio.

PICTURE WHITES OUT

TROUBLE	REMEDY
Raster Only No sound or Pix	Video Detector, IF's, Mixer-Oscillator, Sound Output, Video Amp, Video Output, Picture Tube, AGC
Raster—Sound OK Weak Contrast	
Too Much Contrast	AGC, Noise, Inverter, RF Amp, IF, Video Detector, Amp, Output
Smeary Picture	Video Detector, Amp, Output, Peaking Coil
Negative Picture	Freeze Mist
Pulsating Picture Motorboating	IF Tube, Mixer-Oscillator, RF Amp
Hum Bars	Tuner, IF, Video, Sync, Sound, Color Tubes Picture Tube
Snow	RF Amp—Clean Tuner, B Plus Resistor
No High Band	Mixer-Oscillator
Sound & Pic Won't Tune	RF Amp, Mixer-Oscillator
No UHF	RF—Amp, Mixer-Oscillator, UHF Mix, Oscillator, UHF Diode, UHF Xsistor
No VHF	
Tunable Ghosts	IF, RF Amp, Mixer-Oscillator, Video Detector, Amplifier Output

The main reason for overloaded contrast is usually AGC circuit. First adjust the control.

When there's snow in picture accompanied by audible static, check the RF amplifier.

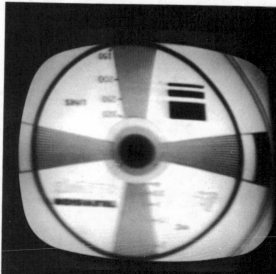

This contrast or Y signal causes the electron beam in the picture tube to flow in full force (a bright spot), cut the flow off altogether (a black spot), or simply reduce some of the electron flow (a gray spot).

The Y signal contains frequencies all the way up to 4.5 million cycles per second (megacycles). For when a change in a TV picture takes place from black to white, the change is taking place in one four millionth of a second. If it doesn't the picture will smear.

As you can see, a video change in a TV is much higher than an audio change since the highest audible audio is only 20,000 cycles per second (kilocycles).

When the Y signal has good frequency response a good sharp picture appears. When it doesn't you'll see one of the following 14 contrast troubles.

TROUBLE NO. 27 —
NO CONTRAST, NO SOUND

When the light is on the screen but there is no contrast and no sound, the trouble usually has occurred in an area before the contrast and sound are separated from one another. This would mean testing the VIDEO DETECTOR, the IF's and the MIXER-OSCILLATOR. As a fast try you can test the RF AMPLIFIER, but when it goes it usually is accompanied by a snow symptom.

Smeary B&W picture is caused by a loss of frequency response. Check video circuits.

Another cause that seems unusual, but is common, is the SOUND OUTPUT tube. In many of the recent TV's the IF's are powered from the sound output circuit, so a fault here causes IF type symptoms.

Lastly, every now and then there is the occasion where two faults occur — one in the sound circuits and another in the picture circuits. As a last resort look for this double trouble that causes this symptom.

TROUBLE NO. 28 —
NO CONTRAST, SOUND OK

This trouble, though resembling the last, is quite different. If the sound is good the trouble spot is probably after the place where the sound and picture are separated. This makes the VIDEO AMPLIFIER, VIDEO OUTPUT and PICTURE TUBE prime suspects. In some color TV's there are separate audio and video detectors. In these sets the VIDEO DETECTOR becomes a suspect.

TROUBLE NO. 29 —
WEAK CONTRAST

The common reasons for this condition are the VIDEO OUTPUT tube or SOUND OUTPUT tube getting weak. Otherwise this is the same as the last two troubles except it's not as severe. To

All diodes have polarity, including this tiny one. Make sure you install it correctly.

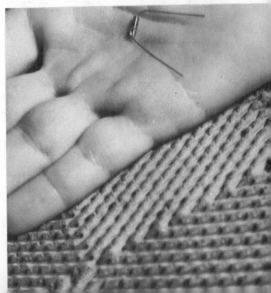

really pinpoint the trouble try to analyze whether the sound is lower, too. If it is, then you have a variation of NO CONTRAST, NO SOUND. If the sound is good then you have a variation of NO CONTRAST, SOUND OK. Don't try to analyze the audio too carefully. If it's not apparently bad or good, test out all systems in both of the trouble types.

TROUBLE NO. 30—
TOO MUCH CONTRAST

Too much contrast usually occurs when there is an AGC problem. The Automatic Gain Control, better thought of as an automatic contrast control, is supplementary to the regular contrast control. It works like a thermostat. When the picture signal gets too strong it turns it down a bit.

The AGC circuit takes a continuous sampling of the contrast signal from the video output. The AGC circuit also has a hookup into the RF amplifier and first two IF's. When the AGC senses that the contrast is getting too strong it instantaneously sends an impulse to the RF-IF that cuts back on their amplification, thus reducing the contrast.

When the AGC circuit fails, the contrast gets too strong. There is an AGC control. First step is to adjust it. Next test the AGC keyer, AGC amplifier,

AGC clamper or any other circuit calling itself AGC. Next test the NOISE INVERTER and then the RF AMPLIFIER and IF tubes. LASTLY, try the VIDEO DETECTOR and VIDEO AMP and OUTPUT. They are all involved and can all cause this symptom.

TROUBLE NO. 31—
SMEARY PICTURE AND
TROUBLE NO. 32—
NEGATIVE PICTURE

While these two troubles are different phenomena they are for the most part caused by the same defective components. A smeary picture occurs when the video frequency response is lost. A negative picture occurs due to whites going black and vice versa.

However, both troubles happen when a defect develops in the VIDEO DETECTOR, VIDEO AMPLIFIER, VIDEO OUTPUT, IF strip or the PICTURE TUBE itself.

Test those tubes and circuits in that order. Should you discover that your problem is the VIDEO DETECTOR and it happens to be a tiny germanium diode, be sure you install the new one with the correct polarity. If you should reverse it the same trouble is likely to appear on the screen and you'll think you have another bad part in there. You'll never find

AGC circuit has job of reducing gain in RF Amp and first two IF's during strong signals.

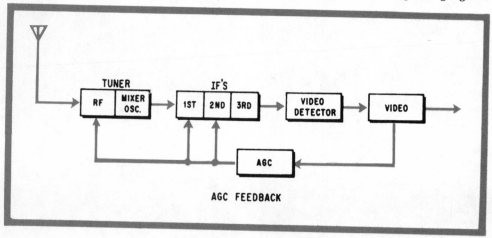

Open peaking coil causes smeary or negative picture. Make jumper wire quick test.

Pulsating picture vibrating horizontally usually means an IF tube that is oscillating.

Common cause of No Contrast is audio output tube, since cathode feeds B plus to the IF's.

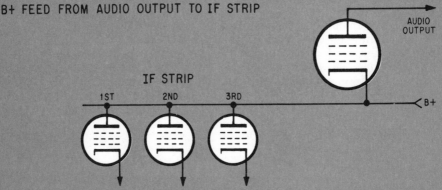

B+ FEED FROM AUDIO OUTPUT TO IF STRIP

AUDIO OUTPUT

IF STRIP

1ST   2ND   3RD

B+

With Sound But No Contrast, condition is after detector. No sound, says trouble is before.

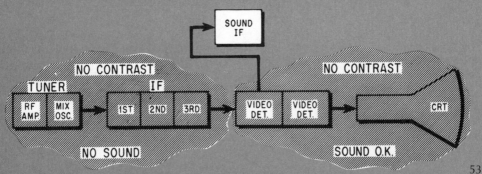

SOUND IF

NO CONTRAST

TUNER   IF

RF AMP   MIX OSC.   1ST   2ND   3RD

NO CONTRAST

VIDEO DET.   VIDEO DET.   CRT

NO SOUND

SOUND O.K.

Be sure to reinstall tube shields when you replace IF tubes. Otherwise they can detune.

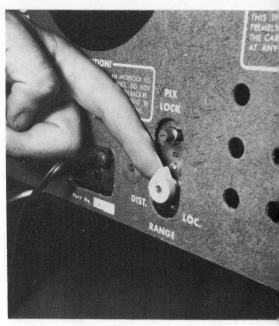

Don't overlook local-distant switches as a cause for Weak Contrast or No Contrast.

that other bad part and will be frustrated in the repair.

If you have a smeary picture and it's not a tube, chances are good it's a PEAKING COIL. The test is easy. Jump the peaking coils one by one with your jumper wire. A noticeable improvement will appear on the screen when you jump the bad one.

As a last resort you can try freezing the components in these circuits. Odds are you'll stumble on the bad one.

TROUBLE NO. 33 — PULSATING PICTURE

The symptoms in this trouble can be quite disconcerting. It comes in three variations. 1) the sound and picture can be popping in and out. While it's in, it's perfect, while it's out just a raster remains. 2) the TV will come on perfectly, then little by little the picture becomes more contrasting, then it begins to pulse and vibrate. 3) no sound or picture will come on at all, just a motorboat noise

from the speaker and a pulsating raster on the screen with a lot of black bars in it.

Most of the time one and two turns out to be a bad IF tube, and number three turns out to be the MIXER-OSCILLA-TOR tube. Try these tubes for both troubles. As a last resort try the RF AMPLI-FIER. If none of these help you probably have a serious bench repair in the tuner or IF strip.

TROUBLE NO. 34 — HUM BARS

Whether the hum bars are in black and white or color they are in nine out of ten cases caused by a heater to cathode short in a tube. If it's not a tube it's a filter and needs filter capacitor techniques as reviewed in Chapter 2's INPUT FILTER section. Only you must test all the filters, not just the input.

The tube testing is best accomplished by direct substitution, although the drug store tester might pick out the bad one for you. The little heater tester is of no use with this trouble.

54

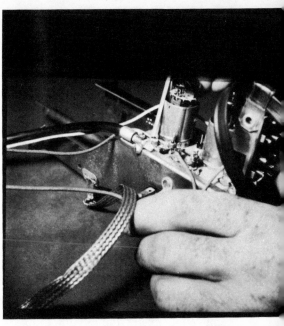

Snow on screen without any contrast means trouble in the tuner and not in the IF strip.

Tuner can be removed from set quite easily. It's compact and can be shipped for repair.

There are a lot of suspects. You'll have to check every tube in the tuner, IF strip, video circuits, sound circuits, sync circuits and color circuits and picture tube. The only tubes you won't have to check are the vertical and horizontal sweep and high voltage.

Front End Fixes: The big confusion in front end troubles is deciding whether the trouble is due to problems in the tuner or in the antenna. Then once you decide it is a tuner trouble you must ascertain whether it is an electrical problem or a mechanical problem.

TROUBLE NO. 35 — SNOW

This is the main tuner trouble symptom. It can occur with or without sound or picture, only on certain channels, be intermittent, erratic or what have you. The main thing is, no matter what else is occurring, there is a snow fall.

The first step is to eliminate the antenna as the trouble source since it too causes exactly the same kind of snow.

Attach a spare pair of rabbit ears to the antenna terminals instead of the antenna being used. This goes for UHF as well as VHF. If the trouble clears, the tuner is not at fault. Should the same condition persist, the tuner is the troublemaker.

An alternative procedure is to take another known good TV and attach it to the suspect antenna. If the second TV does the same thing it's the antenna. However, should the second TV work well the first TV contains the trouble.

Next step is to decide whether the trouble is electronic or mechanical. Rotate the tuner and press it a little bit. If a good picture returns, even momentarily, the trouble is probably mechanical.

After all that, here is what you'll probably find. The trouble is a combination of mechanical and electrical problems. The RF AMPLIFIER tube is weak and the tuner could use a cleaning. Replace the RF AMP and take some tuner lube and spray it into the tuner innards. Then rotate the channel selector knob. This blanket approach is usually a cure-all.

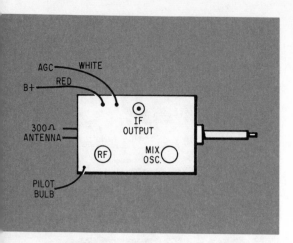

AGC — WHITE
B+ — RED
300Ω ANTENNA
IF OUTPUT
RF
MIX OSC.
PILOT BULB

·If you remove a tuner, make a sketch of inputs so you won't make a wiring error.

Should the snow and erratic action be a little more stubborn you can go further. Remove the cover from the tuner, take a pencil eraser and gently erase the black spots on the electrical contacts in the tuner. Then respray with the tuner lube. That should do the trick. If it doesn't there is one more little trick.

With the TV still on feel the RF AMP tube. It should run quite hot. If it runs lukewarm it means the heaters are on but the B plus voltage is not reaching it. Take a bright light and look over the outside and inside of the tuner for a charred resistor. Quite often you can spot it visually. Then determine its value and replace it. You'll probably effect a cure. Be sure to replace the RF AMP tube too. It has shorted and burnt out the resistor.

Should the trouble remain, stop and call for skilled help. You are getting into deep water.

TROUBLE NO. 36— NO HIGH BAND

As the channel numbers go up, the MIXER-OSCILLATOR must run at higher and higher frequencies. Sometimes a tube becomes defective and won't run too high. In fact, it might run good on the low band, channels 2 through 6, but quit in the high band, 7

through 13. A new MIXER-OSCILLATOR will usually cure. If it doesn't, don't go any further in this trouble.

TROUBLE NO. 37— SOUND & PICTURE WON'T TUNE

This trouble is usually due to a tuner being out of alignment. Sometimes it goes out of alignment due to the tuner tubes. Try replacing the RF AMPLIFIER and the MIXER-OSCILLATOR. If the trouble clears, fine; if not, that's the end of the line for the do-it-yourselfer on this trouble.

TROUBLE NO. 38—NO UHF, VHF GOOD AND TROUBLE NO. 39—NO VHF, UHF GOOD

This requires testing of the tubes in the respective tuners as the first quick step. Then in No. 38 NO UHF there are two more attempts that produce high percentage results. There is a germanium diode resembling a video detector. Try replacing it, observing polarity. Lastly, most UHF tuners today use a transistor. It goes bad more often than the other components in the tuner. Obtain a correct replacement and install it. Chances are good you'll cure No. 38.

TROUBLE NO. 40— TUNABLE GHOSTS

The only ghosts that can occur due to tuner trouble is a tunable ghost. That is, with the ghosts in full view try adjusting the fine tuner control. If the ghosts do not change they are due to antenna difficulties. Should they change drastically as you rotate the fine tuner they are being caused by the TV.

Tunable ghosts is a sister trouble to No. 33 PULSATING PICTURE and the exact same repair measures are used. Test the IF tube, the tuner tubes and also check the VIDEO DETECTOR, VIDEO AMPLIFIER and VIDEO OUTPUT. If none of these measures

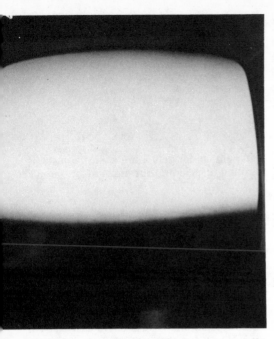

In B&W or color these hum bars are usually caused by a heater to cathode tube short.

Check TV filters by jumping another one across it. If bars go away, that's bad one.

Quick clean job for erratic action is to spray tuner lube into tuner, then rotate slowly.

If spray won't work, use ordinary eraser to get carbon off contacts — and then spray.

At left, this is usually an alignment job. Best repair is simply replace tuner tubes.

At right, older sets were easily adjustable around oscillator, but newer sets aren't.

Below, a common cause of No UHF stations is bad UHF transistor. You should replace it.

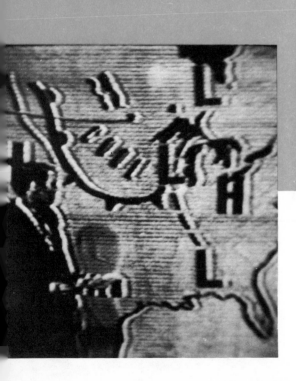

At left, tunable ghost can sometimes be corrected by checking the IF and video tubes.

cure, you probably have an RF-IF alignment job on your hands. Call for help if that is the case.

Now about those little screws and hex head adjustments sticking out all over the tuner. Don't touch them unless you have the proper tools and factory service notes. In the older TV's a do-it-yourselfer could line up the oscillator slugs from the front. Not today, however. The newer portable and color tuners have all kinds of unusual ways of adjustments.

By turning the wrong screw, you can cause all kind of trouble, from losing a channel to killing color.

One thing you can do, however. Once you determine for sure that you do have tuner troubles either electrical or mechanical you can take or mail it to a tuner repair center. Just remove the defective tuner from your TV (be sure you sketch the connections) and send it off to a repair center. For a nominal fee they will repair it and send it back.

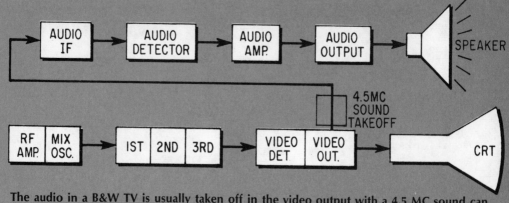

The audio in a B&W TV is usually taken off in the video output with a 4.5 MC sound can. The audio in a color set has a separate sound detector that works alongside video detector.

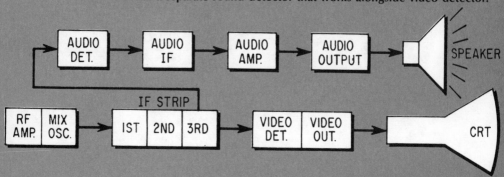

REPAIRING TV SOUND

Always begin the probe at 4.5 MC transformer or germanium detector

The sound section of a TV is almost exactly like the rear end of an FM radio. It gets its signal in a black-and-white TV from a sound takeoff transformer in the video output stage labeled 4.5 MC takeoff. It gets its signal in a color set from a separate sound detector that works like a video detector and is located right near the video detector.

When you have a sound-only trouble you start investigations at the 4.5 MC transformer in a monochrome set and at the germanium sound detector in a color set.

TROUBLE NO. 41 — NO SOUND

When this condition happens in a radio, usual technique has as its first step placing one's finger on the center top of the volume control. The control is about dead center in a radio circuit. A finger touch induces a hum. If one hears the hum it means sound can go from there to the speaker. Therefore the rear half of the radio is good and the trouble is indicated to be in the front half.

Should no hum emanate from the

Buzz controls on chassis rear aprons are popular in new sets. They are easy to adjust.

Business end of audio section is audio output transformer, large resistors, speaker.

Good test for spotting microphonic tubes is tapping. Bad ones cause racket from speaker.

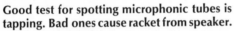

When bars appear in step with sound, try all output tubes. A gassy one can cause it.

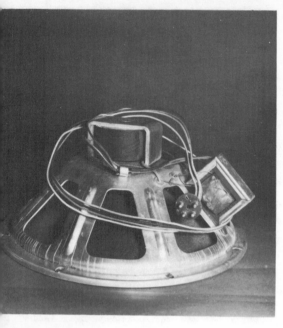

Large expensive sets have large speakers.
Don't puncture paper cone when handling.

Often a minute adjustment of FM detector
will clear up a low or muffled TV sound.

In case the FM detector needs adjustment
it's the coil itself that needs replacing.

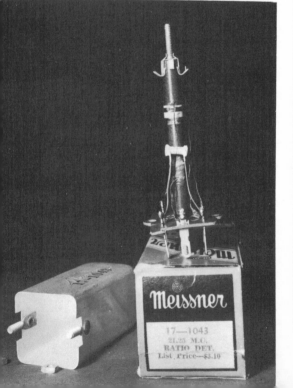

ALL ABOUT FIXING TV SOUND

TROUBLE	REMEDY
No sound Dead Speaker	Audio Output Tube, Audio Output Transformer, High Wattage B Plus Audio Output Resistors
No Sound Background Noise, Inoperative Volume Control	Audio Output Tube, Audio Amp Tube
No sound, Background Noise, Volume Control Works	Audio IF, Audio Detector
Poor Sound	Audio Output, Amp, Detector, Audio IF, Adjust FM Detector, Speaker
Sound Bars in Picture	Audio Output, Vertical Output, Horizontal Output, Mixer-Oscillator, IF Tubes

Rubbing cone or voice coil can cause muffling. The only cure is to install a new one.

speaker the rear half is indicated as the bad half.

In a TV, though, touching your finger to the center top does not induce a hum and might even produce a shock. However, another procedure using the same logic can be used.

Place your ear near the speaker and rotate the volume control with the TV on. There will be one of three results: no sound, background noise but no volume control effect, or a noticeable effect as you crank up the control.

When the speaker is dead test the AUDIO OUTPUT tube, the audio output transformer and any large wattage resistors feeding B plus to the output stage.

If there is some background noise but no volume control effect test the AUDIO OUTPUT and AUDIO AMPLIFIER tubes.

Should the volume control have some effect test the AUDIO IF and AUDIO DETECTOR.

As a last resort test all the audio sections mentioned even though they are not indicated by professional technique.

TROUBLE NO. 42—
POOR SOUND

When the TV performers speak in garbled tones, test all the audio circuits right off. First test is to tap the audio tubes with a pencil. If any of them ping or crackle it's probably bad and needs replacement. Be careful, though, that you catch the right one. The noisy tube is that way because it has loose elements and if you tap an adjoining tube the bad one might still ping.

When a tube doesn't cure the condition, examine the speaker. It might have a hole or tear in it that is causing the problem. It could also have a sticky voice coil. Substituting a good one tells the tale.

Lastly, muffled sound is caused by FM detector drift. Find the FM detector can and adjust it with a hex-head alignment stick. Just a slight turn on the top or bottom core will cure the condition. Should the touch-up alignment cure for a while, but the trouble returns, you'll probably need a new detector can.

TROUBLE NO. 43—
SOUND BARS IN PICTURE

If you have a good picture but the picture quivers in time with the sound, some of the sound output is getting into the video circuit. The sound can get in there due to a defect in one of the output tubes. They are all fed from the same boost B plus supply and when they draw too much current they affect each other.

For sound bars, try a new AUDIO OUTPUT tube, a new VERTICAL OUTPUT tube and a new HORIZONTAL OUTPUT tube. It will probably be one of them. If it's not, try the MIXER-OSCILLATOR and IF strip tubes as a last resort.

The fine tuner is important for proper color. With wrong settings you can lose the color.

PROPERLY ADJUSTING THE COLORS

The four key areas here deal with hue control, color level, color killer and tint control

There are only three and occasionally four adjustments that deal exclusively with color. All the rest of the many adjustments have to do with setting up a good black and white picture on a color screen. These are dealt with in the next chapter.

The color-only adjustments are the HUE control, the COLOR LEVEL control, the COLOR KILLER control and on some TV's a TINT control.

As a color TV set owner and do-it-yourself repairman you must have an idea of their workings.

Fine Tuner: Before touching any of the color adjustments you must be sure the fine tuner is set properly. On a black and white there is quite a bit of range where a satisfactory picture is received. Not so on a color TV. There is only one setting and quite often it is critical.

With a strong channel on, rotate the fine tuner through its range. The picture will vary from a dull, interference-free picture, through a center point where sound bars and picture both appear, to a screen full of sound bars only. The correct setting for color is to back off the control till the sound bars just disappear.

Hue Control: The hue control is a front of the cabinet knob that changes the actual color on the screen. The control was designed to control the change by using human flesh tones as the reference point. Therefore a good flesh tone appears near midrange of the control. As you vary the control from one end to another the flesh tones change from purple through normal to green.

Actually you are varying the phase of the color oscillator around its 3.58 MC operating frequency. Don't try to do anything with the HUE control except get a normal flesh tone.

VARYING COLOR

Color Intensity Control: This is the other companion front of the set control. You can set it after or before you adjust the hue control. It varies the amount of color in the picture from none to weak to intense. Once you have a normal flesh tone, adjusting this control will vary that flesh tone from pale through ruddy to orange. Normal should be about midrange. The control works passably as long as you can get enjoyable colors even though cranking it all the way up won't produce orange.

There is quite a bit of confusion among set owners as to the use of these two controls. Get these two simple adjustments down pat and you'll eliminate a lot of TV service false alarms.

Tint Control: In a lot of new color TV's, Admiral and Motorola, for instance, a third front of the set control is installed. It is called TINT or COLOR FIDELITY. (This is not to be confused with some HUE controls that are labeled TINT. In those cases there is no third control.)

Color subcarrier rides 3.58 MC away from picture carrier on transmitted TV signal.

On this set, color tint is a dual control in combination with the background knob.

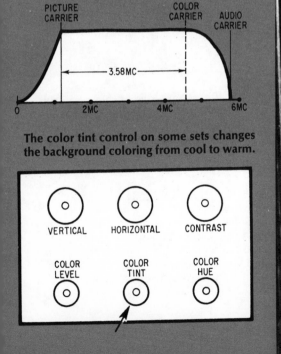

The color tint control on some sets changes the background coloring from cool to warm.

Hue control changes the actual color of picture — flesh from purple through green.

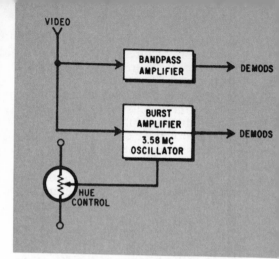

Hue control, hooked into color oscillator, changes the actual color of the TV picture.

Adjusting the Intensity control changes the vividness of color — from pale to brilliant.

Color level control, hooked into the color amplifiers, changes the set's color intensity.

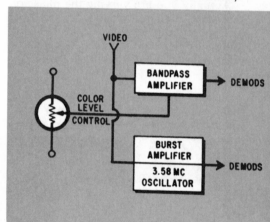

This TINT control is not truly a color-only control since it works all the time whether a color show is on or not. The HUE and COLOR INTENSITY are completely inoperative when a black and white show is being presented. They only work when a color show is on.

This TINT control does this all the time. It varies the black and white picture from shades of green through black and white through shades of blue.

This tint control enables you to vary the tint of the picture from warm (by adding the greens) to cool (by adding the blues). If you have one of these controls, realize its operation or else you'll cause the wrong colors to appear on the screen. Frankly it's a feature I can't see much use to. Best thing to do is set it on black and white and forget about it.

SHUTS DOWN CIRCUITS

Color Killer: The color killer is covered in Chapter 10 with its troubles. The color killer has this job: During a black and white program it turns on. As it goes on it shuts down the entire group of color

Color killer, only color control on rear panel, sets threshold for color signal input.

Washed out color can be due to low setting of AGC control. Always double check it.

Below, leave the gear controls on an older set alone. Use them to set up B&W picture.

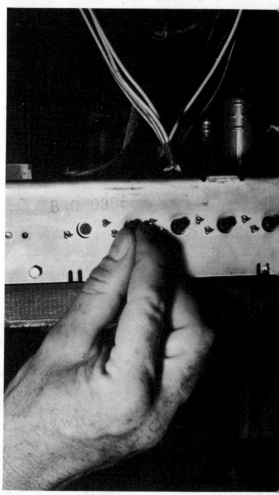

circuits; otherwise color interference will appear on the black and white picture. Such things as colored snow, colored sound bars, colored auto ignition noise, etc., would flash annoyingly across the screen except for the color killer.

When a color show starts, the color killer circuit shuts off and allows the rest of the color circuits to come back on normally.

The killer circuit is critical and needs an adjustment in case minor changes occur in the killer's components. The control is located mostly on the chassis rear

apron but sometimes it can be found on the front of the TV under a service panel or behind one of the knobs. Your service notes will tell you where.

It is adjusted like this. Turn on a black and white program. Turn the killer control up till color streaks come through the picture. Then slowly turn the killer down just till the streaks disappear. That's the correct setting.

If you overadjust you'll place it at a setting where the killer won't permit the color programming to appear at all. Set it right.

HOW TO TOUCH UP THE COLOR

Good black and white assures

you of good color picture

The name of this chapter is really misleading. For all these controls we're going to discuss, although they are exclusively color TV adjustments, are not really color adjustments. They are manipulated strictly to produce a black and white picture on the color TV. Once a satisfactory black and white picture is produced, the color picture will automatically come in beautifully.

These controls that work you toward a perfect black and white picture on a color TV are there to eliminate four color troubles. Let's go through them one by one.

Degaussing or demagnetizing is an easy procedure you can do once you obtain the gadget.

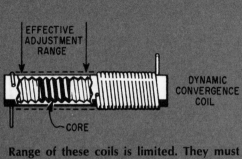

EFFECTIVE ADJUSTMENT RANGE

DYNAMIC CONVERGENCE COIL

CORE

Range of these coils is limited. They must be in a spot where they affect the picture.

Below, if vertical top or bottom is bowed and can't be straightened, check 2 controls.

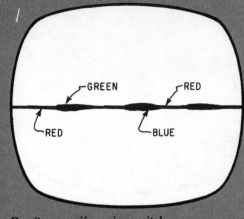

GREEN RED

RED BLUE

Don't worry if service switch causes wrong colors in the line. It's just purity trouble.

Below, if the horizontal, especially blue, is bowed, check the statics once again.

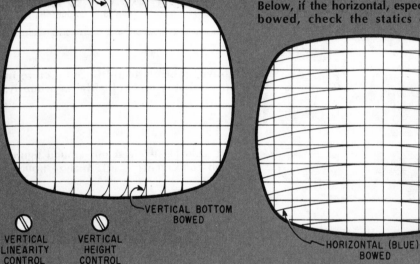

VERTICAL TOP BOWED

VERTICAL BOTTOM BOWED

VERTICAL LINEARITY CONTROL

VERTICAL HEIGHT CONTROL

HORIZONTAL (BLUE) BOWED

TROUBLE NO. 44— TINTED SCREEN

Ideally, you shouldn't be able to tell a color TV from a black and white TV during a black and white show. While you'll probably never be able to achieve such perfection you can come close.

A color TV reveals its identity when a black and white picture comes in tinted. It can be tinted pink, green, blue, yellow or what have you. When it's tinted there-by, all over the screen the obvious service attempts are directed at restoring real blacks, grays and whites instead of the tinting.

The restoration is accomplished by manipulation of the seven GRAY SCALE adjustments. They are found on the rear apron of the TV chassis or under a panel in the front. They are named the SERVICE SWITCH, RED SCREEN, BLUE SCREEN, GREEN SCREEN, CRT BIAS, BLUE DRIVE and

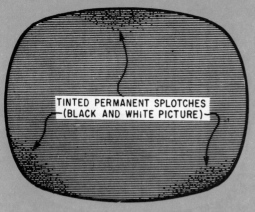

TINTED PERMANENT SPLOTCHES
(BLACK AND WHITE PICTURE)

If picture gets color splotches in a few spots, it's because the purity's not right.

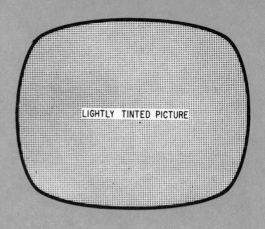

LIGHTLY TINTED PICTURE

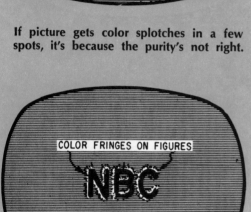

COLOR FRINGES ON FIGURES

NBC

(BLACK AND WHITE PICTURE)

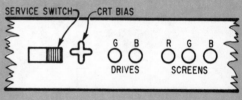

SERVICE SWITCH   CRT BIAS

G B   R G B
DRIVES   SCREENS

Above, controls to rid tinted picture in effect simply mix color lights properly.

Left, colors will bleed out around figures when convergence is off. Analyze trouble.

GREEN DRIVE. Most of the time only the first four mentioned are needed.

You have a tinted picture because the three primary light colors—red, green and blue—are not properly mixed on your TV screen. Here's how you can re-mix to get a good gray scale.

With normal brightness and contrast, turn on the service switch. The picture will collapse into a horizontal line at screen center. Rotate into three lines, one red, one green and one blue. Next turn all three screen controls completely off. The three colored lines should disappear one by one. Then try each screen control on its own by turning it up, then back down. You should be able to produce each color line.

As long as all three lines do appear all you are going to need are the three screen adjustments. Turn up red till you can just see it in a normally lighted room. Then turn up green to the same intensity. Where the lines touch they'll mix to produce yellow. Next turn up the blue till you can just see it. Where all three lines touch, a white line will be produced. Finally, turn off the service switch. A good black and white picture will appear. All tinting will be gone.

All the adjustments around CRT neck in color TV are to set up the black and white.

Flick service switch for good gray scale. This causes three colored horizontal lines.

Next step is adjusting screen controls to mix red, green and blue lights properly.

If one screen control won't cause light, turn up CRT bias till screen shows light.

GRAY SCALE

On some occasions you will try the gray scale setup and run into this confusing situation. You flick your service switch, turn down your screen controls and then begin the procedure. However, when you turn your first screen control back, usually red, a pure red line does not appear on the picture tube face.

In slight cases of this condition a reddish line will appear but there will be other colors in the red line too. There could be a length of white, red-green, red-blue or what have you.

In extreme cases of this complication instead of a red line a green line might appear, or a blue line. This usually throws repairers for a loss.

Actually what is happening is, the red electron stream is hitting the wrong color phosphor. It is an extreme case of POOR PURITY. If you follow the purity procedure in the next trouble number 45 you'll probably cure it. Usually the purity ring is way off its correct setting. Simply restore the vertical sweep with the service switch and work toward a red field. (An upside down purity ring can cause a dull picture with almost no brightness.)

71

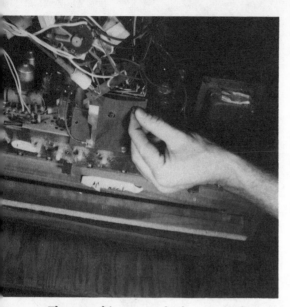

The two drive controls that mix lights are supplementary to the three screen controls.

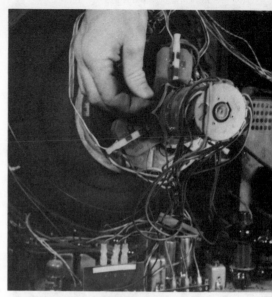

When splotches appear near screen center, you can remedy this with the purity tabs.

Horizontal Hold: On rare occasions a misadjusted horizontal hold control can cause this described effect too. Be sure the hold control is adjusted if the trouble persists.

NEEDS BOOST

CRT BIAS: In the event one or more of the color lines do not appear, it usually means your color picture tube is showing wear and needs a boosting of brightness.

Begin the gray scale procedure again. Turn down all three controls. Then turn the screen up that's not making a line. For instance, let's say there is no red horizontal line. Turn up the red screen control all the way while the blue and green screen controls are turned down all the way. There will be no light on the picture tube face. Adjust the CRT BIAS till the red just appears. Then readjust the blue and green for your gray scale mixture.

That takes care of all the controls except the blue and green drives. These act like supplementary blue and green screen controls. Therefore should you perform gray scale procedure and still note a hint of tint in the picture you can go to these two controls. Don't turn them far. Try to turn them up as little as possible.

If the picture has hints of blue, turn the blue drive down a bit. If there are hints of green turn the green drive down a bit. If the picture is pinkish, turn both blue and green drive up a bit to mix with the pink to produce grays.

TROUBLE NO. 45 — POOR PURITY

The most popular misconception of all color TV rumors is, "you can't move it, once it's set." Like all other rumors, there is a grain of truth to it. The three electron beams in the color picture tube are affected in a slight manner by the earth's magnetic field, just like a magnetic compass. The effect in the TV picture is permanent color splotches, especially around the perimeter of the tube.

The same type of trouble can happen with the TV just sitting in place. Some

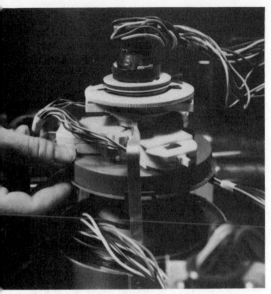

If splotches appear around screen's edge, it's easily adjusted by moving the yoke.

COLOR ADJUSTMENT CHART	
TROUBLE	REMEDY
No Color	Fine Tuner—Color Intensity Color Killer
Wrong Colors	Hue—Tint—Purity Procedure
Color Interference	Fine Tuner—Color Killer
Tinted Screen (All Over Screen)	Gray Scale Tracking
Color Splotches	(Defective Auto Degaussing coil) Degauss—Purity Procedure (Purity Tabs, Screen Center-Yoke, Perimeter)
Bleeding Colors (Screen Center)	Static Convergence (Red Static, Blue Static, Green Static, Blue Lateral)
Bleeding Colors (Around Screen Edges)	Dynamic Convergence (12 controls on Convergence Board)

service manuals advise placing the TV so the picture tube lies in a north-south position. That way there is a minimum magnetic force against the electron beams.

Yes, this does happen and quite often. However, it is usually not too noticeable. Also there are three easy procedures to eliminate poor purity. It turns out also that the easiest one of the three is the one that is needed the most. The other two are not usually necessary unless someone was fooling around with them.

Degaussing: The easiest main purity procedure is degaussing or, to state it simply, demagnetizing. If you take a small pocket magnet and hold it near a color TV picture you'll see the picture distort. This is what happens when a small magnetic field develops somewhere on the bell of the picture tube.

If you demagnetize it, like a jeweler does to a watch, you'll clear the poor purity.

Lots of the newer TV's come equipped with automatic degaussing. One type activates every time you turn the TV on. Another type has a button and you can

degauss manually by simply pressing the button. Other TV's have no provision.

OWN SEPARATE COIL

Unfortunately the set-equipped degaussers are usually weak and will not dislodge a stubborn case of poor purity. It's a good idea for all color TV set owners to own a separate degaussing coil. There are small ones and large ones available at electronic stores.

With a coil, every so often all you have to do is rotate the activated coil around the perimeter of the picture tube. You can do it with the set on or off, before, during or after any repair. It won't hurt a thing. Just keep the coil away from the rear of the TV. You don't want to demagnetize magnets in the set.

Purity Tabs: After degaussing, if some localized splotches still remain, analyze their screen position. Are they around the rim of the tube or near screen center?

You can adjust screen center impurity by adjustment of the purity tabs. Follow this procedure: Turn the blue and green

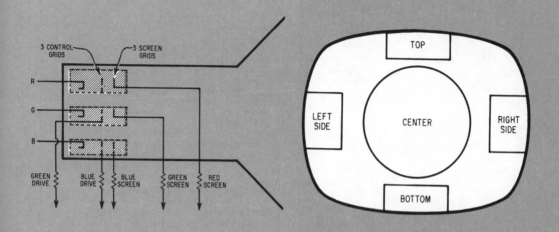

Screen controls turn screen grids up, down. Drive control turns control grids up, down. Right, there are controls for five face sections: center, top, bottom, left, right side.

There are 4 static magnets: red, green and blue statics on convergence yoke, blue lateral. Right, a perfect TV picture will show all dots and bars white and reveal background as black.

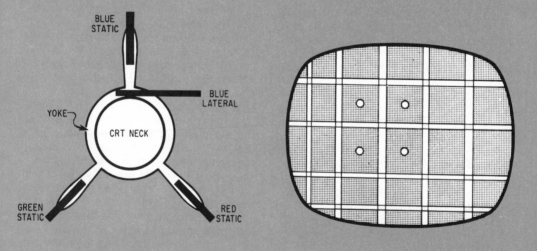

screen controls off. This leaves a red picture. If the picture isn't bright enough turn the red screen up till you get a nicely lit red picture. Then analyze the red picture. It should be uniform throughout the entire face of the tube. If there are any impurities at screen center adjust the two purity tabs that look like centering devices. They will clear center impurities.

Deflection Yoke: The third poor purity procedure is movement back and forth of the yoke. Loosen the bolt that holds it secure. Now, are there any impurities around the edges of the red screen? You can adjust rim and corner impurities by moving the yoke.

There is considerable interaction between the purity tabs and the yoke. The tabs can have some effect on the perimeter and the yoke can cause effect at screen center. Therefore go back and forth from tabs to yoke till a uniform red field is shown. If you like you could even degauss again.

Once satisfied, you can double-check the green and blue by turning down the red screen and turning up the other two one at a time. If the red field was uniform the other two will be too. They are easier to obtain good purity for than the red. However, should you find blue or green impurities go back and check the red. You probably missed a spot on it. Once you get good purity, reset the picture to its proper gray scales with your gray scale adjustments.

TROUBLE NO. 46— BLEEDING COLORS

Bleeding colors are most noticeable during a black and white program on your color TV. Red, green or blue outlines will appear around figures. It looks almost like a ghost image but it's quite different.

As you noticed during manipulation of the screen controls, there are three separate pictures on a color TV—one red, one green and one blue. Each picture must be placed exactly on top of the other. If it's not, one or more of the colors will bleed through. If not, some adjustments are in order.

First step is to analyze where on the picture tube face the trouble is occurring. Is the bleeding taking place at screen center or nearer the rim of the picture? If the bleeding is at screen center the cure is going to be STATIC CONVERGENCE. Should the bleeding be near the rim of the CRT the cure is going to be DYNAMIC CONVERGENCE.

There are four adjustable permanent magnets, called static magnets, stationed strategically on the CRT neck. They adjust screen center. There are twelve adjustable electromagnets also on the CRT neck mounted in a convergence yoke. They cure outer edge bleeding. Their controls are mounted on a printed circuit board called the convergence board.

At this point we run into a complication. You can't make any convergence adjustments unless there is a display of dots and bars on the TV face. The static magnets and convergence board cannot be sensibly touched without the display, for they were designed to be used ONLY with such a display.

DOT-BAR PATTERN

Servicemen use a dot-bar generator. Some color TV's have a special circuit you can switch on that produces dots and bars. Some TV stations transmit a dot-bar pattern. You must get that dot-bar pattern or don't touch the convergence adjustments.

Let's assume you manage to obtain the proper dot-bar pattern. A perfect pattern shows all dots and bars white and the background black. If that's what is seen no adjustments are needed. However, more than likely you'll see in varying degrees red, green and blue bleeding out of the dots and bars. On the still pattern it is then easy to determine where on the screen the misconvergence is taking place.

Static Convergence: For the misconvergence at screen center there are four magnets—RED STATIC, GREEN STATIC, BLUE STATIC and BLUE

STATIC ADJUSTMENTS

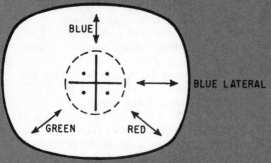

Static magnets move red and green diagonally, move blue up-down or side-to-side.

Right, 3 controls for top, bottom, left, right side, 2 for horizontal, 1 for vertical.

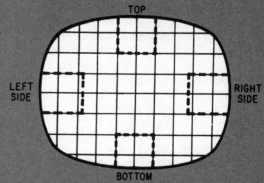

CONVERGENCE BOARD AND SCREEN

	TOP	BOTTOM	LEFT SIDE	RIGHT SIDE
RED–GREEN HORIZONTAL	⊘	⊘	⊘	◉
RED–GREEN VERTICAL	⊘	⊘	⊘	◉
BLUE HORIZONTAL	⊘	⊘	⊘	◉

LATERAL. The magnets come in various shapes such as movable sleeves, screwdriver adjustments and knobs. The blue lateral is on the neck, looks like an ion trap and is the closest object to the plastic socket.

The red static moves the entire red field diagonally. The green static moves the entire green field diagonally across the red field's path. The blue static moves the entire blue field up and down. The blue lateral moves the entire field from side to side.

If you watch the three colored dots at screen center as you manipulate the controls you can get them to merge and form one white dot accomplishing static convergence.

Dynamic Convergence: While you can use either dots or bars to converge screen center, it is easier to use bars around the edges. There are two kinds of bars — vertical and horizontal. There are three color types. This gives us the following six forms of bars: vertical blue, vertical red, vertical green, horizontal blue, horizontal red and horizontal green. If we can merge the horizontals together, the three will turn into one white. If we can merge the verticals together, the three will also turn into one white.

WHAT CONTROLS DO

There are controls to do this. There are three controls to adjust the top of the picture, three to adjust the bottom, three for the left side and three for the right side. The controls are all marked and here is what they do.

1) TOP, HORIZONTAL RED-GREEN: Rocking this control moves the red and green horizontal lines at screen top, up and down.

2) BOTTOM, HORIZONTAL RED-GREEN: Rocking this control moves the red and green horizontal lines at screen bottom, up and down. (Adjust these two together as there is some interaction.)

3) TOP, VERTICAL RED-GREEN: Rocking this control moves the red and green vertical lines at screen top, side to side.

4) BOTTOM, VERTICAL RED-GREEN: Rocking this control moves the red and green vertical lines at screen bottom side to side. (Adjust these two together as there is considerable interaction.)

5) TOP, HORIZONTAL BLUE: Rocking this control moves the blue horizontal lines at screen top, up and down.

6) BOTTOM, HORIZONTAL BLUE: Rocking this control moves the blue horizontal lines at screen bottom, up and down. (Adjust these two together as there is some interaction.)

7) LEFT SIDE, HORIZONTAL RED-GREEN: Rocking this control moves the red and green horizontal lines at screen left side, up and down.

8) RIGHT SIDE, HORIZONTAL

RED-GREEN: Rocking this control with a hex head neut stick moves the red and green horizontal lines at screen right side, up and down. (Adjust these two together as there is considerable interaction.)

9) LEFT SIDE, VERTICAL RED-GREEN: Rocking this control moves the red and green vertical lines at screen left side, side to side.

10) RIGHT SIDE, VERTICAL RED-GREEN: Rocking this control with a hex head neut stick moves the red and green vertical lines at screen right side, side to side. (Adjust these two together as there is some interaction.)

11) LEFT SIDE, HORIZONTAL BLUE: Rocking this control moves the blue horizontal lines at screen left side, up and down.

12) RIGHT SIDE, HORIZONTAL BLUE: Rocking this control with a hex head neut stick moves the blue horizontal lines at screen right side, up and down. (Adjust these two together as there is considerable interaction.)

There are no blue vertical adjustments. Blue vertical is the reference all the rest of the lines are set upon. If need be you

Automatic degaussing circuit helps color TV by demagnetizing CRT almost every day.

Convergence board has 9 screwdriver controls and 3 right side hex coil controls.

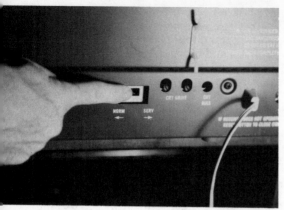

You can gain access to the service switch and activate it without taking back off.

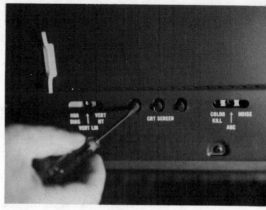

Screen controls might be in front or rear of the TV. Keep looking—they are there!

To loosen yoke for purity adjustment there is a ¼" bolt holding a tightening ring.

The blue lateral adjustment is mounted on the neck of CRT behind the purity magnet.

can move blue vertical with the blue static and blue lateral adjustments.

There is quite a bit of interaction between the static and dynamic convergence adjustments. Even though I have them laid out as separate procedure you will probably have to work back and forth between them.

CONVERGENCE COMPLICATIONS

While I told you what, in general, the convergence adjustments should do, they don't always respond so well.

Most of the time it's because the operator becomes confused and mixes them up. This is natural; there are so

many of them and most do-it-yourselfers do not work on these complicated controls day in and day out like a technician.

The trick to it is mumble to yourself a description of the trouble. For instance, you can mumble, "The blue horizontal top needs adjusting," or "the red-green vertical left side is out." Analyze what lines are out and then reach for the right control. People tend to forget the descriptive terms, especially the horizontal and vertical terms. If you reach for a vertical instead of horizontal control you are completely wrong and you are going to cause a complication.

Linearity Complications I've had many jobs that converged perfectly ex-

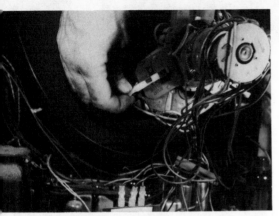

Static magnets are often found in sleeves that easily slide back and forth to adjust.

Sometimes static magnets are adjusted by turning little wheels mounted in assembly.

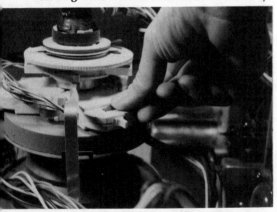

cept for vertical top, vertical bottom or both. They bow badly. This occurs when the vertical is stretched too far and a circle on the screen looks like an egg standing on end. You can try the repair measures mentioned in troubles 19 through 23, especially the vertical linearity and height controls. If they adjust the circle back into its proper shape you'll be able to take the bowing out of the vertical lines. If they won't, the vertical circuits are going to need troubleshooting. You are not going to be able to converge the vertical lines till the vertical linearity is satisfactory.

Bowed Horizontal Complications — According to my discussion I tell you to do the STATIC adjustments first and then the DYNAMIC adjustments. The first time you do the statics it might be true but it is probably not the last time you'll touch them during the procedure. You must go back and back and back again.

STRAIGHTEN THEM OUT

This is to be remembered, especially if you find your horizontal lines through center bowed. When these lines are bowed your first job is going to be to straighten them out. Once they are straightened you'll find they are probably not one on top of each other. However, if you look all over the screen you'll see they are spaced the same distance from each other. The statics move them all at the same time and adjustment of the statics once the lines are straight will merge them altogether. Therefore, when you have bowed horizontal lines, reverse your procedure. Straighten the lines with the dynamic controls then merge them with the statics.

Hex Head Coil Complications — If you'll notice on the convergence board sketch all the "right side" adjustments are made with a hex head neut stick. (Don't use a metallic tool.) All the rest of the adjustments are hand adjustments.

You can give yourself a complication with these coils if you do not notice this effect. With the hand adjustments you can turn them all the way back and forth and you can see noticeable movement of their respective dots or lines.

With the hex head adjustments this is not so. There is noticeable movement of lines on the right side only during one or two turns of the core. Now, make sure you keep the cores in the position where they do cause the lines to move. That is the resonant point of the coil. If you move the core out of the correct position that entire control becomes useless — worse than useless, in fact, since you'll never merge those right hand lines.

Rock each core while watching the screen and be sure all three are in the correct spot.

This chapter, if you can master it, will be worth a lot of money in the years you own a color TV.

Good black and white picture without trace of color means color troubleshooting is needed.

CURING COLOR ILLS

How to combat smearing, weak color, overly bright one color, worms

The color TV from a service point of view is almost exactly like a black-and-white TV except for the additional color-only circuits.

There are about five circuit areas for color and they are usually clumped together. The color signal contains two parts. One is the color sidebands that are going to be processed and then added to the black-and-white picture. The second is the color sync signal, whose troubles we discussed in Chapter 5.

Color Circuit Operation: A sampling of the complete TV signal is taken off at the first VIDEO AMPLIFIER. It is sent to the two entrances in the color circuit area, the BANDPASS AMPLIFIER and the BURST AMPLIFIER. In the bandpass amplifier the color sidebands are extracted from the TV signal, amplified and sent on to the DEMODULATORS. In the burst amplifier the color sync or color burst is separated from the TV signal and sent to the 3.58 MC color oscillator to lock it in step with the station's color. The output of the bandpass amplifier and the color oscillator are both fed into the demodulators.

In the demodulators the color sidebands and the oscillator output are combined and construct the color signal. The demodulator outputs are then sent to the three different amplifiers. The three outputs containing R, G and B are applied to their respective control grids in the picture tube.

Meanwhile, back at the first video amplifier the TV signal is amplified, sent to the second video amplifier and then sent into the DELAY LINE.

The black-and-white signal, called Y, travels faster through the video circuits than the color signal tracks through the color circuits. The Y signal is slowed in the delay line. Then the Y signal is amplified once more in the VIDEO OUTPUT and is applied simultaneously to all three cathodes of the picture tube.

During a black-and-white program, the color killer, as discussed in Chapter 8, shuts down all the color circuits. At that time the only signal that gets to the picture tube is Y, producing a monochrome show.

During a color program, the color killer shuts off, the color circuits come on and the color signal gets to the picture tube control grids. The color signal adds to the Y producing a color show.

Troubles occur to the color when there is a circuit problem in these circuits. Let's go through the color-only troubles.

TROUBLE NO. 47 — NO COLOR, BLACK & WHITE OK

This trouble is to be differentiated from the other losses of color. This is occurring only when there is a good black

When you crank up color intensity control and picture stays B & W, try color circuits.

Smeary color picture is due to loss of Y. Suspect is the delay line in the chassis.

and white picture. Try the COLOR INTENSITY control first. Next there are the tube suspects in order, BANDPASS AMPLIFIER, 3.58 MC OSCILLATOR, BURST AMP and BURST KEYER. If the oscillator gets off frequency the color killer gets an impulse that it interprets as no color burst and shuts down the color circuits.

Lastly, try a new COLOR KILLER tube since it has it in its power to kill color.

Should the color be missing on one or more channels, especially weak channels, but appear on others, test the RF AMPLIFIER, MIXER-OSCILLATOR and IF tubes. (Also see Chapter 11.)

TROUBLE NO. 48—COLOR SMEARED, NO BLACK & WHITE

This is a weird looking trouble. If you look at the block diagram of the color circuits, at the top you'll see the path of the Y signal. It travels through the first VIDEO AMPLIFIER, second VIDEO AMPLIFIER, DELAY LINE and VIDEO OUTPUT into the COLOR CRT.

Since this trouble is loss of the Y signal they are the prime suspects. The colors are actually good. They appear smeared because all you are seeing is the R-Y, G-Y and B-Y that is usually added to the Y to produce pure R, G and B.

TROUBLE NO. 49—WEAK COLOR

When your colors get weak the degrees of the symptom are a dull red instead of a vivid one, to a washed out picture that almost looks like a black and white except for the fact that the sky is a dull blue and flesh tones are almost correct.

First suspect is the BANDPASS AMPLIFIERS. Next try the RF AMPLIFIER, MIXER-OSCILLATOR, IF tubes and VIDEO AMPLIFIERS. Another common cause of weak color is a detuned IF strip. Better call for help on that one though. (Also see Chapter 11.)

TROUBLE NO. 50—OVERLY BRIGHT ONE COLOR PICTURE

Should your TV picture suddenly go vivid, blurry, red, green or blue, that particular circuit is running wide open. This is a different trouble than a lightly tinted picture. Test the color difference amplifier indicating the color. For instance, if

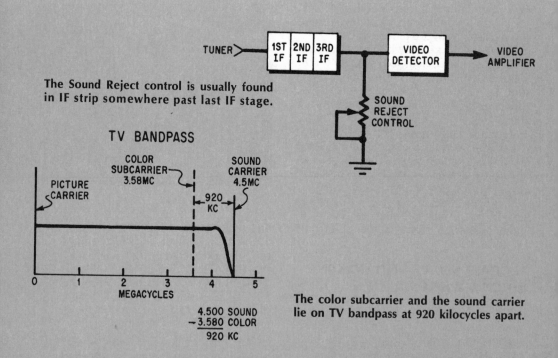

The Sound Reject control is usually found in IF strip somewhere past last IF stage.

The color subcarrier and the sound carrier lie on TV bandpass at 920 kilocycles apart.

the picture is vivid red, test the R-Y amplifier and so on.

A confusing one of these might be a vivid yellow picture. Since yellow is made up of green and red test the R-Y and G-Y amplifier.

TROUBLE NO. 51 —
LOSS OF ONE COLOR

When you lose one color it's a bit confusing to analyze. For instance, when you lose green, your black-and-white picture is lost. It changes to shades of blue, red and purple. When you lose red your picture changes to shades of blue, green and cyan. When you lose blue, your picture changes to shades of red, green and yellow. Black and white becomes impossible.

First step is to try the gray scale adjustments (TROUBLE No. 44 — TINTED PICTURE). If that doesn't cure, try the B-Y, G-Y, R-Y COLOR DIFFERENCE AMPLIFIERS. Next step is to look at the neck of the picture tube to see if all three guns are lit. If one

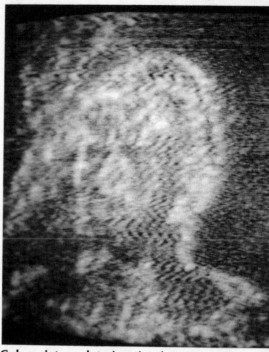

Color picture deteriorating into worms? There's unwanted mixing of color and sound.

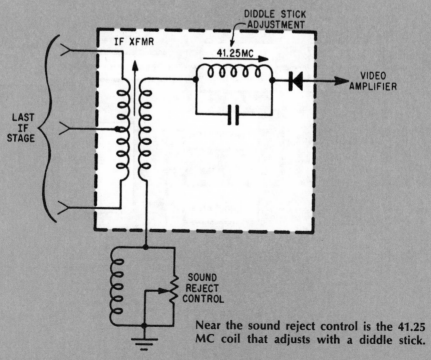

Near the sound reject control is the 41.25 MC coil that adjusts with a diddle stick.

83

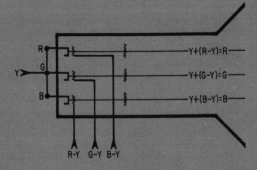

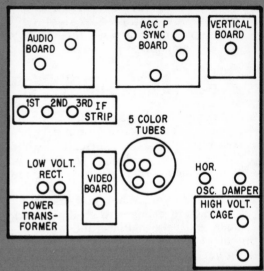

In electron gun, Y mixes with R-Y, B-Y and G-Y, producing pure red, green and blue.

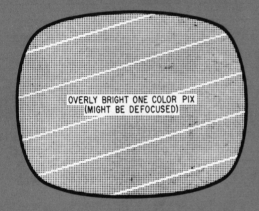

OVERLY BRIGHT ONE COLOR PIX
(MIGHT BE DEFOCUSED)

Above, there are 5 color circuit tubes. They are usually placed together in close group.

Left, picture turning a deep single color is due to the color difference tube dying.

Below, actual color circuits are clear and present no tube-changing problems to you.

COLOR CIRCUIT BLOCK DIAGRAM

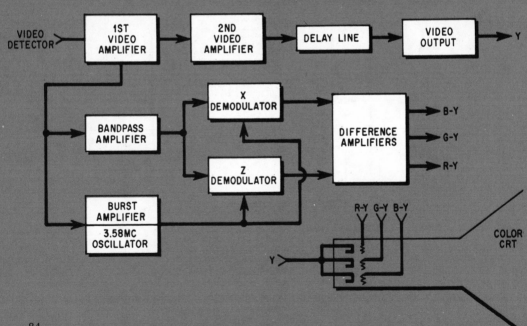

is out that's probably it. A bad picture tube.

Should you not be able to pin down the trouble with the above analysis it's probably bad news. There is a weak gun in the picture tube even though all three guns are lit.

TROUBLE NO. 52—WORMS

If you misadjust your fine tuner you can usually produce color worms in faces of people or in areas where a solid color exists. Readjusting the fine tuner should eliminate it. This interference is a 920KC beat that is always developed whenever a color show is transmitted. The frequency difference between the color subcarrier and the sound carrier is 920 kilocycles.

To suppress this unwanted interference two traps are installed in the output of the last IF circuit. One is a tiny control that is a little potentiometer. You can adjust it with a screwdriver. It's called the SOUND REJECT. One point of information: adjusting this control will not affect the sound at all. Its only purpose is to suppress the sound carrier as much as possible so the sound will not appear on the picture tube face. Sound is to be heard not seen.

Therefore, you adjust the SOUND REJECT while watching the TV screen and adjust it for minimum WORMS. It will be a touchy adjustment and quite often you won't eliminate the worms altogether, just suppress them to minimum position.

41.25 MC TRAP

Right next to and attached to the sound reject control is another adjustment called the 41.25 MC trap. This adjustment must be done with a hex head diddle stick. It is contained in a can and is a coil adjustment. (Do not just try adjusting the nearby coils! Be sure you are adjusting the right one.)

Just realize you are in deep water and do no more than locate the 41.25 MC trap and adjust it with the diddle stick. Adjust no further than a quarter turn

Apparently unrelated horizontal hold control causes color loss when slightly misadjusted.

Visual tipoff of a bad tube is a milky top. This happens when the glass tip cracks open.

each way while watching worms on the screen. If nothing happens, return the core to its original position. If you are lucky you will minimize the worms even further.

Should these adjustments minimize worms, you'll find you have also strengthened the vividness of the colors.

In addition to these two adjustments worms can be minimized by adjustment of the COLOR KILLER, replacement of the COLOR KILLER tube, the BANDPASS AMPLIFIER, RF AMPLIFIER, MIXER OSCILLATOR and IF tubes. Don't go any further than this.

TROUBLE NO. 53—COLOR SNOW AND COLOR INTERFERENCE IN BLACK & WHITE PICTURE

This trouble was mentioned in Chapter 8 under the COLOR KILLER adjustments. Another cause would be the COLOR KILLER tube and the BANDPASS AMPLIFIERS.

A test to determine whether trouble is in outdoor antenna is made with rabbit ears.

REMEDYING ANTENNA PROBLEMS

Safety first with rooftop work;
focus attention on lead-in wire

A TV antenna can cause snow, ghosts, overloading, flashing, static, loss of detail, weak color, no color, worms and other troubles closely resembling set troubles. Therefore your first antenna troubleshooting move is to make sure it is really antenna trouble.

A quick test is easy. Take a pair of rabbit ears, indoor antenna, disconnect the outdoor antenna and install the indoor in its place.

Has the trouble disappeared? Are you now getting normal indoor antenna reception? If so the outdoor antenna is really at fault. If the trouble is still as apparent as before, the TV set is causing the symptoms.

Once you have decided it's really the outdoor antenna system that needs work, you are ready to go. Let's go through the various reasons an antenna fails and the techniques required for the repair.

Safety First: Your number one consideration is SAFETY FIRST! Rooftop work should only be performed by people who have experience with a ladder. It's always the novice who gets hurt. There are two main dangers on a roof, falling and bare electrical wires. Be careful!

WEATHER'S TOLL

Commonest Antenna Breakdown: Unlike the TV that sits indoors like one of the family, the antenna system is exposed to the elements day in, day out. Wind, rain, snow and sun takes it toll. Your LEAD-IN WIRE has a limited life. The wire is subject to deterioration and as a result becomes disconnected, loose, waterlogged, touched by metal, frayed and broke.

Each one of these forms of wear causes TV trouble symptoms to appear on your screen. Each form of wear has its own family of symptoms. A good approach is to simply pull out the old wire and install a complete new length. There are new types of lead-in wire being developed all the time. Therefore if your wire is more than two years old, that's what you should do.

However, if your wire is newer, or was a strong type to begin with, maybe you can repair it. Let's go through the lead-in wire troubles.

Splice twin lead breaks to form permanent repair. The trick is locating the break site.

Photo shows the various things a picture might exhibit when the lead-in is faulty.

ANTENNA TROUBLES	
TROUBLE	REMEDY
Snow, Ghosts, No Color Flashing, Rolling, Bouncing	Replace Wire Check for Poor Connections Snug Down Wire Replace old Standoffs Install More Standoffs Repair or Replace Old Antenna Heads Orient Antenna for Best Heading
Motor Stops or Becomes Erratic	Check connections at Motor and Control box Replace filter capacitor in motor Replace motor Repair or replace control box
Booster Troubles— Snow, Hum Bars, Rolling	Replace Tubes, Transistor or Nuvistors, Replace filter capacitors

If small, cheap antenna doesn't pull good reception, choose a larger expensive rig.

Loose Wire: From the connection on the antenna head to the TV set terminals the wire, ideally, should be snug. However, wind over a period of time loosens it. When this happens the wire flaps from even the slightest breeze. The TV picture becomes erratic. The picture flashes, flops and has color fading in and out. These troubles will have a degree of seriousness in direct relation to the amount of looseness. The remedy: snug down all loose sections of wire.

Disconnected: The wire is vulnerable at connection points — at the antenna head, at any two set couplers, splitters etc., and at the terminals of all the TV's, FM sets or anything else it's connected to. Just one poor connection will cause snow, loss of sound or color, rolling, barberpole effect, worms or ghosts. Check all connections for a complete disconnection, partial disconnection, fraying connection or accidental shorting across terminals by frayed lead-in wire.

It's a good idea to install spade lugs at all connection terminals.

Touched by Metal: If you are using coaxial or shielded cable you can forget about this trouble. With regular twin lead though this is an important consideration. The lead must not touch any rain gutters, drain pipes, TV masts or even lay flat on a roof. Take pains to be sure that the wire is run through enough standoff insulators.

When twin lead touches metal an impedance bump develops at that point. An impedance bump blocks off TV signal like dirt does in a water pipe. The bump not only blocks but bounces the signal back up the wire. These standing waves cancel out some of the incoming signal and combine with some of the signal to cause incorrect impulses to enter the TV set. The metal touching ends up as loss of fine detail, loss of color intensity and ghosts in the TV picture.

NO VISUAL TIPOFF

Broken Wire: If you can see where the lead-in is broken splice it right there. More times than not, though, the wire breaks inside the insulation and there is no visual tipoff. You conclude there might be a break in the wire when snow and flashing appears in your TV picture and the rabbit ears test says the antenna is at fault.

The best approach is replacement of the entire length of wire. Should you want the satisfaction of locating the exact trouble spot, here is how it can be done. You'll need an ohmmeter or other type of continuity device. Disconnect the wire at the set's antenna terminal and short the two ends together. Then working toward the antenna head on the roof, pierce the insulation with the meter probes and shake the wire. As long as the meter reads short you haven't reached the break. As soon as the meter reads open or the needle begins acting erratic you have just passed the break. It lies between that spot and the last one. Zero in on it from there. Then splice in a new section of wire.

Broken or Worn Out Standoffs: These items break, come loose or lose their insulating centers. It is usually obvious when this happens and you can find the bad one by examining them one by one. The bad standoff can cause the lead-in to be loose, break or touch metal. This gives all the snow, flashing, loss of color, etc., symptoms. If in doubt replace the standoffs. They are inexpensive and simple to install.

Worn Out Heads: Antenna heads become defective because they wear out. The bolts rust, the elements deteriorate, fall off, bend, touch each other and cause the head to swing in the wrong direction.

Another more subtle defect occurs when new high buildings are built nearby or a TV transmitter moves its location. The TV picture symptoms usually occur over a long period of time, little by little, and you hardly realize what bad shape you are in.

When you decide to do work on your antenna head, should you repair or re-

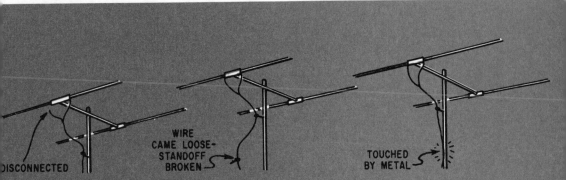

DISCONNECTED

WIRE CAME LOOSE—
STANDOFF
BROKEN

TOUCHED
BY METAL

When lead-in loosens it will flap in the slightest breeze. Broken wire's easy to see.

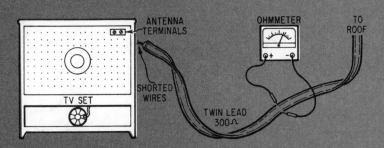

ANTENNA
TERMINALS

OHMMETER

TO
ROOF

TV SET

SHORTED
WIRES

TWIN LEAD
300Ω

Locate actual break by shorting lead-in at antenna terminals and working your way up.

When a new building is erected it can have bad effect on other sets' reception in area.

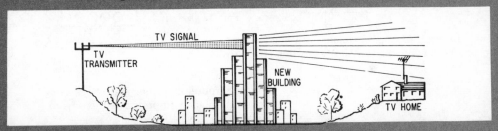

TV SIGNAL

TV
TRANSMITTER

NEW
BUILDING

TV HOME

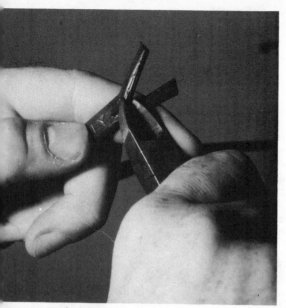

Technique of stripping twin lead is to cut it down center and then take off each side.

If your antenna develops electric charges install ground rod and attach to the mast.

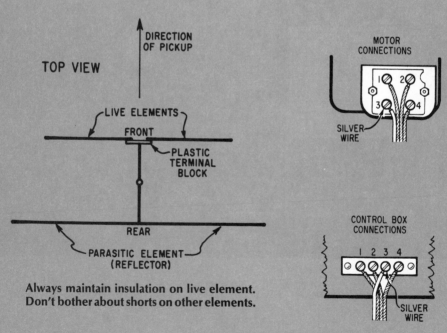

TOP VIEW

DIRECTION OF PICKUP

LIVE ELEMENTS

FRONT

PLASTIC TERMINAL BLOCK

REAR

PARASITIC ELEMENT (REFLECTOR)

Always maintain insulation on live element. Don't bother about shorts on other elements.

MOTOR CONNECTIONS

1 2
3 4

SILVER WIRE

CONTROL BOX CONNECTIONS

1 2 3 4

SILVER WIRE

In motor troubleshooting, first check connections. Alliance rotors have this layout.

place? If the head is more than a year old and is an inexpensive type, replace. It will probably fall apart as you take it apart. If it's a fancy rig the repair attempt might be worthwhile, especially if it's anodized.

REPLACE BROKEN ELEMENTS

Bent elements need only be straightened. Broken elements need replacing. Buy some ½-inch aluminum tubing and a hacksaw. Remove the old element and measure off a new replacement length exactly. Attach the new element.

If it's a parasitic element it's attached directly to the crossbar. You can run screws and bolts through them at will with little concern for insulation. If it's a driven element, one that has lead-in attached to it, be sure you maintain insulation between the elements. Don't short out the spacing between the elements on the insulated element holder.

After you repair the head take a can of plastic spray and put a coat on the antenna, especially around where the lead-in is installed. When you place the new antenna or repaired antenna in place check the orientation. Are you picking up best possible all-around reception? Loosen the mount, rotate the antenna a few degrees at a time and make note of the pictures on your screen. At the heading where best reception is obtained, lock the antenna in.

If you find you need two or three spots for best reception on different channels you can cut a motor in so you can orient your antenna from setside.

Probing the Roof: When your TV picture is a casualty of progress and a new structure has hurt your reception you can probe the roof for a new antenna location and height. This is a two-man walkie-talkie job. One man on the roof walking around with an antenna head on a pole testing different locations on the roof, different angles, and various heights; the second man at setside reporting results. It's time-consuming and dangerous for the rooftop man but often you can get excellent results.

When this produces poor results you can try more expensive rigs and different manufacturers' products.

Servicing Motors: The more complex your antenna system becomes, the more likelihood you'll need service. When you get a motorized antenna in addition to all else, there is a motor, a length of four-wire cable and a control box. These three items are all subject to failure. The symptoms are simple; the motor won't turn.

WIRE NEEDS CHECKING

First check is to make sure all connections are okay. If one of the eight connections, four in the control box and four in the motor, should come off, the motor won't turn. Next check is to look over the wire. It is subject to breakage and fraying due to wind and weather. Be sure to snug it down firmly and replace any standoffs that might have gone bad.

Once you are sure the wire is okay, check out the control box. We prove or eliminate the control box as faulty by in-

Motor failure is often caused by a defective filter capacitator. Change before going on.

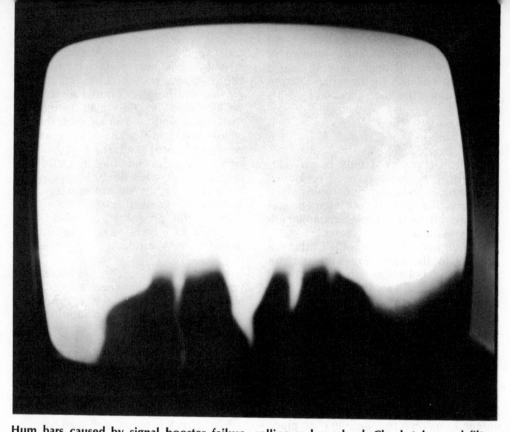

Hum bars caused by signal booster failure, rolling and overload. Check tubes and filter.

Snow is a problem that can afflict your screen when the signal booster has failed.

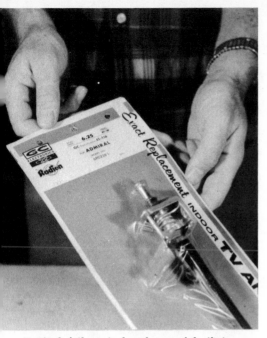

Typical failure is breakage of built-in antenna; replacements available at TV stores.

If only the rod of built-in antenna breaks, buy a cheap, easy-to-install replacement.

stalling a new one and see what happens. If performance is restored then we know the box is at fault. Should the trouble persist we know it's not. Perhaps you can borrow a control box from a neighbor and do the same thing.

Actual servicing of the control box means testing switches, wiring and clock mechanism type equipment. Once you establish that the wire and control box are cleared, the only thing left is the motor. There is a filter condenser in the motor. In a great percentage of motor failures it's that filter that has gone bad. If you can get the motor down, check it first. Everything else in the motor is mechanical, and if you can work on gears and rotation equipment it's all yours. Decide in servicing the motor and control box whether it is worth your while to repair the old equipment or replace it. Unless it's the filter I'd replace the entire motor. It's rough to keep climbing up and down to service it. You can go a little further with the control box since it is convenient. However, too much servic-

ing on it indicates replacement.

Servicing Boosters: Repairing boosters is just like repairing any other circuit. It's electronic work and you need circuit repair technique. There are two troubles a bad booster can cause: Snow in the picture to a more or less degree, and visible hum in the picture to a more or less degree.

The rabbit ears test will pinpoint the trouble as being either in the booster or in the TV. It's very important to use the test. Since the booster is an auxiliary RF amplifier, it causes exactly the same symptoms as the tuner.

The first approach is to replace the tube, transistor or nuvistor. In boosters ninety-five per cent of the time this will effect the cure. If it doesn't, you need a bench repair which you must use your judgment on attempting.

Should you have visible hum trouble, in addition to the tube or equivalent, try replacing the booster's filter condensers. Chances are good you might effect this repair.

THE WORLD OF NEW ANTENNAS

All you need to complete job is an all-channel yagi, an antenna amplifier, motor and booster

Since the strong acceptance of color TV, antenna installations have become a major factor again, just as in the beginning of commercial TV. Large antenna rigs have begun to appear on rooftops in large numbers. Antenna manufacturers have been coming out with families of antennas and antenna accessories. People are quite willing to spend between one and two hundred dollars to pull good TV reception.

The do-it-yourselfer is out in force buying and installing these fancy rigs. There is a certain amount of information from my experience I'd like to impart to you so you can install your rig safely and get good value for money spent.

Shopping List: Once you decide you want to install an outdoor antenna you head for an electronic supply store. The supplies break down into the following items that come in many sizes, shapes and purposes. Heads, poles, lead-in wire, stand-off insulators and mounts. Then if you want a super installation there are motors and boosters. The following lists are the general types of these items.

Conical
Stack Conical
One Channel Yagi
All Channel Yagi
UHF Antenna
Electronic Yagi
Super Electronic Yagi

Poles/5 Ft. Section

Aluminum
Steel
Steel Anodized

Lead-In Wire/100 Ft.

300 ohm light wt.
300 ohm med wt.
300 ohm heavy wt.
300 ohm Shielded cable
720 ohm Coaxial cable

Standoff Insulators

3" wood
5" wood
8" wood
Mast Type
Masonry Type

Mounts

Light Chimney Mount
Heavy Chimney Mount
Short Wall Mount
Long Wall Mount
Roof Mount
Guy Wire/100 Ft.
Guy Hooks
U-Bolts

Motors

Standard
Deluxe
Super Deluxe

Boosters

Tube Type
Transistor
Nuvistor
Double Nuvistor

BRAINS OF THE ANTENNA

The head of the antenna requires the most consideration during the purchase. You must decide what you want from your antenna. Do you want to pull 20 miles, 50 miles, 100 miles or further? The more distance you want the more expensive the job is going to be.

Conical: For short distances up to 50 miles away, unless the terrain is very

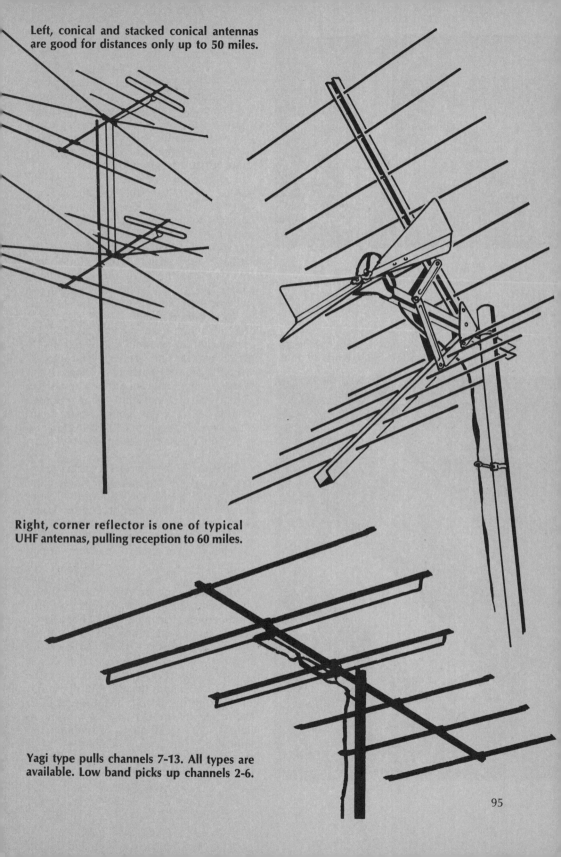

Left, conical and stacked conical antennas are good for distances only up to 50 miles.

Right, corner reflector is one of typical UHF antennas, pulling reception to 60 miles.

Yagi type pulls channels 7-13. All types are available. Low band picks up channels 2-6.

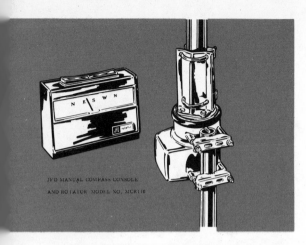

Standard-type rotator works well and it is controlled manually while watching picture.

Flat twin lead is common, cheap and easy to work with. Coax is expensive but durable.

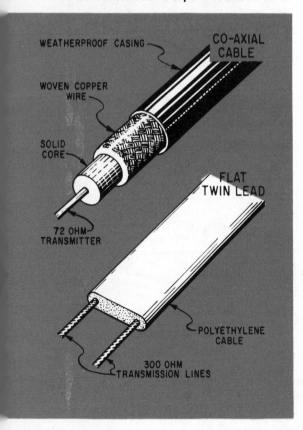

WEATHERPROOF CASING

CO-AXIAL CABLE

WOVEN COPPER WIRE

SOLID CORE

72 OHM TRANSMITTER

FLAT TWIN LEAD

POLYETHYLENE CABLE

300 OHM TRANSMISSION LINES

hilly, a biconical or stacked biconical will do the trick. It has broad band receptive power. It pulls channels 2 through 13 satisfactorily. It is not too directional. You can aim it bulls eye at your weakest channel and the stronger ones are still picked up even if they are to one side or even to the rear. It is cheap, sturdy and snaps together all in one motion.

The conical lends itself well to stacking. Be sure to use stacking bars to separate the two heads. The bars are cut the correct distance to provide maximum pickup of all the channels. Should you stack at incorrect heights, some of the signal could cancel other signal out. Stacking has the advantage of doubling gain in the horizontal plane, which means reduced vertical pickup of interference.

One-Channel Yagi: To pull a single channel a yagi head is useful. It is cut for one particular channel and is extremely directional. This gives it enormous strength on that particular channel and makes it as interference-free as possible.

Yagis also come in low band and high band types. The low band picks up channels two through six. The high band picks up channels seven through thirteen.

Therefore when your reception problem is a single channel or a single band you should choose the yagi for that channel. If that is the general reception situation in your area, suppliers will stock the yagis you want. If not, they can order it for you. For instance, if you want to pull channel two ask for a "channel two yagi."

All-Channel Yagis: An all-channel yagi is in essence a bunch of yagis, one for each station 2 through 83, all hooked together. That's why they get so large and complicated-looking. Four popular all-channel yagis are the Channel Master Crossfires, the Winegard Colortrons, the JFD LPV's and the Jerrold Paralogs. They come in small, medium and large according to the distance you want to pull. There are 50 milers, 75 milers, 100 milers, 125 milers, 150 milers and 175 milers. The larger they are the further they pull and the more they cost.

HOW THE HEAD WORKS

There are only three basic working elements in an antenna array, no matter how complex it is. Any other gadgets are there simply to match the three basic together or trap out unwanted signal. The three signal gatherers are the dipole, the reflector and the director.

Dipole: The dipole is two metal sticks that are physically held together by a plastic terminal block that insulates each arm from the other. The lead-in wire has two ends. Each end is attached to one of the metal sticks where the metal touches the insulator. The dipole is cut at a particular half wave length and is the live or driven element. The energy it absorbs is sent directly to the TV set.

A dipole is quite often the entire antenna without the other elements. When it is by its lonesome it can absorb energy from two directions—front and back. Its general pickup pattern is shown in the sketch.

Reflector: The reflector is not attached to the lead-in. It simply sits behind the dipole. It's known as a parasitic element. It's cut a bit longer than the dipole. It absorbs signal strength then reradiates the signal back to the dipole. It also blocks off any other signal that tries to come in from the rear.

In effect, the addition of the parasite makes the antenna higher in gain and more directional. If you look at the reflector pattern you can see the pattern is reduced drastically. You can think of the reflector as an element that bounces signal back to the dipole and bounces the signal off that tries to come in the rear.

Director: The third element is the director. As the name implies, it is in front of the dipole. It, too, is a parasite. The director is cut smaller than the dipole. It absorbs the TV signal, too, and reradiates it back to the dipole. The director sharpens the directivity of the antenna even more than the reflector. The additional front gain reduces the ratio of front to back gain since the front gain is now stronger than without the director. In effect this makes rear pickup in ratio less.

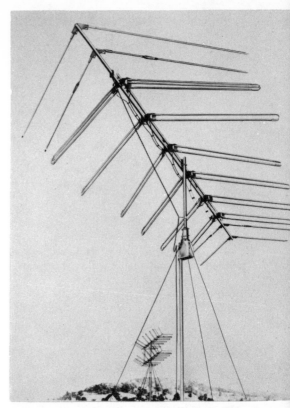

Large antennas, once a rarity, now are extremely popular due to influence of color.

To pull distances of 50-75 miles, a small super antenna installs and aims nicely.

97

Closeup of guy wire ring attachments shows permanent arrangement; it lasts for years.

You must adjust the chimney mount bolts with a wrench till U-Bolt grabs the mast.

LEAD-IN WIRE

The lead-in wire takes the signal the head has absorbed and funnels it down into the TV. The lead-in must have certain characteristics. One of these is called impedance. Most antennas have an impedance of about 300 ohms. Most tuners have an impedance of about 300 ohms. In order for the lead-in to match with the antenna and tuner, it should have an imepdance of 300 ohms. The familiar flat twin-lead possessed this impedance. Under most home conditions twin-lead will be used. It's satisfactory in insulation and interference-rejection qualities.

However, if you have a reception situation where the lead-in must be run hundreds of feet and/or the interference around you is at extremely high levels you'll probably have to use something other than twin-lead. This something is 300 ohm shielded twin-lead or 72 ohm coaxial cable. They are more expensive but are heavy duty and almost interference-proof. Any noise flying through the air will not be picked up by coax as it will with twin-lead.

Unfortunately, in addition to cost, they are hard to work with. If your reception calls for it, you'll have to use it even if you do have a tougher installation job.

STANDOFF INSULATORS (& MOUNTS)

Why use standoff insulators? Why not simply tape the lead onto the mast and tack it to the walls of the house? As a matter of fact, this is just what you do with the shielded cables. With the heavy stuff, you need only to concern yourself about impedance at the antenna and the TV connections.

With unshielded twin-lead, though, the impedance problem requires more concern. If you taped twin-lead to the metal mast, the mast becomes an integral part of the lead wire and the wire-mast combination presents an entirely different impedance to the signal. Should you tack twin-lead to the house, even though the wood and shingle are insulation, when they become wet they change the impedance of the lead.

At an impedance bump the signal waves are dissipated and bounced back up the wire where they came from. These reflections cancel out some of the signal strength and enter the TV at the wrong time causing ghost images.

Standoffs, on the other hand, hold the wire far enough away from mast and wall so no impedance bumps occur. Standoffs come in various forms. There are mast standoffs, short and long wood standoffs and masonry standoffs. Liberal

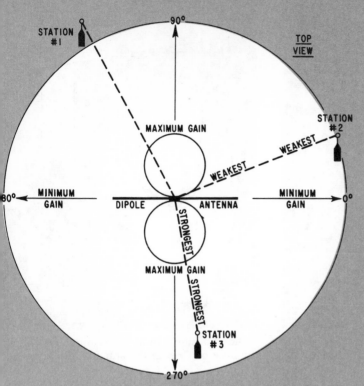

STATION #1

90°

TOP VIEW

MAXIMUM GAIN

STATION #2

WEAKEST

WEAKEST

180° ← MINIMUM GAIN | DIPOLE ANTENNA | MINIMUM GAIN → 0°

STRONGEST

MAXIMUM GAIN

STRONGEST

STATION #3

270°

This is a dipole pattern. The more area in a figure eight a good signal path can cover, the stronger will be the signal.

JFD Zig-a-Log UHF antenna gets sharp directivity, overcomes ghosts, interference.

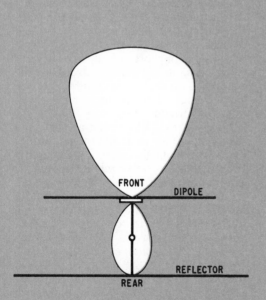

FRONT

DIPOLE

REFLECTOR

REAR

Dipole-reflector pattern. Adding reflector reduces rear entrance pickup and narrows it.

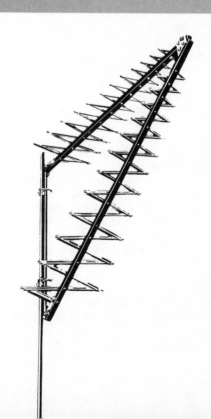

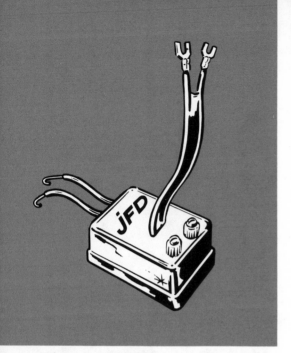

If you use 70 ohm coax you'll need this matching transformer to make input 300.

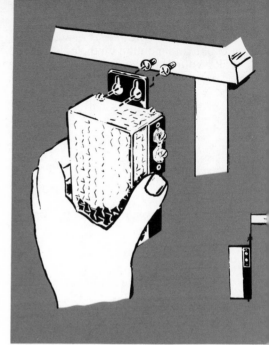

Setside boosters can be easily mounted on the back of TV near the antenna terminals.

use of them keeps wire snug and a constant impedance throughout the entire length of lead-in.

MOUNTS

An antenna mount must hold its ward firmly and permanently in all kinds of weather, from a snowstorm to a hurricane. With a short simple installation you can use a chimney or wall mount. For a high or complex installation you must also guy the array down. Failure to mount an antenna properly will bring it crashing down.

Chimney Mount: The most-used mount for local installations is the chimney type. It is simply two or four steel straps that are tied around the chimney. At one corner a holder protrudes from each strap. The pole slips into and is tightened down permanently in the holders.

Should you install one, separate the two straps as far from one another as possible for maximum holding power. Make sure the chimney is strong enough to hold the antenna system. Do not use a

pole longer than ten feet with a chimney mount. If you do, a strong wind might tear it loose.

Wall Mount: Second in popularity, the wall mount has the same kind of holders as the chimney type. Instead of straps the wall mount is nailed, screwed, bolted or lagged into a convenient eave or wall. They come in short or long sizes to clear roof overhangs. Here again, separate the holders as far as practical and do not use a pole longer than ten feet or your wall might be torn out.

Guy Wires: Whenever an antenna needs a pole higher than ten feet, and/or a heavy antenna array, and/or a motor is being used, or you simply desire a very strong installation, the answer is guy wires. Guy wires are usually many strands of powerful wire with a very high tensile strength. It comes uncoated or with a green plastic weather-proofing. You gauge the number of needed guys by the height of the antenna. You can use three or four guys with a fifteen-foot pole. You can use six guys or eight with a thirty.

If a guy ring is available mount it on

the pole. If no guy ring is available take a U bolt and mount it on the pole instead. Take your three or four lengths of guy wire and tie them to the holes in the guy ring or to the pole above the U bolt. Do all this before putting the antenna into the mount.

Then mount the antenna in position. Find three or four locations on the roof or on the side of the roof to run the guy wires to. The locations, using the pole as the center of a circle, should be about 120° for three and 90° for four, apart from one another. The angle can be off a little.

Put three or four hooks into the locations chosen. Be sure to use some roof tar to seal off the holes made by the guy

hooks. Tie all but one of the guy wires snugly into the hooks without bending the pole. On the last guy wire attach a small turnbuckle. Then run it into its guy hook snugly. Make sure all guy wires are taut and the pole is straight. Then tighten up with the turnbuckle. (After about two weeks you can give the turnbuckle a few more turns for a final tightening.)

You can use guy wires with a chimney mount or a roof mount.

Roof Mount: A roof mount is simply a holder on a swivel. It's used only with guy wires. It's used to seat the bottom of the pole on the roof.

Take a piece of ½″ plywood about 18″ square. Attach the roof mount onto the plywood. Then attach the holder of the

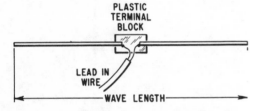

Dipole or driven element is nothing more than 2 metal sticks mounted on insulator.

All elements in an antenna stand broadside in horizontal plane to incoming TV signal.

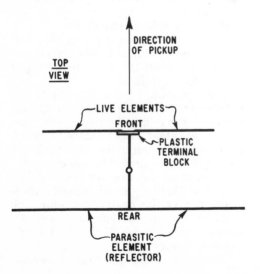

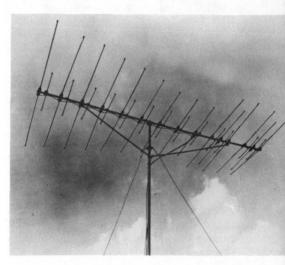

To pull 100 miles or more you need one of these large, complicated-looking monsters.

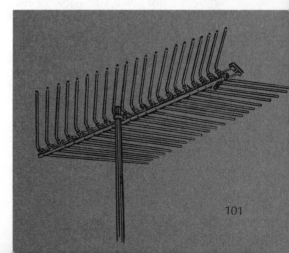

101

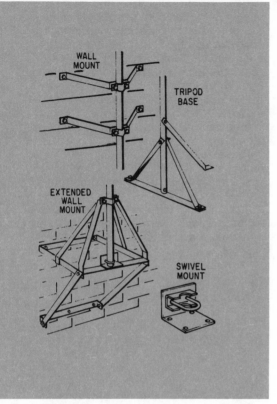

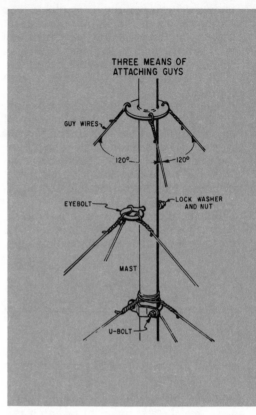

THREE MEANS OF
ATTACHING GUYS

Chimney mounts are more popular, but these wall, roof mounts may be more convenient.

Tie guy wires to holes in guy ring or to mast above U-bolt before mounting antenna.

mount onto the bottom of the pole. There is a swivel on the mount so the plywood can sit flush on any roof no matter how steep.

BOOSTERS

While it's not always possible or necessary to attain an ideal booster here is what one is: A booster is simply another stage of the tuner of the TV; an RF Amplifier that takes the signal before it gets to the TV and amplifies it many times. After the booster action, the processed signal is then fed to the RF Amplifier in the tuner.

The best place to amplify the signal is just after it leaves the antenna array, before it has a chance to make the journey through the lead-in wire. At this time the signal is as pure as the aerial can make it.

No interference or weakening of the signal has taken place yet, as it does in the lead-in wire.

If you are able to amplify the signal at this time, the stronger signal that will force through the lead-in will actually reject and be less pregnable to interference and weakening effects.

The matching of the antenna to the booster to the lead-in is another consideration for the ideal booster. If the output of the antenna has a 300 ohm impedance then the input of the booster should be exactly 300 ohms. The same goes for the output of the booster into the 300 twin-lead. Actually this is almost impossible across the entire low and high bands, but the closer you can come to it the better off you are. Now about amplification devices.

Tube: Available are tube, transistor

102

and nuvistor. The tube is the old reliable and works well. It can absorb great amounts of signal and process them all nicely without going into oscillation, overloading or cross-modulating. It is quite strong for up to about 75 miles. If you want to use your electronic antenna for local as well as distant reception in a metropolitan area the tube booster is a good bet.

Transistor: The transistor type is stronger than the tube type but has the tendency to overload. In a strong signal area this will happen on the local channels. However, if your electronic antenna is primarily for use to pull distance and not to be used for strong local reception, the transistor will outpull the tube.

Nuvistor: The nuvistor is sort of a compromise booster. It has almost the pulling power of a transistor and the overloading freedom of the tube. It works well. In fact, there is the Colortron with two nuvistors that pulls better than a single transistor and won't overload.

Setside Boosters: While the right rooftop booster is ideal, it is not always the practical thing to do. You might not want to go through all the steeplejack work necessary to cut in a booster on your existing antenna or the price might be prohibitive. If so, you can get a setside booster that works well. They come in tube, transistor and nuvistor models with the same pros and cons. The only thing wrong is the boost-up of the noise the lead-in picks up, as well as the signal. This might or might not be a terrible thing according to your particular reception situation.

They are simple to install. All you do is disconnect the lead-in from the TV set and attach it to the booster. Then you attach the booster to the antenna terminals of the TV set. Then turn the booster on. You'll know quickly if you have increased the gain of your signal.

MOTORS

The last major item on the list is a motor for the antenna. A popular misconception is that people think the motor itself performs some signal-pulling job. It

There are many different styles of antenna motors, with many decorative control boxes.

doesn't. All it's there for is to turn the antenna around so you can aim directly at the desired transmitter. If your reception needs do not require movement of the antenna — that is, all your TV channels are arriving from a single direction — you do not need a motor.

However, to install a superhead and booster and not put a motor on is a waste. Even if your primary purpose is a special channel you'll find that by rotating around you'll get all kinds of reception you never dreamt was available.

There are many antenna motors on the market — the Channel Master Rotator and the Alliance Tenna Rotor. They all come in good deluxe and super deluxe type models. Each step up gives you a heavier duty motor. Each step up gives you a fancier, easier-to-work control box. Basically, they all perform the one desired function, though. They rotate your antenna.

To sum up, you can pick up TV stations up to a couple of hundred miles away with the proper equipment. The main items you need are an all-channel yagi, an antenna amplifier and a motor.

There are many on the market; you can pick and choose and ask the advice of the sales person as to which one to purchase. Detailed instructions for each item come with the product.

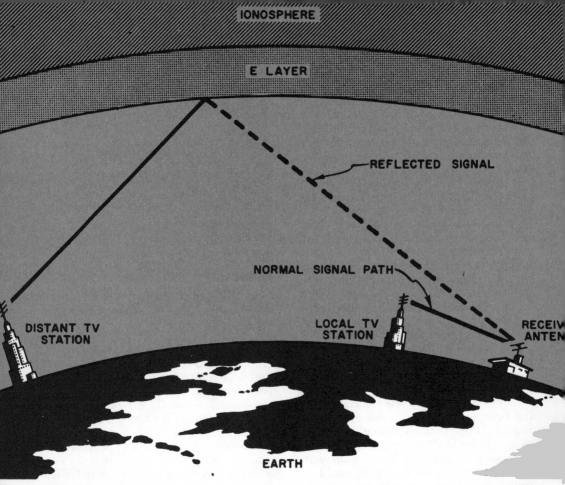

In sun spot radiation periods, ionosphere bounces signals hundreds of miles, causing TVI.

HOW TO TACKLE TV INTERFERENCE

Know the difference between

the erratic and transmitted kind,

then try to locate its source

TV interference was bad enough on black and white TV but on color TV it's maddening. There is nothing you can do about some forms of TVI and you can exterminate completely other forms of TVI. First you must analyze what kind of TVI it is and then apply some detective work to locate its source.

There are two categories of TVI. One is Erratic Interference that is coming from electrical equipment and that is sparking or leaking the electricity off. The other is transmitted interference that is coming from electronic transmitters, has a legitimate other purpose and is arriving on your TV screen unwittingly.

TVI

TROUBLE	REMEDY
Bars & Rippling on Channel 3	Locate defective 3-way or conventional light bulbs and replace
Auto Ignition	Replace lead-in with shielded type—Relocate antenna away from roadway
Electric Appliances	Install plug-in filter at appliance or TV set
920 KC Beat	Increase signal strength with stronger antenna—adjust color killer
Co-Channel Interference	No cure—Wait it out
Adjacent Channel Interference	Install tuned wave trap
Industrial Interference	Locate source of TVI and notify source or FCC
Amateur Interference	Contact amateur

Don't wrap up lead-in behind TV. Besides weakening signal, it's source of TVI pickup.

ERRATIC INTERFERENCE

This is the most prevalent kind of everyday interference. It includes sparking, leaking, poor wiring, etc. Some of it is easy to get rid of and some of it is rough. Let's go through the common types.

Light Bulbs: Electric light bulbs, especially the three-way bulbs, are a major source of trouble. They cause black horizontal jagged lines of ripple to roll through the picture. They take place most often around the frequency of channels 2, 3 and 4.

In the three-way bulbs there are two connection points in the base of the bulb. The higher value connection tends to carbonize due to the large amount of current that flows through it. If you remove the bulb, take a nail file and scrub off the carbonization you can quite often effect a cure. It's also a good idea to file down the connection in the lamp itself.

The same type of TVI can be caused by a one-way bulb, too. Here the fila-

Ignition noise can be blocked off by body of house if you locate the antenna correctly.

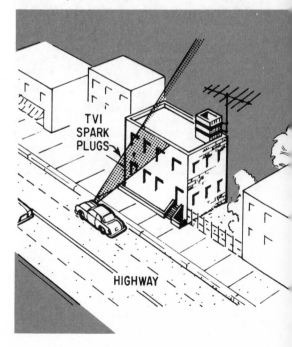

TVI
SPARK
PLUGS

HIGHWAY

Common ignition noise is caused by spark plugs. You can hear engine gunning, slowing.

Three-way light bulbs can cause jagged lines in channels 2, 3 and 4. Replace the bad ones.

You can reduce ignition noise by reducing flat side pickup; a turn every foot is ample.

Installing a line filter either at offending appliance or set itself reduces interference.

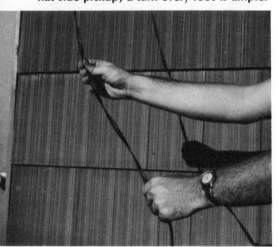

ment cracks but doesn't break. To the naked eye the bulb looks okay and lights normally. Tiny sparks are flying across the break in the filaments, however. They radiate TVI through the air into channels 2, 3 and 4.

By the process of elimination turn off each bulb one by one till the TVI stops in the picture. Replace the suspect.

Auto Ignition: The sparks in a spark plug radiate static. These unwanted impulses can be picked up by your TV antenna system, especially the long length of lead-in wire. They find their way down the wire and into the TV tuner where they ride right through your TV circuits and display themselves on the picture and issue out of the speaker.

DOTS ARE IN COLOR

Ignition noise is common and well known. You can tell when a driver is gunning or slowing his motor by the annoying dots in your picture and the rat-tat-tat out of the speaker. On color programs you see the dots in color. (In a color set, when the color killer is adjusted right, a black and white program shows the TVI in black and white.) There is always a certain amount of ignition noise and you are used to it. However, if the condition begins to get unbearable there are a few corrective measures you can take.

One, try twisting the flat ribbon lead-in every few feet. The flat side has maximum interference pickup and turning the wire reduces flat side exposure.

Two, install some 300 ohm shielded cable or 72 ohm coaxial cable instead of the ribbon lead-in. There is practically no TVI pickup in these.

Three, isolate the antenna as much as possible from the street where the cars are driving. Do this by checking the location of your antenna. If it is not in the farthest spot from the street, placing the solid house between it and the roadway, relocate it there.

Electric Appliances: Vacuum cleaners, power mixers, electric shavers, dryers, dishwashers, etc., all cause erratic TVI in the picture. Most of this interference is not radiated like the last two types. It travels through the power line from the offending appliance to the TV set. The TV set has special capacitors in its line and a filtered power supply to eliminate such noise but it can't get it all out.

The remedy attempt is to install a plug-in line filter either at the appliance or the TV set. These filters are available in most hardware stores. They work well in some cases, not at all in rare instances, and just a bit in others.

TRANSMITTED INTERFERENCE

The less common type of TVI comes from other transmitters. Rather than erratic, their kind is intelligible and operates on definite frequencies. This type can be trapped out to a more or less degree.

920 KC Beat: This is the latest kind and is a direct result of color TV. The sound carrier and the color subcarrier in the TV signal are set exactly 920 kilocycles apart. Whenever the sound is heard, its carrier mixes with the color. This 920 KC beat appears on the TV screen as a herringbone interference in the lighter parts of the picture.

The main thing you need to cure this condition is a good color antenna. Good gain increases the signal to noise ratio and simply rejects the 920 KC beat. Also, you could orient your antenna to different directions. There might be one direction that is best for 920 KC rejection.

Other than that you'll have to judiciously adjust the fine tuner to the best spot. It's somewhere between complete loss of color and loss of picture to the sound bars. It's the nature of the beast.

Should you see little bits of the 920 KC beat in the black and white picture, around small objects, you have a slightly different condition. To cure this condition adjust the Color Killer control till the condition just disappears.

CO-CHANNEL INTERFERENCE

As the name implies, this is interference from a channel with the same frequency. For instance Channel 4 in Miami could possibly interfere with Channel 4 in New York, if the atmospheric conditions are correct.

The interference could be merely lines or ripples (in a moderate case), or in an extreme situation your local channel can be pushed off entirely with a strange snowy picture taking its place. How is this possible?

TV carrier waves normally travel in a straight line of sight path. This gives the carrier an effective range of about 30 miles according to terrain. (Range can be increased by using principles described in the antenna section; Chapter 12.) All other transmitted energy that misses the earth travels on out to space and is dissipated. The 30-mile range was deliber-

When strange snowy picture pushes your local channel off the air it's called co-channel.

This windshield wiper effect on a screen occurs when adjacent TV channel spills over.

ate and permits many channels, with the same frequency of 2, 3, 4, etc., to function near each other without interfering with one another. However, atmospheric conditions sometimes conspire against this well-laid plan.

There is a layer of atmosphere in the sky starting at about 50 miles, on up to about 250 miles, called the ionosphere. The layer between 50 and 80 miles is called the "E" layer. In this region, the air molecules are more sparsely spaced than at low levels, yet not as sparse as at higher levels. They are just close enough together to become heavily ionized by cosmic ray bombardment, yet not close enough to collide and lose the ionization.

The E layer affects RF energy by bending the transmitted waves back toward earth. Most of the time there is not enough bending of TV waves to cause any ill effects. However, during certain atmospheric coincidences, like sun spots, the E layer becomes extra heavily ionized. Then it reflects a lot of the TV waves. The waves can bounce back and forth between the E layer and earth, traveling thousands of miles.

Co-channel can come from any distant station no matter how far, but the strongest type usually comes from a station about 400 miles away. It will shove your local channel off your TV screen. It's

known as sporadic E skip. What can you do? Sit down and wait till it disappears. Try to enjoy the novelty of the phenomenon. It usually doesn't last too many days.

ADJACENT CHANNEL INTERFERENCE

Not to be confused with co-channel, an adjacent channel is the one next to it, not the same one. The TV interference caused by it happens when your TV begins picking up the adjacent channel in addition to the one you have it tuned to.

The victimized channels in our area between Philadelphia and New York are 4 and 11 from New York. Channels 3 and 10 from Philadelphia keep interfering with them. The TVI appears as a writhing herringbone pattern on top of 4 and 11. On occasion, a weak superimposed picture appears moving quickly with the horizontal blanking bar, giving a "windshield wiper" effect.

There's a good reason why Channel 3 and 10 interfere with 4 and 11. The audio portion of 3 and 10 are only 1.5 megacycles below the lowest frequencies of 4 and 11's picture information. This is closer together than the sound and picture are on any one channel taken by itself. The sound and picture on all chan-

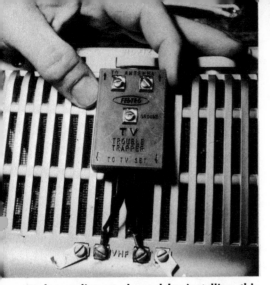

Reduce adjacent channel by installing this trap, which tunes to unwanted frequency.

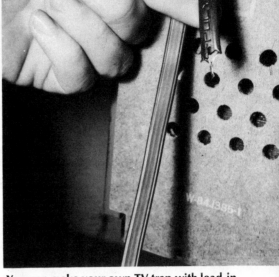

You can make your own TV trap with lead-in wire. Cut stub at the point of best reception.

nels are 4.5 megacycles apart.

Most TV's are not able to tune close enough to keep the sound of 3 from the picture of 4. The sound thus appears as a herringbone overlay. If the channel is strong enough, then it also wipes the windshield. Channel 10 does the same thing to 11.

There are commercial traps on the market that can be installed. One trap is tunable from Channels 2 through 6, while another is tunable from 7 through 13. They cancel out the channel you tune them to. For example, if you want to rid 4 of 3, tune the trap to 3.

INDUSTRIAL TRANSMITTERS

There are many different electronic instruments in common use today. In the main, they are very well shielded and cause no appreciable TVI. However, you might be unlucky enough to be in a position where this is not true. Should you be constantly annoyed with some type of RF interference, it will appear on your screen as herringbone stripes or overlays. To trap it out is going to be a tedious job.

You're going to have to try a number of traps, installed between the antenna lead-in wire and the antenna terminals. The trap that rids you of the TVI is, of

course, the one to install permanently.

For best results, rather than install it at the antenna terminals, install it as close to the tuner input as possible. The closer you get to the tuner, the less lead-in will pick up TVI after the trapping.

A convenient homemade RF trap can be made out of lead-in wire. Cut off a piece about three feet long. Attach one end right on top of the lead-in from the aerial. Then short out the stub every few inches, watching the picture full of TVI at the same time. The spot that is best, cut and short.

AMATEUR TRANSMISSIONS

A word about hams: The amateur radio operator is usually blamed for all TVI from auto ignition to sporadic E skip. Mostly he is not at fault.

True he is on the air and it's possible for you to pick up his transmission. Usually, though, any pickup is due to poor alignment or trapping in your TV. A high pass filter at his frequency, installed at your antenna input, will usually make up the deficiency in your TV.

If the signal still comes in, contact the amateur and tell him how you are receiving his signal. I've never met a ham who wouldn't be happy to help cure your TVI whether he has a hand in it or not.

109

A professional repairman uses a CRT rejuvenation machine to perform many TV repairs.

LET'S EXAMINE
YOUR PICTURE TUBE

Unlike black and white, color tube trouble usually means replacement

When a black-and-white picture tube goes bad, odds are it can be repaired and its life extended for a period of time. When a color picture tube shows defect symptoms, odds are that it has given up the ghost and replacement is the only answer.

At any rate, the same repair measures can be tried on color tubes, but aside from the first technique we'll discuss, results will only occur in a minority percentage.

TROUBLE NO. 3 —
NO BRIGHTNESS, SOUND OK

Yes, this is exactly the same sympton as when the high voltage quits. Only in this instance you'll be clued onto the picture tube because the high voltage is present and strong. You can take your neon test lamp and place it near the cap or the base of the horizontal output tube. When the picture tube is bad the neon lights bright.

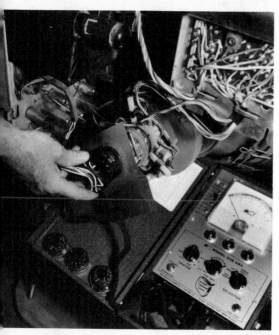

One specific job of rejuvenation machine is to strip poison off the cathode surface.

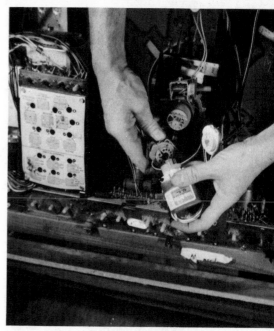

While odds are in your favor with brighteners on B&W, they're against you with color.

Look at the neck of the picture tube. The tube is definitely at fault if the filaments are not lit, or if the neck is lighting up with a bright blue light. When the neck is signaling bright blue you must replace. If the filaments are out you can probably repair them.

A fast check is to grasp the cap attached to the pins sticking out of the neck, and jiggle it. Should the filaments start to light you'll be able to repair for sure.

Whether it does or not, pull off the cap, get a pair of pliers and squeeze the pins sticking out of the plastic socket. (If your CRT is the type that doesn't have a plastic socket and the pins are part of the tube and not the socket you can't do this repair.) Then take your solder gun, heat each pin till the solder runs and try to add a drop of solder into each pin hole.

What you are doing is reheating a corrosive solder joint and restoring a solid

When heaters are out, the first step is to jiggle cap to see if they'll flicker back on.

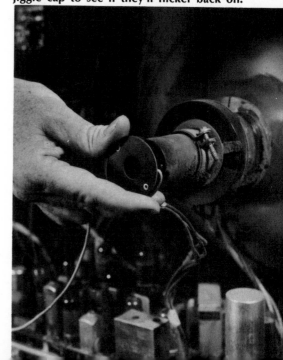

Technicians use CRT pin crimper to squeeze out cold solder joint. Pair of pliers is O.K.

By heating pins with a solder gun, adding solder as well as crimping, repair is sure.

CRT cap is only plastic cover over glass. If cap comes off you can thread it back on.

This dim picture usually happens only in B&W set. A pure form has no shrinking.

connection. This repair applies to both monochrome and polychrome tubes.

Rethreading the Socket: On occasion as you perform the above repair, the socket will come off in your hands. Don't panic, you can reinstall it. Take your solder gun and one by one heat and tap out the solder in each pin. Then take a wire brush and carefully scrub off all corrosion from the wires sticking out of the CRT.

Attach a length of fine wire or strong thread to each protruding wire. Run the extensions through the proper pins in the socket and then thread the socket back on. Run a little solder into each hollow pin. Reglue the plastic cap back onto the glass with some epoxy.

TROUBLE NO. 54—DIM PICTURE

The pure form of this trouble happens only in a monochrome CRT and is accompanied by two other indicators. One, there is no shrinking of the picture. If there is shrinking TROUBLE No. 4 or TROUBLE No. 5 is indicated. They are power supply problems, not CRT.

Two, as you advance the brightness control with this trouble, the whites in the picture get a shiny quicksilver look and the picture might turn inside out or go negative. If the picture doesn't do this but simply gets a little brighter as you advance the control, the trouble is probably not in the picture tube but in the video section.

The corresponding trouble of DIM PICTURE in a color CRT is TROUBLE No. 51—LOSS OF ONE COLOR. That's because it's rare for all three guns in a color CRT to go at the same time. It's usually just one gun that goes while the other two perform satisfactorily. This removes one color from the screen. You can tell which gun is going by which color is missing. If the picture becomes a mixture of purples you have lost your green component. If the picture is blue and green you have lost red. Should the picture be red and green you have lost blue.

The repair attempt is easy. You must install a CRT brightener on the tube. A brightener is simply a small step-up transformer that overheats the cathode by raising the filament voltage from its rated 6.3 volts to 7.8 volts. The brightener won't hurt the filaments since they are 100% overrated and can burn safely up to 12.6 volts. In fact, if your picture tube becomes dim for the second time you can try installing a second brightener in series with the first.

The only real problem you'll have is getting the right brightener. There are between sixteen and twenty different kinds. You'll need the following two facts to get the right one. One, the number of your picture tube. And two, the wiring of your tube heaters, series or parallel.

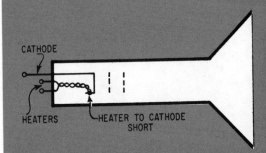

Rejuvenation machine places 1000 volts on control grid, sucking electrons from cathode.

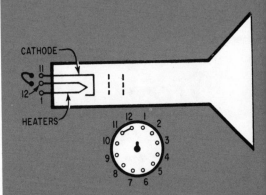

Heater to cathode short effectively shorts out brightness control — rendering it dead.

If isoformer kills brightness it's because cathode's broken. Fix with exterior short.

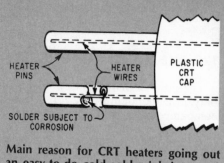

Main reason for CRT heaters going out an easy-to-do cold solder job in cap pin

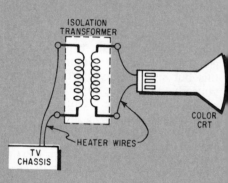

Correctly rated 1:1 transformer can be installed directly to heater leads of color CRT

If CRT is frozen, wedge it loose with screw driver. Don't pull off the entire assembly.

Number of the tube is often needed for repairs. It's usually somewhere on tube body.

Keep in mind that CRT can break into a million pieces. Handle all repairs cautiously.

A professional uses a rejuvenation machine in addition to installing the brightener. This gives the brightener a better and faster start. In fact, sometimes the brightener won't do the trick unless the tube is rejuvenated first.

In a color TV when you restore one low gun by installing a brightener the other two guns work stronger too. The picture will probably get the wrong tint and a gray scale tracking procedure will probably have to be employed. (See TROUBLE No. 44—TINTED PICTURE, Chapter 9.)

TROUBLE NO. 55— FIXED BRIGHTNESS

The pure form of this trouble happens only in a black-and-white CRT. There is a dull-looking picture on the screen, usually with retrace lines showing. Turning the brightness control has no effect. The picture remains the same. There is a short in the electron gun and it is probably a heater to cathode short.

When one brightener fails to do the trick, there's no harm done by installing 2nd one.

Pure form of fixed brightness happens only in B&W sets and shows the retrace lines.

The short in the gun effectively shorts the brightness control right out of the circuit. While the brightness control won't work, the contrast control does.

The problem here is, the heater and cathode must not touch electrically because they operate at different voltage potentials. When they do touch, the cathode is dropped down to the heater potential.

A clever repair can be made by isolating the heater from its low voltage potential. This can be accomplished with a 1:1 isolation transformer.

Isolation transformers can be bought for black-and-white TV's. They look and install exactly like a brightener. Here again be sure you buy the right one. There are also available brighteners that are wound as an isolation transformer. Get one of these and you'll get the brightening action as well as the isolation.

In Case You Lost Brightness: There is the occasional case, where you have fixed brightness, when you install an isoformer and then lose brightness altogether. When this happens it's because the cathode has broken. Most of the time you can restore the picture by placing a short between the heater and the cathode pins on the CRT. For instance, if the heaters are pins 12 and 1 and the cathode is pin 11, by placing a piece of wire between pin 11 and 12 you'll cure all.

The corresponding trouble of FIXED BRIGHTNESS in a color CRT is TROUBLE No. 48 – NO VIDEO, COLOR OK. This means there is no Y but the R-Y, G-Y and B-Y are appearing on the screen. A smeary color picture is the result with no black and white at all. When a monochrome show is on just a raster appears. This happens because the Y is coming in through the shorted cathode while the colors are arriving by way of the clear control grids.

Unfortunately, there is no isoformer made for color CRT's at the present time. You can buy one that will work, even though it was conceived for another purpose. One I've been using is a damper heater isolation transformer that is rated 1:1 at 2 amperes.

Find the heater leads for your color CRT. They are usually coded black and brown. Snip them midway between the chassis and the CRT cap. Attach the primary of the transformer to the chassis lead ends and the secondary of the transformer to the cap lead ends. Mount the transformer conveniently on the chassis or on the cabinet.

If the isoformer repair is going to take, it's an instant success. If it still doesn't work it indicates further shorts in the electron gun and you'll probably have to replace the CRT.

REPLACING OLD PICTURE TUBES

Buying a new or rebuilt CRT —

and proper installation procedure

There comes a time in the life of every picture tube, monochrome or polychrome, when it needs replacement. What then? Let's go through the various considerations.

The Buy: The first question you must answer is, should I buy a new CRT or a rebuilt one? There is no pat answer. It's all according to what kind of picture tube you are replacing. There are three general types. One is the old black-and-white tube that is typified by the 21FLP4. This is a 90-degree tube with a conventional 12 pin socket. In this case a rebuilt tube is probably the best buy. The TV is an older one. These type tubes are rebuilt easily and have a good product result. The only difference between a new and rebuilt tube that is made by a name brand company is that the glass is used over again. A name brand company uses the same quality control and glass inspection procedures on new and rebuilt tubes. You can feel safe with a rebuilt.

The second type tube is the newer black-and-white tube. This is typified by a 17DQP4. These are 110-degree tubes with newer eight pin sockets. They are not quite as easy to rebuild. Shop around and check prices on new and rebuilt versions. Be sure to get a name brand tube.

The correct way to handle a picture tube is by the sides and absolutely not by the neck.

A B&W CRT is easily and reliably rebuilt since the gun is the main breakdown area.

Color CRT has reliability problems with shadow mask, tri-color screen and the gun.

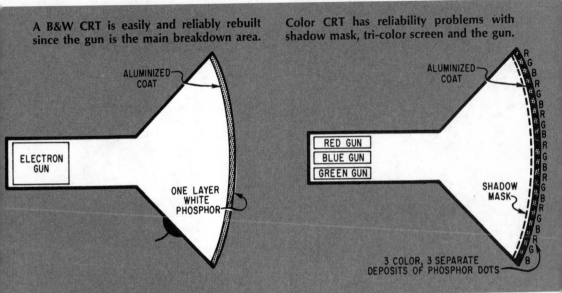

ALUMINIZED COAT

ELECTRON GUN

ONE LAYER WHITE PHOSPHOR

ALUMINIZED COAT

RED GUN
BLUE GUN
GREEN GUN

SHADOW MASK

3 COLOR, 3 SEPARATE DEPOSITS OF PHOSPHOR DOTS

If the price differential is enough you can chance a rebuilt. Should there be only a few dollars' difference take the new, for this is evidence of great difficulty and a large rejection rate on the rebuilts.

If you can, try to make a deal with the company you buy from, that if the rebuilt is not satisfactory you can trade it back in for a credit on a new one. The 110-degree tubes do not rebuild quite as easily as the 90-degree ones.

The third general type is the color CRT. I do not recommend, at this time, the use of rebuilts. I would advise a new tube, with rare earth phosphors only. The black-and-white tube's main breakdown area is the electron gun. This is the part that is replaced during rebuilding. In a color CRT, though, only the gun is changed. There are other major defect areas such as the shadow mask and the tri-color screen. These components cannot be easily rebuilt.

Also if you get a new rare earth tube and your TV didn't have one previously the picture will be better than when the set was new.

Be sure to get an exact replacement tube. It need not be the exact same number but it must be an exact replacement. If it's not you are asking for complica-

Picture tubes come in all sizes and shapes. Be sure you have the correct replacement.

When changing a color picture tube, have it in right. This one has marker groove on top.

117

When CRT cap has been on a long time, pry it off carefully from the rust and corrosion.

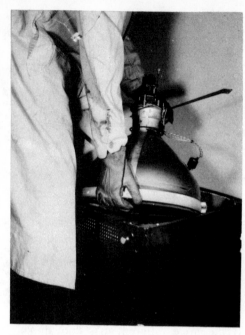

Big consideration to easy CRT removal is to place TV on face, lift up and then away.

When CRT is bolted in with its own bracket assembly, it's usually attached to cabinet.

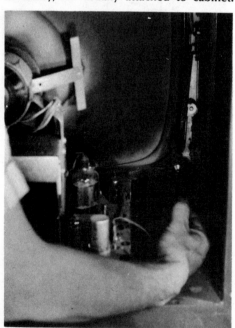

Remove anode button carefully. There are different kinds; sometimes it stores electricity.

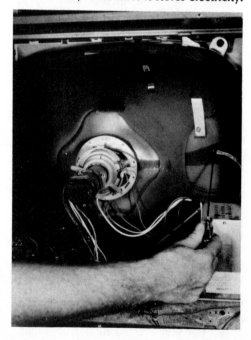

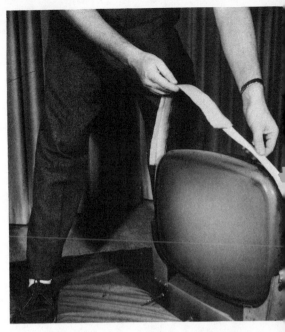

In detaching the CRT from cabinet, remember it's Safety First! Goggles are a good idea.

Some tubes are mounted with a cloth-type strap. This makes for much easier removal.

tions due to incorrect physical size.

When you buy the tube check the labeling on the box. By law the manufacturer must state new or rebuilt. New is designated by the unmistakable NEW on the box. A rebuilt is usually disguised by a label that reads something like this: "This tube is made of all new materials except the glass envelope which might be subject to reuse."

THE INSTALLATION

The big trick in taking out a picture tube is to lay the TV on its face after the chassis and other accessories are out of the way. That way the tube will stay in place with or without its mounting. Lifting is up and down, not sideways.

Safety first is important. In factories gloves, goggles and a long shop coat are required. It would be a good idea for you to do the same if you are going to handle a large picture tube. It can implode with great force and throw glass in all directions.

When yoke freezes to glass neck, it can be loosened easily with special yoke loosener.

A black-and-white CRT is removed easily. Just the CRT cap, an ion trap (if there is one — they have disappeared almost completely from the scene), sometimes a focus coil and the deflection yoke are removed from the neck. Then the high voltage anode lead is removed from the CRT well. The well and the anode lead are discharged to the chassis with your jumper cord.

The mounting bolts are removed and the CRT lifted out. That's all there is to it. The new tube is replaced by retracing your steps exactly. The only stopgap you might run into is a frozen yoke or hardware. In that case you must stop and call for help.

A color CRT can also be removed but not quite as easily. Again with the TV on its face and the chassis out of the way follow the next few steps.

Unplug the CRT cap. Remove the

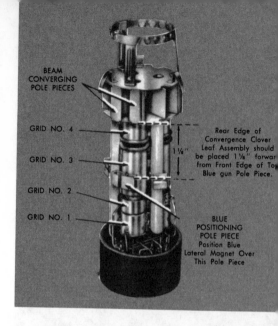

Look closely in the neck at the electron gun assembly and you can pick out pole pieces.

Convergence assembly purity rings and blue lateral magnets must be placed correctly.

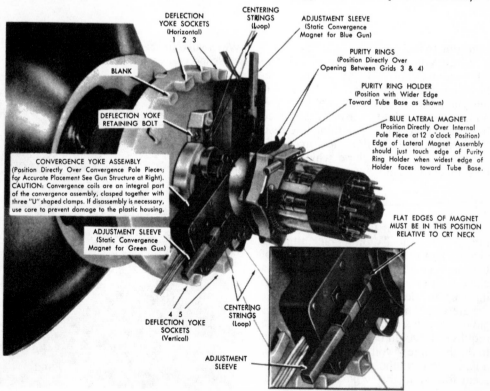

Tilted picture is straightened by loosening yoke, then carefully rotating it into place.

Black shadows in tube corner are caused by yoke being mounted too far back from bell.

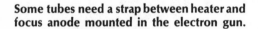

Some tubes need a strap between heater and focus anode mounted in the electron gun.

blue lateral magnet, noting its exact position on the neck. Remove the purity tabs, noting their position. Loosen the convergence yoke assembly and remove it, noting its exact position. Loosen the deflection yoke and remove. Disconnect the anode lead from the CRT well and discharge both well and lead. Then remove mounting hardware and lift out.

The new tube is replaced by retracing your steps exactly. Be sure to place the blue gun at the top just as the old tube was mounted. There is a marking on the rim of the face plate showing the top position. Be sure you get all of the neck hardware over their proper places in the electron gun assembly. Once you get the TV back together you have to adjust the picture back into place.

WHAT DOES WHAT

Tilted Picture: Should the picture return upside down or tilted you can straighten it out by rotation of the yoke.

Shadows in Corners: If you develop black shadows around the perimeter of the tube the yoke is mounted too far back. Push it up closer to the bell of the tube.

Picture Not Centered: Centering devices closely resemble the purity tabs. On a black-and-white tube they are cen-

tering devices, on a color tube they are not. Centering devices on a color tube could be adjustments on the rear chassis panel or strings sticking out of the yoke assembly. Check service folder for the exact type.

Out of Focus: Focus is obtained by adjusting till the lines of the picture stand out the sharpest. Lots of black-and-white CRT's have a focus strap that is a little piece of metal shorting out a few pins on the CRT socket. Quite often it is left on the old tube and focus is lost. If you lose focus after replacing a tube check the old tube for the strap. Check your service folder for exact positioning of focus adjustments.

Color CRT's: After replacing a color CRT, a complete convergence setup is needed. Turn back to Chapter 9 and follow it from start to finish.

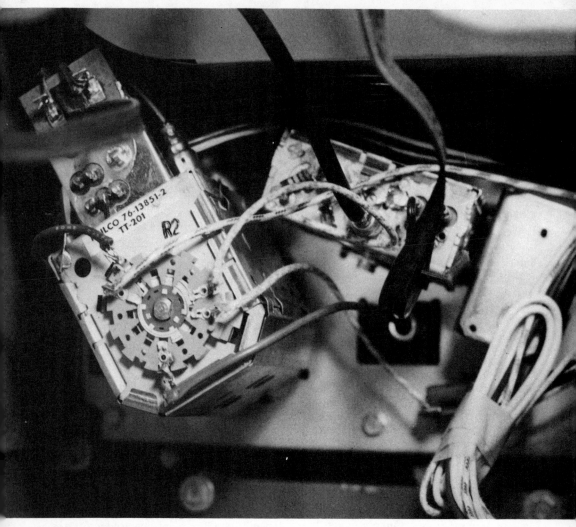

All new televisions have two tuners. The large one is VHF and the smaller one is the UHF.

UHF FOR OLDER SETS

It's quite easy and inexpensive to convert your pre-'64 VHF-only set

Every new TV that rolls off a production line in the U.S. has tuning for channels 2 through 84. However, there were about 60 million TV sets built before April 1964, the date when UHF became law. Very few of the pre '64 TV's had provisions for channels 13 through 84.

There are still literally millions of TV's in use that can't get the UHF programs. If you own one of these it's quite easy and relatively inexpensive to convert your VHF-only TV for UHF reception too.

One point I'd like to make first. Lots of TV sets have a UHF antenna terminal

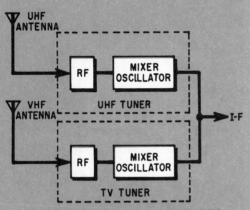

FACTORY INSTALLED UHF TUNER

UHF tuner is separate from VHF tuner and is wired directly into the first IF circuit.

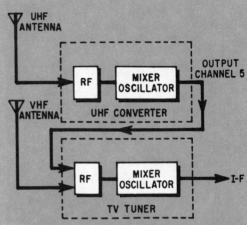

HOME INSTALLED UHF CONVERTER

Converter works by changing all UHF stations to channel 5. Converter dial does tuning.

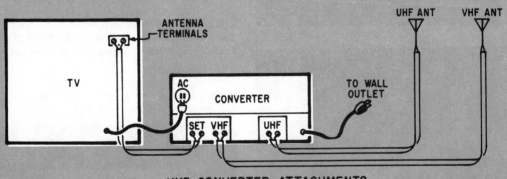

UHF CONVERTER ATTACHMENTS

Converter has 3 sets of terminals: one for UHF antenna, one for VHF and one for jumper cord.

in the rear, and a hole with a cover saying UHF in the front. There is nothing in between. There might be a factory UHF tuner available but probably not. If you can get that special UHF tuner, fine, but since you probably can't, forget that terminal and hole. It is useless.

EASIER TO INSTALL

Converters: We buy and install UHF converters by the case. From a convenience, financial and performance standpoint these converters are better deals

than the factory jobs most of the time. They are usually easier to install, cost less and perform better. Their only drawback is they won t fit your UHF hole. Occasionally you can even use the terminal strip already on your TV back.

There are two kinds. One sits outside the TV and the other mounts inside your TV. Both are converters rather than tuners which actually gives them more signal gain. A factory UHF tuner is tied directly into the IF strip. A UHF converter is connected into the VHF tuner and the signal gets the benefit of the extra circuits it flows through.

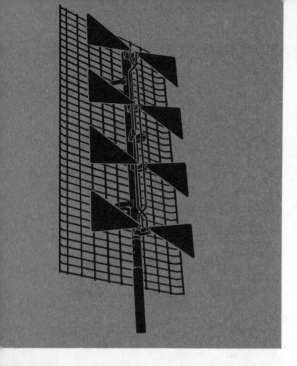

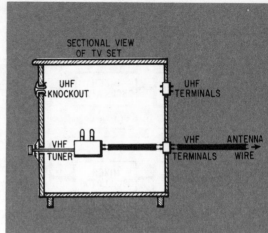

Many sets have holes labeled UHF and VHF terminals on back, but nothing in between.

Left and below, these UHF outdoor antennas are much smaller and shaped differently than their VHF counterpart for tuning.

If your VHF antenna pulls good UHF, you can install a splitter and use it for both.

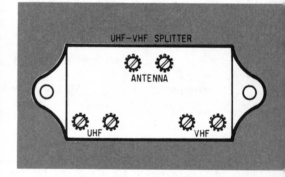

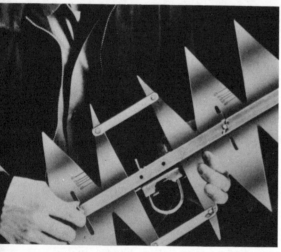

There are about four price ranges and you get exactly what you pay for. The more expensive converters have extra amplification stages, pilot bulbs, fine tuners and AC outlets (so you can plug the TV into the converter and won't need an extra AC outlet in the wall). They vary from about twelve to forty dollars.

Outside Converters: This looks like a little table model radio and is hooked up in four simple steps. 1) Attach your regular antenna to the terminals on the converter marked VHF ANTENNA. 2) Attach your new UHF antenna to the terminals marked UHF ANTENNA. 3) Attach provided jumper lead-in wire to the terminals on the converter marked TV SET. 4) Attach other end of jumper wire to the antenna terminals on your TV. Then plug the converter into an AC outlet.

124

If you don't own a set that possesses UHF channels 14-83, its an easy thing to install.

Simple wire ring with an eight-inch diameter makes excellent indoor UHF antenna.

With the converter off, your TV will operate normally. With the converter on, all the UHF channels are converted to Channel 5. Tune your TV for Channel 5 and then tune the converter dial for the desired UHF stations. It's that easy.

Inside Converter: With the built-in converter, you have a woodworking job on your hands. Drill a hole in the cabinet and mount the converter in the hole according to the instructions you get with the converter. Electrically the converter installs exactly like the OUTSIDE CONVERTER except for the electricity. Most of these show installation of the electricity directly to the AC input in the TV. If you get confused better call for help.

ATTACHES DIRECTLY

UHF Antennas: While many times your regular antenna will pull the UHF stations in fairly well, a separate UHF antenna pulls best. The simplest antenna is an indoor type, a metal ring eight inches in diameter. You can purchase one or make one from a coat hanger. It attaches directly to the UHF antenna terminal, either on the TV if your tuner is built-in, or on the back of the universal converter box. To orient the antenna move it up and down or rotate it.

For something more powerful than the ring, there are various indoor antennas and outdoor antennas. The outdoor antenna can be attached directly to the mast of your regular antenna. There will be no interference as long as each antenna has its separate lead-in.

Splitters: If you take your regular antenna and attach it to the UHF and find it pulls satisfactorily, you can dispense with a separate UHF antenna by means of a VHF-UHF splitter. This is a simple gadget that can split the signal in two.

Once you get a splitter, run the antenna into it. There is a pair of terminals for this purpose. At the other end of the splitter you'll find two other pairs of terminals, one marked UHF and the other VHF. Run a lead from each and attach them to their respective terminals on the converter or TV.

UNDERSTANDING CABLE TV

First used only in remote regions, today it's a fast-growing field

There is nothing new about cable TV. There have been operating systems in existence from the first days of commercial TV dating back to around 1949.

There are many communities that lie physically in a valley surrounded by mountains. The TV signal, direct from the station, is blocked off completely.

Independent operators erected large antenna complexes on top of the mountains and ran cables, containing the TV pictures, into the televisionless towns. They hooked the people into the system and charged them rent. Since this was the only way TV could be received, these operations were quite successful.

In the last few years cable TV has begun to be installed in other communities. In fact, in places where TV reception is quite good. Of what use are these systems?

There is considerable advantage to them. Since color TV began selling in prodigious numbers a serious antenna situation has come about. Old black and white antennas do not pull good color. People want their antennas replaced with a satisfactory color type.

A good color antenna with a motor is expensive. They average in the $150-$200 range installed. Also they are monstrous affairs and subject to wind and weather. Repairs on them are expensive.

For a normal installation fee plus about five dollars a month rent people can get the equivalent from a cable company and there is nothing on the roof.

In addition, cable companies provide distant channels and even their own channel with news, weather and music.

Acceptance is still spotty but seems to be growing. It looks like cable TV will eventually be the main means of TV reception.

Cable TV has been serving isolated communities for years. Now it's moving into all areas.

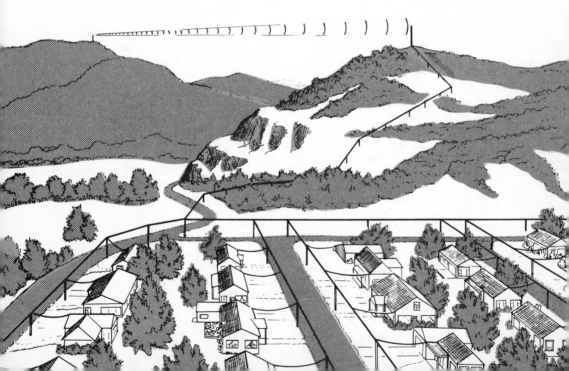

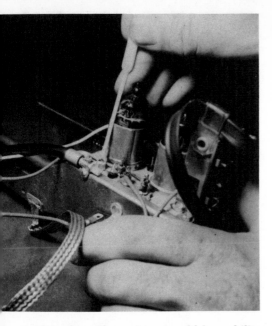

After years of use, tuner could lose ability to receive previously unreceived channels.

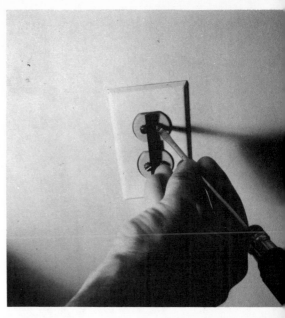

Instead of monstrous antenna system on roof, cable TV substitutes a simple wall plate.

CABLE TROUBLES IN YOUR TV

The cable company provides service up to and including their gadgets they attach on the back of your TV. The TV set itself is still your responsibility. Cable companies so far have carefully avoided any conflict with local TV service companies. The cable company will check out their system with a TV monitor.

Should the trouble be in the cable they will repair it. If it's in your TV set they recommend you to call your own TV service company.

A typical service request I receive from a customer concerning cable TV sounds like this: "The TV was working good till they installed the cable, but they say there is something wrong with the TV, not the cable. Does that sound right?"

It might not sound logical but it is. The truth is, while your TV is working quite satisfactorily on your home antenna system, it might not work at all on the cable.

That is, without repairs that are sometimes major and sometimes minor.

COMMONEST CABLE-CAUSED TROUBLE

At the cable station many TV channels are picked up and processed. For instance, take our area. They will pick up channels 3, 6, 10, 12, 17, 29 and 48 from Philadelphia; also channels 2, 9 and 11 come in good from New York.

Since this is only ten channels they might decide to convert them all to VHF and they install all the ten incoming channels on 2, 4, 5, 6, 7, 9, 10, 11, 12 and 13. Now the channels that appear on the dial are entirely different from the ones that the real stations are transmitting.

In lots of cases the only channels the set owner was receiving were 3, 6 and 10. The other channels up to this time had been unused. In years of disuse and neglect these channel strips have become corroded and won't work. Also on

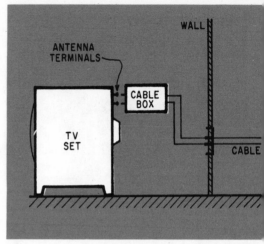

WALL

ANTENNA TERMINALS

CABLE BOX

TV SET

CABLE

Cable company accepts responsibility up to your antenna terminal. Set itself is yours.

Cable operator can buy news-weather machine and transmit his own TV channel.

an occasional repair parts might have been used from the unused channels to repair or replace the ones that were in use.

At any rate, the only good channels on the TV might be 3, 6 and 10. Attaching the cable doesn't do anything except bring in reception on these three channel setups.

What is needed is a tuner repair which could vary from just adjusting all the way to a major tuner overhaul. This is quite common.

OTHER TROUBLES

The other type of cable-caused trouble has to do with the amount of signal strength the cable sends in.

In most cases the signal is much stronger and clearer. If you were operating with a much weaker signal and then received full cable strength, it is possible that your picture will black out and the sound remain good. If it happens while the cable installers are there they will adjust your TV and the problem is solved. However, quite often it occurs days or even weeks after they leave. Then you naturally call for the repairman.

In most cases we find the AGC control was set just a hair too high. With your old weak signal it was fine, but with strong cable reception the AGC threshold is exceeded and the AGC circuit cuts off the contrast. Sometimes you'll need a new AGC tube too.

Another similar-caused trouble will be a new annoying buzz in your audio that wasn't there before cable.

Here again it is due to increased cable signal. You can try adjusting any buzz control setting up the ratio detector and replacement of audio tubes. If that doesn't help you might need a full alignment job so you'll call for the TV men.

A rare case that I ran into once was a good picture with rabbit ears but a wobbly pulsating picture with the cable. I was able to get it to quit by replacing all three IF tubes. They were oscillating with the increased cable signal strength.

The only other trouble I've seen on some older TV's that recently bought the cable deal was windshield wiper on some channels. This is not the cable's fault. It is adjacent channel interference all right, as is described in the TVI chapter, but the TV that displayed it had poor adjacent channel rejection qualities. A new TV cures the trouble.

INDEX

Index Key:

Chapter heads are in capital letters

A

antenna amplifier, 94
antenna booster, 94, 102
  nuvistor, 103
  setside, 103
  transistor, 102
  tube type, 102, 103
antenna elements, 91
antenna guy wires, 100, 101
antenna heads
  conical, 94
  dipole, 97
  director, 97
  reflector, 97
  yagi, all channel, 96
  yagi, one channel, 96
antenna insulators, 94, 98
antenna lead-in wire, 94, 98
antenna motor, 94, 103
antenna, motorized, 91, 93
antenna mounts, 94, 98, 100, 101
antenna poles, 94
antenna positioning, 91
ANTENNA PROBLEMS, REMOVING, 86-93
antenna supplies, 94
antenna trouble chart, 87
ANTENNAS, THE WORLD OF NEW, 94-103
arcing, 35
audio amplifier tube, 63
audio detector, 63
audio IF, 63
audio output transformer, 63
audio output tube, 63
automatic gain control, 52

B

bandpass amplifier, 81, 82, 85
Barkhausen effect, 37
blooming, 30, 33
booster, antenna, 93
brightness, 7, 24, 25, 28, 30
burst amplifier, 81

C

Cable TV, 126
  troubles, 127, 128
CABLE TV, UNDERSTANDING, 126-128
cathode current chart, 31
circuit breaker, 17, 18, 19, 20, 22
color adjustment, 64-67

color adjustment chart, 73
colors, bleeding, 75
color circuit, 80
color controls
  hue, 64, 65, 66
  killer, 64, 66, 67
  level, 64
  tint, 64, 65
COLOR, HOW TO TOUCH UP THE, 68-79
COLOR ILLS, CURING, 80-85
color intensity control, 65, 66, 81
color killer, 81, 85
color sync problems, 39
color touchup, 68-79
COLORS, PROPERLY ADJUSTING THE, 64-67
contrast, 48-59
CONTRAST'S THE CULPRIT, WHEN, 48-59
convergence complications, 78
convergence controls, 76-77
corona effect, 35, 37

D

damper, 27, 30, 33, 35, 37, 43
dead set, 16-23
dead set trouble chart, 17
DEAD, WHEN YOUR SET GOES, 16-23
defocusing, 33
delay line, 81, 82
degaussing (demagnitizing), 73
  coil, 73
demodulators, 81
distortion (the bends), 43
dot-bar pattern, 75
dynamic convergence, 76

F

filters, input, 54
flyback, 33
FM detector, 63
focus rectifier, 33
fusistor, 22

G

gray scale adjustments, 69, 70, 71, 83
ghosts, 56

H

heads, antenna, 89
heaters
  dropping resistor, 21

fuse, 20
  parallel wired, 20
  series wired, 21
  tube test, 21
hex head coil, 79
high band, no, 56
high voltage circuit description, 26, 27
high voltage fuse, 29
high voltage rectifier, 27, 28, 33
high voltage regulator, 27, 28, 33
high voltage symptoms, 24-37
HIGH VOLTAGE, TIPS ON FIXING, 24-37
horizontal circuit symptoms, 26
  bends, 26
  poor linearity, 26
  split picture, 26
horizontal drive, 43
horizontal frequency coil, 41
horizontal oscillator, 26, 29, 30, 37, 39, 40, 43
horizontal output, 26, 37, 43
horizontal output tube, 30, 31, 33
horizontal phase coil, 41
horizontal phase detector, 40, 43
horizontal sync problems, 38-43
  hue control, 64, 65, 66
hum, 93
hum bars, 54

I

identification center, 4, 5, 7
input filter, 22
interference, 104-109
  trouble chart, 105
INTERFERENCE, HOW TO TACKLE TV, 104-109

K

keystone, 34

L

lead-in wire, 87, 88
line cord, 18
linearity, 78

M

mirror image, 34, 35
mixer-oscillator, 49, 51, 54, 56

N

noise inverter, 52

O

off-on switch, 18
oscillators
  horizontal, 26, 29, 30, 37, 39, 40, 43
  vertical, 40

P

parallel wired heaters, 20
peaking coil, 54
PICTURE, TAKING THE JITTERS OUT OF YOUR, 38-47
picture tube, 51, 52
PICTURE TUBE, LET'S EXAMINE YOUR, 110-115
picture tube repair, 110-115
picture tube replacement, 116-121
PICTURE TUBE, REPLACING OLD, 116-121
piecrust effect, 37
pulsating picture, 54. 56
purity, poor, 71, 72, 73
  degaussing (demagnetizing), 73
  tabs, 73

R

rectifiers, 22, 23
REPAIRS, GETTING THE JUMP ON, 4-15
RF amplifier, 49, 51, 52, 54, 55, 56

S

safety rules, 12, 13
  broken glass, 13, 14
  electric shock, 15
  x-rays, 15
series wired heaters, 21
shrink, 30
snow, 55, 93
sound bars, 63
sound, no, 60-63
sound output, 51
sound poor, 63
sound reject, 85
SOUND, REPAIRING, 60-63
sound trouble chart, 62